Gebroken Wit

Off-White

Astrid Roemer

Translated from the Dutch by
Lucy Scott and David McKay

TWO LINES
PRESS

Originally published as *Gebroken Wit* in 2019
by Uitgeverij Prometheus, Amsterdam
© 2019 Astrid H. Roemer
Translation © 2024 by Lucy Scott and David McKay

Two Lines Press
582 Market Street, Suite 700, San Francisco, CA 94104
www.twolinespress.com

ISBN: 978-1-949641-25-7
Ebook ISBN: 978-1-949641-26-4

Cover art: Fares Micue, "Positive Nostalgia"
Cover design by Tiani Kennedy
Typeset by Stephanie Nisbet

Library of Congress Cataloging-in-Publication Data

Names: Roemer, Astrid, author. | Scott, Lucy, translator. | McKay,
David, 1973-, translator.
Title: Off-white / Astrid H. Roemer ; translated from the Dutch
by Lucy Scott and David McKay.
Other titles: *Gebroken wit*. English
Description: San Francisco, CA : Two Lines Press, 2024. |
Identifiers: LCCN 2023043091 (print) | LCCN 2023043092
(ebook) | ISBN 9781949641257 (paperback) | ISBN
9781949641264 (ebook)
Subjects: LCSH: Grandparent and child--Fiction. | Brothers and
sisters--Fiction. | LCGFT: Domestic fiction. | Novels.
Classification: LCC PT5881.28.O333 G4313 2024 (print) |
LCC PT5881.28.O333 (ebook) | DDC 839.313/64--dc23/
eng/20230919
LC record available at https://lccn.loc.gov/2023043091
LC ebook record available at https://lccn.loc.gov/2023043092

The publisher gratefully acknowledges the support of the Dutch
Foundation for Literature, and this publication is supported in
part by the National Endowment for the Arts

For mother H.L.C.

I have used autobiographical structures to write a novel—in other words, a fictional story—and I ask my readers to respect the real-world privacy of potentially identifiable people.

One

Grandma knew right away something horrible was happening. The blood was bright red with small dark clots. She felt tears coming as she flushed her mouth, again and again, with tap water that she spat back into the burnished sink until all traces of blood were gone. She had already lost so much weight. No one mentioned it at the airport in Zanderij. Not even after her granddaughter left. No one saw her anymore. Not a soul spoke to her when she left the house. She was kneeling, murmuring to the figure of the saint, until her knees could no longer bear it. Then she stood, slipped some coins into the donation box, picked out a candle, lit it, put it in place, looked into the small flame, and mumbled, "May my blood start to flow on this very spot and not stop until I'm found." The figure of Christ looked down on her. Blood on his torso. Drops of blood on his feet. Bleeding wounds in his palms. To keep from dissolving into tears again, she moved on to the figure of Saint Anthony of Padua through whose intercession all lost things are found again. She lit a small candle and muttered a quick prayer for Heli, then went to sit in a pew close to him. She could hear the foot-steps of other people who, the same as her, had come to unload their worries and their praises on one of the saints. She sat with her eyes closed. If she gave up the ghost right here and now, then everything would turn out fine. But if death came upon her in her own home, then her lifeless body would fall into the hands of complete strangers, who'd take her away from everything familiar and stash her somewhere no one was allowed to go. And if she regained consciousness because her body wouldn't give up yet, then she would be the only one to hear her screams. And as soon as she could taste this possibility like blood at the back of her throat, the tears began to fall. She'd brought five children into the world who were all good and grown and had even blessed her with grand-children, so why in God's name was she sitting in church so broken?

She had a bag at her feet with bread, cream cheese, a tub of butter, and packets of dried ingredients for chicken soup; these days, fresh ingredients were too heavy to carry to her kitchen. Her daily existence had always been linked to food, to bringing groceries home to nourish loved ones. She'd known a time when peddlers walked the city streets with their wares, some coming to her door regularly for a glass of water and a break from the dusty streets. They were women who lived outside the city, whose families were gardeners or small farmers. Customers haggled over a kubi fish, a black hen, a carton of eggs, but not over vegetables, fruit, milk. Baking, roasting, all types of cook-ing had brought her great joy, because whatever came to the table from her kitchen was, time and again, a feast for her family. Soldiers advanced slowly through the city, chalk-white with fatigue and burned red, too, from the blistering heat, which they couldn't bear. Somewhere the world was on fire. Paramaribo could become a safe haven. She didn't understand a thing about war, despite having married a military man as a seventeen-year-old girl. War entered her house in the shape of a loaf of bread, bars of chocolate, tobacco. Her Anton never brought a bottle of gin home from camp, but she could smell the alcohol on his breath when he talked. She no longer remembered how it had started: cutting a cigar in two and then, in the privacy of her bedroom in the evening, bringing a little match to the stub, drawing it between her lips to hold in the fire, inhaling, exhaling, and feeling herself relax. The large white enamel bucket was her ashtray, her spittoon when she started to chew tobacco, and often a chamber pot at night; the father of her children pissed a loud puddle into the bucket each day before dawn. It was then that she would wake from a deep sleep and get up at once to empty it into the larger tub in a closet near the bedroom. This is how her days began in the near-morning light of the tropics. After emptying the bucket, she usually lingered a while on the stone landing to the kitchen, waiting in her nightgown until the cocks crowed in their pens and her pigeons cooed with passion, and look: dark red fruit strewn over the crushed shells under the cherry trees. For a moment she was back in one of those days—years, years removed from where she sat dreaming—and a tremor of happiness brought a smile to her face. The priest came up to her and said her tranquility touched him; he had no way of guessing the pain that was gnawing away at

3

her. He knew she spent whole hours sitting there. He was just stopping by for a moment to wish her a blessed day. She nodded, even looked up at him to make sure it was the same one: Father Overtoon, the new priest the altar boys kept playing pranks on during the family Mass on Sundays, to the delighted shrieks of the children. He moved on to speak in whispers to other worshippers, but his clogs on the church floor resounded in her mind. She clutched the rosary around her neck and started to take a bead between her thumb and index finger for the first prayer. First a deep sigh escaped her lips, then they effortlessly murmured: *Hail Mary, full of grace, the Lord is with thee…* The murmuring wouldn't stop until the noon siren pierced the silence. Then she'd stand and pick up her bag of groceries, shuffle out of the pew, turn toward the altar, make a deep bow, and walk to the exit. The brown sexton would be there waiting, holding the door open to let her through before locking up the church for the rest of Tuesday.

On the way home, she avoided the streets and the neighborhoods where her friends lived. Talking hurt, made her bleed. Besides, it was so hot downtown in the middle of the day that steam practically rose off the asphalt. She walked on, firmly gripping the bag in her left hand and using her right arm as a kind of oar. She needed to get across town, then pass through a wealthy suburb, to arrive at her own bungalow, margarine yellow, indistinguishable from the neighboring houses. Her bag held a folded straw hat with a wide brim and a plastic raincoat in a little carrying case. She walked in leather sandals from

4

a popular sports brand, a present from her granddaughter Heli, who had gone abroad, so the soles of her feet didn't feel the gravel and bumps in the sidewalk. She was used to closed-toe shoes, but they got hot and damp with sweat in the heat. She didn't really know why she never took the bus. She just liked the freedom of walking. In the old days she had always crossed paths with other women returning home from grocery shopping, and they'd stop to chat, relishing the opportunity to put down their heavy bags. Back then, the city center wasn't so completely covered in tiles and pavement, and it had canals that made it cooler. Besides, the house where she'd raised her children had been closer to the river, not on the edge of town. She stopped under a zinc awning to examine the fruits and vegetables on display. A heavily pregnant young woman with long, straight hair waddled over. She pointed at what she wanted to buy: mangoes with red skins freckled with black, bananas, wild spinach, and ten limes. The saleslady didn't force any small talk as she calmly put the fruits and vegetables into a sack, came up to her, looked on as everything vanished into the tote bag, and waited for her money. As she thanked her and paid, she remembered something: her daughter Louise would be stopping by after work. The bag had gotten heavy. Even so, she tried to take bigger steps to go faster. She was hungry, but without any real appetite. It was getting harder to swallow, even just soup. This past month she'd been getting weaker and weaker, but she didn't understand what was happening to her body and couldn't find the words of complaint to take to a doctor at the military hospital. Her husband's face flashed through her mind, but it was more the thought of the hospital where he'd died a retired sergeant after a brief illness. She hadn't visited him there. But when they came to pick her up after he'd passed away, and she saw him lying there, stock still, smiling even, she'd called him by his nickname for the first time in years and was sick with regret for weeks after. They'd no longer lived as husband and wife, but in separate houses. Anton, clumsy in the kitchen, completely alone in their marital home; her, staying with their son Winston and keeping house there. The hospital loomed. White and towering. Said to be the best medical center in Paramaribo. She was a military widow with a pension and the right to medical treatment until she was gone. She glanced at the building but quickly looked away—*just walk on by.* A growing number of vehicles were racing or lumbering past, and though her eyes had filled with tears, her feet managed to cross the last busy paved road on the way to her neighborhood, where she'd had her own home for four years, and look: her granddaughter Imker came to meet her, smiling, taking the bag of groceries. It startled her. Besides the food, the bag also held some things she couldn't do without: her Bible and a zippered leather pocket Bible with teeny tiny letters she couldn't read. She'd needed both within arm's reach day and night ever since Heli, sobbing, had said farewell to her in Zanderij. Together, she and Imker walked to the front door. And Grandmother took out her keys, saying hoarsely, "Where is your mother?"

Imker didn't answer. Someone had told her mother, Louise, about a dog running around somewhere that looked exactly like their missing guard dog Leika, and

Mama had gone to look, sending her over to Grandma's in her place. A mouthful of information for later, she decided, grabbing her own shopping bag. She walked into the foyer with her grandmother, removed her sandals just like her grandmother, and followed Grandma through the living room into the kitchen, barefoot, with the bags of supplies. The almond-green tiles of the kitchen floor were always striking if you hadn't seen them in a while, and she'd forgotten how cool they felt. Special tiles, which Grandma's son Winston had laid for her in the foyer, kitchen, and bathroom, and on the kitchen patio; in the other living spaces, he'd covered the wood with an expensive brand of linoleum called Marmoleum that looked like marble to him but made Grandma think of crushed seashells. Her grandma had asked for green carpet; Winston laid down an orange one so she would never forget that from then on, his place was in the Netherlands with his wife Lya and the royal House of Orange, a quip that provoked hearty laughter. She took it all in again as if it were new to her, then went to sit next to her grandmother in the living room on the loveseat that still wore its plastic cover. Both had washed their hands and faces with the soap above the granite countertop in the double sink. And because she hadn't answered when her grandmother had asked where her mother was, she now said apologetically, "I'll cook for you, Grandma; Mama sent a fresh chicken, potatoes, peas, tomatoes, and even a big bottle of beer." Her grandmother coughed, responding carefully, "All right, Imker. Get me a glass of beer." Then, after coughing again, Bee murmured, "Make sure all the food is soft, or else I can't eat it." She'd hopped up to grab the beer but stopped in her tracks. She'd noticed

7

her grandmother getting thinner, and the stories about the emotional farewell between Grandma and her sister had stuck in her mind. Her back to her grandmother, she asked, "Are you hurting, Grandma Bee, or are your teeth giving you trouble? You're so thin these days, you really are." She turned around and stared at the woman, as if it weren't her grandmother sitting there but a total stranger. "No, no," her grandmother barked hoarsely, and then, "Go on and bring me a glass of beer, child." She hurried to the kitchen, pausing at the sink, staring for a moment through the frosted glass in the back door out at the patio and then snatching a drinking glass, rinsing and drying it, and pouring in the beer with a nice head of foam. She was only seventeen, but she always gave food and drink her full attention. Her grandmother looked at the beer, complimented her, and started drinking in small, eager sips. She stood close by, watching nervously. She knew something irrevocable was happening to the woman she considered the source of her existence; she didn't often visit her grandmother because her school was too far away and homework took up all her time, but her new training program would be closer by. "Cat got your tongue?" her grandmother asked. She shook her head. "Do you like the beer, Grandma?" And without pause: "You want me to massage your feet? You walk so much; Mama says you never take the bus. A massage, a foot massage?" She'd come up with the idea because it would have been harder for her to say what she felt: *I want to touch you, Grandma Bee.* Instead, her voice too loud, she said, "I can clip your toenails, too, you know." But her grandmother finished the glass and said softly, "Open the windows, pull the curtains aside a little, and get me more of that beer." She did

8

as she was told. It made the living room brighter, cooler too, and she rushed to the fridge in the kitchen down the hall, where her sister's sandals lay on the floor; without her grandmother's feet in them, they belonged entirely to Heli again. She had begged for those sandals herself, but Heli had been clear about who got what, and the sturdy orthopedic footwear went to Grandma, along with the pocket Bible and two new cotton nightgowns. Her grandmother had turned on the radio, and the news echoed through the house; she picked up the second glass of beer and smiled. And as she washed the chicken in a bowl and scrubbed the pieces with half a lemon, tears welled up, for consolation was nowhere to be found. She'd slept next to her sister all her life, shared a room with her for seventeen years, one closet, one desk. Sometimes she woke with a start because she could still hear how Heli had sobbed as she passed through the rooms of their house for the last time before her trip to Holland, while the car waited at the gate with Grandma inside and their mother Louise shouting impatiently, "Heli, come on, Heli!" After her sister had hugged her goodbye, she had shut herself up in their shared bedroom. "I'll be back soon, Imker; don't be sad, Imker; don't cry over me, Imker!" Heli just crying and crying. Leika the guard dog making an awful racket. Her sister Babs and the neighbors looking on in sullen resignation as the car drove off with their darling girl. She hadn't even been capable of that.

She started patting the chicken dry with paper towels. Meat hadn't ever appealed much to her. The family knew she'd rather cook for others than sit down for a meal herself. Her dream: a little restaurant where she'd decide the menu. Heli had promised always to be there for her, and she had promised to earn her preschool teaching certificate and only then become a professional cook. The shards of glass embedded in the top of the brick wall glittered in the sun. No one could climb over Grandma's walls without scratches and scrapes. Except for the yellow marigolds by the front gate, her grandmother's yard was bare. The dark soil was spread with a thick coat of crushed shells to prevent shoots from rising straight and tall in the garden soil, and even though her grandmother had always kept a vegetable garden—a small one, for personal use— she'd completely lost the urge to do anything of the kind any longer; the marigolds out front kept mosquitoes at bay and served as mementos of her childhood years in the British part of the country. Whenever someone started in about the barren lawn, Grandma would stubbornly insist that urban gardens were suited only to certain types of plants: limes and citrus for refreshment, an almond tree for shade, bilimbi fruit to pickle and eat with spicy food, marigolds to keep away insects, and rose bushes for perfume and good luck for the family. As she prepared the meal, Imker couldn't resist nosing around the kitchen cabinets, where she found four of every essential item: drinking glasses, soup bowls, cups and saucers, plates, assorted cutlery, and even four bright white linen napkins and a stack of dish towels. She set the kitchen table for two. Once everything was cooking on the stovetop and the table looked inviting, she fetched her grandmother; after the two glasses of lukewarm beer, Bee had fallen asleep on the loveseat, legs tucked in like an enormous fetus, snoring deeply and breathing regularly. Watching

her grandmother in innocent, relaxed sleep like a baby...
Radio off. Let nothing disturb her rest. She tiptoed out of
the living room and into the laundry room in search of
chores. The laundry basket wasn't full yet. Okay, do a
small load now anyway, then go outside to hang it all on
the rotary clothesline, which her grandmother seldom
used because it was too high for her to reach. Then she
opened the washing machine and saw it. A bloodstained
nightgown. She laid it out flat on the ironing board. The
blood had dried. There on the front. At chest height. She
felt her heart pounding. Fighting the urge to scour this
piece of clothing until it was immaculate, she hurled it
back into the washing machine along with the other laundry. She chose a cycle and was just about to run the
machine when she heard coughing and rushed to her
grandmother's side with a glass of water. The coughing
stopped. "Open the back door wide," her grandmother
told her. And the afternoon trade wind brought sea air
inside. "How far have you gotten with the cooking?" "It'll
take a little longer before everything's nice and soft." A
nod from her grandmother and she flew into the kitchen
to put everything on low heat and run the washer.
Grandma came into the kitchen, apparently on her way to
the toilet. She stopped when she heard the washer running and peered at her. "Is that really necessary?" Bee
grumbled and, without waiting for an answer, said she
was going to freshen up and rinse her mouth with mint
water to chase away the aftertaste of the beer. But she
sank onto the toilet and sat a while. Was Grandma Bee
thinking about the nightgown she'd set aside to show her
daughter Louise, a step that would bring death closer?
With a freshly washed face and a few damp hairs clinging

to her forehead, Grandmother took a seat at the table. Imker was just putting away the half-empty bottle of beer in the fridge. "Are you going to serve me dinner?" Grandma sounded excited. "At your service, Mrs. Vanta," Imker replied, laughing in relief, as she picked up a porcelain plate and carried it over to the pots and pans on the stove. "A little mashed potato, a steamed boneless chicken breast, gravy made with butter and fresh tomatoes, the creamed spinach you bought, and afterward, mango sorbet." She rattled off the menu as she set the plate down in front of her grandmother. Then over to the pots and pans, quick, quick, for her own portion, and then back to Grandma. They sat facing each other across the small table meant to accommodate six. They could look each other straight in the eye and easily touch hands. First Grandma said grace, mumbled but intelligible, and thanked her for the meal. They ate slowly without talking. She kept a close eye on her grandmother. Did the bloodstains on the shirt come from a chest wound, or was the blood from her mouth? Surely it couldn't be heartbreak revealing itself as blood instead of tears: the son Grandma Bee had lived with for so long had remarried and emigrated a few years back, leaving his mother behind like an old appliance, too worn out for his shiny new life. Sometimes, her mother Louise would come down hard on Grandmother Bee, saying she'd never really loved her daughters, just her boys. Winston, the apple of her eye, had even persuaded her to leave her own house and husband to live with him after his devastating divorce, and now look at him, just dumping her in a sterile house in a completely unfamiliar neighborhood, Zorg en Hoop— "Care and Hope"—a good description of her state of mind these days. Maybe her mother was right, but she, Imker Vanta, was sitting across from a woman who'd given away everything she owned, *and then it doesn't matter who you give it to*, Imker thought. The wet strings of hair framing her grandmother's face curled as they dried, and she waited until their eyes met. "Taste good, Grandma?" A nod, a sharp look in her eyes. The next bite went down the wrong way. She took a few sips of water. "Is that my washing machine I hear?" Grandma asked offhandedly. "Yeah, I ran a load of dirty laundry so I could try out your rotary clothesline." And she wondered if now, over their two empty plates, was the right time to ask about the bloodstains. "Then you must have seen my nightgown." Grandma was avoiding her eyes now. She nodded anyway. "And you're wondering where the blood came from?" A shy "Yes, Grandma Bee." Then her grandmother, firmly: "You said something about sorbet, and after that we can figure out the clothesline, dear Imker." She shot to her feet, letting her hands prepare the frozen treat while her mind was elsewhere. They spooned the mango sorbet, her grandmother smacking her lips in delight. She couldn't enjoy it. She was too afraid of what might come next. She suggested doing the dishes first and then going to hang up the laundry. Her grandmother grumbled that it was all very well to dry the clothes outside on the rotary clothesline, but they would have to stay close and keep an eye on things, with all the robberies in the neighborhood. Despite the tall brick wall topped with broken glass? Grandmother admitted it had never yet happened to her, but the elderly parish priest in Zorg en Hoop had warned her to be careful. With one last thump, the washing machine came to a halt. Grandma

13

remained in her seat at the wooden kitchen table. Without placemats, the yellow linoleum tabletop gleamed spotlessly. "How about I take the plastic off your loveseat, Grandma?" Bee granted permission. The living room had no dark wood cabinets with gleaming brass vessels, no elegant side tables with lace doilies, not even a rocking chair anywhere. Still, the bungalow had been converted into a home that wouldn't make Grandma feel hemmed in; it was modern, almost youthful. Glowing with vitality—in her memory, that's how her mother's mother had always looked: beautifully dressed and tirelessly busy, preparing a bite to eat for some elderly acquaintance somewhere in town. The fact that Bee's youngest had moved to Holland to become a pediatrician had inflated her ego, her grandmother would admit, but after Winston's departure three years earlier, it was hard to know how to make it through each day. Her mother Louise would sometimes whisper, with venom in her voice, "Do you miss your boys?"—her tone judgmental, almost rude.

Grandma Bee didn't respond to Imker's question but stood up and wandered to the laundry room in her slippers. She opened the washer door, commanding, "Imker, come take out the clothes and hang them up," but at the same time, she herself was already removing the washed clothes from the drum piece by piece, shaking them out and dropping them into an empty laundry basket with a box of clothespins. The rotary clothesline? Try as she might, she couldn't figure out how to lower it either. But at five feet five inches, she was quite a bit taller than her grandmother and could easily hang up what was handed to her. There were nine items, including a bedsheet and two pillowcases. She fastened them on with the colorful pins and watched the breeze rotate the lines. Grandma's eyes followed the nightgown. So did hers. The color of recycled paper, it fluttered through the air, bright and unblemished. They went to sit on the plastic lawn chairs on the patio, as the sun brought warmth, tempered by the trade wind. The ocean might be far away on a human scale, but the wind reminded her that their city was on the coast at the mouth of a river flowing into the Atlantic. The sky was bluer than anything. No place could be quieter than Grandma's house at three o'clock in the afternoon. She and Grandmother didn't take a siesta, just dozed for a bit. And then, overcoming her trepidation: "The blood, Grandma Bee, where is it coming from?" Her grandmother looked up into the sky; without any clouds, it seemed terribly thin. "Was it at night?" she asked more insistently. "It happens in the morning, Imker. I think it's coming from my throat. Maybe somewhere deeper. I don't understand this bleeding. I never have a fever." Grandma's unspeaking face gazed into hers. "Should I take you to the hospital to have it checked out?" Her grandmother was ready for this question, and her response came pouring out: "Don't even think about it, Imker. They'll keep me there, and I'll never come home again, I just know it. And I don't want any pills. Nothing. No slicing me open, either. And I forbid you to tell anyone I'm bleeding." Her grandmother didn't try to hide her heaving chest. "Not even my mother, Grandma Bee?" "Not even your mother, Imker. I'm the only one who gets to tell people." Silence. Wordless eye contact. "Promise me that, child." Imker, right away: "Yes, yes, I promise, Grandma." A long silence fell between them. Her grandmother sat down at the kitchen table again, staring solemnly out at the clothesline as the wind whirled the laundry dry. Not much longer until the clothes could be brought in again for ironing. She walked along the wall, all the way around the bungalow. Suddenly, she knew what had to be done. She went back inside. Almost excited: "Grandma, I'll go home to Amora now and come right back to spend the night with you. I'll bring a blanket. I can sleep in your room on the rug right next to you. I won't have you going through this alone all day and night." And as she stumbled over what she was trying to put into words, she was overwhelmed by a fit of sobbing, tears she'd managed to hold back when her sister moved to Holland and she suffered through the first night all alone in that big bed, in a bedroom now made of brick and not of Heli's presence. Grandmother looked on, silent, knowing there was no stopping her. She cleaned up and left without her bookbag. On her feet, just for now, were the sandals left by Heli.

It wasn't a request but an announcement with which she disturbed her mother's siesta: "Mom, I'm planning to stay with Grandma Bee." Still lying down, her mother Louise asked worriedly after Bee's health. She got no clear answer, only that Grandma shouldn't be left alone, especially not at night. And like a whirlwind, Imker collected everything she thought she'd need, cramming her little sister Babs's suitcase full of books, clothing, sheets, toiletries, hearing her mother calling, "Don't take our toothpaste and bath soap, buy your own on the way to Grandma's, leave the sanitary pads, too, you hear me,

Imker?" She didn't respond. "How long do you think you'll be gone?" She zipped the suitcase shut, shouting back from her room, "I'm not sure yet, I'll try it out for a weekend and see." She didn't know what the next step would be yet. Mama: "And after that, Imker?" A peculiar silence filled her. Her mother often mentioned how much she resembled her grandmother: same facial features, same skin color, same hair even, only a difference in height. She went over to Mama with the suitcase and sat on the stool at the vanity table, looking at herself and her mother in the mirrors. "Can Grandma Bee come live with us, Mama?" It sounded aggressive. "I know you moved out of your parents' house a long time ago to live on your own, Mama." Her mother responded, sluggishly: "And now there are four nearly adult children between my mother and me." A strange response. As if she were standing beside a large body of water and wanted to wade across without getting soaked. "Mama, what if Grandma gets sick, so sick she needs help?" Her mother was wide awake now, on her feet. "Our house isn't made for that, too small, too crowded." Mama sat down on the edge of the bed and looked straight at her. "Do you miss Heli so much that you'd rather sleep next to Grandma?" This threatened to send the conversation in a new direction. She jumped up and hugged her mother: "No, I really am thinking of Grandma Bee…" And standing in the doorway: "I'm going to miss you, Mama, but I want to be at your mother's house by sundown, bye." And Imker was off. *Keep walking*, she thought, and she realized, *It may be a long stay.*

Babs, poring over a textbook, saw her sister leaving with the suitcase. She got up and watched from the window in the study, staying there until Imker disappeared from view. Without asking, Imker had taken her red suitcase, and God only knew where to. She understood she mustn't give in to her sudden impulse to run to her mother and demand an explanation. Pouting, she kept staring outside. No one in the house really cared about her problems. No cuddles for her. No flattering words. Maybe they thought she was so smitten with Aram that nothing else mattered to her. That was so far from the truth. She would show them. She sat back down at the large desk, making another attempt to fully grasp exactly why and how the Second World War had started. It was a required essay for history, but the question had taken on greater meaning when she'd found out that her father's mother was Jewish. Since then, she'd been better able to accept how her skin color stood out in her family, and once her high school diploma was in the bag, she wouldn't let anyone give her grief. Not even her mother. Even though she was awfully curious where Imker was spending the night, she would let her mother tell her on her own instead of asking. And she stood up again and walked to the window, noticed a fly clinging to the pane of the shutter, grabbed some tissue paper, and brushed the bug outside. She looked up. Her little brother, in his Scout uniform, was pushing the gate open. He probably couldn't see her, but she smiled at him. She could hear his footsteps crunching on the crushed shell walkway. The back door to the kitchen opened and closed. He was inside. Faucet on. Washing his hands. "Take off your shoes first, Audi," she called out, walking out to him. He stared at her with a solemn expression. His eyes glowed brightly and attentively. "I'm so hungry," he said softly. "Where is everyone?" Their mother walked into the room, slowly, lost in thought. "I'll fix you both something to eat. There's still some soup left, actually, I'll heat it up, and who wants bread?" Somewhat apologetically, Louise looked first at her daughter, then at Audi, and said, "I'm not so hungry myself." Babs shot a resentful glance at her mother. "So your appetite took off with Heli?" Mama stood by the stove and did as she'd promised. "You're quiet, Mama," said Audi. "Yes, it's quiet, everything's come to a standstill in this house, kid." Babs's voice sounded accusatory. "Except for the clock, Babs," said Audi soothingly, "and my stomach's growling awfully loud." Braying laughter. Mama didn't join in but remarked that no one had turned on the radio, so there was no music playing in the living room. Babs snapped, "Yep, Heli loves music and the radio, but I don't like all that racket." Mother chuckled. "Then I guess you're glad it's quieter without her?" Babs didn't feel like arguing and withdrew into the study again. "Your food's almost ready," her mother called after her in surprise.

Audi walked into the living room and turned on the radio. A woman's voice was reading a children's story. He sat down at the table where his sister had always sat. He slid his placemat and cutlery closer to his chest. He hadn't been there when Heli left. He'd gone to play soccer with the neighborhood boys, just like any other day. He couldn't face saying goodbye to her. He'd been sitting with his mother when the plan was explained to them: The best thing for Heli was to leave the country instead of using her charms to distract a man who was key to Suriname's development. He and his mother had listened. They were sitting in an office with two unfamiliar men in neckties and one woman. The woman was doing all the talking. Heli had to end the affair at once; they'd give Louise the money, if necessary, to send her eldest daughter to the Netherlands. On the way home, along the shell road running from the ministry building to downtown, he could hear his mother crying softly, without even shedding any tears. He watched the river water shimmer, heard it splashing. Not a word came out of him. Not even when Mama told him to go on ahead and find a clean car at the taxi stand for the ride home to Amora. He signaled to a driver. His voice was gone. Even weeks after her departure, he was still so quiet inside. When his mother and Babs took their places at the table, as if dragged out of a terrible dream, he asked, "Where's Imker?" Mama passed the soup, still holding the ladle. "Staying with Grandma Bee for a while." She delivered the news in a soft voice. "Is Grandma sick?" asked Babs. "Maybe," his mother answered, and then, louder, "Anyone want another piece of bread?" The bread was divided evenly. Everyone made the sign of the cross and said, "Bon appetit." A rattling at the gate. Mama went to the picture window. "Who is it?" They could clearly hear as someone shouted, "Mrs. Vanta, your daughter wants me to tell you she made it to her grandmother's safely. I gave her a lift, just wanted you to know." Mama's voice: "Thank you, Umar." And a motorbike started up and rode away. It was peanut soup. The fragrance of fresh parsley and crushed peanuts filled the living room where they were eating. They broke the bread, dipped it in the warm soup, and ate in silence. The radio played the seven o'clock news. Was anyone listening? Audi turned to his mother with his mouth full and nodded his approval.

I'm buzzing with excitement. It's like I'm about to do something that will change our small world. Mama's eyes and her voice, so close, stir up something inside me. I've registered at the teachers' college, and it's the first day of class, after a September vacation that was much too hot and much too long. I stand in front of the big mirror. The dress I have on was made by the finest tailor in Paramaribo. Went into town with Mama to look for fabric. To the seamstress with Mama to browse through her pattern book. To the atelier with Mama to pick and choose, to be measured and fitted. I look at my reflection. Mama stands diagonally behind me, maybe gazing over my shoulder. I'm all brand new. Shoes, underwear, clothes, and the debut of a new hairstyle—lightly straightened, in a bun I feel resting against my neck. Mother has her perfume bottle in her hand. She asks if I'd like some. With her index finger, she applies a drop to my wrist, two more to my earlobes. Happiness ripples through me, making my heart beat faster. She sniffs under my arms, checking whether I used the deodorant stick. I open my mouth wide. She looks inside, inspecting my breath, too. My schoolbag is on the chair, recently bought and full of new things, like the colorful day planner I got from Grandma Bee. Mother smiles in satisfaction; at the age of fifteen I've been admitted to what for her is a dream education, so Mama pulled up stakes, leaving Nieuw Nickerie to ensure my future. The neighborhood where we live is a public housing development called Amora Village that's still partially under construction. Mama's found a job at the local public school. The long vacation is about to end. Our rent-to-own bungalow is filled with new furniture. She has even found a guard dog and named her Leika. Imker, Babs, and my little brother Audi will start school in two weeks. I'm itching to pick up my class schedule and book list, and maybe I'll catch a first glimpse of my classmates too. Mama looks at me. Our eyes collide in the mirror. I turn to her and smile. "Good luck, Heli." I nod. Something bursts in my belly. I feel no pain. Something warm running down my left leg. I've been agitated for days now. I smell it and stare down at my feet. Drops of blood. "Mama, I'm bleeding," I whisper. "Yes," she says tenderly, and then, "Congratulations." But I don't feel at all like celebrating, because there's no way I'm going out today, or tomorrow, or the day after. I'll have to wait until the bleeding stops. Mother helps me out of my dress, smiling faintly, because just imagine if I'd been out of the house and caught off guard by something like this. We go into the bathroom, and she takes out a pack of sanitary pads. She explains how to use them and how to keep clean from the waist down during these recurring days of female discomfort. She says, "You're not a woman yet, my child, not even close." I take another shower. I cry. I don't want this. The pad between my legs slows me down, and how do I sit and stand up again? My panties are soaking in sudsy water. I look at them. Mama says, "I'll go to the school myself and let them know not to give your place away, and I'll pick up your books and class schedule." But I want Mama to stay home with me and answer my questions. I've read about menstruation in a medical handbook and know it's healthy and normal, but I want to speak to a woman who's gone through this experience. "No," Mama says, and, looking me in the eye, she says, "I'll buy you a present from a goldsmith in town, then head over to your school." I give in. "College, not school," I say, irritably. "Your college," she repeats, happy to grant me that.

I pace around our living room. I sit. I stand up. I jump. I keep going to the toilet to see if anything has changed. And I remember Nanda. And I see what happened to Nanda again. She sat next to me in sixth grade—she was called to the chalkboard—she didn't want to stand up—she wouldn't say why—our teacher waited—the class waited too—she still wouldn't stand up—she burst into tears—she sobbed until the recess bell chased everyone onto the playground. I stayed in my seat next to her. Our teacher asked if I knew anything. It was Nanda who replied. "Miss, I'm bleeding, I have blood on my skirt." I looked at the seat, at the floor, and saw no blood. I wanted to go, but the teacher asked me to stay with Nanda and left the classroom. "Are you sick?" "Not really," Nanda said. "I just can't get used to it." Our teacher, a friend of Mama's, was newly married and heavily pregnant with her first child. Like us, she came from the city and had been assigned to teach in Nickerie, where we'd been living for about a year. Mrs. Snow came back and took Nanda with her. A strange bloodstain on the wooden seat that no one came to clean off. Nanda didn't return to school that day. The spot had dried by the time we went home. It was a hot Friday, and I thought Nanda would die. A girl of twelve losing blood?

I lie on my mother's bedspread, thinking about my own body and its secrets. I must have fallen into a deep sleep around eleven in the morning; when I wake up it's two p.m. and my mom Louise still hasn't returned. My two younger sisters and my little brother left for summer camp two weeks ago and will probably get home this afternoon, tired, grumpy, filthy. And in a week a relative will be moving in with us—Mama's youngest brother, a medical student, who's decided he'd rather live with his sister than in his childhood home in Jacobusrust. He bought a new scooter. He's been on a camping trip. And he'll decorate his bedroom himself. Through the lives of others, I am beginning to understand that life presents opportunities for charting your own course, and I'll figure out the details without anyone's help. On my mother's vanity table lies a large Bible. She read to me from the Bible this morning. Mama likes to say God is her co-pilot. And I believe her. My mother was assigned a bungalow at a T-intersection. A bad location, because in the evening the headlights of passing cars shine into our living room. It's not a busy road, but the lights get on my nerves. Mama won't even shut the blackout curtains before ten at night. She assumes that by then everyone has made it home for the night, but as long as there are still people out, she wants to prove she has nothing to hide. There are half-finished roads between the houses: dirt tracks without sidewalks, grassy roadsides still teeming with slippery creatures. The construction worker my mother hired to lay tile in the yard, build a boundary wall, and install a heavy gate is very dark-skinned and very good-looking. When he sees my mother, he breaks into a flirty grin. He tells us the sewer system here in Amora Village is very good, and the clogs and floods that plague the city center in the rainy season won't trouble us in this outer district. As a pre-school teacher, my mother needs to live close to work, according to her principal, who came by once to meet her children. My mother would much rather live downtown in a big house with a flowering garden. Maybe she can't afford that. Maybe after more than four years away from the capital, she's taking the time to catch her breath with her family in a quiet neighborhood. It's a day's journey by river between Paramaribo and Nieuw Nickerie, and I haven't forgotten that the move to this new house was a hellish chore for a husbandless woman with three young girls and a son not even ten. We couldn't bring anything but some clothing and a few personal items that didn't take up much space. No books. Not my bike. For days, I kept a sheet of paper deep in the pocket of my new jeans with the names and addresses of my friends in their own handwriting. Lost it. Don't know where or how. Maybe in the laundry. However hard I try to dream of the street in the district where we lived, it doesn't work. The dream images that stalk me in the morning, ever since we've moved back to Paramaribo, come from Jacobusrust. I see the faces of my relatives, of sisters and brothers and their parents, attacking each other with words. And I can't forget what Grandma Bee called my mother, even though I wasn't even ten and didn't know what the word "hussy" meant, just that it was hurtful because it made my mother cry so hard. Crying is what you do when blood pours from your body, because you may be in mortal danger. But sometimes a woman bleeds and no one can see it. Tears run down my face unhindered. My mother might come home any moment now. And the campers must also be on their way. For two weeks now, it's been Mama and me and no one else, just the two of us. In conversation, in silence, in laughter. Shopping, cooking, eating, singing, lazing around.

The tears flow freely. My suitcase lies open on the rug. My name, *Heli Vanta*, on the silk lining. It's my first Sunday morning in the Netherlands in the guest room at Winston and his wife Lya's place. They've invited me to Sunday Mass.

Bee could hear her granddaughter Imker's deep, calm breathing. She herself couldn't fall asleep even though she wasn't tossing and turning; her throat was suffocating her. To make matters worse, she had a terrible craving for the taste and aroma of a cigar. In the kitchen cabinet, hidden away in a cookie jar, was a tin of cigars, a good brand. She yearned for a large one, like the ones she'd smoked every evening for years, sitting on a stool in her bedroom, legs wide, leaning over to spit in the chamber pot. A cigar calmed her, smoking soothed her. The smoke that curled past her nose, the way she vanished with each breath, all her thoughts dissolving and her head emptying out completely, as if she were drunk. And then—if she'd reduced the cigar to a fat stub and still hadn't puffed away all her pain—the chewing would begin. Chewing and spitting and chewing again and spitting again until her tongue and throat burned from the tobacco's bitterness. Then she would rinse out her mouth with tap water flavored with mint leaves, which she kept in a carafe next to her. She swallowed nothing. Everything ended up in the chamber pot. She would stare into the dark liquid for a long while before putting the lid on. By then, it was usually around midnight. Her husband Anton would be asleep and the children who were still at home gone to bed. It became so hard to lie down next to the father of her children without feeling him there. And she didn't want to feel him there. That uneasiness from years ago came over her again.

Imker mumbled something in her sleep. She wanted to get up. She wanted to do something, fetch the clothes for ironing, for example, unfold the ironing board, heat the iron, and smooth out the wrinkles from each piece of clothing, one by one. Imker would wake up, startled, and ask her all kinds of questions. Her granddaughter would worry. She reached for the silver box hanging from an unbreakable cord around her neck. It held the baby teeth of her last child. Rogier had brought her the pillbox with his name engraved on the inside, along with the names of his parents. He came to tell her he had to go to the Netherlands for a residency. She was shocked. She hadn't been expecting anything like that. After all, he'd grown close to a girl who didn't want to live in a foreign country far from her family. Her son had said, "Don't cry, Ma, I'm leaving with my girlfriend, we'll get married in Holland, and when I become a pediatrician, we'll move back with grandchildren for you to spoil." Gripping the pillbox, she'd gone on grumbling, "Your father hasn't even been dead a year, and you're going so far away from me." He'd nodded. He'd also said, "Pa never spoke more than ten sentences to me, Ma; he never talked. He went to his job

27

at the army base. He came home on time. He sat in his chair. He listened to the radio. He ate. He took a bath. He read the paper. He went to bed." She listened and watched him in fascinated silence until he finished. She waited for more. She expected Rogier to mention how caring she'd always been. But he fell into a deep silence, which she broke half an hour later: "I still have your baby teeth. I'll put them in a box and have a goldsmith solder it shut with the gold from our wedding rings." Her son didn't respond. He looked impeccable in his white shirt, gray trousers, and dark brown moccasins, with a healthy glow to his skin and his hair cut short. "How old are you?" she asked. "Not quite thirty, but I get older every year on March 16th, Ma." She almost let slip that she sometimes felt unwell and had trouble swallowing, but instead she asked in a voice as sugary sweet as a girl's, "By the way, why didn't you stay here with us?" And he stood up abruptly, her son did, because he couldn't stand being reminded of his sister Laura. "I'm leaving in ten days," he said brusquely. "On a plane?" "Yeah, Ma, we're leaving on a plane." "And where are you going to live?" "In Utrecht with my girlfriend's family and later in our own place, Ma." "Do you have the money to live there?" "I have a scholarship; the Surinamese government is paying for my studies, Ma." Her, blubbering: "You're taking away everything I live for, but I'm happy for you all the same, Rogier!" He wrapped an arm around her. "I'll come back, I'll come back to you, Ma, I swear." And off he went, out of the living room, outside to his scooter. "Will you come say goodbye?" "Of course, Ma." The conversation kept repeating in her head, especially in the mornings and nights when sleep wouldn't come. As promised, he came back to hug her and thank her for everything, his girlfriend waiting out in the street by the scooter, watching. "Is she good to you?" "Her father likes me." "Why won't she come in?" she'd asked, but he wouldn't answer that question either. And she remembered what she thought as he drove off with his girlfriend behind him on the scooter Anton had paid for: *She's even blacker than your father!* And that thought had disturbed her; she never got over it, that feeling that her son had fallen into the wrong hands. Her daughter Louise thought her fear was unwarranted, even mean-spirited. But she couldn't shake it. She walked to her familiar church in the city center each day to light a candle for Rogier and do a rosary for him. She hadn't missed a day since he left...

But she must have nodded off, because when she looked up, the room was bright and warm. Imker was no longer swaddled in sheets in her friend's sleeping bag on the rug. "Imker, where are you?" And she was greeted with a cheerful "Good morning, Grandma Bee." The sweet smell of warm cocoa reached her nostrils, and she forgot the nagging pain in her throat. Even though bright sun was shining into the bedroom and the sunflowers on her curtains seemed to be dancing, she smelled blood. She slid her feet into her slippers and smiled because her granddaughter had already cleared away the sheets, sleeping bag, and sleeping pad from the spot where she had slept; Imker was already up and about. "What are you doing, dear child?" she called, coming out of her bedroom. Then she saw it. Imker, ironing the previous day's laundry, looked up. They met each other's gaze. Her granddaughter's eyes were bright with tears. "You don't need to be on your way?" "Yes, soon, Grandma." "Are you

29

going back home?" "No, Grandma, I work Saturdays at a clothing store downtown for pocket money. The pay is pretty good." She started pushing the curtains aside to let in more sunlight, mumbling, "That's good. So you'll come back to my house?" Imker stopped, put down the iron, came up to her. "I work until five, then I'll pick up some ingredients for dinner and come back." In Imker's hand was the piece of clothing the blood had stained. But her granddaughter said excitedly, "Look, Grandma, all clean! I remember when Heli bought a dozen nightgowns with the words OFF WHITE, and everyone at home got two, including our little brother Audi and the lady next door. She even saved one for you, huh?" She'd turned on the radio for the morning benediction. "Did you sleep well, Grandma?" She knew Imker really wanted to talk about something else, something that went far deeper than a good night's rest. "Off-white is the color of bittersweet almonds once you've peeled away the dark brown skin," she said warmly, and, "Yes, I woke up feeling so much better than yesterday." Keeping her eyes on her grand-daughter, she picked up the ironed nightgown. "I gave one nightgown to Laura." She froze for a second, think-ing of her child. "Sweet of you," mumbled Imker. "Yes, everything is better than yesterday, Imker," she repeated, heading for the bathroom to wash up, but most of all to rinse the taste of blood from her mouth and throat. "Grandma, do you want me to rake outside?" The yard didn't really need raking, but it was one way to collect your thoughts in the early morning, and she heard Imker calling again and at the same time she saw fresh blood in the sink. From her throat? Panic. She heard Imker unlocking the front door. A stream of cool air breezed inside. She called out to her granddaughter. "I'm bleeding again." Imker saw it and began to cry uncontrollably.

Although the bleeding soon stopped, its traces washed away with warm water, a scrub brush, and soap, Saturday remained bloodstained. And although she slowly but resolutely worked her way through a small bowl of oatmeal, fear lingered at the table with them. She made Imker go outside and do the raking. But first she explained to her granddaughter that the bleeding always happened in the morning. It had been going on for months, initially at intervals of days or even weeks, but then, all of a sudden, every morning. Once in a great while the bleeding hurt. "Badly?" Imker asked. She sighed. And she reached her left arm across the table toward her granddaughter, palm up. At first, Imker stared in silence at the open hand, doing nothing, until finally she said, "What's keeping you?" And when she felt another person's warm hand against hers, she said, hoarse, "Pain is something else altogether, ask your mother about it, because I didn't have any mother I could ask questions…what I feel is like a fire in my throat, no more than that." And she let go of Imker's hand. Withdrew her own hand. And Imker fixed herself a mug of cocoa. She had a glass of water to which she'd added a drop of an antiseptic home remedy. Saturday morning slowly blossomed into a day that brimmed with light. The trade wind brought a breeze that wound around her neck, her cheeks, her head, her legs. "I'll stay here and live with you," Imker said softly. She was surprised. "You'd better discuss it with your mother first, Imker." Her granddaughter nodded vaguely. She said a prayer of thanks. Imker went to rake the yard. She went about her routine. Read a Bible passage. Said the Hail Marys for her rosary. Laid out her clothes. Made the bed. Meditated. And then, around nine, she and Imker left the house on Passiflorastraat. Imker took a minibus into town.

Bee walked to Zorg en Hoop Church, where she spent her Saturdays polishing brass candlesticks for Sunday Mass. She arrived at the church door at the same time as the curate. This assistant priest could have been her grandson, he was so young. He greeted her with a handshake. "I'll air it out first, Mrs. Vanta, stay out here in the fresh air." She nodded and sat down on the cool stoop, but the young man brought her a folding chair and made sure she was seated comfortably. He knew her. He knew that her sons had gone to Holland. He knew about her sadness in front of the statue of Mother Mary, where he'd discovered her crying, and his mentor, Father Teloor, who'd been her confessor for over twenty years now, had told him to welcome her on Saturdays by laying out the candlesticks for her along with the polish and buffing cloth. She sat on the folding chair, thinking about the assistant priest and Father Overtoon: the conversations they'd had with her about their own families, their mothers, their country of birth, their hometowns in Holland. Their house calls had helped her and them to endure certain things that had seemed unbearable. He came out to get her and walked with her to the sacristy next to the altar. "Would you like a cup of tea?" "No, thank you." And she sat down at the table with the brass work. "Okay, maybe later then," the

32

young man in black said affably before he left. There was a bell nearby she could use to summon him. The room also had a sink with a faucet and a small counter where drinking glasses were kept. Hangers with altar boy robes in various sizes. The constant odor of incense. Somewhere high above in the wooden walls were glass-louvered windows with security bars; they were open, and cool air drifted down on her head. She took off her hat, ran her hands through her hair, and tapped her sandals back and forth along the parquet floor as if drumming. She set to work. Leaving the brass polish unopened, she picked up the buffing cloth and started on the base of a huge candelabrum. The pieces in front of her were parts of large brass ornaments too heavy to move without disassembling. She didn't exactly know which ones went together. She enjoyed polishing the brass until it gleamed. The ticking of the clock on the wall nearby kept time with her thoughts as they raced backward, coming to a stop at the engagement party. More than a hundred eggs had been baked into pastries, pies, and snacks by more than ten women cooks, who'd spent days whisking, kneading, shaping, stirring, and whipping up the "small party" her daughter Laura had requested into something bigger and bigger. Laura had said yes to Bram; at last, her daughter had found the man of her dreams. And if Bram had discussed the festivities with Bee and not with her son, she could have kept everything in proportion, not let it get so out of hand. Impressed by Winston's connections, Bram had given the 2,000-guilder budget to him instead of placing it in the trustworthy hands of Laura's parents, Anton and herself. She attacked the brass with new vigor, set the piece aside, and picked up another one. Grandma Bee polished with great care, and whoever saw her absorbed in the task would have assumed her thoughts were on the candelabrum. An hour went by, and another. The curate's footsteps. No, it was old Teloor. He had reached her side long before she could tear her thoughts away from her daughter Laura. She could see Laura standing there just as if she could touch her; her daughter in her engagement gown, and oh, how beautiful she looked in off-white taffeta. Perhaps a mother shouldn't develop a preference for any one of her five children, but who could really say where feelings came from, or whether the thing we call love even exists. Her elderly confessor stood next to her. She heard him saying that with every loving act, she was combating the evil of the human world. She got up for a glass of water. She washed her hands. She grabbed a glass, turned on the faucet, drank. Teloor asked how she was doing and if he could stop by again with the young curate. "God willing, Father." And the house call was added to his appointment book. Grandmother Vanta put on her hat. Said goodbye.

My grandparents' house no longer stands. The neighbors' homes are long gone, too. It's not easy for me to admit that what I'm seeing is real. A vast expanse looms before me, overgrown with the kinds of plants that will never grow tall. Pieces of rubble reach no higher than my knees. I don't exactly know where our house was, because nothing remains of the tall almond tree. The houses across the street are still there, wooden houses, freshly painted, even. Almost every night, I dream of the house from my earliest childhood, the one that stood on this street: dark brown stained wood with olive green doors. In my dreams, I'm not the six-year-old child who lived there; I am as old I am now. I dream that I enter the front yard from the street, step up onto the deck, and go inside. That's all that happens. Except that when I wake, I'm overwhelmed by a violent feeling of unease. And now I'm actually standing on Weidestraat, where I walk in my dreams, but there's no building here for me to enter, even though the street remains unchanged. The house was too small for all the people who wanted to live there. I remember the altercations and bitter silences between my mother, Louise, and her sister, Laura. I held Mama's hand tight during those arguments as I took in Aunt Laura's face. It was her mouth I watched, her wide mouth, with lips painted dark red. I didn't know what the fight was about. I was too scared to ask what was going on once the name-calling was over and my mother sat dead quiet in a lawn chair facing the street. The expression in her eyes was ominous. I see the same expression in them again these days, and I feel the same unease. My grandmother now lives in an entirely different part of town. Grandpa Anton has passed away. Mama wants me to go and see her sister Laura. She expects me to accompany her to Kolera for a hospital visit before leaving my homeland. But I'll be damned if I will.

Amazing how sunlight makes a landscape shine in shades of ocean blue, blood red, grass green, and everything in between. A tree with orange blossoms high in its canopy of leaves; blossoms that sway in the wind and flutter downward, slowly, pirouetting like miniature dancers. Everywhere I look, I see young people, and a sense of exhilaration takes hold of me. I enter the yard of the teacher training college for the first time. I have to report to the administrative office to pick up some documents from the registrar. Thanks to my period two weeks ago, I missed the big orientation day. The gold bracelet on my wrist is a gift from my mother. I glance at it: a rosebud on a stem curved into a band. I stride onward, in search of something that doesn't resemble a classroom. The building complex overwhelms me. I'm too nervous to speak to anyone. Don't spot anyone from my old school: Nieuw Nickerie is far to the east. But my mother secured a recommendation from my principal there, so I could skip a year and register for teacher training here in Paramaribo. Parents typically believe it's safer to have their daughters finish school before moving on to vocational training. Not my mother. I didn't have any say in it. Her decision was final: I could no longer remain in the rice district of Nickerie. To her, a daughter of fifteen is still a child; she'll grow into a woman in time but is under strict parental supervision. And if I suddenly feel lost when a gong sounds out of the blue, spurring everyone around me to confident action, well, Mother doesn't need to know. I stand there, looking around, and wait for the schoolyard to empty out before I go up to the elderly caretaker by the gate and ask him how to get to the registrar's office. Half an hour later, I'm walking across the same square with the school director. He escorts me to the temporary classrooms for the first-year students. "The program is packed," he mentions. He knocks on a moss green door and lets me enter first. He says with a smile and a nod in my direction, "Heli Vanta belongs in this group." And then, turning toward the class, which has fallen dead silent, he adds pointedly, "There should still be a desk for her somewhere." A boy in jeans and an immaculate white shirt rises, pulls up another desk and chair, looks at me, and says, "You can sit here, my name's Umar, and what should I call you, Heli or Ms. Vanta?" The director smiles, but the class erupts into laughter. I take a seat and watch as the man who introduced me walks back across the schoolyard, saying nothing until my classmates settle down. Then I glance over at the faces that I can see clearly and ask bluntly, "No lessons today?" If I'd read the documents, I'd have known that the start of classes has been postponed, as a few instructors still hadn't arrived from the Netherlands. Umar explains this to me in a whisper. A blond man comes marching straight toward our classroom. After entering, he hesitates at the blackboard, fiddling with the chalk. Mirrored sunglasses. Beige clothing. Necktie. He looks around in silence. Then he writes his name and title and the class he'll be teaching: Standard Dutch. He wishes us a good morning and bids us welcome. He speaks clearly. His gaze is piercing. He's tall and wiry. He's our homeroom teacher, and he tells us he has a few things to explain about our chosen program of study. It seems as if everyone is listening breathlessly, just like me. His blue eyes twinkle, and as he reads our names off the roster, he shoots an amused look at each of us in turn: fourteen young women and nine young men, six Chinese, five Hindustanis, two Javanese, two Indonesians, eight Creoles. A smile parts his lips. Then he says distinctly, though it's masked as a mutter, "Whoever fails my class won't get a teaching job anywhere!" No one budges. We have nothing to say to that. Not one of us leaves in protest. I glare at him. He stares back. In a bored voice, he adds,

"You can pick up your books and worksheets in room 27." He leaves us. My classmates start to gossip about the teacher. He's strict and fair, apparently, but has nothing good to say about Hindustanis, maybe Javanese either, and spends his free time photographing Arawak Indians deep in the hinterland. The Arawak? The original inhabitants of the Amazon forest? I notice we're all from outside the capital. They've put us together in one group, and most of the others already know each other well. I don't want to hear their stories about teachers I haven't met. I stare outside. I wonder why Grandma Bee's girls all chose teaching. Umar says I should come get our books with him now, because it's a long way to walk. We leave the classroom together. The housing complex built for professional soldiers and their families has been wiped off the face of the earth. The times have changed. I walk down the broad sidewalk along the broad street as if expecting a sudden miracle. A sinkhole back to my preschool years. Memories bomb me flat. I pick up my handkerchief and inhale the perfume my mother and her sister love so much. Maybe all my experiences fit into a single handkerchief, which, like a conjurer, I can crumple in one hand and then unfurl wherever I may go, to bring the past to life again like distant lightning. In the Jacobusrust district of Paramaribo, or somewhere in Holland, in the north wind. Humming, I walk on. Laura will see me, but this time without my mother, who can't even answer my question about why her sister was turned away from our house when she stood pleading at the door one night. Mama says, "Life will teach you to forget, and even to forgive, Heli."

To reach her destination, Grandmother had to walk half-way across Paramaribo. Her feet were doing so well in the sports sandals that she took more risks than usual. She knew she might suddenly bleed from her mouth. She knew she might abruptly trip and fall. But her body was propelled by willpower. She walked briskly, knowing only too well what it meant to long for it all to end. She stopped at a bookstore to catch her breath. The streets she took were so familiar that the shopkeepers recognized her, and she knew exactly which loose paving stones to avoid. She even recognized the neighborhood houses, although she didn't know who lived in them anymore. Bit by bit, half the city had moved to Holland. She took another break at an intersection. The pedestrian light turned green, and she crossed. It still bothered her that her son Winston, with whom she'd lived for years, hadn't even invited her along when he started planning his move. "Must have been his wife's doing," she muttered, almost out loud. He'd always picked girls who didn't have a kind word to say to her. She stopped in front of the display window of a car dealership, this time to scrutinize her reflection. A salesman hurried over. Startled, she walked on. Her mirror image was a dreadful sight anyway, even for less than five seconds. The judgment she passed on her own body was damning. Still, she could clearly see that whatever made her bleed in the morning had not taken over every facet of her life. And so, revitalized, she pressed on, her face hidden behind a pair of sunglasses, her head covered with a sun visor, her feet comfortable. Farther, still farther. The striped dress she wore had two pockets that held cotton handkerchiefs. She arrived at the street where she'd happily looked after her family for years. A narrow brick path, which unexpectedly curved into a bridge over a canal. They'd been assigned a lovely house by the colonial army. When the Jacobusrust building complex was complete and her husband Anton was no longer of much use as a sergeant, they'd had to move. He could have bought the house when they'd first moved in, a sound suggestion from the senior officers, but he'd absolutely refused. Anton didn't care about his children, no, he didn't care about *her* children, he didn't care about *their* children! No one else could hear her voice ringing out so clearly in her mind. As mother to five little ones, she'd had her favorites, but every child she bore, she loved. So little remained of those feelings now. Truth be told, nothing remained of all those feelings. When she thought of her children, she couldn't help but cry. She gazed into the street. Market stalls shimmered in the sun. There were women, all dressed up, buying all sorts of things and tucking their purchases away in their bags. She observed them. Nausea swept over her. She always started feeling unwell when she approached this avenue, which led straight to Kolera. Her breathing grew labored as if she were dead tired. She knew exactly what the Javanese peddlers were hawking under their canopies. Bami with stir-fried chicken. Banana fritters. Nasi goreng with sambal. Oranges, peeled and chilled, and soft drinks. Also cigarettes, pouches of rolling tobacco, and even cigars. She gazed at the view of palm trees. She wondered if she could still stand it. Walking along those walls. The last time had been when Winston was about to leave the country. Through her sobs, she'd begged him to come with her, to say goodbye to his little sister for heaven's sake, begged him never to forget Laura. And he'd picked her up on the Wednesday morning before he went to the airport, and they'd driven there in silence. She walked as slowly as possible to the food stalls. Bami with chicken to go, two soft drinks, two cigars, a pack of unfiltered cigarettes, and a bunch of bananas for the head manager. Then, head held high, she went to check in at the security booth. Received permission to enter. Went to visit what remained of her favorite child. As the nurses saw her approaching, they began to call out her daughter's name: "Laura, Laura Vanta, Laura!" One even shouted, "Laura Vanta, where on earth are you, your mother is here to see you!" And then she saw her child standing there. Her dress was too baggy, hanging loosely around her thin body. Laura stood still, looking at her. They hadn't seen each other in so many months. Months that had turned into years. Her daughter's frizzy hair looked like it hadn't been combed in days. Tears rolled down her cheeks. She wanted to take her daughter with her, into death, if need be, and so she walked over to where Laura remained frozen in place. "Mama, Mama," said Laura softly. "Come, let's go have a seat over there at the table." She went with her. It was a round table, entirely empty. Laura fetched a chair. "What have you brought me, Mama?" But she couldn't speak. She didn't take a seat. She stood at the round table, unloading the plastic bags. She laid it out on the table: bami packed in aluminum foil, soft drinks, bananas. Then she stood by her daughter, watching Laura unwrap the meal with eager fingers, eating it with her hands. A nurse hurried over with cutlery, but Laura responded, "I don't want anything from you, just leave me alone with my mother." Not harsh but firm. "Sit down, Mama. Got any cigarettes for me?" She nodded, sliding the pack across the table. Laura grabbed it and tucked it away, maybe into her bra. She watched her girl eat. She popped the soft drink open and waited. Using an ironed handkerchief, she wiped the grease off Laura's mouth. Laura drank, burped, and looked at her. She lowered her gaze. A woman came over with a laughing mouth and large eyes, "Miss Laura, give me a cigarette, please." And the woman reached her arm out to Laura, palm open. Her daughter froze, wiped her fingers clean on the handkerchief, rummaged around in her bodice, pulled out the pack, tore it open with her teeth, and slid a few cigarettes into the open hand. The woman ran off in a flash. "Do you have cigars, too, Mama?" She took them out of her bag. "For me?" "Yes, for you, Laura," and she tried to look her daughter in the eye. If only she hadn't. Bee's fourth child broke down in uncontrollable tears.

Imker didn't have to wait long to be let inside. Her grandmother came to the door with a friendly "I saw your friend driving off." And her: "Yes, he has an art class to get to, yes, he's good at painting, Grandma." And because her grandmother was waiting for more, "Umar is actually Heli's friend from her teacher training program, but now that she's gone, he's come to me looking for a little consolation." Grandma chuckled. "And where are you looking for consolation, child?" And gave her the keys to unlock the deadbolt. Her grandmother went inside first. She picked up her shopping and followed her into the kitchen. Wash hands. Rinse face with cold tap water. "I've got a cold beer for you, Grandma Bee, you want it now?" Grandma had headed straight for the bathroom. She sat down at the kitchen table, tired. Too many problems that needed solving. Worries about school. Doubts about her choice of major. Grandmother came back refreshed, opened the kitchen door wide, saw the cans of beer, and picked up one of them. "Dutch beer? Boy, oh, boy. Just for me? Boy, oh, boy!" She nodded. "Want me to pour you a glass?" Grandmother fetched a glass and sat down close to her. "Pour me one, Imker." Foam escaped when she popped the tab. "Imker, what's to become of my daughter when I die?" She watched her grandmother bring the glass to her lips. Hesitantly, she tried out a reply: "But they take such good care of her there, Grandma." Her grandmother appeared to be engrossed in tasting and evaluating the canned Dutch beer, taking sip after sip even though swallowing was difficult, and nearly finishing the whole can in one go. Then she placed the glass upside down on the tablecloth and stared at the trickles of foam oozing out, finally saying, "They're holding my daughter prisoner there; it's as simple as that." The words sounded hoarse. And instead of saying more about visiting Laura, Grandmother started talking about confessing to priests, who knew almost everything about you, except for the things no words can express. "Do you ever feel that way, Imker?"

Imker had never been able to keep up at school. Her thoughts wandered off to other matters, her handwriting was illegible, and when she complained she could barely read the words on the page, no one took her seriously. And in her new program, she still couldn't take in what the teachers were talking about. Typically, she sat there doodling while the other students took notes, and when she had no choice but to flip open a textbook, it was as if the letters clumped together and all she could see was black. She no longer mentioned it at home. Heli and Umar knew. The assignments she had to turn in every now and then were knocked out on a typewriter, by her sister at first, and more recently by Umar. The teachers complimented her on what they believed to be her typing, and she passed those compliments along to her boyfriend. She'd just begun her first year of training to become a kindergarten teacher, and along with the excitement over how new and different everything was compared to her old girls' school, there was also the fear of failure. In one of her workbooks, she used felt-tip pens to draw colorful cartoon figures that expressed her feelings. That helped her put up with the women and girls who upset her. "Why do so many women want to become teachers?" "It pays well, Imker, and once you become a mom, you're home early for your kids, and you have the same summer break and days off as they do. Besides, children are wonderful to work with, especially the very little ones." That was her mother's credo. And Louise added, "Would you rather be a nurse emptying out bedpans?" *My own restaurant, Mama, and a small family.* She kept her plans to herself. She took classes with male teachers for the first time. That was fun. She enjoyed their voices, the way they looked, the way they flirted with students. When Grandmother started in about her "daughter in prison," she quickly came up with a pretext for leaving the table: "Grandma, I'm listening, but I need to put the raw chicken and fish in the icebox." Her grandmother talked about what she'd seen on the ward for mentally ill women at the hospital and made no secret of how hard her daughter had cried this

44

time. The nurses said that Laura never shed a tear otherwise and found a way to get through each day undaunted, but when she saw her mother, she broke down. And then she'd remain inconsolable for days. Her grandmother had wandered off to the living room and turned on the radio. "Get some rest, Grandma." And she told her she'd make chicken soup with potatoes, not the packaged kind, but from scratch. Grandma was crazy about chicken soup with Dutch potatoes. Her own restlessness was apparently contagious: Grandma was roaming the house, going to wash up, coming back in a bathrobe, trying another radio station, dawdling in the doorway with her eyes on the boundary wall, suddenly admitting she didn't know what to do with herself. Her grandmother's voice sounded strained and very hoarse. She looked at Grandma's face and felt shivers run down her spine. "Want to peel the potatoes, Grandma?" She got a paring knife, a bowl for the potatoes, and a dish towel for Grandma's lap. A calmer mood slowly returned. The radio was playing a string of pop songs. For the next hour, not a word. Grandma on the sofa listening to the news. Soon the soup would be simmering, giving off its comforting aroma, but not yet. Ranting voices on the radio. She had no interest in how the country where she lived was being governed, and news from abroad left her cold. As she gathered the ingredients for the soup, she dreamed of her own little restaurant, where customers on a budget could have a good meal. No separate seating, but long tables where mothers and children would be welcome. Her daydream was interrupted by the voices of the politicians on the radio, who sounded as if they were on the brink of a fistfight. Umar was the only man she liked, but she was also a sucker for her little brother, Audi. She washed the chicken in a bowl of tap water mixed with salt and lemon juice, saying, "I need a pot with a lid, one big enough for this whole chicken, Grandma Bee." Grandma was already at her side. "Cut the chicken for the soup into pieces, Imker. Everything in this house is for the convenience of an elderly woman." All the same, Grandmother brought over a braising pan large enough for the entire chicken, and it even had a lid. "No real stockpot? This'll be a challenge, Grandma." She put the small aluminum stockpot back in the cupboard. With capable fingers, her grandmother cut the potatoes into cubes; effortlessly minced onion and garlic, parsley, and vegetables; and handed it all to her. It vanished into the pot. And as the chicken was coming to a boil with two bouillon cubes, and Bee was scurrying around as if searching for more things to dice, the answer came to the question her grandmother had asked earlier: *Who's going to look after my daughter when I die?* She said, "Grandma, what can I do once you can't be there for Laura anymore?" The answer was immediate: "First, you should get married, Imker." The smell of parsley and cilantro rose from the pot where the chicken had come to a rolling boil, and the only other sound was "Jesu, Joy of Man's Desiring," which signaled the obituary notices. She needed time to put her thoughts in order. "Then you'll have to live for many more years, Grandma, because marriage isn't on my list." Her grandmother persisted, "But you have to get married, my child, even if it's to a fool." And Grandma nimbly slung a dish towel over her shoulder. "A fool? Is that the best you can offer me, Grandma?" A cough: "Well, or a handsome priest from Holland, but he isn't supposed to marry." And Grandmother started to laugh, first a soft chuckle, then a full-out cackle. Imker took off her apron, looking on in amusement.

Louise had never accepted what happened to her sister. She thought it was unacceptable that her mother's grand-children didn't know her. Her brother Winston's children made fun of Laura, and her brothers' wives never talked about their sister-in-law. She'd just started working in Nickerie when Laura lost the will to do the things con-sidered normal for women in Paramaribo. A woman who had once biked briskly to her school each morning with a bundle of notebooks tied to the cargo rack had turned into a loaded gun: menacing, unapproachable. She could have refused to move for the new job in the easternmost part of the country, but her children had so badly needed that fresh start. It had kept her from sleeping. Four long years, 1,500 days away from Laura, who'd fallen into the hands of a mental hospital with a gruesome reputation. She could've died of shame, sorrow, fury; her children were what kept her in the daylight. And far away in the rice district, she strove to recover from that defeat. The whole city knew Laura had been committed. The whole city was outraged. Friends and acquaintances went to the gate at Kolera complaining, yelling, and even cursing at the hospital director, a man as "black as soot" who'd sul-lied their "flawless pearl"; for who could sing Doris Day love songs better than their beautiful Laura Vanta? But she'd kept quiet, rushing back and forth with her four children between the school where she worked and her home, that old wooden house on Dwarsstraat, where everything was getting out of hand. As she reflected on all of this, she stared through her window out into the street. One Monday at the school in Amora where she had been hired as a kindergarten teacher, one of the other teachers had suddenly gone into a Winti trance. And one of the things she'd said in her trance was that "Mrs. Vanta" had to move because nothing good would come of living at a T-intersection. She'd shrugged her shoulders at the news and matter-of-factly informed everyone that she wouldn't be looking for a new neighborhood until all her children had finished school. But the woman had refused to leave it at that and kept showering her with solutions to the problem, which wasn't a problem to her. Her co-worker's fanatical ravings were all the more insane in view of everything she'd done to find a house and a job in Amora—the tough negotiations with the bank and with an influential politician. Amora Village was much sought after by single working mothers. Besides, she thought as she stared at the dirt road, a woman's life couldn't possibly have more trouble in it: nothing was harder than raising a family without a husband to share the responsibility. She never complained. She faced society with a smile. Not because it was her way of dealing with adversity, but because she, like her baby sister Laura, was greatly admired for her good looks. Even when she was livid, her face maintained a friendly expression. After leaving her parents' home in tears, she decided she'd survived the hard part. Crying was for kids and babies, for lovelorn teenagers rejected for the first time. The pain of living was for adults, and why avoid it? When Heli broke down sobbing saying good-bye in Amora and again at the airport in Zanderij, she'd told herself—in order not to drop dead—*Only God knows why this is happening.* This would be the first Sunday without her eldest child. Imker had found her mission at her grandmother's. Babs was out to lunch with her father Boyce. Her son Audi was wandering around aimlessly, as usual, until it was time for Scouting. It hadn't escaped her notice that one of her neighbors had stepped off the mini-bus and was looking toward the window where she stood; perhaps the woman wanted to ask if Heli had arrived safely at her uncle's home in Holland. She didn't know yet. She had faith in her brothers, who were rescuing her daughter, after all; nothing could be worse for a young girl like Heli than an affair with a man of that station. Rage rose inside her. There was something not quite right with a lot of men in her country. She'd been on the lookout for more than four hours already. Her guard dog Leika had suddenly vanished, and she was mortified to admit to herself that she missed her golden-brown pet so much more than her daughter. She pulled away from the window to start cooking. One day, her daughter Heli would come back to her. Heli had promised to write her long letters. As long as the letters kept coming, Louise could get by perfectly well for a while without much more.

Babs had arranged to see her father Boyce. She picked him up, and he took her to the cafeteria. Members only. And as he sat playing mah-jongg with whoever was available, he treated her to one dish after another. "Eat, eat your fill, Babs," he said, looking at her. All he wanted was soup with fish balls. She wasn't a big eater, but for the chance to have lunch with her father, she stuffed herself with food like a spoiled brat. The cafeteria was really just one big kitchen with set tables. Hardly any daylight or fresh air came in. Air conditioning and glaring bulbs. Cooking. Eating. Playing. A gathering place for like-minded folks. Boyce had denied that any serious gambling went on. "Would I bring my little girl into a den of robbers? It's a clubhouse, Babs, where us folks with Hong Kong roots can do what we enjoy doing: cooking, eating, playing." He was right. She could see that for herself every Saturday. The boy who served her didn't speak a word of Dutch. Doesn't need to, her father told her; if he just does his job well, the rest will take care of itself. The young cook smiled at her, and she kept mumbling, "Thank you, thank you." Her father looked at her with a smile now and then, always asking the same question, "Yummy, Babsie?" Then she would nod. To have enough space for his ivory mah-jongg tiles, he always chose the same table, the one closest to a huge porcelain Buddha with a belly that never failed to make her smile. Striking up a conversation with her father was virtually impossible. She stared at his lightning-fast hands sliding, shifting, stacking. She loved the rattling of the tiles. Players didn't talk to each other during the game. Later, at the dining tables, was when tongues would loosen. She loved her father. She knew he lived in a big house with his wife and kids. She knew where the house was. She occasionally met him there. One day, she asked, "What are your kids' names?" And right away, he reeled off a list of names. "Wait, how many kids do you have?" And he couldn't help but cackle at her question. He still owed her an answer. After coming home that Saturday night, she'd posed the same question to her mother, who had replied indignantly that only her father could say for certain. She wanted to live with him. She wanted to belong to that exotic family. She thought she looked more like what she'd seen of them than like her mother's other children. And as soon as she had her diploma in hand, she'd write her father a letter with her request. There was another reason they met every Saturday: he gave her his weekly child support contribution for Louise. Cash, usually the same amount, and he always added a little something for her, some pocket change. Then he'd glance at his wristwatch, saying, "Time to go home, kid," and hand her the envelope with the banknotes. She'd take it, open it, count the money, and thank him with a nod and a smile. Then she'd hop up and leave her father's unusual restaurant. *Hong Kong Specialties*, said the sign on the building. Each week, her mother gave her a scrap of paper with a penciled shopping list. Usually, it was the same things: toothpaste, detergent, soybean oil, butter, dog food. Each week, she went to the same stores. It was too hot to shop around. Besides, the greasy Asian food made her slow and sleepy. The sidewalks downtown were dusty, packed with mothers and shrieking babies, the traffic loud. She quickly worked her way through her shopping list. Calling her boyfriend to say she was free wasn't on her mother's list, but it was the reason for her good mood. It was appallingly busy at the pay phone. She bought a telephone card, got a number, waited her turn. There was also a window for international calls. That line was much longer. The people in it were more agitated, impatient, arrogant. The tourists were easy for her to pick out, even when they were standing still and not saying a word. Tourists from Holland always demanded attention one way or another. It was her turn, and she entered the booth. Insert card; dial number; use scented tissue to try to remove makeup, facial oil, sweat, and other grime from receiver; and bring to ear. Aram picked up right away. "I'm fifteen minutes away from your neighborhood. Usual place, at Spanhoek?" She hung up. She looked around, picked up her shopping bags, and left the building with the pay phones. *I want a big house with a working phone on each floor*, she muttered to herself. Babs Vanta was convinced of one thing: she hadn't been born for poverty.

Audi Vanta just couldn't push his religion teacher's question out of his mind. The class of twelve-year-olds at the boys' school had lapsed into intense silence. He was quite a bit younger but had ventured to raise a finger. The windows were wide open, letting the scent of freshly cut grass inside. Ten o'clock in the morning. Koprokanu, brass canon—their teasing nickname for the teacher, Mr. Blaasbalg, because he was lanky and bony, with beige skin and big front teeth—repeated the question in a booming voice and looked in his direction. "Are we awake, boys, or is Vanta the only one with the answer again?" He hesitated but responded boldly, "Having no money, sir, to meet your needs." Blaasbalg perched on the edge of his desk and kept staring at him. "May I know what your needs are?" Classmates snickered, "Girls, sir!" He didn't join in their laughter. "Sir, poverty is for adults, not for children; my mother makes sure my needs are met." The teacher nodded, hesitated briefly, and said, "Don't have a father who takes care of you?" And looking at the other boys, "Who has a father who brings home money to Mother to put food on the table each day?" Some hands were raised. Not his. He looked around, wondering what this all had to do with religion, so he said nothing. Suddenly, Blaasbalg changed his tone: "Audi Vanta, you're right. Poverty is suffering from not being able to get what you need. That could be food, clothes, or education, but also love—yes, love in the form of attention from your father, your mother, brothers, sisters, and others close to you. And does anyone know where love comes from?" The silence in the classroom was almost hostile. The teacher's tawny face shone against the dark blackboard, his teeth flashing as he wrote the answer there in big letters: GOD. The teacher left. His classmates scattered. He didn't say another word that day. He wondered why his father never showed himself, never gave him any attention. He couldn't bring it up with his sisters at home. Imker and Babs with their dollhouses, their doll families, making him play the father on demand. He was very good at the game, even if he did let the girls whisper to him what to say and to which doll. They'd had to leave their colorful dollhouses behind when they moved to the city, but the rag dolls came with them, and after a couple of weeks in Amora, Louise hired a carpenter to put together two three-story dollhouses and give each one a flamboyant paint job. The sisters picked up the game with a vengeance, including him as needed. He came when they called. He made up his own answers to the questions they asked. The girls sometimes complained that he didn't understand what was going on at their dollhouse. Then he'd just walk away. Outside. To Leika. To the boys. At the new school, he joined the soccer club and the Scouts and became an altar boy. He suffered through meetings with only boys and men. But at home, he sat at his mother's table between the girls, and was sometimes defiant because his last name didn't come from a man who gave him attention, but from his mother, Louise Vanta, who loved him so.

One day, after picking up a pack of sanitary pads for his mother at the corner store, he snuck into Heli's study with the pack while she was working at her desk. She looked up. "What's the matter?" He placed the package of Kotex on her desk and asked, "What's this?" He'd once heard Heli say to Umar that she'd do everything in her power to help make a good man of her little brother Audi. She picked up the package and said in a friendly tone, "They're pads for older girls and women, to absorb their monthly blood flow; yes, they put it in their underwear, and the bleeding has to do with making babies." He nodded. "Can you die from it?" Heli rewrapped the pack in the newspaper he'd brought it in. "Bleed to death, you mean? I've never heard of that happening. Stomachaches, headaches, pimples, all sorts of little aches and pains, maybe, but I'm still waiting for my first time. Mama's already set aside a box of pads for me." Smiling, she handed the Kotex back to him. "Take this to Mama, and as soon as you turn twelve, I'll give you a booklet about boy stuff, okay?" His sister was the only one at home who took him seriously. He was proud of her; the teachers at school sent her their "warmest wishes," and young men whistled at her. Years later, once she'd started to use Kotex, she called him aside and showed him her gold bracelet shaped like a rose. He'd asked if she was in any pain. Heli wasn't. Mr. Blaasbalg's questions were tormenting him, which was why he said goodbye to his friends after school that day and hurried home to talk to his mother in private. She was standing by the wall around the front yard, talking to the lady next door. She looked up when she heard the gate opening. Her face sparkled with delight. "We're getting a puppy," she said. He wasn't about to spoil her mood. He waved at the neighbor, nodded at his mother, and went to the backyard. No sanitary pads for him to prove that something was maturing inside of him. Something that really hurt, but without bleeding. He sat on the stoop by the kitchen door brooding until his mother came along. "It's a female puppy, Audi, but I'll have her spayed early so she won't go into heat and attract males." She stood tall next to him. "After all, Audi, you're still too young to protect our house." Key in the door. Turning the double lock. His mother continued, "You know, Paramaribo isn't as safe as Nieuw Nickerie." Opening. Pushing. She paused to wipe her feet clean on the floor mat in the kitchen. And suddenly, it tumbled out of his mouth: "Mama, where is my father?" She was turned away from him. He'd stabbed her in the back. She placed her work bag on a kitchen chair. And as she washed her hands, she kept staring at the water streaming from the faucet. "Are we going to have a problem here, boy?" It was scorching hot in the house. He walked past her to open the windows. And as the fresh air poured in, he thought, *I will never abandon my own children*. No one saw Audi's eyes filling with tears.

Winston picks me up at Schiphol Airport. I recognize him right away, even though the man next to him is a stranger and not Uncle Rogier. I have on a moss green jacket made by my mother's best friend, a professional dressmaker. I chose the fabric: soft, silky cotton that's wrinkle resistant.

Waiting for my suitcase, I watch the two men; both are wearing dark suits, and I haven't seen them talk to each other. They keep looking in my direction too. My suitcase surfaces, and with my luggage in hand, I first walk over to the glass partition wall behind which my uncle is waiting. He waves me toward the exit on the other side. I'm wearing shoes with heels an inch higher than I'm used to, and they pinch. Around me are other travelers from Suriname, making comments in the language of our streets and marketplaces. White travelers everywhere. I know I've left behind everything I trust and love. And I know why. Winston is waiting at the exit and stoops a little to welcome me with a hug. It dizzies me when he whispers, "I'm with Gordon, your father." I follow my uncle with my suitcase. The man he starts talking to looks at me and smiles. "I'll leave you two alone," Winston says in a warm tone, and he disappears into the crowd of travelers. There I stand. There Father stands. I don't know what to say. My father, Gordon, must not know either, because he says nothing. Then I look at him head on to etch his facial features into my memory. I want to hear his voice. I come up with something. "My mother will be glad to hear we've met." It takes him a while to respond. "Forgive me for being such a bad father. I was so young. Girlfriends all over town. I've been a no-good bastard to you and your mother, but forgive me." And without waiting for me to respond, he asks if I had a good flight and mentions he works at Schiphol's largest airline. I listen in silence. Winston comes back. We say goodbye to my father. As soon as we're outside in the parking lot, Mama's brother says, "Did your father give you any money?" I mutter an answer, and Winston growls, "Gordon's always been a

56

cheapskate." My uncle's wife joins us. She draws me in for a warm, friendly hug. My uncle loves gorgeous women, and this one is a looker, maybe fifteen years younger than him: dark brown curls around a white face with bright, twinkling eyes that match her clear voice. "Good to have you here, Heli." I was the bridesmaid at their wedding. I nod: "Everyone sends their love." Then we get into the car. Winston at the steering wheel. "Did Heli talk to her father?" she asks her husband. "Yes," he says in a loud voice. I look around. The Netherlands? He hits the gas. Suddenly, I miss my mother like crazy.

The house where my uncle and his wife Lya live has both a front and a back yard. Not as big as in the tropics, more like postage stamps, but every corner is well maintained. No high-rises in this neighborhood, but rows of single-family homes, ramrod straight, signaling their owners' prosperity. It is the middle of the week and my relatives have taken a day off to get me settled in. It's September and cold. Inside you can hear a pin drop, it's so quiet. The double living room is tastefully furnished, and Lya brings me to the guest room, which has been prepared for my stay for the coming months. Uncle carries my luggage upstairs to my room. Lya is tender hearted, and I see tears in her eyes when she says, "I know what it means, Heli, to be so far away from your mother for the first time; I've gone through it myself, but you have your whole life ahead of you, and the Netherlands is a good country." She takes my hand and shows me around the rest of the house: the other bedrooms, the bathroom, and on the way to the kitchen, a safe distance from her husband, she whispers, "If you're ever feeling heartsick, come talk to me; I know all about that too." And she wipes the tears from my face and hers and leaves me on my own. Back in my room, I look outside through the big window, seeing gray skies and the neighbors' garden patios with empty lounge chairs. I see a woman hanging white laundry on a rotary clothesline. My grandmother leaps to mind. With the help of the curate assigned to her neighborhood, she and I set up her rotary clothesline in a spot in her backyard that she could easily reach. And, of course, Grandma gave me presents for her sons. She gave me one for myself as well, a bottle of almond syrup, knowing how crazy I am about the orgeat she makes from scratch. She felt boneless when I threw my arms around her, squeezing her body against mine, thanking her for everything she'd done for my mother and me since the day of my birth, and kissed her on her head, ears, face, nose, lips. And then I let her go, taking one last look at my mother, and without shedding another tear, I headed for the departure terminal. There were two guys in the terminal I hadn't expected to see there. Derik and Umar. I had ignored their unbroken stares. Still watching the woman who is hanging her bedclothes out to dry, I think about my Dutch teacher and how, overwhelmed with feelings of shame, I didn't say goodbye to him, not even after he'd sent me a present—a collection of poetry I haven't yet dared to open. On the wrapping paper he wrote, *Dutchmen aren't so bad, dear Heli Vanta*. Downstairs I hear the lively voice of my mother's brother Rogier, who's doing a pediatric residency. He's dropped by on his lunch break to see me and is excitedly calling my name. I let go of the past and descend the two flights of stairs to the living room, where my family is waiting for me with coffee and pastries.

Evening fell at Grandmother's house, and the rooms were bathed in artificial light. The aroma of freshly made chicken soup was so pervasive that it roused her spirits. And she hadn't even had one spoonful yet. She lay on the sofa listening to the radio, which was playing so softly that nothing entirely intelligible reached her. Even if her granddaughter Imker was with her now, it had been mostly the radio that helped her not to die of a lack of human contact. "Human contact"—those had been her granddaughter Heli's words when she brought over a very fancy portable radio and set it up for her. Heli had clearly and patiently explained how to change the stations, how to turn it on and off, how to adjust the volume, and even how to lock it up. "Close your doors and windows securely when you go out in the street, Grandma." She'd replied, "Yes, you're going abroad just like my two sons, so now there's even fewer loved ones around to keep me alive." Heli had admitted she was right. And her granddaughter reminded her that her husband Anton used to listen to the radio all the time at Jacobusrust. And when they took away first his wife and later his radio, he died within a year. Heli had loved Anton so much and visited him daily in the old family home, where he sat in his upholstered chair staring at the gate. Heli had prepared a hot meal for him every day, clipped his nails, washed his clothes and bedding, done the ironing and mending, and tidied up the house. And Heli had been horrified by her decision to move in with Winston and wouldn't say a word to her uncle, because she held him responsible for Grandpa Anton Vanta's isolation. Radio gone. Brass serving ware vanished. Antique furniture taken. Heli was livid. Filed a complaint of theft. Named names of likely perpetrators. But Bee's separation from her husband had deeper grounds than her grandchildren would ever be able to fathom. There on those deeper grounds, things had taken place between Anton and her so cutting that a fracture was inevitable. She sat up to catch a glimpse of her granddaughter Imker, who was setting the table for dinner. She heard her rummaging through the kitchen cabinets and called out, "Imker, under my bed there's a cardboard box with the rest of the tableware." Speaking so many words in one breath had become an effort. She gulped down a clot of blood. She was in pain. She was losing weight. But she really wasn't interested in bleeding to death. She sprang up lightly from the sofa and tiptoed to the kitchen. Imker was putting the box of tableware on a chair. Peeling off the tape. Opening the lid. Removing the plates and soup bowls from the soft wrapping paper. "Nice china, Grandma Bee." A wedding present for Winston and Lya, left unopened just like her other gifts and dumped on her when they left. Realizing no explana-tion of the box or its contents would be forthcoming, her granddaughter silently went on setting the table for two. Imker had even unearthed a pastel yellow tablecloth, but she stopped her from using it because even new things needed a good washing first. And when they were finally seated across from each other with a tureen in the middle of the table, they smiled. The ingredients had simmered long enough to become chicken and potato soup, but the dish had also cooled down enough to be as smooth and tasty as possible. Imker, as a granddaughter, knew that her grandmother still appreciated fine food, and she, as a grandmother, knew that her granddaughter had done more than her best to cater to her tastes. They said grace. She wanted to serve the food, and as she did so, she knew Imker was watching her like a hawk, because the real point of making the soup had been to give her strength and truly satisfy her hunger. She ate slowly. Every ingredient came through distinctly. She said slowly, "Imker, should we take some soup to your Aunt Laura tomorrow?" Imker, knowing her grandmother expected an answer right away, nodded heavily, doing her best to smile. The food was so good that she wanted to share her enjoyment with her girl in Kolera. Smile. Bite. Chew. And she took pleasure in Imker's pleasure. "Is there enough?" Imker said, "More than enough, Grandma, have some more." But as she stood up for a second helping, she said firmly, "Because if you plan to take care of my daughter when I'm no longer around, then you have to learn to love her like I do." Imker had a pat answer ready: "Yes, Grandma, sure thing, eat up." Reassured, Grandmother Bee settled down again in her seat.

Imker was the only one in her household who didn't go to Sunday Mass. She was religious but had learned it didn't suit her to do things she didn't understand. Mother didn't force her to go but expressed her hope that she would find a congregation whose services made sense to her. It made no difference to her how the world worked anyway. In Nickerie, she'd had loads of friends and had been the only family member always invited to other people's birthday parties. It was a mystery to her why everyone thought her features were so much prettier than her sisters'. Her mother would let her attend, all dressed up, and a few hours later she'd return home and give her family all the details of the party, even more than you might expect from an excited little girl. The architectural style of the house; the furniture in the rooms; the family structure; the smells, colors, tastes that had characterized the party. It was as if she were consoling the others, who were never invited anywhere. But back then, she had a head full of Shirley Temple curls and was slightly bowlegged, which made everyone laugh. After turning nine, she started to grow tall and everything straightened out, and even before they returned to Paramaribo she had her curls cut off, which made her look boyish for a while. After dinner with Grandma, she needed a shower, as well as clothes that didn't smell of parsley, onions, and chicken. Clean up the kitchen. Put the soup away in the ice box. *Would you like to shower now, Grandma? Yes?* And her grandmother got up right away to go cleanse her body in the bathroom after a day of windblown dust. She stood there staring again at her mother's mother, overcome by questions that maybe only Grandma Bee could truthfully answer. But talking was hard for her grandmother. She could hear her taking a bath with the bathroom door open. Grandma, scared? There was no reason to be, because she would stay to look after her. If anything did go wrong, she'd call for help, and she'd stick close to Grandma, no matter what. She had decided to move in with her grandmother. She needed to tell her mother she couldn't live at Amora now that Heli was gone and, in any case, Grandma needed her. Funny how some things fall neatly into place. She

made the sign of the cross, stuck her tongue out rebel-
liously at the crucifix hanging on the wall, and went to her
and her grandmother's bedroom to get it ready for bed-
time. As she dragged out her sleeping bag, Umar came
to mind. How he'd waited next to his scooter and asked
if she wanted to go with him to the market, wouldn't it
be nicer than going alone? Imker flushed at the thought
and smiled.

On the south side of Paramaribo, the remaining members of Louise's household were watching TV. Louise
and Babs and Audi had turned down the sound after the
eight o'clock news and now looked on in amusement as a
muted preacher harangued the viewers in perfect silence.
And on top of that, he was using Sranantongo, the language of the street, instead of the country's official language, Dutch. The man was known for his blunt opinions. As a scion of a wealthy family, he could even lash
out at politicians. His family owned pharmacies, and a
private school just for the children in his congregation.
He was the blackest gentleman in town. His was also the
blackest face on national television, and if poor reception
sometimes made his skin indistinguishable from the dark
background, his eyes always conveyed a clear message.
Raised in Germany and married to a German woman,
he had settled in the town of his birth. He spoke lucidly,
slowly, intensely. After thirty minutes, he said goodbye,
and she said, "Finally. Turn the volume back up, Audi."
The TV was supposed to be her window on the world,
especially the latest news from Holland. The preacher
had discussed community building and the importance of

belonging—even if you paid no more than the minimum dues—to a club, a political party, or—why not?—a church congregation. She tried to keep her children away from groups, afraid that peer pressure would carry more weight than parental authority. She had her preferences when it came to politicians. It was no secret who had helped her get the house she now lived in, and so fast. Babs was watching the commercials. Audi had gone to get something to drink. They were waiting for their weekly TV show. The children at her school kept talking about it; even in her kindergarten class, it was all they chattered about. Audi broke the silence by sharing a memory from four years ago. This was his latest attempt to bring the conversation around to their guard dog, which hadn't returned since Heli's departure. Tensely, she listened. He sounded nervous. "Remember the time our family had another mouth to feed, because Mama brought a puppy home and named her Leika." And Babs continued, "I dashed around town in search of a pet store to buy good food for that dog, and a chain with a collar." She said nothing, waiting. Listened in amusement to their conversation. The children were in a hurry to get a new puppy to comfort her. "Not yet," she kept saying. "Leika will come back to us soon, and you can keep buying dog food on Saturdays, Babs." But Babs balked. "Not for now, Mama, those bags are pretty heavy." Her gaze shifted from her daughter to her son. Did they know something about Leika's disappearance that she didn't? She thought about what had happened one recent afternoon between her and Audi. She kept her voice even, saying, "I can't believe Leika is never coming home again. It's like I haven't lost one child, but two. The dog isn't replaceable, either." The

TV series started. Lassie bounded onto the screen, looking her best. Enchanted by the sight, Babs said, "Mom, I'll buy a purebred dog for you, and you can raise it to be a healthy guard dog, and I'll keep taking care of the dog food, okay?" She didn't respond but kept watching how the Scotch collie bounded into the frame, longing for contact. She stood up and pulled open the heavy curtains. The evening breeze streamed in through the open shutters. She stared blankly into the street, saying, "I wonder how Imker's doing at Grandma's." But in her thoughts, Louise was still in the departure hall in Zanderij, watching her daughter walk away.

Two

Tuesday is deep-cleaning day at the downtown church. It is Father Teloor's parish, the one where, as adults, her children became Catholics again. Bee goes to polish brass at the church near her house, but her heart and soul belong to the church downtown. When her time comes, it's where she wants the mourners to pay their last respects. And she's there again for the first time in weeks. She's set herself up in the Saint Anthony Chapel: left transept, second row, first bench. The cleaning crew always does this chapel first for the weekday visitors who drop in for a donation, a prayer, a votive candle. Saint Anthony of Padua performs miracles and brings back what is lost. And to top that off, he's also the patron saint of women and children, lovers, spouses, sailors, the poor. She reads and rereads the engraving. Of course, she isn't the only one who comes here for solace: tea lights are burning all around her, and the glass coin jar is nearly full. Behind her, spread out among the pews, are four women and a man. The cleaning crew is making muffled noises in the background. After the six Sunday masses, a thorough cleaning is necessary, partly because people accidentally leave things on and under the pews. There are also people who leave something behind on purpose to get rid of it anonymously. She's found a purse full of money—once, years ago—and women's jewelry, too. In both cases, there was a handwritten letter with a request. But most of the time, no note is included. The cleaning crew hand everything they've found over to the priest. And the church keeps mum. Even during sermons, not a word about "found objects." Anyone who absentmindedly left something behind is always welcome to come and pick it up. A few times, they've found something truly scandalous: once the corpse of a baby. Then the police are called in. The cleaning crew has a code of silence. She smiles because she can clearly hear them talking to each other. They're supposed to whisper, not raising their voices unless it's an emergency. Every Tuesday afternoon, the choir meets to prepare for the next Mass, and the organist, a heavyset brown man, comes between twelve and two. He makes the church organ resound in an almost deafening manner. They know her. Most of them also knew her children. Especially Winston and Rogier. Winston used to come with his wife on Sunday mornings, and sometimes Rogier brought his girlfriend along to evening Mass. In front of Saint Anthony, she can let everything she misses flood back into her mind again. In a whisper, she asks the wooden saint with the dark brown cloak over his shoulders to bring her father back, and as the statue looks down at her, she closes her eyes and waits. Her father, Julienne, is standing next to her. The same questions always come up. *Why did you make me marry that black boy?* Father doesn't answer. Then she asks, *What did my mother die of?*

68

No response from her father. She was always at his heels in the house where she wasn't allowed to stay, because Mother wasn't coming back and Mother's brother, Mr. Cru, a brusque locksmith, was planning to move in with his boys. A young girl didn't belong in a household of men, Father said when he took her to live at the convent. The nuns knew her already from school, and there were other girl boarders. She was still too young, but her father paid double, and he'd built and painted a wooden bed and a wooden chest to store all her things. He often traveled for work and was usually away for months at a time. A new job with new possibilities, admittedly in French Guiana but with men from his own country. He wanted to make sure his daughter was in the safest possible hands. He visited her as often as he could. He brought her presents. He told her their house was getting a fresh coat of paint for her brother Scott, who planned to marry. The chest in her bedroom filled up with colorful feathers, puppets made of rubber, animal fangs, a wooden cup, a pan flute, and woven clothes. The nuns were willing to turn a blind eye as long she didn't talk about it with the other boarders. She didn't. Throughout her years at the convent, she shared a large room with a nun. She still doesn't know if the nun was young or old. The other girls slept in the dormitory, each on the same kind of narrow bed with storage cubbies. Eating together. Playing together. Going to church services together early in the morning. Suddenly, she turned sixteen. Her father Julienne had a marriage partner for her. The young man was tall and skinny like her brothers, but their skin was the color of pancake batter, while he was as dark as a raisin. A narrow face with wide eyes, and the whites shone so bright that all the black within them seemed like twilight, like something unsettled. He spoke like someone from the capital—softly, clearly, often. Yet she couldn't tell Mother Superior exactly what he'd said. Maybe his tropical uniform was a little too large. Maybe his boots were a little too shiny. Maybe his teeth were a little too perfect and his mouth a little too wide. But when the nun asked if she was willing to marry the young man, she gave a clear *yes*. "Yes, Sister, I will." What they'd hoped for at the convent would never come to pass—she wouldn't become a nun. The wedding would take place within a year. Father was making arrangements for a trip to a big city in France, because his hearing was getting worse and he wanted to consult a doctor in his country of birth. He had a lucrative job in Cayenne, recruiting workers for a large French construction project in French Guiana. Her father would never return to his job and house in Nieuw Nickerie. His letters, which contained important news, took far too long to reach his sons. The wait was almost unbearable. One day her youngest brother, Napo, went to visit him and never came back to Gouverneurstraat again. Mother's brother Mr. Cru, unmarried and taciturn, kept what was left of the family warm, and maintained the enormous brick and wooden house as best he could until one of the boys was ready to start a family. Never happened. The beautiful house grew paler, emptier. Her father Julienne visited to set up her marital home with furniture that he'd bought at auction and refurbished. After the wedding ceremony, she and Anton rode in an automobile, horns blaring, to their new home: a rental under army management. It was only then that she truly understood her husband was a career soldier. Then her father took her to place flowers at her mother's grave. And that very night, after the wedding reception, he boarded a ship to the country he'd left behind as a seventeen-year-old boy, with no intention of ever returning, he'd told them, because his parents had seen so much bloodshed and were worried it would happen again. She springs to her feet. The sound of the organ thunders through the church. She thanks Saint Anthony for the memories. When talking doesn't hurt, she can spend the whole day gabbing; even when she's alone, she grumbles to herself, and the stream of words usually veers into songs of praise. One day, her husband Anton bought a big radio, a radio cabinet, and two easy chairs with arm and back rests. He upholstered the chairs and properly installed it all in the living room in Jacobusrust with the words, "Bee, this is mine, so no touching, but one chair is for you." And without consulting her, he took the two rocking chairs—the ones they'd had since she was pregnant with Rogier—out to the back yard and burned them. "You just don't listen to me," she chided, and he retorted, "Bee, I'm a man." He meant he wasn't like those women from her book club, the ones who cooked and baked and brewed drinks, talking and laughing the whole time. Anton was twenty-one when he took her as his wife before God and country, and he'd never touched a girl. Her father couldn't have found a more decent man for her.

It's Tuesday; yesterday she went with Imker to bring Laura some lukewarm but still perfectly delicious chicken and potato soup. Now she finds a place to sit tucked away from everyone. God can find her here, in this forgotten place with no statues, no figurines. In this spot she once caught the organist with one of the cleaning ladies; she still can't make sense of what she saw, even after giving birth to five children herself. In any case, all the memories of those years full of life will soon fade; disease doesn't spare your memories; they will die the very instant she does. She asked Laura why she had to cry after every visit. "Because you love me" was the answer. And her daughter kept repeating it, as if she wanted to make clear what mattered to her. "Because you love me, Mama." And Imker nodded, too. And Laura explained, "Mother, I make you so sad, you see?" It was crowded. So many visitors on a Monday afternoon, and more staff members walking around than usual. Her granddaughter did her best to focus on Laura and establish a rapport. She'd never been able to get permission to see more of the place where Laura lived than the visitors' hall. "Would it be all right if I combed your hair?" Bee was startled. Would Imker's proposal upset Laura's fragile moment of balance? She looked reproachfully at Imker: *No one touches my daughter's hair!* No response from Laura. "Would it be all right if I came to visit without Grandma?" With the sweetest possible smile, Laura answered, "Bring me cigarettes. And a pretty skirt." Wordless eye contact. "Will a pretty skirt make you happy?" But then Laura broke the silence, and she knew exactly what would come next. And it came. In a voice as gentle as an evening breeze, Laura sang in English, "I'm glad that you're happy with somebody else, but I'm sorry it couldn't be me…" And continued until the last note, the last word. The song brought tears to Imker's eyes. Her daughter began to mutter as if there were others seated at the table, and her words weren't intended for the real people before her. "The Germans killed Bram's relatives, sssshhhhhh," Laura whispered, pressing a finger to her lips. Blood rushed to her head. "Your questions are hurting her, Imker." Her voice tense and shrill, she said, "Laura has other guests and is wandering away from us, bidding us farewell. She wants to be alone with her memories and rave like a madwoman!" Out of nowhere, footsteps and the organist's voice, the cleaning lady's laughter. She springs to her feet. Wipes her tears away, fast, and creeps out of the church.

The raincoat Lya lends me is brown, like the leaves of an old almond tree. I see myself standing in the mirror in the spacious front hall, and Lya nods at me encouragingly. When I go on staring at myself in that piece of clothing I don't entirely understand, she says, "As soon as your money reaches your account, we'll go into town to get you new clothes and so on." I nod, buttoning up the jacket because it's rainy and windy. My uncle's wife goes with me to the bus stop. Hood up. Scarf on. Boots. She gives me a bus pass and directions. She waits with me until the right bus arrives and, oh, gosh, wipes away a tear: "Good luck, you'll find your way." I get on, concentrating on what I need to do. The driver will give me a shout when I need to get off. So I sit in an individual seat as close to him as possible. The heavy traffic fascinates me, as do the many Dutch people zipped, buttoned, and wrapped in autumn clothing. And then the sudden golden swaying of the trees—what a sight, and will the branches really end up completely bare? "You need to get off at the next stop." The bus driver's voice.

"Thank you," I say, and I hop up at once, taking my first look back into the bus, which turns out to be chock full of people, and squeeze my way through them to the exit doors in the middle. The bus stops. People get off. So do I. I don't need to follow the directions to my training center, Orange-Nassau, because there are so many other Surinamese people around, probably students like me. "Orange-Nassau?" I ask. "Walk with us, it's our first day, too," someone says. I join them, walking in silence until I see the building complex. Yesterday's conversation with my relatives about the girls' boarding school run by nuns somewhere in the south of the Netherlands weighs heavy on me. Uncle Rogier thinks the best option for me is to go to boarding school and then to university; he knows me well because he lived at our house for a short while. His brother Winston has his own interests: providing me with "room and board" earns him a little pocket money for his evening bridge games. Is the decision really even mine? I've washed up in a situation with a structure of its own. Two hours after leaving Winston and Lya's house, I'm sitting in a classroom with two dozen total strangers. It's barely a week since I left Suriname. I sit up front. There's an empty seat next to mine. The other Surinamese students sit at the back—when you come from far away, it can help to survey the whole landscape. It's all because of the man I love; he's the reason I've landed in this limbo. A teacher comes in with a list. He speaks, but I only half-listen. The presence of the man I love is powerful in me. My mother has gotten me as far away from him as she can afford. But where did I find the strength to confound her expectations so completely? An ocean lies between us. The teacher calls my name: Heli

Vanta. "Present," I say, too loud. And I don't know why it makes everyone laugh.

They all stand in a cluster during the break. A broad-faced boy and another in an ill-fitting suit. They live in a Moravian boarding school in Zeist, and one of them already knows he'll go on to become a priest. A breath-taking Hindustani boy looks familiar to me. A Muslim with a remarkably deep voice. And the girls. Two who are always chatting with each other and another who never says anything. I just stand there with them, in my travel clothes, someone else's raincoat over my shoulders. I don't know what I'm supposed to talk about. Look around a bit. Can't tell the Dutch students apart from the others. In less than a year, I'll be a fully qualified instructor and can travel back to Paramaribo to run an elementary school there. No one goes back—after that long, expensive flight to Holland there's no going back. The boy with the wide face has been explaining that he'll start by becoming a priest. Now he leans toward the boy standing next to him: "And you?" Not everyone has a cut-and-dried plan. I have absolutely nothing. He cackles in my face. During the bus ride back to the neighborhood where Winston and Lya live, it dawns on me that my stay in Holland is real. I have a stack of textbooks with me. A course guide. My class schedule and the pages of rules for students make me feel trapped. As I walk back from the bus stop to my familiar address, a cyclist comes to a standstill next to me. A head full of curls. Dark glasses. He'd helped me pick up my textbooks—his name is Hans. "May I walk with you?" he asks. "Yes," I say. And I'm so glad he doesn't say anything else. We walk in silence. Rust brown coat. Mouse gray coat. Winston stands in plain sight in the window, maybe waiting for me. Hans doesn't ask any questions. He says goodbye and pedals away. *This is real*, I keep thinking. *I'm living in a foreign country, and the people I love are out of reach.* As I press the doorbell, the thought buzzes painfully in my head.

We were sitting at our desks listening to the pedagogy instructor in a temporary structure some 500 yards from the main building. In the sweltering midday heat, that was my favorite classroom. The wind could find us, and I felt safe there, so low to the ground. Carefully pruned almond trees bordered the field, and the ground was covered with a fresh layer of crushed shells. I could smell the sea. I was listening to the voices from the street and to my teacher lecturing. Then I spotted her outside, coming toward us: a wide canary yellow skirt; a lacy, pure white blouse; wine-red lips; hair pulled back in a bun like a Javanese woman; and long, strong legs in yellow pumps. Before I could make sense of what I was seeing, she was in the doorway to the classroom. "Your mother's here," shouted Umar. There was no getting away from it. Her smile exposing a perfect set of teeth. The day came to a halt. The teacher glanced at me as he walked toward the woman at the door, saying, "What can I do for you, ma'am?" And my mother answered without missing a beat: "If your teenage daughter is especially fond of one of her teachers, it's a mother's duty to come and look him straight in the eye." My classmates were in hysterics. My heart pounding. My teacher frozen in place. I don't know how many seconds passed before he found his voice again, saying, "Is Heli Vanta your child?" Later, on occasion, I'll remind my mother of this unconventional school visit of hers, because I was by far the youngest in the class and very childish compared to my classmates. And she'd defend herself with a resolute "That's exactly why I was there." I didn't understand back then. She braved the risk of being humiliated by my teacher. Now, as I ask her brother how to mail letters back home, in my mind I'm composing the first sentence of the first letter to my mother Louise.

Everyone was excited to see Louise Vanta back in the teachers' lounge. Having taken a few days off to get her eldest daughter ready to fly to Holland, she was finally showing her face again. The principal pulled her into his office to tell her he thought she was brave. "Louise, Heli's misstep could have been your downfall, but you've turned it into a victory." She wasn't pleased by this compliment. He'd occasionally talked to her about the fact that her daughter was screwing one of his buddies, a guy who had absolutely nothing to offer her. She never responded because it felt like a personal attack. It was his married friend who needed a talking to, not the girl's mother. She still saw her daughter Heli as a blank page, chalk-white paper, sky-blue purity. Her daughter and sex were light years apart. Another female teacher had asked her how she could be so sure. Louise knew that the woman took a night class from the man in question and had no reasonable argument to make other than "God watches over my daughter." Her words rang out like a gong. The woman backed down, but Louise still felt uneasy. And even on this sunny workday, with a daughter she'd defended up and down and sent off to live with her brothers in Holland, she was still seething with rage. Maybe it would've been better if she'd never become a mother. She crossed the schoolyard straight to her own classroom. For the first time, she was afraid to unlock the door. She waited at the door until the bell. She waited until the small children were all lined up, until they stopped talking, until they grew restless and started to shuffle. She turned the key in the door. She felt dizzy. She didn't fall. She'd grabbed the doorknob. She pushed the door wide. The students breezed inside and did for themselves what she was supposed to do: picked up their chairs from the long play table and carried them to their individual desks. They made a bit of a racket, but everything went just fine. They sat down. They looked at her. She resolved to have her blood pressure checked. Or maybe it was just that time of the month. The little kids she'd been entrusted with stared expectantly at her mouth, expecting a good story to pour from her lips, because she'd never missed work before and they'd had to spend a couple of days with a substitute teacher. She had some explaining to do. So, she started with a question. And was astonished to see how many little hands shot up. Holland had gobbled up some of their loved ones too. Mrs. Vanta was relieved to discover that she had a quite relevant topic for class discussion.

The school doctor did as she asked and told her the blood pressure readings weren't high enough to be a cause for concern. They knew each other, these two women, and the doctor said in passing that it was a terrible shame Heli had had to go to the Netherlands. She shrugged off the remark, because that horse had bolted. And, as the doctor handed her a course of birth control pills and she buried them deep in her purse, she mumbled that the relationship between Heli and her had been deteriorating. "My daughter and I can't even have a normal conversation," she explained. The doctor said nothing; she had only one child—a daughter of ten. There was a photo of the girl in a gold frame in the office. They went over to it and took a good look. "Sometimes as a mother, you wish they'd stay small forever." The doctor laughed at her own comment, but the woman with four children joked, "Sometimes you wish they'd never been born." She said goodbye with a smile, closing the door to the doctor's office a bit too hard. Her daughter Imker was waiting outside. She walked over to meet her. "Wouldn't they let you in?" Imker nodded and didn't ask why she'd been to the doctor. On their way home, shouting children and cars honking and swerving to avoid accidents created a chaos they had to navigate with care, and she found it too distracting to talk as they walked. They kept close to each other on the sidewalk. She knew where the cobblestones were loose, was familiar with the treetops at the horizon and the houses she walked past daily. She had no nearby friends to visit. No afternoon courses to take. She lived for her children; the route to work in the early morning sun and the route back home in the blistering heat never felt like a burden to her. Should she not have let Heli go? Her eyes filled with tears. It was true: she should have kept her daughter with the family. Imker, by her side, stayed silent all the way to their front door. She knew exactly what her daughter had come to do. But she wouldn't let her go without raising objections. As she watched Imker gather her things to go stay with her grandmother, it struck her how thin the girl was. "Are you getting enough to eat?" Imker laughed a little. "Mama, I make a home-cooked meal every day and eat with Grandma." She nodded in approval. Imker had always been a picky eater, and it did her good to hear her daughter speak with confidence about her choices. "What about money?" "Grandma can live comfortably on a military widow's pension and benefits, like shopping at a discount in the city's most expensive department store. She hasn't been taking advantage of that, Mama, but I'll soon change that," Imker said playfully. "Is Grandma doing well?" Her daughter flinched and gave her a worried look. "No, Grandma isn't doing well at all; that's why I need to be with her." Silence. "My mother's still walking to church every day in this hot city?" Imker nodded. "It would be better if Grandma came to live with us, but that doesn't work for you, and it won't work for her." And so their uncomfortable conversation drew to a close, right before Babs and Audi burst into the house. "Are you going to live in town?" Babs asked, upset. Imker shook her head firmly. "I'm helping Grandma. No one else is there for her anymore, and none of you visit her, either." And the emotion in Imker's voice hushed everyone. "Will you stay for dinner with us?" But Imker grabbed the backpack with all her stuff and asked, "Did Heli make it to Holland okay?" Her brother said, "I keep wondering that, too, you know." All three turned to her. Of course, she didn't know either. She hadn't received word yet. "Your sister promised to write us long letters. I'm waiting." Imker hugged her gently and walked out the door. Audi went to his room. Babs headed for the bathroom. Louise, suddenly alone in the living room, went to the window to watch her second daughter stride away.

Imker walked with a straight back but could feel the pressure of her mother's worries and understood what was behind them. She wondered what she could do to make Mama's life easier besides what she was already doing: moving in with Grandma. She still didn't have any interest in training to become a schoolteacher, but her mother wanted to see a diploma, and she was determined not to disappoint her. In Paramaribo, a woman who couldn't provide for herself became a plaything for men. She knew what her mother had meant by this warning and was determined not to fall into the hands of someone who might take advantage of her. Her mother had grown gloomier and more silent since Heli had left, but was sure to brighten up as soon as she received a letter with good news. She felt like tearing Derik limb from limb for chasing after Heli for years. How was it possible that her sister had given in to that leering glutton? For weeks, she'd observed his comings and goings in the teacher training program, watching as he joked around with the other teachers while students looked on. Popular, huh? She'd wanted to go up to him and beg, *Man, just leave our Heli in peace.* The arguments. The tension at home. Her mother's desperation, and Heli's. She'd been afraid of how it would end. She made sure her and Heli's shared bedroom remained an oasis of peace; she wouldn't even let her mother inside. "Mom, can't you leave just one place in our house where Heli isn't under attack!" She was terrified that one day her sister just wouldn't come home. She didn't take sides. She lay awake until her sister came home late at night from a date with the guy. She watched Heli clean her face calmly with cotton balls and something fragrant, wipe her feet clean with a washcloth, brush her teeth and gargle, brush out her hair, put on her nightgown, and then fall asleep like a log beside her. Heli smelled like flowers that have no name. Of course, a man like that would fall for her. If only he understood how rotten Heli felt inside—then he'd set her free. Umar would have made a good husband for Heli. From her seat in the minibus, she waved at him, and he watched her as the bus pulled away and drove off. She'd avoided Umar this time. At the medical school, she was going to meet up with a college buddy of Uncle Rogier's who was in contact with her relatives in Holland. He seemed trustworthy to her; someone had to inform Rogier that his mother was terribly sick even though she walked a marathon every day. She'd learned from her mother never to ask any man for a favor, but for Grandmother Bee she'd try anything. She asked the driver to turn down the music a little. He refused. The bus was overcrowded. She was ready for anything.

Albert was the best-looking young man she knew personally, which she noticed, not for the first time, when she saw him waiting for her by the gate of the national hospital. He'd told her he was interning with the midwives because he wanted his work to make a difference for the women in his country. He came up to her with a smile and said, "Hey, gorgeous. Shall we talk in the clinic, or would you rather stay here and keep it short?" Hesitation. "Stay here," she said, avoiding his eyes, and she added, "It's not about me." He nodded, took her hand, and led her to a spot in the shade of a huge tamarind tree. "Talk to me," he said. And when she began to describe the state of Grandmother's health, it was hard for her to keep her tears at bay. Albert let her tell the whole story. He didn't ask questions. He promised to get in touch with Rogier right away, and when he finally let go of her hand, he said, "Won't you come train with us? We're always short of nursing staff, and you can earn some money while you study." It was confusing for her, such an unexpected question. "Just think it over, Imker," and he walked off in his white doctor's coat. She remained behind in the shadow of the tamarind tree. She'd betrayed her grandmother. She'd asked a young man for a favor. She'd left her mother's house. The traffic on the street grew into a long row of cars that people on bikes and motorcycles wound their way through. Bedlam. She was getting more and more used to Paramaribo, downtown in particular. She stood in front of the hospital where she'd been born. She traced a mental route home to her grandmother. She didn't take a bus. She wanted to "hoof it" through the city, as Grandma called it. The bag was getting heavier, but Albert had remarked on how healthy she looked. And after being around so many doctors—a situation that usually sent her into a panic—a walk could be just the thing to settle her nerves. In fact, Albert had said that very thing about the long walks that Grandmother took across town. And he should know. Imker started walking.

Grandma sought respite in her bedroom earlier than usual. Perhaps because it started to rain hard at sundown. The pitter-patter on the roof filled her head. The sudden drop in temperature sent a cold draft whipping through the house. Downpours like this made her dizzy. With her granddaughter nearby, she didn't need to walk from room to room in her housecoat, muttering every kind of prayer to force God to keep close to her. Imker had spoiled her with bean soup that went down easy. Her granddaughter's care had undoubtedly made her stronger. And warmer. On top of that, the morning bleeding had stopped. She lay in bed, wrapped up in a warm blanket, listening almost breathlessly to the full-moon rainfall. Imker was right beside her, on a sturdy cot that Albert, her son Rogier's friend, had brought over by car. He'd spoken to Imker, he told her, and he understood she had a good sleeping bag but no guest bed. He'd taken an interest in her, asking how she was doing and if there was anything he could do for her as a doctor and a family friend. She'd assured him she'd take him up on his offer just as soon as the need was pressing. Imker had set up the cot and now lay nearby. "Did you make sure to shut the doors and windows tight?" "Yes, Grandma." "Did you have a good talk with your mother?" "Yes, Grandma." "Do you like staying here with me?" "Yes, Grandma Bee." It got very quiet. The strength of the downpour had diminished. It wasn't all that dark in the room. The light from a streetlamp crept inside. "I need to tell you something, Grandma." Imker's voice sounded hollow. "Tell me something, child? Are you pregnant by Umar?" A loud "No, no, what I want to tell you isn't about me but about my mother." Then her granddaughter seemed to hold her breath as if dreading this moment. "I want you to know about it, Grandma." She kept quiet. She wasn't in the frame of mind to hear anything that would make her sad. The last time she'd seen her daughter Louise was when Heli left. The airport had been so crowded. They'd barely spoken to each other. They'd both felt awkward in the presence of Albert, who'd given them a ride. Both afraid. Sick with grief. Isolated. She said, "Imker, give your mother time to get used to a house without your sister." The words came out of her mouth in bits and pieces, but Imker understood she was putting up a wall to stave off whatever was coming. "Something happened, years ago, Grandma; yes, it's about Laura." And because she started coughing, Imker said at once, "Never mind, just forget it, Grandma, I'm sleepy, good night." She let the silence settle in before saying softly, "Sleep well, girl; God will keep watch." And yet she couldn't manage to fall asleep herself. She stared at the ceiling. She looked at the nightlight. She was comforted by Imker's easy breathing, her gentle snoring. She was surprised by a storm that came along with lightning and claps of thunder. As far as she was concerned, it could rain the whole night through.

In the morning she woke up gasping. Short of breath. Her granddaughter shot upright. "Don't die, Grandma!" She helped her to her feet. "Maybe let's go to the bathroom?" But she managed to start breathing normally again. She'd had such an awful nightmare, about black men dancing in a clearing in the woods, dancing and singing until they dropped, Anton was there watching, dressed in a white tropical uniform with a helmet, a child in his arms, looking at a woman he thought he recognized—his mother's grandmother, who'd been bought into freedom in real life. But in this nightmare, she sang in an unintelligible language and waved cloths at the dancers to cool them and didn't notice Anton, even though he was screaming for her attention. Imker listened. "It sounds jumbled up, child, but dreams are incoherent memories from sleep, Rogier always said. Your grandfather was wearing his white uniform from when we first met, but he was old and haggard." She took a deep breath. Her husband hadn't appeared in her dreams for years, and then out of nowhere, there he was, so real she could touch him. And that white child in his arms? She walked to the closet where she stashed her tobacco box. A cigar would make the dream complete. She grabbed the box and sat down with it at the kitchen table. "You're not supposed to smoke, Grandma." Imker was right. She should try to keep away from cigars. Outside, dawn was breaking. Her granddaughter stayed put. "I smoke so I won't cry." Imker nodded, taking a seat close to her. "Better to cry, Grandma, until it's over." She shook her head. "It's never over." She opened the box, fished out a cigar, and stared at it for a long time. It was a fat cigar. She grabbed matches, placed the cigar between her lips, and lit it. Her granddaughter remained at her side, running her fingers along the edge of a brass ashtray with a little lid. The smoke left her mouth in small plumes. Anton had sometimes rolled his own. Anton could roll a thin cigarette so fast. She tried not to inhale yet still to enjoy what was forbidden to her. She thought of her married life and her marital bed. After Laura's birth, everything had ended. He'd stood by as her daughter was cut out of her stomach.

He'd worn a white doctor's coat so he could stay with her, because everyone thought she would die and the child would live. When she opened her eyes, he was standing by her bed with a face full of tears. She knew what he was thinking. "Do you know what your grandfather was thinking, Imker? He was thinking, 'No child on earth is worth this!'" And after a whole human lifespan, for the first time she pictured how she must have looked to her husband, lying there and staring up at him and whispering, *Anton, I don't ever want to do this again.* And she'd asked the midwife to put the newborn in her husband's arms. "He stood there, Imker, with the girl who'd nearly cost me my life. And everything hurt. Sex was off limits." Fragments of memories that she, for the first time in her life, spit out. Cigar smoke hung around her head. Imker had gotten up to unlock the kitchen door to the backyard and let in the daylight. She saw her granddaughter fill her lungs with the crispness of wind after rain. Imker's voice evenly uttered a message without the slightest meaning: "In my mother's house, there's no sex." She was putting away the cigar stub. And as she walked past Imker to flush the ashes down the toilet, she said blandly, "Your mother should just marry you all off, like the other communities do." The sink was running, so Imker shouted, "What makes you say that, Grandma?" She turned around and slowly went to the radio, switched it on at low volume, walked over to Imker, and said hoarsely, "Because none of you will find a decent spouse on your own." Imker, pertly: "I'll pass that message on to Mama; maybe she can find a better match for me than your Dutch priest?" It came out as a question. Her granddaughter fled outside to the terrace, still in her nightgown; she could hear the footsteps on the crushed shells. Then Grandmother heard her granddaughter raking, even though there wasn't a single withered leaf to be found.

My first letter to my mother. *Dear Mama*. But as I spread out the airmail stationery, I change my mind. *Darling Derik*. My pen glides across the paper. It turns into more than a love letter. I let Derik know that I see no future for myself in Utrecht. I let him know that staying with Winston and Lya brings me sleepless nights. I want to return home, and I end with this underlined sentence: *I love you, but don't tell anyone*! These will be the closing words of every letter I write to him. I fold the letter and stuff it into an airmail envelope. As for the stamps I got from Winston, intended for the letter to my mother, I give them a moist, lascivious lick and stick them on the envelope, on which I've written a post office box address and Derik's full name and title. I don't know how I can explain it to him, I don't know what he really is to me, I can't figure it out. My uncle and his wife aren't home. Playing bridge with friends. It's around eight o'clock at night. I've been away from my mother for about two weeks, and I now write to her, start to tell her I'll become the daughter she wants to see, and that this will take time. I write that I won't forget how touched she was when I came home with my first paycheck and slid the envelope in her hands. I write that everything I do is meant to let her know that I'm so very grateful to her. Also I say that I've met other Surinamese students at the teaching program. I tell her the program is at a Calvinist college. It ends up being a short letter. I can't have her knowing how excited I am about Derik coming to spend New Year's with me somewhere in Europe, far away from prying eyes. I add that I'm having no trouble with my studies and that the school year will fly by. I don't tell her how often I feel utterly baffled by the circumstances I've wound up in. And I slide the letter to my mother into a second blue airmail envelope. Then I read the texts to be discussed in the study group in the morning. Then shower. In bed, I think about the fact that my scholarship has been disbursed and part of it was transferred directly to me. Along with a leaflet about an opportunity to go on to a university with continued financial support. "Ground under our feet," that's what my compatriots call it, and a "very fine gesture" from the Netherlands to their overseas territory. The room is spacious and light, with big double-paned windows offering a view of the outdoors and colorful wisps of sunset. In the evening, the neighborhood remains shrouded in calm. The room has a large bed, a chest of drawers with a mirror, a desk, and a proper chair. The flooring and curtains are an identical shade of light brown. A guest room too tastefully furnished for an extended stay. "True beauty should be preserved in museums," our art history teacher recently said, while showing us a movie of three masterpieces by Dutch painters. "But there's also the kind of beauty that flares up when exposed to the eyes and immediately vanishes again and can never be captured." "True," the teacher said. "Dutch masters have made an attempt to convey that kind of beauty to us." My thoughts had wandered to Umar. He even made an oil painting of me—to get me to stay in the country, he said. And as I sat for hours in his living room posing before his easel, he spoke, looking at me, about his fear that he might never see me again. Umar confessed, "I spray-painted his car, slashed his tires, aimed my headlights at him when he was parked somewhere in the dark. I haven't quite reached the point of setting his car on fire." He asked me, "Do you love that man?" and I couldn't answer. The memory surfaces, not because I want it to. What happened at Umar's house is as tangible as the bottle of almond syrup from my grandmother on my desk, still wrapped. It may be the reason my philosophy teacher was astonished by my interest in a subject most of his students loathed: Edmund Husserl's phenomenology. "And you're still just a child," he said. The other Surinamese students in my class laughed mockingly. But they couldn't have known that the distinguished college director went on addressing me as "dear child" even when I was no longer his student. Or how close he came to making me his wife.

Derik asked if I wanted to help him at the office. His secretary was on vacation, the new bookshelves had been delivered and the old ones hauled off, and the books had to be shelved in order. The job would take a week. I could bring a classmate along, and we would be paid, he said. I told him I didn't want any money from him, and I was sure she didn't, either. Nolda and I reported for duty and worked our way through the books. Each day, Derik dropped my friend off at home first. Then he took the highway toward Amora. He said little. I said nothing. But when the job was over, he wanted to go out for a bite to eat—just with me, if I didn't mind. I was faint with hunger, but I told him I had no appetite. He said that he would really miss seeing me everywhere—on the school grounds at the teachers' college, among the students in his classroom. "I fell in love with you at first sight." A shiver went down my spine. And after a confession like that I didn't think I'd ever see him again. But a few days later, Derik picked me up. I was sitting at Uncle Rogier's desk nosing through a medical textbook. The room faced the street. My heart leaped to my throat when I saw his car waiting at our gate. He stepped out. I ran to Mother. "Say I'm not home, please!" As I waited in her bedroom, I heard his voice. Mother laughed heartily. I heard his car drive off. Mother said, "He had his wife and children in the car, that man..."

I jolt awake. Downstairs, the front door is being unlocked. The married couple come inside arguing. Their squabbling is playful, never hateful. My uncle is so clearly in love with her. She enjoys his flirtatious bickering. Now and then, Lya says, "You and I need to talk, but Winston can't know about it." And she widens her big eyes at me. They're in the house, they're home. I make the sign of the cross, pull up the covers. Mother's face looms. And I fall away. The post office where I take my two letters is horribly large, with droves of silent people standing in line, and I don't know which line to choose, and I'm worried my letters will never reach their destinations. I jolt awake again. A church bell strikes three o'clock. Someone is in the bathroom taking a shower. Laughter. Wow, they make love in the master bedroom right below me. Something moves in my underbelly.

From the depths of her work bag, Louise's fingers dug out the strips of birth control pills. They weren't all meant for her; the doctor had prescribed the same kind of pill for Babs's irregular cycle. But she didn't give them to Babs. Pointless—she was much too young. The very idea offended her motherly feelings. Babs's boyfriend Aram had given her a large-format edition of the Kama Sutra as a gift on her fifteenth birthday. The three girls got it out every day to pore over the illustrations with shining eyes. Audi, who wasn't allowed to look, had tipped her off. She gathered her courage, demanded the book, and encountered no resistance. But instead of returning the book along with a scolding to the young man who'd saddled her house with it, she ended up taking it to her own boyfriend's house. He grinned, teasing, "So these pictures get your daughters all worked up? And what do they do for you?" "Not much," she said defensively. He took the Kama Sutra to the military base, allegedly to keep his boys away from the whores. That didn't make much sense to her, but she was glad she could keep her daughters away from that sex book. And she kept an eye on Babs. But with the girl's irregular periods, monitoring her was a royal pain. She didn't avoid conversations about intimate matters. Since Heli had gotten into in a relationship with an older man, not a day went by without her treating her daughters to a new variation on her rule: "There's only one person in my house old enough for sex, and that's me." The girls didn't respond. They'd stared at her. Then she looked at them one by one and thought, *How will I know when one of my children is mature enough for sex?* And one day, after a big swig of whisky from the bottle her boyfriend Lester kept at her place, she'd spilled the story to them. The story of the Hindustani in Nickerie, who'd come to ask for her eldest daughter's hand on behalf of his son who was in the same class as Heli. The family had become millionaires in the rice trade, and his son was headed for a career as an agricultural engineer. And as all the details came back to her, she said pensively, "It was the first time in my whole damn life that I needed a man at my side, to act as a father to all of you." Since Heli had left, she'd often felt that need. She couldn't keep her children in check. A mother doesn't want to arrange her daughter's marriage. That's a job for a father. Meanwhile, the long wait for news from Holland had left her incapable of focusing on anything except waiting for news from Holland. She didn't want to see her boyfriend and had sent Audi off to the army base with a note to let him know. The letter said she needed a break to work out some things; she felt more loaded down than liberated. He sent her money for something pretty, and warm wishes. He was an easygoing kind of guy. A professional musician. And a career soldier, just like her father, Anton. She fell for big men in military dress. She loved the uniform, a symbol of safety and power, self-discipline and order. She'd never felt attracted to civil servants, educators, doctors, policemen, politicians, businessmen, and their ilk. She lay in bed considering this; Audi and Babs were turning the vacated bedroom into a den so she and her boyfriend could sit in the living room without the kids around. Babs's boyfriend had bought a color TV and wanted to give his old black-and-white one to Babs. She meant to shout out to her kids that it was fine to use the bedroom for something else, but it would always remain available for Heli and Imker. But she didn't. What would be the point? Her two daughters had left their home in Amora forever. She sank into a deep sleep. When she woke, hours later, her son was sitting next to her reading a book. He snapped it shut when she began to yawn. He looked at her, narrowing his eyes into slits. "Mama, I'll live with you forever." It was such a sweet thing to say that she couldn't object, even though she had very different plans for him. The fact was, she owed him so many answers. She understood her daughters, but not her son. She didn't dare go into the bathroom to get anything when he was in the shower. She knew his voice. The way he moved. She knew his face. But there was still something enigmatic about him, and she never went to any trouble to figure him out. Sometimes she asked her boyfriend Lester for advice, but he always said the same thing: "Just let your son go his own way; make it clear to him how much you love him, Louise Vanta." She said, "Audi, if Heli stays in Holland and goes to a university, then I'll send you to live with her after you finish school here, is that okay?" He didn't know what to say and asked if she would trim his hair. "Yes," she said. And she thought about how strange it was that he had more hair on his head than all three of his sisters combined. Thick, dark, coily hair that grew super fast. Could Louise bring herself to talk to him about his father?

Audi knew his mother never really answered his questions. Her responses had a way of keeping him at arm's length. Even so, he slept next to her in bed until his first holy communion. None of the girls had shared the big bed with Mama for seven whole years. His mother put

94

him on a pedestal, so he tended to stick to her like glue. Wherever she was, he could be found. When she returned to work three months after he was born, she took him to her classroom at a private school for rich kids downtown. After that, she brought him along to a series of classrooms—her own and, when he was older, other teachers'. He could have spent hours going through all the photos parents had taken of their own children with the teacher's little boy. Black-and-white images. Tiny. Chubby. Well dressed. A handsome kid. As soon as he was old enough, he was placed at a boys' school. And he figured out that the difference between him and his sisters was in his underpants. It made him more of a quiet little man. When Uncle Rogier stayed with them for a while, he had to share a room with Babs, but even then he remained an alien in the house. He sat next to his mother, watching as she slept. He knew every detail of her face. He had stared at it so often. He loved his mama's face, even when her eyes opened and her lips burst into speech. His book, which he'd laid on the floor, was a gift from Heli with a scribbled dedication: *To the best male human being in the whole wide world.* It was an informational guide for boys on the verge of adulthood. He wasn't there yet. He had finished the whole book and kept coming back to it, unable to resist. Mother looked at him, half-yawning. "Babs is with Aram," he sneered, "watching TV in the back room." It must have sounded like an accusation. "And you're sitting with your mother," she replied. He said, "Yes," and then softly, "It's not like I have a dad I can do things with." It was meant as a joke. But Mama wasn't about to let it go. She sat up, looking at her reflection in the door of the linen cupboard. "Well now, Audi, what kind of things would you like to do with your father right now? At this hour, a whole lot of fathers aren't home with their children, and the ones who are home are watching television. Shall we do that?" And Mother gracefully got out of bed, stretching her arms up into the air. Had he gotten the answer to what was starting to dig at him more and more? Wanting to show his frustration, he said, "I'll never abandon my children." Mother grabbed his big head of hair and spoke agonizingly slowly. "Boy, sometimes it's the father who's abandoned, not by his child but by the woman carrying his child." She was standing so close behind him. Audi let his head rest against her waist and squeezed his eyes shut. Ready for his trim.

Imker felt like she was on a rampage, instead of doing what she'd so often seen her mother and grandmother do: make slow, thoughtful scratches over the crushed shells. She didn't sing as she worked the way Grandma Bee did, nor did she mutter a psalm as her mother liked to do. It was as if her head were full of soap bubbles bumping into each other and leaving behind a drizzly, soggy liquid. She needed to concentrate on raking, because she heard her grandmother shuffling over. Grandma kept her distance, looking at her granddaughter, to whom she'd made an unwelcome remark. Her long bathrobe was almost as blue as the sky. Calmer now, much calmer, Imker went on raking and ignored her. Grandma vanished into the house to make something warm to drink, since her granddaughter hadn't. On purpose? She'd woken up too early, thanks to Grandma's anxious wheezing, penetrating cigar smoke, and disturbing admissions. At Grandma's house, the yard received an early-morning raking. Out of necessity. She'd left her textbooks lying around unopened. Zero interest in spending her days in front of a kindergarten class. She could just hear mother raising her voice, "All my daughters have to earn a teaching certificate at the very least!" And because she had threatened to play hooky and become a saleslady at a Portuguese shop, Heli took her along one day for a home visit. A backyard tucked away in the center of Paramaribo. They first saw the wooden house fronts, which looked well-maintained. Then a gate. Then the long courtyard, right in the middle of the city, like a public square surrounded by cramped barracks. All around them were women, children, barking dogs, and maybe clucking chickens too. It had rained, and the ground was pitch-black, wet, and muddy. Somewhere nearby there must have been a well; young girls were carrying buckets of sloshing water. Heli was looking for a student who had stopped showing up at school because she was pregnant. Heli Vanta stopped and shouted into an open window. The head that popped up was the girl's. Heli asked her student if they could talk somewhere private. Neighbors were fixing them with hostile stares, their black faces gleaming beneath crowns of coily, dull black hair. Paramaribo isn't just what you can see; most of all, it's what stays hidden. She, Imker Vanta, might think she's as special as the Holy Virgin Mary, but without a degree or a secure job, there'd be a pit like that one waiting for her to fall into it, somewhere behind a well-maintained façade in the middle of her hometown. Her mother and Heli had scared her straight. Shop girls were brutally groped by their bosses and their bosses' sons, and then snarled at by the girls and women in the family, who wanted to make it clear whose side they were on in case of conflict. But a job at a hospital can't just mean emptying chamber pots, can it?

She stood in the doorway with a rake. Inside at the kitchen table, Grandma was sipping at something warm. She breathed in the sweet aroma of the cigar. If cigar smoking was her grandmother's greatest pleasure, it was all right with her. Everyone in the family knew Grandmother Bee had been married off. Because she never had the chance to choose a life partner for herself, her husband Anton became the man of her dreams. On birthdays, when children and grandchildren had gathered in the living room, they would listen once again to the tale of the Frenchman who'd married the daughter of an Englishman and whose daughter, set on the path to becoming a nun, was instead married off to a boy from a slave plantation somewhere on the bank of a tributary. But then Grandfather would mutter, "No Dutchman influenced our choosing each other, right, Bee?" At least once a year, they would map the territory of their past and dig up the roots of the family tree for a brief inspection. And then the adults would conclude once again that, regardless, they were all off-white. And they would drink a toast to that. Though there was some sadness to it. Bee's father Julienne sent letters and even shipped food to his children, but the voyage from Paris to Paramaribo was risky, and everything arrived behind schedule, including the last letter from France—a death certificate and the announcement that his son Napo had picked up his estate: two full shipping crates.

She looked at her grandmother. Grandma looked

at her. She wanted to take a bath. Wash up. "I wonder where my daughter Ethel is." Grandmother's voice. "Do you think about her at lot?" No reply. Off to the bathroom. Many of life's questions can never be answered. She told Grandmother she was going to take a shower. She let the streams of water soak through her like Grandma Bee's thought-provoking recollections. When Ethel had been shown to Grandmother after her birth, panic almost broke out. The newborn was nearly jet-black, but her hair, which didn't have a single curl, was a few shades removed from blonde. The midwife, who handled all her childbirths, called the baby a jewel, mixed from a formidable network of bloodlines that included so many different people. They were in the small military hospital. Dressed in his military uniform, Anton went to report his child's birth at the civil registry office in Nieuw Nickerie. "Ethel Vanta," he said with pride. The midwife's name and his last name, which meant "black" at the plantation where his mother came from. He must have looked unusually happy with the birth of this particular child—his third—because he bought a round of beers for everyone at the canteen at the base. Much less delighted were the members of his wife's family who came to see the new baby. They leaned in for a close look, shaking their heads in astonishment. Ethel's older siblings, Winston and Louise, had come out a just barely respectable shade of light brown, but the skin on this one had gone a step too far toward an undesirable extreme. Even Bee was stunned by what she'd carried for nine months, and blamed herself for possibly having eaten too much of something or other—sugarcane stalks, she'd been crazy about those, especially the dark purple ones, which she loved to chew on. She cuddled her daughter lovingly in her arms, nursing her tenderly at her ginger-colored breasts. And Ethel was such a sweetheart. It did Anton good to see her lavishing affection on their newborn. To him, this child was a link to the history and indigenous origins of his ancestors. He'd tried to explain to his English-speaking brothers-in-law and to all his nieces and nephews that Ethel was his masterpiece. "All of you are off-white, but her skin absorbs every wavelength of light; yes, our Ethel is whole." Could anyone begin to make sense of this explanation? The family kept saying disappointedly, "Yes, Anton, Baby Ethel certainly is dark-skinned." It wasn't an easy year for the family, and when Laura came into the world fourteen months later with the right complexion, the family relationships were restored. Yet Anton stubbornly insisted that Laura's birth was a terrible tragedy and that his wife had nearly died in childbirth. When he'd been drinking too much, he'd swear that no other child would ever be born in his house after Laura. His fellow soldiers laughed right in his face. They knew Soldier Vanta through and through, and he wasn't cut out for going to the whores or cheating on his pretty wife. They predicted he'd find himself standing beside her hospital bed again one fine day, as full of self-pity as ever. And they were right. Years after Laura, there was another pregnancy, not in the vicinity of Bee's blood relatives and Anton's army buddies, but in Paramaribo in the beautiful home of a Jewish family who'd fled from Hitler. She toweled herself dry, wiping away the chilly past. Spread fragrant jasmine oil over her skin. Then Imker, washed, dressed, and perfumed, reported to her grandmother.

On Friday afternoon, I find Lya waiting for me. Is there some problem? In silence, I walk with her to her car in the parking lot. No Uncle Winston to be seen. The good news, she finally says, is that my stipend has reached my account, but she hesitates before saying, "Your grandma is coughing up blood. She's practically skin and bones." She opens the door, and I get into the car. It's such a warm autumn day, no harsh wind, sunny. The city center is postcard-perfect. I sink into the loveliness of nature, feeling my own shortcomings nipping at me. Laura gets behind the steering wheel, turns on the ignition, and says, "I managed to intercept a couple of letters from someone calling themselves Billboard." I flinch. She opens the glove compartment and hands me two sealed envelopes. I take one, nervous about what may come next. "You're not going to thank me?" she asks. I do, right away. Then she makes it clear to me that her husband knows nothing about the letters and doesn't have to hear about them. She takes her time pulling out of the parking lot, saying, "My heart goes out to you, Heli, my mother also sent me to Holland because I was having an affair with an older married man with children, and I worked in a Catholic hospital." It's so quiet in the car that I can hear the city noise, the leaves rustling in the wind. Lya doesn't drive me to her house. The city library? She personally takes me inside to help me register for a card. Once it's in my hand, she says in a friendly, encouraging tone, "Go to the reading room to read your letters and reply to him. Cut them up afterward and throw them all away." Her copper-colored irises glow bright: "Never bring anyone else to this place." I know she's advising me not to bring my escapade with Derik into their house, not to confide in anyone about it. I nod and say, "Maybe I'd better go to boarding school after all?" She reassures me. "Let's see how the first semester goes. Don't forget I'm here for you, Heli." I watch her through the glass in the revolving door, smiling at how effortlessly she finds the exit. Did she once come here to write love letters? The reading room is crowded. I walk around for a bit until I find an empty seat at the newspaper counter.

I still remember the first time I looked into Derik's eyes. It was in the hallway of the main school building, and he walked up to me in a white shirt and tie, dark trousers, and black Oxford shoes with polished leather. I had on a form-fitting velvet tiger print dress. I'd read in Rogier's medical textbook that eyes are just lenses capturing material information for the brain, which then does with the images as it pleases. I was like dry kindling set aflame by the sparks that flew from Derik's eyes. The light hitting me just right and the way everything came together created an unexpected moment for both our brains. Years later, for the first time, his hand on my skin and his voice describing his irresistible desire for me from that moment in the hallway to the first wet kiss in his car parked on the street… I sit at the counter for a while before finally taking the envelopes out of my bag: my name in his handwriting. I look around to see if anyone's spying on me. Rip them open. Both envelopes in a single motion: pages of airmail stationery covered in small handwriting. I want to scream with happiness. My eyes absorb, my brain processes, my body receives what it needs to quicken my heartbeat. I'm sweating with delight. Derik describes what he wants to do with me this New Year's; I can feel it, every detail. I'm tingling in places in my underbelly that I hold sacred and guard tenderly. My throat fills. I swallow. And then Grandmother's image comes to mind: beautiful, tough as a woody vine, wasting away. I gulp for fresh air. I'll have to tear up the letters and toss them into some can of filthy garbage on the street. My consolation is the belief that the most beautiful things reveal themselves only once but leave an enduring imprint on my brain, which I'll see reflected in every following love letter. I don't reread. I tear. Into tiny pieces. Then I get up. Head outside with my shoulder bag. Coat pocket full of shredded passion. The afternoon shines. I want to hear a song. My god-mother's voice spreads through me, singing the hymn that she performed at the party for my first communion, her voice as light as the beating wings of a hummingbird seeking nectar deep within me. Everyone applauds, but my eyes are full of tears. My new shoes pinch terribly. The photographer asks for a smile, but I don't want to. Aunt Laura comes to give me a hug, and in the photo, my face is beaming with affection. A few years later, she'll disappear into Kolera. Hesitantly, I pause to breathe in the city. Mobs of schoolchildren, hungry after a fantastic day at school, excitedly wind their way to their mothers. The city center is swamped with children. Colorful coats, bags bouncing on their backs, hats on their heads, and hair blowing in the autumn wind. I won't run into anyone I know. I walk slowly to the bus station. A wide boulevard with buses constantly coming and going. I hardly see anything happening on the other side of the road. Then an enormous dark building looms up on a corner. The post office? A heavy revolving door. A counter full of postcards and other packaging. Mama gave me 200 guilders in spending money, which I exchanged for 400 Dutch guilders. I still have enough left for a planner, airmail paper, envelopes, pens, stamps, postcards, tape. I join the back of a long line. As I wait, I fill postcards of Utrecht with little messages for my loved ones in Paramaribo. Even one for Laura, to send her the sounds of a street organ. Do my letters to Mama and Derik have sufficient postage? "Yes, ma'am." And I get free airmail stickers for priority delivery. To the trash can with a handful of paper scraps. And then back out into the daylight.

For Louise, a man could have everything a woman wanted in a husband and still be unappealing as a life partner. Bohr had had affairs with every one of her four closest friends, each resulting in a child. He would never get married; he'd said so openly. The idea of living together with a woman scared him. Yet during his medical residency in New York, he got married to an African American woman, who wouldn't stay in Suriname for man or money. He soon divorced her, moving back in with his parents. Her fingers combed through Audi's hair in search of knots. Bohr had been born somewhere in Europe, maybe in Italy or in Poland—no one knew for sure, he always talked in circles—and had fled with his parents to Brazil, winding up in Paramaribo at a luxury residence on the river right next door to the hotel owned by Babs's paternal grandparents, and the boys had grown up together like brothers. She and Laura knew him from the medical school. Always hanging out with the girls and always joking about being addicted to mulatto women because the maid employed by his parents had been the sweetest human being he'd ever known; he'd even dedicated his final thesis to her. But as she, sunk in thought, kept digging through her son's hair, she tightened her face, pursing her lips. He'd chased after her for years without any success. He attended the first party she threw at the big yellow house where she lived with Babs's father. One day, in an unguarded moment, he cornered her in her own bedroom and fucked her. My God, how she puked the next morning and sobbed. A pregnancy like a hand grenade, sending her joie de vivre up in smoke. But when the midwife said, "It's a boy, Louise," she understood that at last a man had come into her life to stay. And she would love him unconditionally. Her fingers combed through her son's thick hair. Audi didn't make a peep. They never talked during his haircuts, and he sat where the mirrors in Mother's room couldn't reflect the two of them together. She knew he didn't care what happened to his hair, as long as he felt his mother's hands on his head. She set him loose so that she could go to the living room; on the way there, she coughed pointedly to assert her authority to Babs and her boyfriend Aram, who were watching television out of sight. "Are you still in there?" she called out, because it was so quiet. Laughter from Babs, as if that would reassure her no rules were being broken. Suddenly, Aram's figure in the hallway with a cheerful "How are you, Mrs. Vanta?" That was good enough for her. But when he asked if they'd had an update from Heli, she didn't know what to tell him. With a gesture, she made it clear to him that Audi was getting his hair cut. Her eyes drank in the evening sky as it rushed in through the window and the celestial exhaust that was fading from view in colorful trails of light. Her eyes settled on Aram's sports car. She took a deep breath. With scissors, clippers, and a salon cape, she returned to Audi, who slid to the floor so that she could sit down. She draped the cape around him. He shifted, grumbling, "I have a strong feeling you're thinking about my father, Mama." She replied in a stage whisper, "You shouldn't raise sensitive topics when you're in the hands of someone with sharp scissors." Audi slapped his thighs, laughing. The trim could begin, and as she took hold of the first lock: "Everyone thinks you're a fool when you're pregnant and you leave a man as soft as a three-minute egg to move in with your family at your parents' home, which is bursting with strong opinions." She leaned forward to see the face of her beautiful boy. And then the first lock of hair slid to the floor. Louise hummed a tune whose words she had forgotten.

For years, Babs had been keeping a black-and-white photo in which the flash bulb seemed to be reflected in the eyes of every member of her mother's family. A square piece of paper the size of her palm with deckled edges. Herself as a little girl. She could look at Imker as a seven-year-old. She couldn't help chuckling at the confused face Heli had made on her tenth birthday, but what stunned her most was Mama with baby Audi on her shoulder. The photographer had stumbled smack into the anguish of that moment, the lowest point of Mother's existence. And the pale blonde girl standing among the nieces and nephews and a bunch of local kids from the neighborhood? It was Josje, the favorite child of a Dutch couple who ran a bakery on a pretty shopping street. Heli and

Josje attended the same school and were inseparable, her mother had explained, adding that Josje's father was the one who went around startling everyone with flashbulbs at parties. The pastry shop had delivered all sorts of treats. But what people talked about for years afterward was the enormous chocolate birthday cake with whipped cream and burning candles for the birthday girl, all blown out in a single breath, a present from Josje and her parents. Heli was wriggling with joy, but Mama, who had pressing concerns, was happy when the little kids cleared out of her house with the party favors she'd put together: colorful little parchment-paper bags with a variety of sweets carefully sealed inside with a cute ribbon. There was music from a street organ grinder, who also did magic tricks that kept the children shaking with laughter. Drinks in abundance. But the bike Louise had promised Heli would have to wait. Babs treasured Mama's every word about her struggle to keep it all together. She was well known for asking questions that were blunt to the point of rudeness, and when the answer was evasive, she would keep badgering until she started an argument. Then she'd lie in bed crying, not because she hadn't gotten her way, but because she'd pushed away someone she'd meant to pull closer. Sometimes she had the feeling she'd dropped out of the sky and landed in a house that could never be a real home for her. She was always sullen and acting out. Unfriendly and obnoxious. This was how others talked about her, but she never got the chance to tell her side. At school, she'd started stomping her feet when she had to sit next to a black girl, and when assigned to a black homeroom teacher, she'd refuse to go to class. Her father, Boyce, had personally enrolled her in a private school where everything was different from her daily life. And that distanced her from her family, more than she could manage. Everyone at home was almost afraid of her, and she was even estranged from her sister Heli, who'd always been a comfort to her. So she took over the vacated room, without guilt, and transformed it into something that suited her. She said good night to Aram, waving as he drove off. Then went to Mother's bedroom where Audi was getting a haircut. She couldn't go in. She hung back in the doorway. She watched. Her eyes welled with tears. She wanted to offer them some of the Dutch apples and red grapes and maybe a piece of the Gouda cheese that Aram had brought her, but her voice choked up. She went to the living room window and stared outside, where evening was bleeding into night. Babs thought, *There must be someone somewhere that I can truly love? Someone I can really connect with?*

Grandma couldn't shake the thought of her daughter Ethel. And for the first time ever, she didn't feel like "hoofing it." Her granddaughter was surprised and understood that saying nothing and just staying with her would do more good than anything. "Sometimes, it feels like she's watching me, Imker. My priest says it's the voice of my conscience. He may be right." Even though she was close to Ethel, she hadn't grieved her for long. After all, she soon had another baby girl, who left her practically no time for little Ethel and the others. The children were growing up fast. She could hardly handle the four of them, and Anton proposed hiring one of his nieces to help with the housekeeping and childcare. As if he didn't know perfectly well that she'd refuse. It led to yet another argument. As she loaded him with abuse, Winston, Louise, and especially little Ethel and baby Laura all watched and listened, mouth agape, eyes bulging with fear. That must have been the day Anton made up his mind—not only to sleep in the attic from then on, far away from their marital bed, but to also liberate his favorite child from a situation that he couldn't handle. And the opportunity came sooner than he thought. She hadn't expected her accusations to cut so deep that he no longer saw any solid ground for their marriage. She shook her head in self-reproach.

"What did you scream in Grandpa's face, Grandma Bee?" Her granddaughter had snuggled up right next to her. She took a deep breath and spit it out: "Slave, plantation nigger, Black Peter, devil, brute! And he shot back that he wasn't any of those things, and I shoved him over to the big mirror in our parlor and asked if he saw a human being there when he looked at his reflection." An act of desperation. Imker grabbed her hand, whispering with a face full of horror, "You need to beg my Grandpa Anton for forgiveness, go to his grave and tell him you're sorry!" But she wrenched away her hand; she could picture him leaving the house early in the morning in his military uniform, without eating breakfast, and returning in the evening when the children were asleep, Sergeant Vanta, unsteady on his feet, because he killed the hours in bars with gold seekers and fishermen, hard-drinking, hard-gambling types. He wouldn't touch the food she kept warm for him. He wouldn't answer her questions. One afternoon he came to pick up Ethel. Grandma walked to the faucet and drank some water, not bothering with a glass. Imker said, "So Grandpa told you he had come to pick up the child who resembled him the most for a visit to his relatives at Lustoord Plantation, but then he came home without Ethel?" Grandmother said nothing and looked for a place to sit a little farther away from her granddaughter, so she could tell her story her own way. She continued forcefully. "Your grandfather had so often said, 'Dame Bee, a slave is for selling, a plantation nigger is for beating, a devil is for cursing, and a brute is for killing.' He gave away his own child so she could have a better life than he could offer her in our family." To punish his wife for her "big talk," he kept the location of her daughter's new home a secret from her. And seeing how much she'd already shocked her granddaughter, she didn't add that she herself, along with the rest of her family, blamed her father Julienne for having married her off, his own daughter, to the lowest of the low—a descendant of slaves. "You'll bleed for what came out of your mouth!" Anton once said that right to her face, and he never uttered another word on the subject of Ethel. Even as he remained her husband. Even as he went on loving her. On his deathbed, he whispered to their granddaughter Heli, "I adored your grandmother, let her know Anton Vanta was thinking of her." Isn't that a sign of forgiveness? Imker nodded. "But even after so many ugly words, you and Grandpa still managed to have one last child together, huh, Grandma?" No more words were left in her. She was worn out. Hungry. She'd eaten a boiled egg that day and nothing else. Sleep, that was what she wanted, long and deep.

Imker drew the curtains all the way open so that the fresh air and light could pour in. Straightened up her bedding. She saw Grandma stretching and reaching for a pillow to cuddle. Despite their problems, her grandparents had created a safe haven at the house in Jacobusrust, she thought. Even though she had no definite memories of the place. The houses where Grandma Bee and Grandpa Anton had lived were no longer standing, and even in the Nickerie district, the forefather of Grandma's English family hadn't been able to protect his plantation from the ocean's voracious destructiveness. To her, that piece of history seemed gone forever, along with the slaveholders. In her appearance and in her blood traces of them were still visible, but dreams free of violence grew wild in her head. She stared at the woman lying in bed. She felt certain that bottled-up grief was the main thing sending Grandma to the grave. It must have been so hard for a young woman to find an escape route in a society born of other people's violence. She collapsed the cot. She heard Grandma breathing, snoring as if her mouth had dropped open. She looked at the body on the bed, which she cared for because there was no other choice. There was no point in planning for the future because the compulsion to stay at Grandma Bee's side controlled her. She carried the sleeping bag and sheets to the big linen cupboard in the laundry room. The sunlight slanting into the room made her smile. Buy budding flowers in pots and hang them next to the kitchen door. A bouquet of sunflowers for the living room. Determined, she put on a clean apron. First the bathroom, then the kitchen, and after that a nice bowl of porridge for the patient. It had to be this way. And if it was God making it impossible to lead a more privileged life, then as far as she was concerned, Grandma Bee could keep on resting comfortably in her bed instead of trotting over to God's house. She grabbed a cloth to dust the crucifixes that hung on various walls. What if Ethel were to turn up at the gate one day? Some thoughts were easier to dodge while sleeping. Grinning, she polished a small brass crucifix until Christ's body shone. Would the life of a nun be a good fit for her? Looped the crucifix back on the hook again. As she stretched, she noticed the orthopedic sandals in the hallway. She went to sit on the sofa and be with Heli in her thoughts. But then she realized Heli must be fast asleep somewhere in Holland. And if a young woman went to live in a convent, was it only for the sake of her own future? She knew Grandfather had given Ethel away to German Moravian missionaries. Perhaps one day Ethel would show up at the gate, skinny and worn out from spreading the gospel, her eyes burning with the desire to see her parents again. Nothing for Ethel to come back to besides gravestones among clumps of tough grass. She would force Grandmother to visit Sergeant Vanta's grave. Or had he been a Sergeant-Major, or a Private First Class? She walked to the window, yanking open the curtains to let the new day into the living room. Unbreakable quiet all around her. Only Grandmother's breathing was audible, along with Imker's own footsteps on the Marmoleum floor of Grandma's bungalow.

Young children can annoy adults more deeply than they intend to. Louise had often seen the aftermath of a young child being beaten by an adult family member for some imagined offense: the child asked a question, made a comment, didn't want to speak. She didn't like corporal punishment and, whenever she was asked for advice, what she tried hardest to explain was that a beating never made anyone—not even a child—behave better. But a child can work your nerves, like Audi, who'd been whining on about his father for years. And children know instinctively how to press their parents' buttons. She trimmed her son's hair until she was happy with it and fell asleep, exhausted, on the sofa afterward. She jolted awake when she heard loud barking from the neighbor's dogs and someone pounding at the gate. The man next door, who was from a family of gardeners, had tried to set her at ease, saying that their dogs sometimes barked at nothing more than shadows and passing lights. She wasn't happy about it, but she didn't dare get up and turn on the outside light to see why the dogs were making such a ruckus. She had borne four children and raised them without anyone's help, but, truth be told, she was as afraid of the dark as a young girl of thirteen. The dogs barked, growled, jumped against the gate. She could feel her heart pounding as she broke out in a cold sweat. She went to check on Babs, who turned out to be sleeping soundly; she went on to Audi's room, and he too was fast asleep. Gripped by fear, she turned on the outside light. The dogs calmed down. She'd planned to take a bath, but now anxiety wouldn't let go of her. Finally, to bed. Audi had swept up his hair; it was still there in the dustpan. She could still hear the dogs, but they were no longer barking. Was it possible Leika, her guard dog, had turned up again after all? In the darkness of the night, her house was awash in artificial light, and now she'd have to answer questions from the neighbors:

"Oh, Mrs. Vanta, is your Leika back home?" Still, she didn't feel like turning off the light. Wash face with tap water. Brush teeth. Scrape tongue. Gargle. Spit. Put on night balm. She undid her cleaning apron and hung it up, then slid between the sheets. Her feet hurt from standing all day in cork sole slippers. Slippers Heli had left behind. Scary to be wide awake at night and then pounced on by what you'd rather not remember: horrible experiences. She knew why she was feeling dizzy at work; she spent all her time thinking about her daughter in Holland, among total strangers. Heli was afraid of things like sleepovers and was attached to her mother's house like a fetus to the womb. How could she have succumbed to pressure from others and brutally uprooted her child? At Nickerie, she had experienced what it meant to not feel at home anywhere. She reached for the Bible next to the pillow and switched on the reading lamp. But the small light bulb glowed only briefly before immediately flickering out. Was it burned out, just like her? She couldn't just fade into darkness. Her children were counting on her, even Heli, who'd become unreachable. She didn't know why, but she got up to turn off the outside light. And if the dogs started howling again, she'd just stay in bed and wait until morning. That was how she wanted to drift off, with her right hand on the Bible. She lay on her right side with her back to the street. *If* she'd married off Heli to Umar, the son of that rich Hindustani family, *then* she could have settled permanently in Nieuw Nickerie, *then* her son-in-law would have gone to Wageningen as an agricultural engineer, *then* Heli could have finished high school and jumped right into administrative work at the rice merchant's office, and *then* perhaps Imker, Babs, and

Audi could have led more stable lives. But hold on—Heli Vanta as a Hindustani mother? It was God who had offered her daughter this opportunity to escape her own limitations. And with that thought, Louise fell asleep, full of faith in her Heavenly Co-Pilot.

Three

We've been at Amora Village for less than a week when Mama gets a surprise visit from a man who claims to be a close relative of her father, Anton. He's wearing an elegant suit, leather shoes, and a fedora. With a grave expression, he says he's come by for a private talk with my mother. I stand next to her in the open front door. I can sense her irritation as she tells him she won't be having any private conversations with a perfect stranger. "Since you claim to be family, I'll let you in, but my eldest daughter will join us." We let him inside, and Mother offers him a place to sit on her brand-new chaise longue, its throw pillows still wrapped in plastic. It isn't easy for Mr. Vanta to start the conversation, and Mother clearly has no interest in encouraging him. We look at each other. We say nothing until the man explains where he stands in my grandfather's family tree. My grandfather has only one sister and he's the son of that sister, so he and my mother are full-blooded cousins. But Mother protests. "Not necessarily full blooded; my father and your mother could have different fathers." As if he didn't already know that. He nods but holds firm. "Louise, children from the same womb are full-blooded family because we can never prove who the father is." Mother neither accepts nor rejects this. "Go on, then." "The Vanta family bought Lustoord Plantation through its combined efforts, you see, and Anton Vanta once played a role in those efforts. Now a momentous event is about to take place." "Well, what?" "The whole family is being summoned to a multiday celebration. We'll pull out all the stops." "A Winti séance?" Mother's slender figure rises from the chair. "How did you get my address, anyway?" "Your father," he says. "Have you spoken to my brother Winston?" He doesn't hesitate. "Yes, Louise, Cousin Winston will be there." Mother sits back down so that she can look at the man from a distance and asks sternly, "What kind of work do you do then?" He looks up, removing the hat from his head and mumbling, "I do whatever odd jobs come my way and earn my bread with honest work, Cousin Louise." Then the conversation comes to an abrupt end as Mother spits out her answer, too loud, into the living room. "I'll give you some money, but my family will not be present at your gathering." The man jumps up, saying, "Cousin Louise, the gods will make your household pay for this, believe me. They want everyone with Vanta blood in their veins to show their faces there." He stares at my mother aggressively. "Not happening," she says firmly. I sit beside her with no idea what to say, but I try anyway: "May I represent our household?" Mother's startled, looking at me in surprise. The man suddenly understands there's nothing more to get out of this visit than some money from mother and my willingness to visit their plantation. Mama sees him out. I can hear her ask her cousin not to come to her house again and not to her place of work either and not to get Winston involved in her business; she instructs him to leave any messages for her with her father Anton if strictly necessary. Door closed. She dashes over to me and gives me a scolding I'll never forget. She says without raising her voice, her eyes piercing straight into my gray matter like an awl, "Heli, in a conversation with other people, you always take your mother's side." I nod. "And what about you?" I ask.

It took a day or two, as I recall, for my mother to respond. "Heli, even when I won't take your side in a conversation with other people, please remember I'm just acting in your best interest." Five years later, she provided proof of this, in the form of my one-way ocean crossing to Holland. Before that, she'd given me the opportunity to go to the teachers' college in Paramaribo. The Dutchman who served as the high school principal for years and years in Nickerie had guaranteed at every parent-teacher conference that I was smart, but also warned that I was too pretty to go unsupervised. She'd taken the comment with a grain of salt until Derik chose me over so many others. But by then, years had gone by, and we were living in the big city.

I take Imker with me to a workshop on the theme of VIRGINITY. There it is in black capital letters on red posters throughout the city. I'm teaching at a girls' school, and my co-worker Cate invites me along. It's a Saturday morning, and only eleven women have come to listen. The space is too large, and we all decide to sit close to each other at two big tables. Fans on. Windows closed. *The First Association for the Rights of the Surinamese Woman* is subsidized by the government, so even the soft drinks are free. The woman who comes in with a Dutch lady looks familiar to me. She doesn't say her own name, but immediately introduces the white woman, who begins her talk. Right away we're all on the edge of our seats. Even with the noise of the fans, I don't miss a single word. We're shown a big color illustration of the vulva and vagina. Eleven pairs of women's eyes stare at the thing. The Surinamese woman leaves the midwife-gynecologist-sexologist alone with us, maybe for reasons of privacy; we didn't have to give our names, either. The moderator has a question for each of us: "Are you in a relationship and how old is your partner?" She doesn't ask who's still a virgin and who is having sex. She obviously isn't interested in lies. I say I have a boyfriend and give his age. She blinks. She even smiles. She says, "Best not to get stuck in that type of relationship, no matter how romantic it is, because by the time you get a handle on what your body needs, he'll be too old to satisfy you and get you pregnant." I say nothing but feel myself growing tense. "Would you like to know what makes me say that?" she asks. I nod. "Because by then his penis will no longer be capable of maintaining an erection, and his sperm will have decreased in both quality and number. Is that clear?" Not really. Not much more than that gets through to me that afternoon. I clap along with everyone else and thank the lady from Holland, shaking her hand. Back out on the street, we all decide to go to Spanhoek for ice cream. Imker and my co-worker Cate and I walk arm in arm behind the other women in silence. Then Imker says softly, "The woman who introduced us to the doctor is Derik's wife: she's straightened and dyed her hair, but

I know her from the training program; she teaches arts and crafts." I don't respond. "Are you taking one of her classes?" my co-worker Cate asks sweetly. "Yes," my sister whispers. "You poor thing," Cate says, giving my arm a hard, painful pinch. I should say something to Imker, but I don't know what. And suddenly my sister declares in a loud voice, "I'll love you just the same, Heli, whatever you do!" I pull free and hug her in the middle of the street. I promise to share everything I have with her for as long as I live. Since I'm a student living on a scholarship, this promise doesn't yet mean very much. I'll need to come up with something to make my absence bearable for Imker. There will also be someone else who'll miss me. I feel it. And I don't understand why it's so terribly hard for me to go say goodbye to her—it's better to shed sorrowful tears than to leave Laura wondering, "What's keeping Heli?"

Grandma considered her life small and her worries big. It sounded ridiculous. Physically, she was a petite little woman, who had married a boy over six feet tall. That difference influenced her view of the world. "A carpenter needs a spirit level to avoid building crooked rooms," she would say enigmatically, usually in a mishmash of French and English. A spirit level? "And a woman without a healthy, pinkish-red tongue is useless in the kitchen." Makes more sense. If any woman was born for the kitchen, it was Bee. She could brew concoctions that made you tipsy, tonics for coughs and all sorts of tropical diseases. She whipped up ointments for warts, sores, and pustules. And she could cook and bake like nobody's business. After Laura's birth, she'd stopped the bleeding with special foods she prepared herself. The things she could do with wooden spoons, cooking pots, and fire even caught the attention of older women. She wasn't yet thirty then, but when she walked through her hometown market on Achterstraat, men would approach her to talk, women to hawk their wares, girls to get advice. Her father Julienne had left her and her brothers a villa with a large but poorly lit backyard, full of tall trees yielding seasonal fruits. The boys didn't allow her to go there as a child, so she would wait patiently until the harvest was carried into the kitchen. And even though she was only a head higher than the stove, everyone gave her free rein in the kitchen. Her mother was pale and delicate as meringue and was slowly fading away, right when their father Julienne often needed to be in French Guiana for work. She was sent to live with the nuns. Their kitchen gardens at the convent were her passion and her life. Her husband Anton remembered this well; not long after their wedding, he hired a Hindustani to install a vegetable garden. She watched him work. It was up to her what to grow there. And in the evening hours when she and Anton withdrew to the bathroom for closer inspection of each other's bodies, he had to crouch down so she could soap his back. And she did, meanwhile telling him how the growth of this or that plant was progressing or what surprising and unfamiliar herbs the gardener had planted. Neither one of them was ready to start having sex yet. Their greatest pleasure was taking a bath together. And that went on and on. She may still have been in the shadows of a morning slumber when he physically took her as his wife. Over time, he became the only man that she could turn to. Her father Julienne didn't come back; her uncle Mr. Cru left for Scotland; and her brothers drifted away one by one, not to Paramaribo but to French and British territory. Her brother Winston, after whom she would name her eldest son, stayed in the villa to be close to his little sister, until he fell head over heels in love with an older lady from Demerara. Nothing could keep him in Nickerie. He said goodbye to her while she was recovering from the ordeal of Laura's birth, leaving his address and some money, because he'd sold the villa to a Chinese merchant who wanted to turn it into a store.

She lay on her back, daydreaming. If she hadn't heard her granddaughter in the kitchen, she might have begun to doubt her own existence. She, the woman known as "Bee"—Bernadette Vanta van Julienne, she who once wore prêt-à-porter dresses with lace and frosted buttons, usually in an off-white color to keep herself cool—did she still exist? Her brother never passed up the chance to send her clothes and shoes from Georgetown. He and his wife dealt in textiles and clothing and made good money, according to the couriers. Anton received white shirts from him, socks, neckties, and even a men's bicycle. She received a baby carriage so beautifully decorated that passers-by would stare. She sent her brother jars of guava jam, birambi fruit, pickled limes, and orgeat syrup. Now and then, Anton and the gardener would go to the villa to pick birambi fruit, oranges, limes, olives, soursop, guineps, and bright yellow mangoes. As the men picked fruit, she would cut sunflowers to make a big bouquet for the house. She had trouble keeping the rose bushes in check. They were neglected, wild but still capable of flowering. It took the Chinese merchant more than a year to bring over a few relatives from his home country to help with his new shop. And when the Chinese family was well established in the villa and the backyard was littered with building supplies, the priest said in his Sunday sermon, "To every thing there is a season," and on behalf of the parishioners, he dedicated a Holy Mass to "the family of the late Mr. and Mrs. Julienne." Her past had become like a seascape she woke up to each day, and sometimes she took a sobering dive straight in. She got up and more-or-less dragged herself out of bed to the kitchen. "Do you think God exists?" Imker looked her straight in the eyes and slowly answered, "Yes, Grandma, and today He still doesn't really love us." Laughter gushing from both of them. It was time for Grandma to eat breakfast with her grandchild.

Imker had no memories of her mother Louise as a pregnant woman, and since Heli wasn't there to jog her memory, she decided to approach people who could shed more light on some of her experiences. Daily contact with Grandma was opening her up like an unfurling map, revealing some spots whose existence she'd forgotten. *Mama has left Grandma Bee to her fate*, she thought. *She never stops by, never seriously asks how things are going in Zorg en Hoop.* An old grudge? Louise had once taken her and the others to stay in a hotel for several days, before they moved to Nickerie. She and Heli and Babs had to stay in the room, and every morning their mother had gone out in search of suitable housing with their baby brother Audi in a sling. Tears shot up at this memory. Mother was so silent. Even though she was only six, she could sense her sisters' panic at being locked

124

in a room with two beds, a toilet, a shower, and large windows that didn't open. They were green windows, and the daylight came in through glass panes above the green shutters. They didn't talk. It was in the heat of the long September school vacation. She never saw her mother cry, but the way Mama moved among them in the small room was worse. Heli had once claimed that Grandma had kicked their mother out. The woman sitting across the table from her had a bowl of polenta and was taking small sips of elderberry tea. When their eyes met, Grandma said, "I hope my daughter Ethel's living somewhere with good people and is married to a kind man." Her grandmother was at it again, starting another difficult conversation. "And why did you kick my mother out of the house a year after my little brother was born?" Grandmother, looking surprised, poured herself another cup of tea. "Imker, child, that happened so long ago, and how old has Audi gotten since then?" Right away she regretted her attack, saying apologetically, "Grandma Bee, if you don't remember anymore, you don't have to answer." Grandmother kept shaking her head, as she answered hoarsely, "I remember quite clearly that it all went helter-skelter. There were election campaigns going on in town, and Laura'd had a falling-out with a friend and arrived unexpectedly from Saramacca, where she had a job and her own house, and demanded her room, yes." She let Grandmother catch her breath, and then, "But couldn't you have made it clear to Laura that it would be better for her to go to a hotel, because Mama had to build up her strength again after having a baby and was staying at your house with her children?" She needed to catch her breath too, caught off guard by her own bluntness.

Everyone knew that conflicts among Grandma Bee's children were more than she could handle. Her grandmother hadn't grown up among squabbling sisters and thought all that name-calling was tedious, nothing more, and she let it all happen, too, in the belief that a fire set by accident will eventually burn itself out. The silence between them went on for some time. It was clear that Grandma was taking the question seriously. She could see her mulling it over, perhaps searching for words that would be fair to everyone involved. "Imker, I asked your mother to leave because Laura was furious and drinking too much, while your mother, even under the most difficult circumstances, remains level-headed and finds the best way to press on." After a sudden pause, Grandma wailed, "My God, just look at Laura!" She didn't budge from her seat at the table. Neither did Grandmother. She said in a more relaxed voice, "Yes, Mama found a place on Dwarsstraat within a week. Uncle Winston helped her move, but Grandma, something truly horrible happened there in that house." She could feel Grandma's sharp eyes cutting into her skin. "I can't tell you, Grandma, because it's too awful for words, and Mama just kept throwing up until it nearly killed her." She brought a finger to her lips to stop herself from talking: Ssssshhh. Grandma nodded as if she understood what couldn't be spoken. The teapot was empty. She was the one who thought to make a shopping list so that she and her grandmother would have something else to occupy their minds. Grandma said, "Item one: a new dress for Laura, new underwear too, even though the others keep stealing it, and..." But she interrupted: "Item two: a bunch of sunflowers for my grandmother." They had found a way back to the outside world. Grandma told her to turn on the radio, good and loud. And Imker was happy to oblige.

Babs knew she'd pass her finals. But she didn't know what to do next as a sixteen-year-old with a high school diploma. Mama had always insisted on a teaching certificate but was now on bad terms with the director of the teacher training program, so that whole plan had now been thrown into uncertainty. Every time they talked about it, her mother would start hyperventilating, which was not the path to a solution. She was the only one who knew that Umar had been the first to tip off her mother about Heli's affair. And she was the only one who had witnessed her mother fuming through the house. And the following day, when she asked if she could still register, Mama had said she couldn't take responsibility for a second daughter "in that program with that man." So she was on her own again. She spent hours lying in bed wrestling with questions that couldn't be answered. Even at Aram's, she never gave any sign of what was on her mind. He came from a family with a reputation for being as tight-knit and strong as a monastic order, a family with a long, storied history. And she didn't want to burden her father with her mother's problems. Boyce wasn't any better than Derik. He'd maintained two families living in two separate houses. He had two wives. He wasn't married to either woman, but his other children carried his last name. Not her. Her mother had refused. Louise didn't want to say if Audi was also one of Boyce's, and Boyce had stonewalled when she confronted him about it. So she went on tormenting herself with images from her earliest childhood in the big yellow house on a street not far from the Dutch naval base. Her birth must have been a godsend for Mama, Grandma said, because Boyce was white and rich. He was the one who had rescued Mama from her parents. Winston brought him to the house to admire his sisters, and although Boyce had laid eyes on both of them before, he fell hard for Louise. Right? Maybe he'd wanted Laura too and Mama had forced him to choose? She could connect the dots effortlessly, consider the underlying interests, and articulate them easily. "How can you be so sure of what happened, Babs?" Imker and Heli always pouted. "You weren't around back then, and Mama wasn't even pregnant with you yet." They said it was disgusting, the way she poked her nose into Mama's most intimate stories. Then she would stalk off, more resentful than ever; but that piece of history stayed with her like the moon stays with planet Earth. In any case, it had been her existence that saved their lives: her father bought a pretty house, had it beautifully decorated, and invited their mother to live there, and that was how she became his woman. Mama had two Javanese girls who helped her run the household, and when she was born, an older woman stayed with them for months as a live-in nanny. If her mother's life had ever been a barrel of laughs, it was there in that big yellow house that her father had provided.

She bit her nails to the quick. She had gone ahead and registered for the training program with Derik after all, but she didn't need any special treatment from him. Still, she had started taking birth control to keep her cycle regular while she was studying. Aram had assured her he wouldn't take advantage. "There are girls all around me,

Babs, and women I can fuck whenever and however I want." She was disturbed and relieved; her virginity was for a wedding night somewhere in a faraway land. She was the only one who knew that Aram was more of a dear friend than a future husband. She was privileged, and no one could do anything to change that. She was almost as white as her father, and skin color was her yardstick for good fortune in life. The proof of that was plain to see every day in their own society, not even to mention the rest of the world. All the same, one day Mother, heavily pregnant, left behind the life of luxury Boyce had given her to go live in Jacobusrust with Babs on her arm and Heli and Imker on her back. Her father refused to divulge the reason but had assured her that for him, there'd been no question of another woman. Indignant, he exclaimed, "I would never have abandoned your mother, I'm no heartbreaker, I have too much respect for my own late mother." And then she didn't press him further, knowing that his mother was Jewish and had run away from her Sabbath-keeping relatives at the age of sixteen to live with his Creole father out of wedlock. The heat and the trade wind made her drowsy. And the instructor couldn't hold her attention. Thoughts piled up within her, making her defiant. She rejected the hypothesis that a child comes into the world as a blank slate; she was the product of her parents, already written, and when she searched for an escape route, a way to be "new" in spite of everything, it just gave her a headache. She felt like taking a nap at her desk at the teachers' college. The instructor refused to take her point of view seriously, because the theory they were discussing hadn't been invented by her, but by a highly educated man. "Just admit defeat, Babs," Derik's co-worker teased her. All her mother had ever heard at parent-teacher conferences was that her daughter was "impertinent but sharp," and God, who could deny it? Not even Babs.

Audi couldn't understand why people were always telling him he was so good-looking. He was fed up with it, but he couldn't do anything about it. He sometimes stood in front of the mirror to see and judge his own appearance for himself. The inspection yielded no results. Compliments and attention were wasted on him, if they came from men, and as he grew older, he even started lashing out. *Mapima*, he would snap, not knowing that meant "your mama's cunt." His mother hadn't given him his dad's last name, but she had said his father was one of the city's most desired men. How could he settle for knowing nothing more about his own father's than that he was handsome? Good looks were his mother's thing. She had admirers. She went through life as a single woman with children, but around Christmas, guys who admired her and wanted things from her would shower her with gifts. He liked all the attention she got, as long as her suitors didn't show up in person. "My mother already has a man," he'd told some guy in a car who was sending her his best regards for the umpteenth time. Sometimes he passed the message on, but usually not. While playing with their dollhouses, Imker and Babs had taught him that a mother has only one man and that one man is the father of her kids. He saw examples of this in their neighborhood, but a different standard prevailed in his mother's house. She had a boyfriend who wasn't the father of her children, and why shouldn't she? She had adopted Leika as a puppy and trained her to guard the house. They were a family, complete, entire, finished, and whole. And then Mr. Blaasbalg, the teacher they called Koprokanu, said something that destroyed everything. It was as if his head sprung a leak. In Nieuw Nickerie, they'd lived in a house with a huge attic full of bats. It made no difference to them until one dark day a board in the attic floor came loose and the things that had been shut away came flying into the innermost spaces of their lives. He'd been just a little boy, but that gaping hole had scared the hell out of Mama and the girls. His sisters no longer remembered this. He and his mother still remembered what life was like with that hole, because the attic floor was their bedroom ceiling, and it was hard to find a carpenter to take the job right away. The man who finally came to close the hole put them at ease, saying that bats don't fly toward indoor light but toward outdoor light in the nighttime and that the little critters are terrified of humans because they're too big to be prey. Now a hole like that one had formed in his head and was letting thoughts inside, thoughts that kept getting bigger and bigger and could swallow him up. As a little boy, he'd wanted a bat on a string to play with and a cage in the hall to keep it in. If only he could chain up his thoughts. The handyman had closed the hole neatly, telling his mother that the noise from the attic at night was made not by bats but by owls. Hadn't they heard the beautiful white owls hooting in the darkness? "Yes," Mama said. "But in the corner shop, people say it's ghosts moaning." Owls, just fluttering nocturnal creatures, harmless to humans. And now that everyone in the Amora house was looking for a way to fill the hole of Heli's absence, he felt it was time to do something rebellious: tell Mama her beloved guard dog Leika hadn't run away but had been run over by a minibus the day Heli left. Leika had run after the car taking Heli to the airport. Friends from his soccer team picked him up at noon and took him to the stretch of highway where it had happened. They'd already dragged the body to the side of the road. He stood there wanting to scream in agony, but in front of his teammates, all he did was gasp. One went to get a burlap bag from the Chinese shop nearby. Together, they put Leika in the bag and took her to a grassy field, dug a hole with a shovel, and lowered Leika into it, bag and all. And he filled the hole with soil. It was damp and black. He knew that his mother sometimes turned the porch light on in the middle of the night, hoping Leika would recognize her house and come running and whimpering with happiness, as she always had when she saw Louise coming home from work. He often dreamed of Mama, of showering her with everything her heart desired. Days went by. He couldn't find the right moment to tell her the truth about the dog. Even though he was longing to spit it out, not a word about it would come out of his mouth in her presence. Maybe he'd be better off talking to a career soldier. As he saw it, death by violence would always be men's business; women bring forth life. Audi decided to pay a visit to Mama's boyfriend Lester at the military base.

My interactions with other Surinamese students in my study group remain superficial. I don't run into anyone I know downtown. The black people I see are in a hurry.

So am I, actually—it's just that I'm a slow walker. Lya has brought me two new letters from Paramaribo—one from Mother and one from Derik. I read the letters at the agreed location. My mother writes that everyone misses me and everyone has confidence in the future. She asks if I'm going to church on Sundays and requests that I keep up with my duties as a Catholic girl. And there's a third commandment: she urges me with all her heart to pray. I found a pocket Bible at the little store near the cafeteria. I don't do anything with it, but I keep it in my purse. That's what I tell Mama when I write back, and also that I don't feel like doing church stuff. Uncle Winston got me to go one Sunday, but I felt so out of place among all those churchgoers in their Sunday best that I never went back. In the guest room, I take my time writing to Mother. I prefer to write to Derik just before bed, but I control myself—everything Derik-related is for the reading lounge at the library. It's become an established routine. Sometimes Hans is waiting for me at the bus stop. He walks me to the front door, asking each time, "Are you liking it here in Holland?" And each time, I answer, "I haven't seen much of Holland yet." Then he laughs. To make it clear I'm not encouraging him to ask me out on a date, I always add, "I need to make this academic year a success so that I can get a good scholarship, you know?" He gets it, and he's hoping to be admitted to a seminary himself. I don't know what I'd like to study. At the dinner table, Winston has remarked that Hans is a "nice young man" and that I'm welcome to invite him over for tea and cookies. He says it with a grin. Lya looks dubious. I smile wanly. Uncle asks if my classes are going well. I nod. Then I inquire about his mother's health. "Not good," he says, adding that my grandma is shuffling her way toward death. I ask why he didn't bring her with him to Holland. He laughs, loud and hollow, and says, "Lya left behind an elderly mother in Paramaribo too." I nod as if this makes perfect sense to me, thinking, *Grandma isn't even seventy yet*. His wife is a good cook, and I compliment her after every dinner. Then I make the sign of the cross, thank them for sharing their meal with me, and offer to help clear the table and do the dishes. But they don't want me to do either. They enjoy being near each other. They clean the table together, do the dishes together, and then sit side by side on the sofa together. He watches television, she reads a book. Sometimes he says, "Babe, look at this." Sometimes she says, "Babe, listen to this." They make a perfect couple, and it's not right to pass judgment if neither of them misses their mother. It's none of my business. They personally set the bottle of orgeat from Grandma Bee on top of one of their kitchen cupboards. No one can reach it without a stepladder. The syrup stands out against the pale green shelves, the walls, the ceiling. When I enter the kitchen, the first thing I do is look up there and mumble, "Off-white." I want a jacket in exactly that shade so I can make it through this cold. Not a dark winter coat, as Lya recommended. I want to know my grandmother is with me.

Cate, my former co-worker from back in Suriname, spotted me at Sunday Mass with my aunt and uncle. A phone call here, a phone call there, and she knew within an hour where I spent my weekdays. And on Thursday afternoon, she's there waiting for me. I can't believe my eyes. "I left two days after you did," she tells me, her laughter roaring through the cafeteria at Orange-Nassau. We hug each other and grab a seat at an empty table. "I live in Utrecht too, in Overvecht, with a married couple. The husband remembers seeing you skipping around Nickerie as a little girl." I settle comfortably into her eyes, enjoying the sound of her voice. "The children at Fatima School are going to miss us so much," she says, adding, "School vacation in Suriname will last another two weeks, and then…" Her voice trails off into silence. I say nothing and get tea for us both. "Did you break up with Derik?" she asks, in a dark voice. "No," I say, "Cate, with every blink, what I see is my classroom; their heads, arms, and little bodies poking out above the desks; their braids; their long, thin legs and their bright eyes always following me." She nods. Smiles. "Derik has asked for time off to be with you in Holland." Cate can't keep it to herself a moment longer. "He wants to get a divorce, then remarry, start a new family!" Catie's a few years older than I am and a kindergarten teacher just like my mother. "Have you come to continue your studies?" I ask, nervous. "No, no," she protests, "I'll spend my whole life working with little kids; I'm looking for a new job." "Do they pay well here?" She pinches my cheek. "Heli, ten times better than back home, with small classes, white children, caring parents." I sigh. She looks at me with her light eyes. "Without you, another school year back home wouldn't be much fun for me, anyway." I write down my current address and exchange it for hers. She gets up. "Come on, let's go into town: the stores are open late, and I'm in urgent need of a warm jacket." Me, too, I think, but not one in a wintry color. As we walk toward the bus stop, feeling other Surinamese eyes on us, she whispers in a staccato voice, "I broke up with that bastard I was dating because he couldn't understand that a woman like me wants marriage, kids, a nice house, and a long life together, and not him screwing around like the cock of the walk." I don't crack a smile, even though she's trying to make me laugh. I know how much that bastard really meant to her. After spending the night with him, she'd tell me the next morning at school, "He has a short penis, but so thick, it's addictive, Heli, I'm staying with him until I drop dead!" In silence, we wait at the bus stop. The first thing I'll do once I get a job is buy a car. And then suddenly, "Is your family supporting you financially, Heli?" A bus glides up to the stop, and as we board, I respond, "A scholarship." It's tricky, but we find a spot to sit together. "Did you hear what I said?" I ask. Cate nods. She laughs, exposing her teeth. "That'll be hard work, Heli, years of drudgery, unless you make sure Derik doesn't go back to his wife." She makes this last observation not in Dutch, but in the lingua franca of our homeland. In the two years I've worked with her, I've never heard her use Sranantongo, and I nearly burst out giggling. The city center approaches, sparkling and gleaming. Catie hums a pop song. As we get off the bus, she says, "Heli, you know what rhymes with 'thick penis'?" Just like at school in Paramaribo, I respond, "Hot Venus!" She offers me her arm, and we venture into the unknown.

In the living room, Imker tried to persuade her grandmother to stay home instead of coming with her to do the shopping. It had rained. Too many puddles on the street. Grandma Bee would get splashed. Or maybe slip on the muddy cobblestones? It had become clear to her that being at home by herself was increasingly difficult for her grandmother. Bee wanted to be around people, and her daily getaway to church wasn't just for religious reasons. "I'll be back in two hours," she tried to say, but her grandmother wanted to go into town, too. "You don't want to be alone?" Grandma hesitated, as if the question offended her. Then came the reply: "You don't want to be seen with me?" Startled, she had to admit that forcing her grandmother to stay in the house was ridiculous. *Grandma wants to go into town to do her own shopping, and that's that.* Why was she blowing it out of proportion? "On foot, Grandma, or by bus? How about a taxi this time?" No response. Grandma dictated a list of everything they needed to fill the pantry. Once Imker had jotted it all down, she took a seat beside her. Her grandmother seemed to want to ask what had happened in the house on Dwarsstraat, but instead said, "I know I'm falling apart, but I won't accept treatment, know why?" Grandma answered her own question. "I want to live like I'm not about to die." It made her shiver. "How do you know you're about to die, Grandma?" She might as well ask, she thought. *How can I help Grandma live as if there's no death?* It dawned on her that the woman sitting there next to her had been admired for years for her practical knowledge of the human body. "Good that we're going to do the shopping together, Grandma, after all, you know your way around downtown better than I do, whatever the weather." Her grandmother squeezed her hand and walked over to the radio to listen to the obituaries. Right on time. A sad Bach melody filled the living room, and Grandmother hummed along. Noise and chatter from the street. Mail. The mailman at the gate handed her a post-card. A cry of surprise. Heli's handwriting. Words from her sister: *Dearest Grandma, I Love You So Very Much.* She didn't know where the tears were coming from. She dropped the mail in Grandma Bee's lap and walked back to what she'd been doing in the kitchen, pulling herself together. She saw that Grandmother had settled into a more comfortable seat, eyes glued to the postcard, and was cuddling it against her face, patting it again and again. If Grandma's two sons in Holland or their wives would make the effort to send a postcard to Bernadette Vanta *née* Julienne every week, then perhaps death could be deferred. The white envelope bearing the parish logo was set down on the sofa for later. Hands resting on the post-card on her lap, Grandma Bee sat gazing out as if she saw the future being born from deep within the past. Mama would just have to do without her dear Imker, because Bee needed a granddaughter. Louise had remarked that Grandma saw pieces of herself in her grandchildren and how restorative that was. Winston's children had gone away even before they had learned enough words to make any sense of the world around them, moving permanently to Aruba with their mother after a messy divorce; and Grandma's youngest son Rogier had, without any discus-sion with her, chosen a woman with skin as dark as night, or as Grandma moaned, "even blacker than his father Anton." Imker thought of it this way: she herself, her two sisters, and her little brother were the descendants that Grandma could touch, even if only in a postcard from a distant country.

Grandmother had given Imker that prescient nickname at childbirth, but she'd missed the deliveries of Heli, Babs, and Audi. She always demanded to be involved in cutting the umbilical cord, but circumstances didn't usually make that possible. And her eldest daughter meant so much to her. Not for nothing had Grandma named Louise after her English-speaking mother, who had died too young; she was so happy to have given birth to a daughter after Winston, she said with a laugh, because his willy as he lay in the tub had given her goosebumps. No, she wasn't happy about her daughter having so many children, because every pregnancy widened the gap between them. As a mother, she'd hoped that Louise would stop at one child. At Heli. Maybe because she found out that Heli's father came from an English-speaking family in Nickerie just as stuck up as her mother's. Her hand caressed the postcard, and no one was close enough to see the tears streaming along her nose to the corners of her mouth, where her tongue licked up the last traces of salt from her heart to flavor the days ahead. It was somehow disquieting when long-ago events came looming up in the future, and she wished that instead of crying she could scream. She got up, put the church letter on the coffee table, and took the postcard to the high kitchen table, where it would be easier to talk and think things over in the abundant morning light and cool sea breeze. In the open back door, her granddaughter stood like a brushstroke, a green stalk in the light, and she knew that Imker was bullied and called names by the boys in Amora Village: beanpole, twig, beanpole, twig. The Amora boys whistled at girls with curves. She could see her granddaughter as a newborn, an infant, a toddler, a preschooler, until she left along with Louise's other children for Bee's old hometown near the eastern border. In memory, she heard Anton calling, "We must redeem ourselves from the shortcomings of the place called Suriname. The Europeans abandoned their overseas plantations, but they forgot to liberate their overseas workers from the hell they lived in. No, it's not just slavery that's intolerable, but also this swatch of sweltering jungle on the ocean!" Anton Vanta didn't care for his mother country.

She said, "Imker, does my son Winston have anything to do with the story you haven't quite told me yet?" She had laid down the postcard on the tablecloth and was trying to tear open the white envelope that Imker had brought her from the living room. "Yes, Grandma." The words came out plain and flat. "And now will you tell me, child?" Her voice was barely a whisper. And Imker started to talk, pacing around the kitchen, without looking at her. And Grandmother's eyes followed Imker's every movement, and for the first time, she saw who Imker really was.

Louise Vanta saw the mailman walking across the schoolyard. Her heart was racing. The man came to her classroom. He smiled, unearthed something from his mailbag, and handed it to her: two pieces of blue airmail. She thanked him and returned to her seat in front of her thirty-two children, who were hard at work with colorful pieces of paper and glue. The mail might as well have been a wild animal, she was so scared of it. It was dead quiet. Two letters from Holland. Read her daughter's first? But she couldn't. She didn't want to be interrupted by anything or anyone. The letter from Winston could wait, too. She walked to the deep closet at the back of the classroom and did something she'd always thought of as vulgar—she stuck one letter in the left and the other in the right cup of her bra. Her button-down shirt made it easy. The mail tickled and felt uncomfortable. She waited in suspense for recess. If there wasn't a safe moment to read then, she would just have to wait until she got home. Time on the clock crawled by. The letters scratched against the softness of her skin. The principal dropped by to ask if there was any good news to report. She admitted that she hadn't been able to read the letters yet because she had to focus on her schoolchildren. "That's what I'm paid for, right?" As a young woman, she could have continued her studies and climbed the ranks of the educational ladder at her organization. The principal was aware of that, and he also knew Louise Vanta was too much of an individualist for that. She always knew best. As she surveyed the heads and faces of her little kindergarteners, thoughts washed over her, trying to teach her lessons she preferred to forget. She'd so often fought to liberate herself and build a life for herself, and she wanted something different for her daughters, even though she still wasn't entirely sure what in the world a woman like her would need to feel good about life in the long run. The letters from her daughter Heli made her blood churn and tingle. And even as she carefully went through her daily routine, the excitement didn't go away, not even as she gathered her things, led the children across the schoolyard to their waiting parents, locked the classroom door, slid the keys into her purse, and called out to her boss, "See you tomorrow." She took a few deep breaths before hiking back home.

Right after her brother Winston had moved their mother away from their father Anton, she gave Heli friendly instructions to stop by her grandfather's house in Jacobusrust straight after her classes at the teachers' college. Her daughter was happy to take on the task and performed it without complaint. It was as if her firstborn child inexplicably knew that Grandpa cared more about the survival of his descendants than was generally believed. She wanted to show her enduring appreciation for his protection the day he beat his son Winston half to death in a room where Heli was bawling in her cot, while she herself looked on, half-dressed, frozen in place. It wasn't the first time her brother had sexually assaulted her, but it was the first time anyone had pulled him off her. Anton didn't just beat his son bloody but also showed him the door once and for all. When Bee came home from the market, she heard just one thing from her husband, the only thing that really mattered: as long as Anton lived, their son Winston would not set foot in his parents' home. Months later, Imker was born. She can still see them playing together on the terrace at her parents' house—Heli on the three-wheeler and Imker crawling after her. And her, staying close. After the incident, the gap between her parents seemed unbridgeable, and Bee treated her eldest daughter more or less as the enemy that had driven away her beloved Winston. A difficult time, partly because Gordon, the man she really loved, was about to emigrate abroad with another young woman and another small child, and he didn't even visit to say goodbye to her and his daughter Heli. And she still remembered how her eyes roamed Jacobusrust, as she thought, *How in God's name can I get away from here with my girls?*

Meanwhile, she'd taken out the letters pressed against her flesh and set them on the coffee table. A feeling of disgust kept her from opening one of the envelopes. Memories like pouring rain, and she knew of no defense but to let them crash over her until the storm passed. Audi got home first. Then Babs. She waited until the three of them were seated at the table for a hot meal of salt beef and beans, white rice, and boiled ripe plantains. A family favorite. And instead of starting the meal off by saying grace, she opened Heli's letter, unfolded the thin pages, and read it out loud. There were three full pages, with a section for each member of the family. How often had any of her children done anything against their will? No reaction from Babs or from Audi to the letter from Holland? They ate in silence. As they ate together, her children nodding in satisfaction, what was never said aloud was followed by something like an extended olive branch, something she wanted to tell them. Without each of them, she couldn't have kept going, not in her family, not in the city, not in the country, and maybe not even in day-to-day life. Babs and Audi listened but said nothing. First, she would make it clear to her brother Winston by letter that her daughter Heli was only a child and her precious treasure. She'd write Heli and thank her for accepting the responsibilities shoved into a child's hands and beyond her understanding—fearlessly representing their household at the Winti prayer ceremony; a family séance at a plantation among unknown relatives; and before all that, helping, out of necessity, to raise her baby boy because she was too weak after an abortion, and unrelentingly keeping Winston away from their house. At the table, she didn't spell it all out for them, yet her confession was understood. The silence that fell was oppressive. When she clasped her hands to thank God at the end of the meal, her son said to her in a choked voice, "Mama, I don't understand how Heli can still love you so much." Louise Vanta slid the letter from Winston over to Audi so that her son could read it to them. Her brother had finally admitted he had been wrong, apologized, and asked for her forgiveness.

Father Teloor had tried to make many things clear to Grandmother during the home visits in Jacobusrust. Children are dependent on the adults around them and have no concept of love, so claiming your children love you is foolish, because one person can love another only with an adult heart that is filled with the love of God. After the domestic conflicts between father and son and daughter, she had called on Teloor to consecrate her house. Anton didn't oppose it as long as all he had to do was attend in silence, without any kind of active participation, and on the condition that his son Winston stayed away. Seventeen-year-old Laura had announced that she had better things to do at that time of day. Louise was there, looking ready to flee, with her little girl on her lap and Rogier, age six, leaning against her. She was the supreme Christian woman in the house. And after the consecration ceremony, the black brother religion of Winti no longer existed for her.

The letter on church stationery was a reminder of an appointment: Teloor wrote that he would come by that weekend for a private conversation. The tone seemed stern. She hadn't shown up at Father Overtoon's church downtown for a few days, and she hadn't gone to the church nearby to polish brass for the assistant priest, either. In the end, she hadn't even gone into town with Imker to do the shopping. She apologized, saying she needed to save her strength for a Sunday visit with Laura. And Imker left with the shopping list and the shopping bags. Watching her go, she tried to call out, "Don't stay away too long!" But not a word came out of her throat as she saw her granddaughter, out in the street, stop for a moment to look back in concern at the house she was leaving behind. She'd felt it. It was a look of love. Imker had an "adult heart," and so did Heli, with her postcard: *Grandma, I Love You So Very Much.* Her priest firmly believed that love emanated from God and no human is capable of it, but said it was still worthwhile to keep trying to love. That sometimes made her feel discouraged. And when her father confessor asked, "Do you love everyone else as much as you love your children?" she would answer right away, "Yes, Reverend, all exactly the same." But after she did her penance and left the church, she would mumble on her way home, "Is there one special child I couldn't do without?" Ethel had been taken abroad by foreigners, and no one mentioned her name anymore, not even Anton. But right after that, something had happened, quietly, like a crack in the ground under her feet, a crack that grew wider and wider as time went by. The better off their family became year by year, the more Anton insisted that one day they'd have to move to Paramaribo. She had a nice house full of pretty things and a vegetable garden full of flowering plants. Her children were healthy, and her family and good friends lived nearby. She could visit the convent whenever she liked to put her thoughts in order, and to treat the women who had raised her homemade goodies. Her brothers could check in on her easily. She had deep roots in the soil of the district. In fact, she had just been figuring out how she could fit into the Nieuw Nickerie community, with the help of working-class women who shared their stories, and she'd just told them her husband was content with their way of life. Sergeant Vanta would put on his bottle-green military uniform and go to work at the army base, where his duties were mostly clerical, and whenever he had the least opportunity he would play cards with the other grunts, betting loose change. Sometimes he had one too many. Sometimes he said something nasty. On Saturdays, he tinkered with the radio transmitter he'd built. On Sundays, they went to church with the children. They were all so well dressed that people said her late father had been the adventurous heir to a French family fortune. She couldn't imagine how they came up with that, but every word spoken about her father was a comfort to her. Her brothers Scott and Léon were still adjusting to life as small tradesmen, and Winston Senior had escaped, once and for all, from the torments of timber harvesting, balata bleeding, and gold mining in the primeval Amazon forest. Now, dressed like a gentleman, he ran a successful company in British Guiana. There was no reason to panic. And women came to her for recipes and for vegetables from the garden, and to bake with her, making English tarts, braided sweet bread, chicken pot pie. The Dutch army was her husband's bread and butter, and the authority and perks of his status extended to his family—bread, butter, and cheese every week, and once a year Christmas presents and ginger cookies for the children. There was no cause for tears. In the morning, she took Winston and Louise to a nearby school and hurried back home, where she'd left Ethel behind in her playpen, and she picked up her children with Ethel in a sling on her back. And after the drama of Ethel's departure, God proved that His love for her family was undiminished, because Laura kept getting prettier and prettier, and her singing brought the family together again in joy. Bee Vanta's life in the village where she'd been born was far from unhappy.

Louise Vanta knew what had caused the breakthrough— time, the ceaseless transformation of everything. She'd been there but hadn't seen it happening, the slow trans-formation of her own body from object to subject. Her physical self became part of her, more and more over time; still worse, without her body, she didn't exist. She was her flesh. She was only ten, but to her little sisters Ethel and Laura, she became a playmate, sitting with them at a low table on the veranda, drawing, coloring, cutting, pasting. The bits of soft rubber that her cous-ins gathered during the weeks of timber harvesting and balata bleeding were transformed in her hands into dolls, animal figurines, balls, and other toys. From time to time, her father Anton watched her work, picking up one of her creations for a closer look. He would say, "Nice job, Louise," and nod encouragingly. Her mother Bee would bring her scraps of fabric for clothes, seeds for eyes, frayed rope for hair, buttons, and a sewing box. She didn't have much interest in her mother's kitchen secrets. Mama liked to say diplomatically that her daughters' greatest talent was making clothes. That was all Bee would say, except that Winston should go work for the Dutch soldiers until the war was over. Her father would shake his head in refusal. Once, when Mama asked what all that head shaking meant, he went upstairs to the veranda and, looking out into the street, shouted, "Voorstraat, Achterstraat, Gouverneurstraat, and all the fancy street names in the world don't make a town a city, and my children will be civil servants in Paramaribo, working in offices, not barracks!" It sounded like a death sentence. And the war hadn't even begun yet. Her mother started to cry. He had put a curse on a border town that remained English-speaking and would never become Dutch. Maybe Hindustani, Indonesian, Chinese even, but never Dutch. Anton stared wide-eyed at his pacing, wailing wife. She looked on with her brother and little Laura, and she understood that something precious was on the verge of breaking. At that time, she wasn't sure what, except that her little sister Ethel really wouldn't ever come home again and that Laura had become the measure of all things. Louise and Winston, they'd come out brown. Brown like milky coffee. A niece on Mother's side of the family suggested that the brown was a case of a "dirty womb," as if she couldn't see the father, Anton, there in his radiant blackness.

Never bring up the move from Nieuw Nickerie to Paramaribo, where Grandmother lives now. Even decades later, the sheer distress might make her gasp for breath. The notice lay on the kitchen table: Sergeant Vanta must report to Paramaribo with his family within a month. Off-white stationery, black print. Winston was excited.

At the age of sixteen, he felt the pull of the city. Louise was flustered by the news, because she liked the idea of a job in the military, especially when her father talked about ladies in uniform, working as telegraph operators or as drivers. Her father was agitated then, too—by the mosquitoes, which attacked him day and night. The plumes of smoke rising around their home every evening drove away the mosquitoes and brought relief to everyone except him. "I'm black, and they have a taste for my blood," he complained. Over the years, they'd given him so much trouble that he was eager to move. "Besides," he said after thinking it over, "you and Winston are done with the local school here and ready to learn shorthand, typing, law, and bookkeeping. It's high time we left this mosquito coast behind." Their mother and father didn't shout or curse each other; Mama had run out of words to explain how she felt. Her mother cried, unable to face the thought of packing up. Bernadette couldn't imagine another existence for herself. Her father had received a monthlong furlough, and the army would make sure his household goods were loaded into crates and delivered safely by riverboat to the port of Paramaribo. Winston helped. She packed the kitchenware, clothing, and other fragile things in cardboard boxes. Mama lay in bed face down, her back to her family members. Laura stayed at her side, playing quietly with a set of nine colored billiard balls that her father had brought her to keep "that spoiled child" out of everyone's way. But leaving behind the house where she was born proved more difficult than she'd expected, and when she asked her brother Winston how he made himself feel better, he pulled down his blue-black trousers and his underwear and let her see how he bounced his penis around and asked her to hold onto it until it settled down. And she did. And it got so hard, and a wad of something white shot out. She loved using both hands on his thing. She started to do it more often, and she started to crave it so badly she couldn't do without it—it was the best feeling ever. It would have gone on longer than just a couple of days if Winston hadn't tried to stick his hand down her underwear. That really shocked her. That wasn't allowed. Suppose she started bleeding? And the urge to grab her brother's penis, rub it hard, bite it, slide it into her mouth, suck until he nearly screamed from the pleasure of release—it vanished in an instant. Sometimes he grabbed her, pushed her against a wall, pressed his lower body against hers, but she kept dead still even if sometimes she started panting. She understood she had to keep away from him so she wouldn't get stuck to him one day, like the stray dogs she'd seen in the street. It wasn't until the week of their departure that their mother Bee showed her face again. Winston Senior had come from Georgetown with his wife to say goodbye, and the couple had brought more gifts than their family could accept. Travel clothes, tailormade, with comfortable shoes for everyone. Sweets. Bedclothes. Underwear. They promised someday they'd visit Paramaribo and invited the family to Demerara. The family home had been sold, but they wanted Bernadette to know there was a house in Georgetown where she would always be safe and welcome, either with her whole family or just with Anton "for the summer holidays." As the eldest sibling, Winston Senior felt responsible for maintaining the family ties, not just with her but also with their brothers Scott and Léon—and maybe Napo would show up again, who could say. Their parents had died too young, and they couldn't help being the children of fore-fathers rooted in a Europe of which they'd seen nothing, aside from Jewish refugees, priests and missionaries, soldiers, and abandoned plantations. All the conversation in English and in French helped Louise's mother stay afloat until the day of their voyage.

On Saturday, the priest and the young doctor Albert arrived at Grandma's gate at the same time. She'd been expecting old Teloor and opened the front door right away. For a moment, she was alarmed to see him with their family friend Albert. Graciously, she welcomed the men inside and took them not to the living room but to the kitchen table. She'd made tea and baked sequilhos. Her confessor was almost eighty but quite fit. In fact, Father Teloor was the chattiest of them all. "We miss you, Mrs. Vanta, and we've been wondering how you're really doing." She looked at her son Rogier's school friend and couldn't stop her eyes from filling with tears. "I miss my sons, I don't know if I'll ever see them again..." And she went on like that. The visitors listened patiently, took sips of tea, and didn't turn down her cookies. Albert asked if she had any physical complaints. The question came as a shock. She got up to make a fresh pot of tea, and when she sat down again with her hands folded on the table-top, as if about to start praying, she replied, "My body is getting older, I don't fight it, I feel like I've been alive for centuries..." She brought the men another plate of off-white sequilhos. They each took another, polishing off every last crumb and washing the sticky sweetness from their teeth with English tea. Grandma explained that

Imker was at her Saturday job as a shop girl and that her granddaughter was just an angel, helping her with everything. The priest asked if a doctor's appointment and a thorough examination at a military hospital might shed some light on her health issues. But before Albert could say anything, she cut him off. "Yes, but at the moment I have no interest in that whatsoever. If my sons want to see me before I'm gone, they'll just have to fly back to their home country." Her voice sounded angry and firm. She was well aware that her visitors were trying to force her to do something she didn't want to do. Out of the question. She looked Albert straight in the eyes, and then Teloor. It was the young doctor who responded first. "I'm here for you anytime, Mrs. Vanta." And the elderly priest added that both the downtown church and the one in Zorg en Hoop greatly appreciated her and prayed for her recovery every day. She thanked them. Then they said the Lord's Prayer at the table and, at her request, another prayer as well: "Hail Mary, full of grace…" Albert had appointments at the hospital and hurried off with a "Give my regards to Imker." The priest stayed behind and asked how things were going with her two daughters. He listened carefully, unable to suppress a smile, when she playfully remarked that the young assistant priest from his monastery would be a good husband for her granddaughter Imker and that it was high time to do away with celibacy anyway. The priest was familiar with her wicked sense of humor and didn't let it distract him from asking whether she could still get to church without help. No, not really? And finally: "In case you die unexpectedly, Mrs. Vanta, and can no longer speak, I mean, do you have any special requests?" Her face broke into a smile. She had filled a plastic container with sequilhos for him. And she answered in a single breath, "Let me be like a Christmas night, dark with candlelight that burns out slowly, leaving only a puddle of wax behind to toss into the garbage." The priest was taken aback. "Have you thought long and hard about it, Mrs. Vanta?" She nodded solemnly, and as she opened the front door to let him out, she kept on mumbling. "The human world is nothing more than a pile of garbage." And Grandmother followed her confessor with her eyes, even after she could no longer make out the fluttering of his bright white robes.

With Cate so close by, it's almost like I'm living in my hometown again. She also brings back memories of making out with Derik. We never went beyond kissing and long drives through dark villages bordering our capital city, with my body snuggled as close to his as possible because I was terrified of the dark. Once in a while, he turned onto a road where his wheels got stuck in a mudhole. My heart would pound then, because his headlights revealed little more than darkness and overgrown paths. That was my usual adventure with Derik, about two times a week. And when Cate and I supervised children on the playground, she would try to get it through my skull that sooner or later that man would decide the time had come to screw me, with or maybe even without a condom. She would ask straight out if I was prepared. Usually, I'd give a vague answer, something along the lines of not wanting to be screwed yet and certainly not in someone's car in the middle of nowhere. Then she'd laugh and I would too, and we'd buy ginger beer and streusel rolls from the vendor who came to the schoolyard with her wicker basket. Who could have imagined back then that, before too long, Cate and I would be meeting up every day somewhere in the middle of the Netherlands? We have hot drinks at the cafeteria, walk to the bus stop, board the bus together, and get off at the same stop. She tells me the latest news about her job hunt and introduces me to a world beyond the ken of Uncle Winston and his Lya. I find out the city is brimming with Surinamese; they live all over, but especially in certain neighborhoods. "So what do they do?" Cate brushes aside my ignorance with a laugh. "They work, they study, they look for jobs, yes, they live just like they were back home in Suriname." She takes me to a downtown diner, where Dutch is not the only language I hear around me. The menu is astoundingly varied. The waitresses, the guests, the chefs—they're all Surinamese. I sit across from Cate at a little table, feeling like a child at a terrific birthday party. I scarf down my chicken casserole with rice and Chinese long beans with salt beef, washing it down with passionfruit juice. Cate is clearly no stranger to this joint. She jokes around with the cooks and the young Javanese woman who brings us the food and slides the restaurant's business card over to me with a smile. It is the first time since landing at Schiphol that I've felt good, as if what was in danger of falling apart has just now become strong and whole. "How do you feel, Heli?" And I ask, "Are you thinking about seconds of the cassava soup too?" She's beaming, just like I am. Then she leans in and whispers, "You and I are pretty young things; we'll soon find good husbands in this land of liberated women…" But her voice trails off. She stares at the entrance behind me. I turn around. He has followed her to the Netherlands and found her at the Sranan Sani Diner. "Hot Venus," I mumble. "But I've had enough of him," she says, ice cold, adding, "I flew across the ocean so I'd never have to see him again, Heli Vanta." She doesn't move from her chair, fishes a napkin out of a glass, and wipes the grease from her lips. I can sense the tension and don't dare look. I want to go back home to my room with my family. "Do you want to know what that guy did to me, Heli?" I shake my head no. "Let's pay up," I say, and the waiter hurries over. "The check, ladies?" I nod. Cate has lit a cigarette. Shows no sign of planning to leave with me. I pay for us both, tell her goodbye, and leave. I run to the bus stop as fast as I can, hoping I'll soon be someplace where men and women get along. I flew across the Atlantic Ocean too. And I would break down inside too if I ran into Derik here unexpectedly. I shiver in the cold autumn wind. The city throbs around me. I'm not ready to be screwed yet, especially not in this Dutch winter.

I haven't yet written to my mother about meeting my father at Schiphol. It didn't make a lasting impression. The way I see it, he was more like one of Mama's flings, with me as the byproduct, than a man with ambitions to become a father. I don't feel an ounce of resentment toward him. It's worse than that: the man is a stranger to me, that's all, and I don't have any secret dreams of getting to know him. But if I explained my attitude, Mama might feel hurt, so in my letters I ignore him into absence. And my textbooks are really starting to speak to me now; if I go on like this, I'll have done the reading for the whole program in a single term. I've found something that captivates me without literally holding me captive. As for Cate, I haven't seen her in a couple of days now. So I've gone back to my old routine: after class each day, I sit and read in the library, write a letter to Derik, and dash off loving messages on postcards for the girls at Fatima School in my hometown. And when I get off at the bus stop, there's Hans on his bike. We walk slowly toward my house. We talk softly about unimportant things. Then I tell him about Cate, who looked me up and has entertained me for days. He says he's happy for me and he wants to take me out sometime too, to a fun party. I don't respond. Umar once invited me to Eid al-Fitr with his relatives in Moengo, a bauxite mining town in the west of the country. It was also a major wedding anniversary for his parents. I had just graduated from teachers' college with remarkably good grades, and he personally asked my mother's permission to take me along. His older sister and a brother who'd sat next to us in class were also on the bus to the party. My mother was very fond of him and hoped he would fall for one of her daughters. She entrusted me to him and even gave me permission to stay at their house overnight. The night of Eid al-Fitr, he approached me in a way I didn't like. He was insulted. I was upset. Later he apologized for his clumsiness, trying to French kiss me as the first step toward a relationship. I was not quite ready for something wet that made me think of sex. As I see it, any date with a boy can get out of hand. Even here in Utrecht. Hans doesn't insist. He gives me a book of photos about the history of the city where we live.

A longing for shelter can run so deep, deeper than hunger, a powerful bodily urge. I said this to Derik the time he asked what exactly I wanted out of life. A sheltered feeling. He argued that the best strategy would be to find a person who made me feel that way. Did I feel sheltered with him? I couldn't think how to answer, uncertain what he wanted from me in his busy life. He thought time would make everything clear. Mama was synonymous with shelter. Yet something can always happen to make even the warmest relationship feel unsafe. For example: I choose Derik. Mama rejects Derik. Mama packs me off to Holland. I want to stay in Paramaribo. My longing to feel sheltered has started to resemble a spaceship with highly sensitive instruments on board, scanning other worlds for signs of intelligent life like me, because we earthlings can't stand to be alone with each other after all the endless bloodshed. A memory of a night in the house on Dwarsstraat: I wake up to a deep moan from Mama's bedroom. I listen closely and the moaning turns to wailing, whimpering in pain. I slide out of the top bunk. Tiptoeing to my mother's room where the door is open like always and the moonlight shines through the window onto the bed where my mother lies with a man on top of her and he roars and it all goes quiet. "Mama, Mama," I say out loud, running toward her. The man who leaps up is naked, and I know him, and I want to say his name... But maybe someone hit me hard because when I woke up again, I was in bed. Mother said I fell out of bed and bumped my forehead. She said I must have had a terrible dream. But how does a mother look her child in the eyes when the child knows something the mother would rather forget?

My intrusion was a dust cloud across the blue skies of Louise Vanta's life.

With difficulty, Louise had found a house where her entire family could live, not too expensive and in a nice neighborhood, until behind the bottle-green façade her daughter Heli discovered the courtyard with small houses and saw the people living there. But she'd left Jacobusrust behind and no longer had to put up with Laura's outbursts. She had to enroll Imker and Heli in a new school. Babs could stay at the private school Boyce paid for. They needed school uniforms and other materials. Audi was still too young for a child bike seat, and the house had a steep staircase to the attic, so steep that she kept warning them, "If you fall down the stairs, you'll die instantly!" She could even smell death, like rotting blood and morning sickness. She was so afraid of losing one of her children. And Winston had shown up again after a year of lying low. He'd heard from their mother about her plans to move to a place of her own. He brought her sandwiches on soft rolls. He made sure the necessary household items were moved from the big yellow house to the address on Dwarsstraat. He didn't give her children hugs but chocolate bars. He didn't even ask why she'd left her husband Boyce. She'd heard in passing that his wife had divorced him and begun a relationship with a wealthy American who wanted to take her and their five children abroad. He was bitter and cursed their father Anton for bringing him into the world so low on the social ladder. Maybe it would've been better, he thought, if they'd never left Nickerie, where their mother's relatives had a plantation, connections, a good name, and opportunities for him in the sugar industry as a trader with a network in British Guiana and beyond. She listened as he ranted on. She didn't contradict him. When the house was fit to live in and the long school vacation was over and she'd found a babysitter for her infant boy nearby and was biking to her kindergarten class every day again, bringing the girls to the school bus, her boy to the babysitter, when it seemed like a sort of peace had settled over her house, right at that moment he asked for a house key. "Why, Winston?" And him: "Now and then, if I come across something nice, I'll buy it and bring it to your place." Things had gone too far for her to say no. And she was too tired to keep her body from him at night. She started vomiting in the morning. She was desperate. She couldn't take the look in Heli's eyes, and Louise Vanta knew if she struck her daughter again, the blow might be fatal.

Imker owed her Saturday job as a saleslady to one of her grandmother's relatives by marriage, who ran a successful downtown clothing boutique and had found the position for her at the Lebanese store where they bought their fabric. There she didn't have to worry about being groped by the men or snubbed by the women. She was happy to be at work because for a few hours her thoughts were focused on something other than her own family. The sweet scent of the rolls of fabric, the colors, the patterns, the girls and women who came by, chattering, for a few yards of fabric in florals, stripes, checks, and more, and lunch together afterward in the family kitchen, where the table was always covered with Lebanese dishes. With a few ten-guilder bills she'd earned herself, she breathed in the Saturday afternoon on her way to the market. Umar was at her side; sometimes they even walked hand in hand. Babs no longer came barging into the business with Aram in tow since she'd moved in with Grandmother, and that didn't sit well with her. She'd give Umar a note for her brother. Maybe Audi would visit her, and she could treat him to a lunch at a place young people liked. Being stuck in Amora wouldn't help him to forget how far away his sister was. For years, she and Babs had relied on him to play with them and their dollhouse families. And Christmas was still too far away. Then he would throw himself into building a Nativity scene in the fullest possible detail, from the moss on the trees to the three kings. Their brother certainly had his quirks. Their mother downplayed them: "Audi has to become a man, not a woman." She couldn't explain his fear of dogs either, and it had always bothered her when he chained up Leika for no good reason. Louise had saved so that he could study abroad when the time came. And as these thoughts went through her mind, she remained alert, helpful, and friendly to the customers at the clothing shop. She bought four pairs of white underwear for Laura and a housecoat with polka dots. She'd buy sunflowers at the market. And something small for Umar, a set of handkerchiefs, even though one of Uncle Scott's granddaughters had said you should never give handkerchiefs as presents because they bring tears. So many girls and women went to her grandmother's relative for custom-made clothing and told all sorts of anecdotes, which the woman's daughters picked up and tossed out as life lessons. She enjoyed spending time with the grandchildren of her grandmother's brother Scott but never mentioned it to other people. Her Saturday job gave her the sense that life was worthwhile as long as the right people came along. Umar occasionally said, "You're the prettiest girl I walk around town with, but you're still just a child." Hearty laughter from her: "A child who wears the smallest women's size—a lot like you, Umar, a wolf in sheep's clothing." Hearty laughter from him; maybe he didn't know she disapproved of his role in the Heli-Derik affair. And when he asked with concern how her studies were going, she grew quiet. Maybe working at a hospital would be more suitable for her to start with. Her heart was with her grandmother. As if he didn't know. "A place had been left empty, and you filled it," he said, and maybe both of them were think-ing of Heli's departure. At the market, they came across one of Cate's brothers, who told them, gesticulating in enthusiasm, that his sister had gone to Holland too and had looked up Heli there. By the time it sank in, Cate's brother was on his way again, leaving her behind in aston-ishment. No other place perked up her mood as quickly than the waterfront market. "The place where our country shows its true identity." Umar lectured. "After all, how does our multi-ethnic society trade its cultural treasures at the market? By haggling in an artificial language that everyone speaks." His point didn't really sink in. "I'm English," she said boldly, adding, "French and African, too." Then Umar paused, giving her a serious look. "I'm mixed race, too: Asian with a touch of African. Believe me, Imker, if we have children together, they're likely to be as diverse as our compatriots at the market." Laughter. Moving on. Enjoying a cold glass of ginger beer, carefree. "Do you have a handkerchief on you? No?" She gave him a set of four. "Imker, look at the clouds." She saw the blue of the sky. She felt his lips on her chin. The trade wind is so good to everyone. They put on their caps with the bills down. He said, "Anyway, I love this country." Resting the postcard against his back, Imker wrote sweet words to her little brother Audi.

Audi had been helping to paint the clubhouse. The Sea Scouts of Amora had never seen the ocean, but that would change very soon. A week at the seaside in Nickerie during the Christmas break. He saw Umar drive up and knew it was for him. A postcard? No, not from Heli but from Imker. He snatched the card, read, smiled. "Want a ride home, Audi? It's getting too dark to go on paint-ing." He said goodbye to the painting crew and jumped on the back of the scooter. They didn't talk. He normally kept his distance from the young men who were in love with his sisters. The motionless landscape around them, dotted with bungalows where all sorts of people lived, was familiar by day but could seem strange and even hostile at night. At the gate to his own house, he hopped off the shared seat with a sigh. "Thanks." Umar revved the engine and drove off. He opened the gate, closed it, watched the streetlamps light up. He should have stayed behind and hung out with his friends until eight, as Mama expected. Her boyfriend Lester would pick her up then, and he'd be all alone in the house. He didn't feel like watching television. He dawdled at the gate. "Audi," Mother called out. "Why are you standing around out there?" He didn't answer but stepped into the light. "Is something the matter?" He nodded. "You're leaving in two hours, Babs won't be home yet, I don't know what to do." He could clearly see the tears well up in her eyes. "Do you want to come to the base with us? There's always something to do there—music, games, snacks, cans of Coca-Cola." He hesitated. "I'm not eighteen yet." She laughed, her teeth flashing. "That's why you'll have a guardian with you, my boy. So you'll see Dutch soldiers with their girlfriends and couples dancing, so what?" He shook his head firmly. "I'd rather stay at home, then it'll still be a secret how you spend your Saturday nights, Mama." Her expression turned solemn. "A secret? I don't want to hide anything from my son." And him: "Mama, some things are just too serious to tell anyone about." He saw her consider this. "Do you want me to make you a pancake? With salted cod?" He nodded. "As you wish, my son." She walked to the kitchen, washed her hands with soap, put on an apron, and mixed the ingredients. He watched, amused, and thought, *Without Mama I'd be alone in the world. Without her to take care of me, I'd be lost...* He thought, *I should be good to this woman even when I don't need her anymore.* He headed for the bathroom to take a shower and change before dinner. She stopped him. "One day, I'll tell you all my secrets, son." Her tone of voice took him by surprise. "All your secrets, Mama?" She nodded, serious. "When I'm eighteen?" She chuckled. "As soon as I can, when I'm ready, it'll all spill out one day." "And the girls?" he ventured. His mother shook her head. "God gave me a son to deliver me from my sins." And she stirred the batter, muttering, "Secrets almost always have to do with sin, but you go take a shower—it may be years before this woman is ready to confess to all her sins." He said nothing. He thought about her dog Leika, run over by

163

a car. He went to the bathroom. He tried to whistle a Sea Scouts tune. As he got undressed, Imker's postcard slid out of his pants pocket. Oh, right. Even if there was only one person in the world, besides his mother, who thought about him, it was enough to get him through a Saturday night alone. That and a book, if need be. There were so many books in the study, left behind by Rogier and Heli. In the shower, the water refreshed him like a cloudburst. The aroma of Mother's pancakes reached him in the bathroom. He dried off with a clean towel Mother had laid out for him. He tingled as if coming back to life. And suddenly he knew exactly what he would do—write a poem about loved ones disappearing and mail it to Heli. He was pretty pleased with the face that smiled at him in the mirror as he brushed his teeth.

Mama's boyfriend arrived promptly at 8:30, driving up in his small Saab. Audi opened the door to let Lester into the house, where it smelled of delicious perfume and Mother was waiting in a red dress that gleamed like bathroom tiles and perfectly matched her red lipstick. Her face was framed by a crown braid and she wore black high heels. "Not too shabby," Lester said when he saw Louise. The man gave him a firm handshake. "How's it going, kid?" Rising onto his toes to look "Mama's beau" in the eyes, he responded gruffly, "How are things at the military base?" Lester laughed. "All right. The boys are always fine in peacetime." And swerving to face Mama: "Most of the time the marching band keeps me busy there, but Saturday night is for your mother." Silence. Mama stood next to him, looking a little self-conscious. The rumor in the family was that she kept falling for charming guys who were very popular. It was no secret to any of them that this was a source of friction between Mama and her boyfriend. He was the one who, in periods of absence, ferried letters of reconciliation between the two of them. They left, the man in a long-sleeved white shirt and the lady in a passionate red. He watched the car drive off. The advantage of living at the top of a T-intersection is that the view from the rear windows stretches far and wide, and since there wasn't too much traffic in the neighborhood, he could spend long minutes staring out to the blank horizon. In the days leading up to New Year's, the quiet had often been disrupted by strangers who left offerings at the crossroads at night—wooden boxes stuffed with food and unopened bottles of strong liquor. That was because of a folk belief going back to slave days that gods and deceased relatives gathered at certain crossroads at the end of the year. Mother had mixed feelings. She didn't put any stock in such things, but she asked him and his friends to let the offerings be, meaning: don't say anything about it and don't touch anything. Each year, the same warning. After a few days, the offerings would vanish without a trace. Sometimes stray dogs tore them open, feeding on whatever they could stomach. As long as there was anything left out there, Mother kept the blinds down. Just like she kept them down on New Year's Eve, when the neighbors set off tons of fireworks at the offering site, with the intention of sending the spirits and gods back to their own realms. Each year, it was just as exciting. An idea came to him: he would buy his mother a Christmas present that would make her jaw drop. A young purebred dog? He still didn't know how he'd pull it off, but it was a fact that Mama had the right to a new guard dog. He would have liked to close the curtains completely to turn his mind to the poem, but Babs was still out, and for her, their house had to remain bathed in lamplight. So, to the kitchen for another pancake. No? He had plenty of appetite but changed his mind. What about Aram and Babs? Babs loved salty, filling dishes. Better wait. And in the meantime, to the study for a book of poetry. He plopped down into Rogier's spacious armchair at the wide desk, his eyes browsing the shelves not for poetry but for a medical encyclopedia. After all, he wanted to know all about the organ stuck to his underbelly, even more than he'd read in the book *Dotted Lines for Boys*. Door locked. And then he searched through the pages to see what girls had. He heard Aram's sports car. Babs's voice at the gate. Relieved, Audi took a deep breath and let in the Saturday evening.

Babs came inside talking excitedly to Aram, who followed with bags. She went to the kitchen, where he put everything down. "I can take driving lessons as soon as I have space in my class schedule," she said. "Boyce promised me a car, too!" This news had her even more worked up than the annoyance she felt every time she saw Heli's Derik loitering in the corridors between classes. It gave her a headache. She felt sure that, as soon as she came near him, everyone started gossiping. Aram had listened and offered a few tips for facing up to her troubles in a more relaxed way. Her father Boyce had showered her with presents beyond her wildest dreams. She'd hugged him, promising him not to rush into visiting Heli. She still had a couple of years to go at the teachers' college. "Audi, will you come with me to my driving lessons?" The boys had other things to do. "Who's paying?" her little brother asked, looking at her boyfriend. Aram motioned to the shopping she was stuffing into the cabinets. "Will you come with me or not?" She raced to the toilet. Peed. Wiped. Flushed. Washed her hands. "Is there something for girls to wipe after they pee?" Audi asked the person who knew best. Aram laughed and teased him. "You'll find out one day, kiddo." She stuck to the topic that mattered to her. "Audi, I don't want to spend a whole hour alone with a driving instructor, driving down deserted roads to practice parking in an empty parking lot, you get me?" Her little brother nodded. Aram said she was exaggerating the risks, but she snapped at him, "Aram, shut up!" and he did. And her brother asked sweetly if anyone was still hungry for pancakes with salted cod made fresh by their mother. She went to the study to close the large door, and noticing the big book lying open, she leaned over, seeing in full color: vulva, vagina. She slammed the book shut on impulse and returned to the boys. "Sure, Audi, I'm in the mood for a pancake, and I bet Aram is too, and how about watching a nice movie on television together after that?" "No way," Audi said. "I'll serve you the pancakes and then I have to hit the books." She felt the blood rise to her head but said nothing. *There's something about men I don't understand*, she thought, fetching plates and napkins, and she asked the boys if they wanted apple syrup, and seeing that Audi was caught up in a conversation with Aram about pure-bred dogs, she started serving the food, attentively and carefully. She couldn't bear sloppiness, in either herself or the people around her. She brought Aram and Audi's plates to Mama's sofa, along with cutlery, big napkins, and drops of syrup. She picked up her own portion, folded in half. "I love you guys," she said softly. "Are you talking to your mother's pancakes, or does that include me?" Aram asked. She looked up. "I'll let you know as soon as I know, boy." It didn't sound friendly. And the living room went quiet. They ate together. But eating made her think of Grandmother Bee, who might soon die of a sickness in her throat. She wondered what a boy, not even a teenager yet, wanted to know about a woman's sex organs, a subject that didn't even interest her. She thought about her father Boyce and how much he loved her. And Babs missed her two sisters something awful.

Four

I skip class and hide in the library reading lounge so no one can find me, except Lya in an emergency. It's early in the morning, and two men are at the newspaper counter reading. The table where I read and write letters is completely empty, free of printed matter. I unbutton my jacket and yank off my gloves and lay them on the table. Sit down. Because of me, they had a fight yesterday, Uncle Winston and his wife. Even though I kept my promise to Lya, a letter from Derik wound up in Winston's hands. It must have been the mailman, a new one, who didn't know that mail to the Vanta family shouldn't be tossed through the mail slot in the front door but slid neatly into the mailbox at the front of the house. Only Lya has the keys to that mailbox. Every marriage has a weak spot somewhere. Everyone knows to watch out for that spot, and for Lya, it was managing the mailbox. I'm in their guest room working on a pedagogy assignment when her voice hits me: "Winston, you had no right to read a letter addressed to Heli!" I eavesdrop from the stairs. My heart still hasn't returned to normal after everything I heard. Two people who treated each other so tenderly, so furious and reproachful and insulting. I went downstairs. They froze and said nothing. "I'm so sorry," I offered, looking at them both. Winston nodded curtly, walked to the foyer, and picked up his jacket. Lya and I heard him slam the front door. I wanted to remove myself from the premises. "Sit down," Lya said. "Winston isn't really angry with you but with me, about things that happened before he was in my life. He thinks I'm still attached to someone from back then. A complete fantasy, but can you believe it, he thought the letter to you looked fishy." She smiled wanly. "We get more mail for your uncle from the women he flirts with at his insurance agency than we do junk mail." And then her fountain of words ran dry. Lya has beautiful eyes, and they lit up when she heard her husband come back inside. And that evening, they were sitting together on the sofa again, her with her book and him engrossed in a sports program. Derik's letter to me lay in front of the door to my room, neatly sealed with Scotch tape. I couldn't find the courage to read it until now, and it occurs to me that my mother Louise would've ripped up a letter like this one before my eyes. Heartless, right? I read. Derik writes that he's enclosing 500 guilders I can use to travel during my fall break, with Cate, maybe. *Go to the North Sea*, he writes. I haven't seen Cate again since that time at the diner. What's more, there's no money in the envelope. Letter in my bag. I get up. Jacket on. Gloves on. I plunge into the city, making my way to the train station. The countless lights streaking past overwhelm me, as if the city center has exploded into shards. At the station hall, I have trouble finding the ticket window through the throng of people. "A roundtrip ticket to

the sea, but not too far from Utrecht." The man scruti-
nizes me. "Are you a tourist?" I nod. "Pick a destination,"
he orders me. "The Hague," I finally mutter after a long
pause, sensing the line behind me growing. He sells me a
first-class roundtrip ticket without any transfers. I find a
quiet corner and take a good look at my ticket, breathing
the atmosphere of the concourse in and out. Everyone has
a destination that's familiar, a familiar home. Not me. I
ask how and where, left and right, until I reach the correct platform. Why am I going to the sea? I don't really
know, but I'm on my way. I belong here, even if all the
seats are taken. The intercity train pulls out of the station.
Memories of childhood billow up like colorful autumn
leaves, twirling down somewhere in me that I can't reach.
School field trips on the slow train from Paramaribo to
Lelydorp. I let it all in, the images and feelings, and look
at what's gliding past the window. At the terminal station, I hurry outside for a taxi to Scheveningen. Make
small talk with the driver. Get out and walk, as he recommended, straight into the Kurhaus. Coffee and apple pie.
Yes, whipped cream. No, I'm not meeting anyone, sir.
Yes, I've come for the sea and the sand. The waiter leaves
me in peace. I can't stop staring, drowning in the luxury
of the Kurhaus. Outside, the sea charges at me. So many
shades of sky blue. Walk. Don't cry. Move on.

I received my first salary as a licensed teacher in an
unsealed envelope presented by an employee of the
Catholic Church. A long row of educators stood waiting
for their monthly pay. I signed the receipt for it and, head
held high, walked out into the street where my mother

Louise was waiting. I had invited her along, and the laughter and hubbub of more than a hundred co-workers at the education union clubhouse didn't escape my attention, but she was the only one I wanted to see. I walked right up to her and pushed the envelope into her hand. "For you, Mama." She shook her head. "It's your money, Heli." I nodded, asking her to check if what was in the envelope matched the amount on the receipt. She did. And at my request, the money disappeared into her purse. Sometimes, happiness is as simple as a gesture. And this moment of happiness with my mother was at least twenty-four months in the making. She'd instilled the belief in her daughters that the only money worth the trouble is the money you earn by working. Weren't we destined for wealth, then? "Yes, you are," Mother said, "or should I never have brought you into this world?" She expected her son to become a rich man, and she'd go to great lengths to make that happen.

I saunter along the paving stones of the boulevard, gawking at the hotels, restaurants, cafés, and whatnot. People out walking with their dogs on leashes. Holland moves me. Whichever way I look, I can't make out a bright future with Derik ahead. With the wind at my back, I reread the latest letter. I tear it to pieces to shred our promises and scatter them to the wind. I zip one piece into the side pocket of my shoulder bag. That's where I keep the pet names he uses for me in his letters. Sweet nothings, exquisite as perfume, dazzling as heavy jewelry. Although Derik's words are only paper and ink, they slip inside me like something I don't yet understand but my body recognizes. It's a longing for deep physical contact with him. The flame of my own existence as a living being has been stoked, and the heat is flowing through my veins. After wandering for hours, I find myself back at the Kurhaus. I hesitate before taking a streetcar to The Hague city center. Strolling past store windows without the slightest impulse to buy anything. Walking as if the world is a platform on which everything moves with no destination but death. I end up at Central Station. At the cafeteria there, I wind my way to a seat as though I've spotted someone ahead, coming to join me. An hour. Another hour. Then I disappear into rush hour and end up in Utrecht again. Walk through the center. Amble toward the Sranan Sani diner. Go inside, unaccompanied by Cate. The waitress recognizes me: "What happened to your red-haired friend?" "Cate's at work," I lie cheerfully. "She found a job as a kindergarten teacher." The waitress nods, understanding, and asks if I'm waiting for Cate. I shake my head and order the daily special. And a bottle of sparkling water. I miss Cate and can't finish my order. Head outside. Homeward. "Where've you been, Heli?" It's Winston. Overly friendly. "Just playing hooky," I answer evasively, pulling off my gloves and jacket by the coat stand. Lya walks over. "Hungry?" she asks. I confess I've already had dinner, brown beans and rice. She smiles, and Winston asks, "Were you with that Dutch boy, Hans?" At the same time, he reaches into his inner pocket. "I wasn't with anyone at all," I stress, irritated. "Look, I've exchanged your 500 Surinamese guilders for local currency, count it, almost 1,000 Dutch guilders." I take the money, not knowing what to say or do. I give the entire bundle of banknotes to Lya. "Can you please send this to my mother for me?" She nods and takes the money. And at last I pass through the kitchen, where the

173

bottle of orgeat high on the kitchen shelf makes me think of my grandmother, and hurry up the stairs to the guest room. At every turn I glimpse the azure of the North Sea as if I were still right beside it.

The ocean voyage from Nieuw Nickerie to Paramaribo had stuck in Bernadette's craw. Although she hadn't gotten seasick like her husband Anton, she'd caught a bad cold. Shivering and too hoarse to speak a word due to a sore throat, she'd stared out over the city harbor. Louise took care of Laura, who was nearly ten but small and frail. Winston and his father kept an eye on the family's luggage. Bee did nothing but gaze at the storefronts of the city where she would live from here on out. She wasn't in any state for contemplation. She clung to what Winston Senior had said when they were leaving: "Bee, leave everything to your husband and the military officers and try to be good to your children, then you'll be happy again." As he spoke, he brought his face close to hers to look into the eyes of his only sister, and for the first time she saw the blue of their father's eyes flashing in the darkness of his. *Sky blue*, she thought, looking at the coffee-brown river water lapping against the dock. All around were black men with bare backs in wooden canoes. Her husband's blackness shone in the skin of the men who waved and laughed at the riverboat *Perica* as it dropped anchor in the capital. The girls were nervous, especially when some young white studs in military dress came over to help them disembark safely. Step by step, they went down the walkway, taking in all the unfamiliar sights. She kept a tight grip on Laura, whose other hand clutched Louise. Passengers were welcomed by family members, who showered them with kisses and warm embraces. No relatives were waiting for the Vanta family. They and their household possessions were driven by military vehicles to provisional housing. Her brothers Scott and Léon had stopped by at the last minute to bring her presents, but even though they'd both married city girls, they hadn't given her their in-laws' home addresses. Anton seemed to be perking up, and Bee's children were glowing with curiosity. She'd survived without a mother's care. Without a father close by, she'd kept her marriage intact. And she still had God, who was always there. As she had a cold, her family had booked a large, well-furnished cabin for the overnight river voyage. She'd spent the journey slumbering on a firm bed. She'd given her girls permission to bring chocolate bars, which they could keep cool in the cabin. Yes, her family had been treated so much better than all those poor souls who had to suffer through the voyage with their children on wooden benches out in the gusts of chilly ocean wind. They had made it ashore, and even though no one had asked if she'd a good trip, she'd had a privileged arrival in Paramaribo. Louise thought the city stank of fish and sweat. As for her, she couldn't smell a thing. She saw how people were looking at her and the "pretty children" she and Anton had brought to Paramaribo. And Ethel? A face with tearful eyes—her husband's. He too must have been thinking of his daughter who was no longer with them.

She couldn't dodge death too much longer. She knew her end was coming, in the span of one calendar page.

The pigeons she'd kept during her married years in Paramaribo fluttered inside her like flashes of light. Some settled on her shoulders and even on her head. Other pigeons stayed just out of reach, always, as if saying, *I love you so much but don't touch me and don't pick me up and never slaughter me.* Precious little things, too darling to stay close to humans. At Jacobusrust, Anton had a tall pigeon cote built for her in the backyard as well as a henhouse where she kept chickens and a single rooster. And when the rooster crowed, she'd go at once in her housecoat to the backyard, where no fewer than sixty pigeons would fly to greet her, and the chickens would cluck in their closed coops to be relieved of their eggs, but especially to be allowed to run after her, pecking at the corn and other food she tossed around, scratching in the off-white shells with their feet just as she did with her rake. And even on such mornings, death was present, because she always had a pair of pigeons and a chicken in mind to slaughter. Once every three months, year in and year out, she killed two pigeons and slit one chicken's throat. These acts didn't excite her. On the contrary, hours later she was still as unapproachable as a crocodile that has tearfully devoured the thing that kept it alive, which for that very reason it hadn't wanted to kill. Once, in a moment of carelessness, she had slaughtered the rooster's favorite hen. He kept coming at her with his spurs until he got over his loss and was willing to mate with her hens again. And when she threw a party, she insisted on getting the meat somewhere else.

She took tiny steps across her living room, looking at the crucifix on the wall, which bore the image of a man who'd hoped his violent death would bring peace to the

176

world. She said a prayer of thanks out loud. Her family had been convinced that when Laura married her fiancé Bram it would heal their unspoken suffering. Ethel's disappearance, the journey to the city, Louise's pregnancy with Heli—events that were never discussed but gave her and Anton high blood pressure and could instantaneously transform a pleasant conversation into an argument. A slight difference of opinion could reduce her to tears. And even though it never took the family long to make up, and they had no problem sitting together at the table and enjoying the dinner she cooked for them each day, the threat of emotional outbursts could not be contained, until Laura showed up with a young man fresh from abroad. He was as white as milk bread, and his words came out as soft and sweet as bread pudding. Laura would always put on music that mellowed the mood in the house, and when she added her own voice, she made the songs ring even truer than the unfamiliar ladies on the records. Singing for an audience and educating children were the two things Laura excelled at. When she brought Bram home to meet her parents, it came as a surprise. Her other boyfriends had floated in and drifted right back out again. But everything was different with Bram. He found a job at a private school, and he made one thing clear: he would do whatever he could to get to know Laura, her family, and Paramaribo. He went away only to return to Laura with engagement rings made of Surinamese gold and the promise that they would live in her country after the wedding ceremony in Holland. The engagement party was much too elaborate, in Anton's opinion, and not what Laura herself wanted, in Louise's view. Winston had managed to get his hands on some of Bram's savings and use it for "grand gestures."

The betrothal ceremony was carried out in great style on a Saturday and sealed with a priestly blessing and a lavish reception. Winston Senior and his lady Mathilde came down from British Guiana to the flat coast of Paramaribo. Scott and Léon attended with their families, and Anton's sister joined them with four of her children. Some relatives didn't show up, and others attended but were studiously ignored, yet Laura's party seemed to be a magnet for everything beautiful and joyous. And don't even ask what or how much was eaten up and drunk down, because she was still receiving compliments weeks later. Bram left to settle his remaining business in the Netherlands, but mostly to prepare for the wedding at his parents' home in Apeldoorn. Laura waited and waited in bewilderment. And even she couldn't get a single word about Bram out of her daughter. One day she found Laura's engagement ring next to her napkin on the table. Laura would never depart by white ocean liner or blue airplane. Laura stayed in Jacobusrust. Whenever anyone asked for an explanation, her daughter would stare blankly as if no one was standing there waiting for an answer.

A kind of dread overcame her. She went to lie down on the sofa. Imker had removed the plastic and draped a striped blanket over it. Invitingly soft. She stretched out her legs. Leaned her head against an armrest. It had been unbearable to leave Laura in the hands of strangers in Kolera. The thought that her death would leave her daughter unloved in this world was grueling for Bernadette Vanta and a reason to resist her own decay. Jacobusrust had only the one street. The street where the home of Louise's parents stood. And even though she knew the neighborhood consisted of a hundred homes built specifically to provide decent housing to former soldiers and their families, for her, there was just one house: her Ma and Pa's house. She had never made the effort to explore the neighborhood, and even the path along the backyards, which connected a whole row of neighbors, remained untrodden for her. She had just turned twenty when she went to live there, and of course, her mother Bee hadn't really wanted to move to a new house where all the neighbors had the same employer as her husband. It led to squabbling. And they'd had other options—her father Anton could have bought the house where they were living happily at a very low cost. He refused again. Everyone still lived at home. Her sister Laura had just started the most basic level of schoolteacher training—fourth class, they called it. As for her, she had a Schoevers secretarial certificate. Two years later, the war broke out in Europe, and she was hired by the military.

Major Lester knew that on Saturday nights the first place he should drive her was the waterfront. He would park his car at a spot where she had a good view of the river and the play of the lights on the water. The drive that took her away from her house and out of Amora always came as a relief. A long road, well paved and bathed in the lights of the houses on both sides. A guy with a motorcycle, one other car, and Holband at his cart, surrounded by voracious fans of his blood sausages. A little farther away were walking paths, strung with scantily clad hookers. The city lay motionless on the water, and the almond trees along the shoreline seemed to say that time, which was so important to her, meant nothing to them or to

179

the river. And that decay hardly mattered to Paramaribo either. She couldn't get enough of peering out into the distance, toward the ocean. Lester asked if she wanted to get out for a short walk with him, maybe someplace more private? She got out but stayed close to the car, peering toward the far bank of the river where the darkness was complete. The young girl of fourteen who'd stood by her parents at the harbor had become a woman who'd somehow ended up with four children and had been robbed of her most beautiful dream—living in London and working in the high fashion industry with a handsome man as a life partner. "Nothing to see but water," Lester said coaxingly, wrapping an arm around her. She went on gazing a little longer at the white of the Governor's Palace and the statue of the Dutch monarch in the illuminated, grassy square. With her back to the river, facing Lester head on, she said in a sultry voice, "Let's get to the base, my dearest."

The wooden house on Tafelmanstraat had four huge bedrooms. It was part of a row of well-maintained houses along a narrow asphalt street on the outer fringe of the office complex. They had a yard with four dwarf trees; sweet limes and lemons; a tall, zinc-plated wooden fence; and a swing without a seat. It was a neighborhood for senior officials. Their family didn't fit in there, and her parents often couldn't relate to the brown men in white shirts and neckties who spoke Dutch as fluently as the soldiers from the Netherlands. And even though they were better dressed than the women and children of these urbanites, they hardly dared open their mouths when spoken to. The

Dutch they knew and had spoken in Nieuw Nickerie was saturated with the other mother tongues passed down to them by their English and French forebears and sounded like a Hindustani love song. Anton made it his constant mission to clean up their speech. He earned the respect of his family with his way of addressing the high-and-mighty neighbors. Mother came to admire him and talked to him with new words in a new way. She no longer called her husband "Mister Vanta" but "Pa Anton," which sounded like "Panton" and sometimes "Ponton." She made a point of speaking to him only in her best Dutch, which no one but the two of them could understand. It made them laugh, but Bee persisted. A year later, Bee was pregnant, and in a blindingly white room of the military hospital, Rogier was born. Twelve years after Laura. Mrs. Vanta-Julienne was declared infertile for the remainder of her life. And then God re-entered their lives, because Rogier had to be christened, the house had to be blessed, and so they would have to make their way to the Catholic Church downtown. But Anton put a stop to this, registering his children and his wife as members of the "black church," the Moravian congregation. No priest would be coming to their door for all kinds of discussions. Instead, the Vantas let in a Protestant minister, a black man in a tailored suit who spoke the Dutch that the family seemed to need for social advancement in their new city, among creoles, the unfettered descendants of a violent era.

The base was dark, but the clubhouse shone bright in the twilight, and the Dutch flag still flew. What was called a clubhouse for the sake of convenience was a chic lodge with distinguished members. Lester was quite high in the ranks even though he'd never carried a gun. His drinking became a threat to his marriage and eventually to his wife and children as well. They'd moved to Florida, where she'd found a good stepfather for her children and a better husband for herself. Lester was okay with it, he said. Brass player and professional musician—he was a popular man, even in civilian life, where he was best known for his artistic contributions to many cool dance festivals. Turning music into a deeply human pleasure takes more than a score filled with notes and other squiggles; it requires a place with wide-awake women, good food, strong liquor, and a dance floor. These were words Lester muttered without embarrassment, without regret, without pain. His time on Earth was devoted to music. "Living is a natural process and unfolds spontaneously, my dear Louise, but my darling, survival is an art, because to do it you need your own driving force." Even his days off, his instruments were onstage, ready for use. She knew that. She also loved him because he was so big, so black, so musical, and so wise. And if once in a great while he happened to get as drunk as a skunk, she would have a close friend drive him to her house in his own Saab, and she'd let him lie down in her bedroom and toss and turn and churn and retch until he was back to his old self again. Her children understood that Lester, the alien being their mother cherished, had entered their private domain to stay. They had no choice but to accept and respect him. She and Lester liked to sit where they could hear and see the band properly. Guys in ironed uniforms really brought her to life—their green that wasn't green, their decorations that weren't decorations, their strength that wasn't strength, their lust for life that wasn't lust for life. And, of course, she found in every soldier something she'd lost when the man who'd made her a woman and a mother had left her once and for all. Gordon had taken her breath away when he came up to her in his white uniform and matching cap and said, "I've never been into brown, but you're showing me how crazy I was." *Don't hyperventilate*, she'd thought. "Are you on later, Lester?" He took her hand. "No, I'm sticking with you this time, and the band is going to play one of my songs, written just for you, Louise." Her fingers slid over the coarse stubble around his mouth. *That's Paramaribo for you*, she thought, *winning or losing is all a question of skin color*. More couples came to where she sat with Lester. They knew each other. They greeted each other with light kisses and firm hugs. The women smelled divine, as always, and their husbands were dressed in light tailored suits with loose jackets. Some whispering went on among the women. The men shouted all sorts of jokes at each other in the language of street negotiations, as if to make it perfectly clear that the difference between natives and foreigners would never disappear, even if they did serve the same monarchy. She never had much to say. Truth be told, she was usually reserved in the company of married couples. She was on her guard. Responding in a friendly manner, but only when spoken to. Her boyfriend Lester knew he shouldn't give the ladies' husbands any opportunity to dance with her. "My lady's here for me," he said, and she nodded, almost glad. Since her daughter's affair with Derik, she'd become even more guarded. Heli's behavior had made Bee quick to anger and often even unable to experience sexual pleasure. She stared at the band members setting up to play. *Good thing Heli's gone*, she thought as she sipped a gin and tonic, because Heli's presence at home was worse than a toothache. Louise Vanta had never had a toothache but couldn't think of anything else that could possibly work her nerves like a defiant, sexually mature daughter. The band started their set with "Louise."

At Zorg en Hoop, Imker had already brought home everything Grandmother had asked for: coconut oil, soybean oil, canned sardines, preserved Dutch butter, aniseed, vanilla, Quaker oats, raisins, liquid honey, unsprouted potatoes, white eggs, brown beans, canned powdered milk, condensed milk, Demerara sugar, flour, baking powder, cleaning supplies, toothpaste, bath soap, sanitary napkins, powdered detergent for the washing machine, castor oil from the pharmacy, new mops. Lying next to the groceries was a giant bunch of long-stemmed sunflowers for a special purpose. She put down her heavy load in the kitchen under her grandmother's watchful eye and said, hurriedly, "I'm going back out again to go see Laura." And leaving Grandma behind in the kitchen with the food, she took the back door out, raced to the gate, and slid onto the minibus beside the other passengers. It was almost noon, maybe lunchtime at Kolera, but Laura's birthday was coming up and she wanted to let her aunt know that the family was thinking of her. The presents could wait, but there should be flowers someplace where Laura could see them whenever she wanted until the big day. Persuading the department head at Kolera wouldn't be easy, but Dr. Albert had promised to step in if her request was denied. The bus driver hit every pothole in the road on the way to her destination. "Kolera," he shouted, with emotion in his voice. She hopped off the bus and grabbed the bunch of sunflowers. She'd already paid the fare, and the driver and several passengers gave her encouraging nods. She went to the gatekeeper. It was almost lunchtime, but she was expected. She had barely set foot inside the asylum walls when Laura approached her with quick steps. Her aunt laughed, eyes glowing. "Flowers for me!" There was no turning back now. Laura grabbed the heavy bouquet by the stems with a firm grip and pressed them to her upper body. "Sunflowers because the day after tomorrow's my birthday," and she lowered her face into the yellow of the large flowers. She herself was so surprised that she didn't know what to do next. She'd never seen her mother's sister so happy and excited before. "I'll hold them close," Laura said, "until they're all wilted, Imker, because we're not allowed to put flowers in vases with water, you see." She took a moment to calm herself. "Yes, Laura, but still, maybe we can find someplace in here for your birthday flowers." Laura nodded. "Sunflowers, and so many! Maybe a bucket of fresh water would be better than vases anyway, don't you think?" Together they went to the visitors' lounge, where there was a reception desk. The other patients had all gone to the dining hall. Laura had no appetite but wanted to walk around outside. "Did you show up out of the blue to bring her flowers?" The nurse chuckled. And Laura started muttering, "Where are we going to put them, these pretty sunflowers for my birthday?" The nurse called over another staff member, and they whispered to each other. She and Laura couldn't make out what they were saying. The whispering dragged on. She grew impatient and moved in closer to them while Laura waited at the reception desk. And suddenly the words came flying out: "May Laura visit her mother until her birthday?" She whispered it so Laura wouldn't hear, because the plan seemed ridiculous, practically doomed to fail. "First the flowers," the nurse said. And the other spoke with raised eyebrows, "I'll take your request to the attending physician tomorrow morning." She nodded gratefully, and they looked at Laura, still clutching the flowers without moving an inch. "Come, Laura, let's find a place to sit and have a smoke." But Laura shook her head, wanting to know what the nurses planned to do with her bouquet. It was foolish to have brought so many cut flowers to a place that offered no nourishment: no vase, no bucket, no fresh water. And nothing at all resembling a mother's love. Even animals can't do without that. The nurses just couldn't figure out where to put Laura's bouquet, and meanwhile there stood Laura, her face dusted yellow with pollen. It was a peculiar scene. And to everyone who saw it, one thing was clear—Laura wouldn't give up her flowers. Would Laura like something to eat from the Javanese shop outside? No? Not hungry? "I've waited for flowers for so long," Laura said softly, adding, "You can go back to your house." But how could she do that, under the circumstances? "What are you going to do with the flowers?" Laura's response was very simple and, at the same time, the correct solution to a nonexistent problem. "I'll go see my friends now and give each of them a flower." Fantastic. "What about you?" She sounded anxious. Laura stared at her in surprise. "Imker, they're still my birthday flowers even if there's no water for them." She and Laura stared at each other solemnly, nodding in agreement. Waiting side

186

by side for Laura's friends to finish their hot lunch. Each flower would be held in a woman's warm hand. She would see to it that Laura was allowed to keep one for herself, as long as she wanted, until the last petal was gone.

As she left Kolera, she pictured women with both hands wrapped around tall sunflowers on sturdy green stems, their eyes on her and Laura. She walked through the palm grove and listened to the rustling of hundreds of palm leaves. Walking slowly, hearing the trade wind singing for Laura. The request to bring her home must be soaking like a marinade into the brains of the authorities at Kolera. Laura Vanta at her own mother's house in Zorg en Hoop, even just for one night? There might never be another chance. She could see for herself that her grandmother's strength was ebbing away. Even though Dr. Albert claimed it might take as much as a year thanks to Grandma Bee's strong heart, she—a granddaughter, by her grandmother's side each day—was prepared for the worst and had no use for his reassurances. Grandma had a right to see Laura, period. And could she, with no training as a nurse, handle Laura for twenty-four hours? The question seemed silly to her. She always felt so clear-headed with the women at Kolera, and she had a good relationship with Laura. The palm grove seemed deserted in the middle of the day. She looked up along the smooth trunks that were firmly rooted in the ground where she stood, and all the waving foliage resembled the face of one woman, who didn't know the first thing about the northeast wind. The women with the sunflowers still blazed in her mind's eye. She blinked a few times.

Before her brother Audi could even talk, when she, Heli, and Babs were still camping out with sleeping bags and pillows in the wooden townhouse with the steep stairs to the attic and the unfurnished rooms, she woke one night to the sound of knocking, on the door, on the windows. Mama was awake, too, pacing the rooms, and suddenly asked in a frightened voice, "Who's there?" And then the voice of Mama's sister: "It's me, Louise." Soft and clear. "What do you want, Laura?" And again, "It's scary outside, I want to be with you, open the door for me." And Laura kept asking to be let inside. She looked at Mama. She, Heli, and even little Babs, who'd woken up too. Upset and silent, they stared at their mother Louise, who called out loud and stern, "Go away, Laura, go back to Jacobusrust, I'm not letting you in!" Silence fell outside, as complete as the sudden silence in the house. They could hear their mother's sister walk away in the night, her high heels tapping on the asphalt. Maybe her mother and grandmother could explain to her what had happened that night. The next day, Laura didn't show up for work or call in sick. Her employer gave her three weeks' paid sick leave. But what was wrong with Laura? She was determined to learn the whole story. In a family kept so small, they couldn't let past events just evaporate like steam from boiling water. She was a Vanta, just like Laura. They went through life with the same family name, and Laura's history wouldn't just magically disappear if they pretended she didn't exist. Albert said she'd make a good nurse. Who could say? Her ambition was to be a good blood relative. Nothing else. Footsteps approaching. Voices too. She got up. Left the palm grove. Where in the world could she buy a couple of pigeons for pigeon soup? Her grandparents' Paramaribo no longer existed. Or did it? After all, who could Imker turn to these days if not her grandmother?

Five

Grandmother's life-threatening delivery of Ethel, which went down in fond memory as the little angel's arrival in the household, ushered in a respite from the carnal side of her marriage. Another child almost every year, when you haven't yet entirely become a woman yourself—everyone around her might have seen it as healthy, even a blessing, but it left her exhausted. After Ethel's birth, she could send the women who dropped by into peals of laughter by saying that her three children were consuming her life, not only by sucking her breasts dry but above all by being completely dependent on her. She would also describe her embarrassment during the delivery: how she lay there, naked and moaning with her legs spread, pushing with all her might as others observed what was coming out of her nether regions... Then the visiting women would all cry, "No, man!" In her circle of friends, this conclusion even became a cliché, used for every occasion and persisting in corrupted forms: *nò mang, no way, don't even think about it!* And Grandma could still laugh when memories from long ago rolled in. Meanwhile, Imker mainly wanted to talk about Laura. She didn't. Against her will, she found herself back in the townhouse in the city, tastefully decorated by others, who'd suddenly had to decamp to a secret address in a foreign country. In the house, among things that didn't belong to her, she was sometimes haunted by the feeling of being an intruder, a housemaid, or an unexpected guest. After their own furniture was unloaded at the dock, the crates remained closed for a long time under a protective tarpaulin, stacked against the corrugated fence in the backyard. Their new dwelling was already fully furnished, even with bedding and towels. The army command had requested that they treat everything with care while waiting for another house to become available for their family. They were told it might take months. It took years. Keeping the townhouse in good shape was tiring. She could've gotten help from one of her husband's nieces; she refused. A daughter of her brother Scott, born out of wedlock, came by looking for domestic work, but she sent that girl away too. Winston and Louise each had to clean their own room and help around the house when needed. So what was the problem? The problem lay in her own bedroom, where her husband Anton again claimed her every night. The almost ten years she had spent without the fear of getting pregnant had in truth been the most glorious years of her marriage. It was then that she had started to see her husband as he really was, orphaned just like her, and maybe she'd learned to love him back because he was no longer demanding her body. As long as that lasted, she hadn't begrudged him his drinking more than was good for him, or his gambling, a frequent alternative source of pleasure. She had taken good care of him, lovingly, as if he were her idol. In Paramaribo, he didn't drink, and he didn't gamble. But he took her nearly every night, in an unknown couple's tall marriage bed. An almost opaque mosquito net in an off-white color hung over the enormous mattress. That color even seeped into her dreams, and when the morning light fell through the window, Anton wanted her again. When he finally got out of bed to go to the base, she could hear him whistling in the shower as she lay staring at the netting, half undressed, until she heard him ride away on his bike. Then out of bed to make breakfast for Winston and Louise, who had to get to school. And within a couple of months she was pregnant again with Rogier, just when Laura most needed support from her and Anton to grow beyond the old identity of Nickerie schoolgirl and emerge from her cocoon, ready for life in the city.

But she really couldn't talk for long stretches. She had to try to fit an entire life, one that issued from her and had usually remained close at hand, into little anecdotes, the same way she piped cheese filling into bite-sized puffs, because her granddaughter Imker needed to sample the flavor of her own main ingredient: family blood. But she brought it all back to something nearly spiritual. "Imker, bring Laura to me, then you'll witness a miracle." As if a single loaf of bread would turn out to be enough to feed the entire Vanta-Julienne bloodline. And she advised her granddaughter to lean especially on their family friend Albert for help, saying, "Doctors will bend rules like pretzels for one of their own." And when Imker was back at home, she tried to sing, but it came out as humming. "I've turned into a honeybee, Imker." And her granddaughter

didn't know what to do but hum in reply: "Hmmmm."
News of deaths drifted through the rooms, and each day
she listened, taking in every detail. Beside the radio, she
turned around and gathered the strength to say, "Being
at home with me on her birthday will be enough because
Laura doesn't have to spend the night because—" She
pressed her lips shut. She sat back down. Imker had the
hand mixer on and couldn't have heard her. What had she
really wanted to say, anyway? She looked at the sunflowers her granddaughter had brought in with the groceries,
which she'd happily placed all over the house in vases of
fresh tap water, lovely vases that brought to mind the fes-
tive wedding of Lya to her son Winston.

There were years when Laura's birthday was a date everyone ignored. No one spoke to Bee then of her daughter, who'd been kept out of sight for so long. No one in
Paramaribo knew about her other daughter Ethel, whose
birthday likewise passed unnoticed—except by Anton,
who would be impossible to talk to all day and drink himself into a stupor in the evening. She alone knew about it.

Before, Laura had made a name for herself around
town, mainly as a beloved schoolteacher. Parents wanted
their children to be in her class and no one else's. She
had everything that makes a woman appealing to all ages,
Bram had declared adoringly when they became engaged.
And as Laura's mother, she received and put up with all
sorts of compliments on her daughter, under all sorts of
circumstances. Ethel's birthday never went unnoticed in
their house, but Laura's was wrapped in silence. A week
after, as if everyone had been corked up for days, they

would throw a much-too-lavish birthday party for her youngest child Rogier, inviting hordes of children to Jacobusrust, where Laura had been so happy for years as a young schoolteacher. She used to see her daughter outside on the spacious patio every day after work, thumbing through notebooks, reviewing her lessons, and glancing out into the street, where acquaintances often passed by and waved at her. After dinner, the record player would come on, softly so as not to disturb anyone, and as the mellifluous voice of Doris Day wound through the room, Laura's housemates could enjoy hearing her sing along: *I'm glad that you're happy with somebody else, but I'm sorry it couldn't be me.* And the calm regularity of the years was in no way distressing. And yet she would still think, as a mother does, each time she saw her daughter sitting so serenely: *God, why didn't she just marry Bram?* And even as she told herself she didn't know the answer, panic seized her. And a coughing fit rose from deep within. That was the very thing she feared most, because coughing was unimaginably painful. She panted, glancing at the figure of Christ on the wall, imploring him not to let her go before she could wish her daughter Laura a happy birthday. How had that girl persevered for so long through so much wordless suffering there within the walls of Kolera? Even though the coughing fit never erupted, Grandmother was still in pain.

I celebrate autumn in the Netherlands. Astonished, I take in the beautiful colors of the trees and roadsides. I use Saturday to venture downtown, but as soon as I start to feel crushed by the throng, I flee the city center without knowing where to. Hat on my head. Scarf around my neck. Coat open. Boots tied tight. Do I feel tired? I step inside a restaurant. Order a ham, egg, and cheese sandwich and a bottle of sparkling water. I don't walk in parks or on forest paths. I don't want to give the impression of searching for something I can't find. The jubilant decay of autumn moves me. I am not even twenty-one yet, probably too young to map out a clear-cut life path for myself. Autumn leaves cover the sidewalks. So soothing. Derik is still writing letters that leave me unsettled for hours, but like my favorite pop songs, they turn me on and then offer me no satisfaction. I've often heard my mother Louise saying to other women, "My children flesh out my daily life." I understand her better now. It wasn't an apology but the reality. She's often told me the story of how I met my father, though I couldn't begin to picture the dapper soldiers, army trucks and jeeps, or cute girls in combat uniforms. There was chaos in Europe. The spreading mayhem of the war had demolished cities and shot countless families into mourning. My grandfather Anton had refused to serve in a foreign military unit and been demoted. He was dispatched to the jungle as punishment and emerged months later in terrible shape, with a case of malaria from which he never fully recovered. My father had chosen a career in coastal shipping. With his white uniform and bold expression, he was the type of stud that girls fell for easily. Everyone but my mother? Or everyone, including my mother? She sometimes says, "Gordon took my body without me giving it to him." "Didn't you love him? Didn't you love him an awful lot?" Mama no longer knows for sure. She knows her pregnancy was a disaster for the Vanta family in Jacobusrust and that her mother started smoking thick cigars in the evening and chewing tobacco at night. She's never forgotten how her father Anton's eyes teared up as he looked at her. "And what did you think then, Mama?" She can't remember. She left her parents' house behind with me under her heart, not knowing where she'd spend the night. "Then where did you sleep, Mama?" She always answered softly, "My sister came to get me and even shared her room with me." "Her bed, too?" "Mother Bee had locked the other bedrooms. The floor by Laura's bed was cold. And when I started to show, I handed in my army gear." My mother started taking classes, paid for by her brother, who was scoring one promotion after another in the sales department of a freight shipping company. "And where does your Gordon live now, Mama?" "His employer forbade him to remain in contact with me." "The colonial army? Why didn't you get an abortion, Mama?" She was taken aback by my question, but even so, she answered offhandedly, "I was so scared of my child dying that I did everything I could to keep you and me alive." "Was your mother at the delivery, Mama?" I can see her shiver. "I called for her, I don't know if she came because I lost so much blood, child, but in the heart of Europe they were hunting for people, gas chambers were roaring, rivers turning red… Paramaribo was a safe place to bring you into the world, Heli." And now, twenty years later, I'm sitting somewhere in the heart of the Netherlands, dryly enjoying the autumn all by myself.

Uncle Winston has no contact with his children, but at every opportunity, he tries to convince me that calling my father more regularly could mean more money for me. I ask if he supports his own children. His bellowing laughter leaves my question in tatters. "My children are lucky enough to have a rich stepfather!" I explain to Winston that I don't need money. He insists that my mother has the right to money from Gordon. I explain that in that case it's up to my mother to take my father to court. This shuts my mother's brother up. He spent many years studying law but never entered the profession. According to him, he has too much "slaveholder blood" to be offered any opportunities by the descendants of freed slaves, what he calls the "Creole society of Paramaribo." His forefathers on his mother's side became filthy rich through the violent system of slave labor, and even though he never saw a cent of it, the Creoles around town made him pay for it. My mother Louise and grandmother Bee harbor the same resentments but have chosen to smother their rebellious thoughts. Rogier has found a wife who claims with pride not to have a single drop of "slaveholder blood"; Wonny sometimes lets on that it's awkward for her to have taken a surname like Vanta that was coined by a racist, even if over time its significance has changed from threatening to healing. Rogier lets her talk. Her ambitions may be inspired by our country's history, but they're focused entirely on creating new human life. Besides, nothing blacker than Vanta exists; that's a necessary condition of the universe. And no one can escape it. And on Sunday after church, coffee is served and the cream scooped out of the chocolate-covered cream puffs that the Dutch call "Moors' heads," as people joke about how fresh the distant past tastes in Holland. Sometimes, I briefly become the butt of the jokes, with my two purebred colonist ancestors. That stings. I've never enslaved any human being, and

I never will. Anyway, Uncle Winston knows my answer. My father and I will cross paths again sometime in the future. I get ready for a presentation; the theme assigned to me is family relationships. Lines of ink are transforming into bloodlines, and it's not my doing. I don't plan to talk about the days of slavery but about my grandfather's last name, which his mother took when she was redeemed from slavery. I want to talk about his parents' community, which he fled in his youth, preferring the life of a soldier to everything else. He saw no future for himself in that plantation community. The outside world, whether overseas or just around the bend, seemed like a hell from which the base offered protection. Private Vanta's commanders knew the boy was deathly afraid of weapons, blood, corpses. But what would Paramaribo have to offer a plantation boy like him? Nothing. What did such a dark-skinned boy think about the people of his home country? I don't know. He was deployed. A small-town military base. Site: Nieuw Nickerie. His equipment consisted of paper, pen, ink. By his name, the title of *clerk*. Not once did he hurt anyone. Today is his daughter Laura's birthday. I've sent her a postcard with glossy sunflowers from Vincent van Gogh and a lot of sweet words from me. Will she smile? Imker and I heard Mother refusing to open our front door and let her inside when she was desperate. I squeezed Imker's hand as we stared at our mother and heard our aunt disappear into the deep darkness of the night. Even a girl of ten is old enough to have a vague sense of right and wrong. In my eyes, my mother became evil for the first time. And then something happened that was even worse.

One evening, Cate is at the door. She's come to bring me good news. She's found a job as a substitute teacher. In my winter coat, gloves on, hat on, I stand outside the front door talking to her. Even the garage door is ice cold. Can I let her inside? It's windy and dark out on the street. I hesitate. "Should we head downtown, Heli?" I shake my head. Cate pouts. "They're keeping you prisoner in their house." I shake my head again, denying it. Cate doesn't talk about her boyfriend, who's followed her to this country, and I don't ask questions. We decide to meet downtown next Saturday in front of the Sranan Sani Diner. "You should rent a room of your own, Heli." I ask where she's headed. "Off to dance at a place where the Surinamese are in charge." Her voice sounds hoarse. She still hasn't given up smoking. I walk with her down the street, watch her go, head back in a hurry. The Oog in Al neighborhood is airy and enchanting in the moonlight. At the front door, Winston asks if Cate came to pick me up. "No," I say, cheerful. "She's found a job in education." He chuckles. "No meetings in our house with Surinamese guests," he says with a smile. "Sure," I snap, walking past him down the hall to the kitchen for a glass of water. I look at the orgeat syrup atop the kitchen cabinet. No one is allowed to uncork it without my permission, and no one has. Rules are rules. I learned this from my mother Louise.

Louise Vanta knew her brother Winston had battled his way to the top spot at a Dutch chain of stores managed by the Protestant Church, a bastion of power in Paramaribo. He'd successfully pushed to bring about a merger between the members of the "black church" and the white Protestants. It was fortunate for him that his parents weren't in contact with the Catholics. Mother Bee went along without complaining, loyally attending services at the Grote Stadskerk, which was on a beautiful plaza in the garden district downtown. The family was effortlessly absorbed into the Moravian church community. She and Winston had to make their professions of faith and be publicly acknowledged as new church members. They attended Bible study together every week. And her mother Bee had no trouble keeping her Catholic hymns secret, as Moravian canticles resounded through the house. Uncle Léon came by one Sunday afternoon to explain, at length, that it was their French father Julienne who'd "infected" Bee's Anglophile family with incense and holy water. Everything Catholic had been an abomination to the English and Scots along the colonized coast. Mother Bee had gone along with this story out of necessity. Couldn't understand why men argued over the outward trappings of a God who was invisible. She said nothing. Uncle Léon hung around the city to start a small business but kept secret what type of store it would be until the grand opening of Léon Shoe Repair Shop. He'd sworn off religion. Winston helped his uncle with the paperwork and marketing. Custom-made clothes and especially shoes were the height of fashion in the capital city and beyond. The well-off professional class had no other means of standing out amid the impressive green military uniforms than through their sophisticated fashion sense. Women indifferent to white men's religions scraped together vestiges of African traditions, designing their own vibrantly colored variations on the kinds of clothing their enslaved ancestors had worn to protect their bodies from the heat of the sun and the overseers' sexual brutality. Their own family, likewise, seemed to have struck just the right balance in a city that was a mass of contradictions. Darling Laura and little Rogier never got sick and were coddled by everyone. She and her brother Winston were hard-working students. Father Anton's blood relatives made a long trip by river and crossed inhospitable chenier plains to be with the family. They brought coconut oil, nuts of all kinds, sweet potatoes, salt fish, smoked meat, and tasty berries. She can still see her cousins sitting at the kitchen table, saying nothing. Her father's sister, who came with her daughters, full heads of curly hair in thick braids, white teeth, flashing eyes. They didn't talk, except to answer questions. No one asked them anything. They carried the smells of the plantation and of the food they'd gathered on their journey. The girls sometimes played games with Laura and Rogier in the yard, while their mother and Bee looked on, sipping glasses of ginger beer garnished with bobbing cloves. The swing without a seat remained untouched on the small lawn. *Jewish children played there*, she thought. And her sister Ethel broke to the surface. She looked and looked and listened and wondered why her mother, known for being a motormouth, was so quiet around these relatives from the plantation. Dad said it was an issue of comprehension. The languages Mama and his sister spoke were so completely different they couldn't understand each other. She couldn't stop thinking about it and had blurted out her astonishment in catechism class. The instructor explained, "City people, small-town people, plantation people, and the people who dwell in the forests of our county have had such harsh lives that they've developed complexes, which imprison them even today." She hadn't yet learned what complexes were, but at least he'd offered some explanation of why guests from the plantation never spoke. And when she heard her mother Bee talking a mile a minute with her other guests, she couldn't do anything other than offer a comforting smile. "Complexes" came to mean something like not being able to put into words what really matters, for fear you might never be able to stop crying. Did she have that problem too? At the same time, she'd noticed more and more soldiers patrolling downtown. She often stood gawking in dismay at the heavy military vehicles, fast jeeps, and motorcycles with sidecars. Winston had told her about the bloodshed: millions of people dying in countries overseas. Their country couldn't be dragged into a war, though, because it had nothing to offer and nothing to defend. Suriname was a country to flee to. A country of refuge. There was aluminum and bauxite, but not where you could get to it. There was gold and hardwood. For the trade in these commodities, teams of workers were hired and supervised by the military. Her father Anton, after a few drinks, had been persuaded to explain a few things considered state secrets. Dutch soldiers were collecting gold from creeks and tributaries deep in the Amazon forest, where even nomads didn't like to stay too long, and shipping the raw gold to Holland, where their countrymen smelted it into bars that they stored in their bank vaults. Her father said, "We can't discuss this with anyone, as a matter of military honor. Wars cost not only human lives, but also unfathomable sums of money." She could still hear him saying it. Winston summed it up frankly. "Pa, Suriname

203

is involved in what's happening in Europe. What do you think all those troops from abroad are doing over here?" And she went to bed with all this sensitive information and woke up to it again in the morning. Her homeland was Holland's territory, so they too were at war. She'd sign up at the base as soon as she turned twenty. The thought cheered her up. Among the girls and young women, there was a popular war song, and whenever she could, she sang along: *Farewell, farewell, for sad to tell, I cannot take you with me, I'll love you truly, My brown-skinned beauty, My heart longs only for you.* The move to Jacobusrust went smoothly. Their own furniture was there, polished to a gleam. The dolls had a place in the display case. Winston was engaged to a pretty city girl and would soon be married. She'd rarely felt this cheerful. She'd been accepted into the colonial army. And then she saw Gordon.

Early in the morning before the rooster had started to crow, she lay awake thinking about the nameplate on her door: LOUISE VANTA. Sometimes, dreams nudged her out of sleep. The gigantic bird showing up regularly in her dreams seemed to her to be a messenger, even if she couldn't puzzle out whether it was bringing her messages from the past or from the future. They came naturally, these fragments of memories and events, premonitions. She didn't have anyone close enough to share her deepest thoughts with. Besides, she was afraid that kind of person might try to teach her things that didn't fit her way of life. She hadn't been raised to seek aid from the gods of water, wind, and sky. Her father said sternly, "What you can't see doesn't exist." And then her mother would chime in, telling her we have senses to understand what surrounds us. It was a lighthearted, carefree way to grow up. She didn't plan to go into science and think beyond her senses. Since the journey to Paramaribo, Bee had decided her girls would become teachers and nothing else. Winston could work only at a trading company, since the prospect of making big money drew him like a magnet. And only after they'd been living in the city for a while did it finally dawn on her that her mother didn't see her daughters as future housewives and maybe not even as future mothers. Weren't there any charming young men to be found for Bee's nubile daughters? One Sunday after church, her father, in his church suit in someone else's living room, sat on the stool of an unplayable piano, gazing through the open windows out into the street as if pondering the sermon. At the table after her mother said grace, he'd say flatly, "Bee, I'm not religious, drop all that praying when I'm around." But her mother wouldn't. And sometimes he'd erupt into a slow, loud declaration: "All over the world, good young men in uniform are dying in wars they don't understand, so I should be grateful to your father for pairing me with you and protecting me from being deployed to some terrible foreign place." Then her mother would nod, saying proudly, "My father was a God-fearing man, Anton Vanta." And Bee would repeat this in a mixture of languages and a variety of ways. She would keep quiet, and so would Winston and Laura, as they enjoyed all the special treats at the Sunday lunch. It hadn't escaped her how openly people would stare at the Vantas in and after church. Her brother Winston would collect donations with a poker face. "We're not black, and we're not white," he would sometimes say, meaning that the Vanta-Julienne family didn't belong anywhere, not in the black church and not with the white-robed Catholics. And then their father would lose his temper: "Nonsense, Winston, you're both, whether you like it or not, and treat these values as your start-up capital, because I don't have anything more to offer you." At the table, talking back was forbidden. Even Winston kept his mouth shut tight. And she would pull little Rogier out of his highchair into her lap and feed him patiently.

On one such enervating day of rest, Mother's brother Léon came by after lunch with their brother Scott's twin daughters. Bee was so happy she couldn't stop hugging her brother and the girls, and they talked in their family's mixture of languages until her father Anton invited her mother's brother out to the backyard to play bingo under the extended awning while sharing the bottle of gin Léon had brought. Every now and then, Léon would stumble inside to pee and stop for a brief chat with his sister Bee about family matters. He let her know how work was progressing on the space station in French Guiana, a project in which their father had once been involved. A place to launch rockets into the sky. He always said, "You should go out at night once in a while to look at the stars in the sky, Bee." Inside, the children raced through the rooms, enjoying the thrill of hearing the wide stairs to the bedrooms groan under their weight. They were allowed to go all over the house, but their parents kept loudly reminding them of the rules: "These things belong to white strangers, so keep them clean!" The former occupants were a sergeant major, his Jewish wife, and their four children, who'd emigrated to the United States. At breakneck speed. They never returned to their house on Tafelmanstraat. After some years, they renounced their rights to their furnishings, donating them to the new occupants of their house. For her mother and father, the letter arrived too late; the family had just moved to Jacobusrust. Winston had gone to see who the new residents were. He found a Lebanese family who didn't speak a word of Dutch or English and were also on the run. In the shower, early in the morning, whatever had been stirred up by sleep and dreams would slide off her like water. Some remnant always clung to her skin, like gold dust she'd see sparkling out of the corner of her eye. Whatever it was would influence her mood for days. That didn't bother her; she loved the children entrusted to her in her professional capacity and at home. No one had anything to fear from her. Not even when anger seeped into her heart like pus.

He'd arranged everything for her. The rental agreement. The moving truck. He'd made sure the electricity was connected and the water turned on. After some discussion with Babs's father, the man she'd left, he'd even gotten her a set of keys to the big yellow house, so that she could pick up furniture and anything else she thought she needed. He'd sent two Maroon women to the rental house with spray bottles and chemicals to scrub it clean because it had been empty for years; the owner had resisted renting it out for a long time. He had drummed up two Hindustani construction workers with painting experience to paint the wood floors dark green and install carpeting where she wanted it. He'd also had a new toilet put in. And when she moved in with her four children, she'd lost twenty pounds, not because the only thing she ate was salted cod sandwiches he brought her during his lunch break, but because she was consumed with fear of living alone with her four children in a rental house where she and not her husband had the keys to the front door. He'd supervised as one of his employees installed a new lock in the front door and offered her two of the three keys, telling her he'd keep the third in a safe at his office. But she wanted all three, so he gave her his copy as well. As yet another surprise, he'd hauled off her old bike and brought her a new woman's bike, with a child seat for her boy who was going on two so she could take him along to work. She knew he was going through hard times, too. His wife wanted a divorce and had gone home to her mother's, taking the children. At work, others were after his job. He hadn't told her himself, but she'd heard from her little sister Laura that the man that his wife was leaving him for was jet-black, and the man who might get his job was a blond Dutchman, fresh off the boat from the Netherlands. Sometimes his problems kept her awake and she forgot her own. One day she found a babysitter who could look after little Audi when necessary. Riding her bike in traffic with such a young child every day had proved to be no picnic; he was often tired and cranky, sometimes crying the whole ride through until she got to school, slid the bike into the bike rack, and took him in her arms. Audi needed a babysitter close to home. The neighbor had spoken to her and even offered her services. They had agreed on an amount, and it seemed like a done deal. Heli and Imker found their way by bus to the Catholic girls' school on the other side of town. Babs's private school sent a taxi for her. There was nothing to fear. In the evening, after putting the whole passel to bed, she took a long shower. What a relief to finally stretch out on a Friday like that, with the prospect of two days off in the company of her children. She could take the time to look them in the eyes, touch their feet and hands, listen to their voices, and check the teeth in their fresh, clean mouths. That would help to reassure her that all four had truly developed out of her body into beings that belonged nowhere but with her. Somewhere in the middle of these thoughts, she must have fallen asleep. She jolts awake. He is lying with his full weight on top of her, and the heat of her longing for pleasure courses through her body like a burning flame, and she pants with him. She wants to feel him grow hard in her hands. She wants him in her mouth. She wants him in her womb. She wants him everywhere, hard and deep and persistent, and she rolls with him in a dance that mustn't end. Don't stop, don't stop, their voices sigh into each other's ears as she feels him squirt semen inside her with powerful thrusts, exploding into her vagina. My god, how can this pleasure end, unless it kills her? A scream gurgles up from the depths of her throat, climbing into her mouth, surging out of her body like the slimy gobs of sperm she sees gleaming in the twilight through her tears. Then she hears her daughter's voice beside her bed. He jumps up. He flees her body, her room, her house. She's still shivering as the door to the house slams shut and locks. Heli looks at her, saying, "Uncle Winston was hurting you, Mama!" She gets up and strikes the girl in the face with all her might. The whites of Heli's eyes break. For weeks, she keeps seeing the ruptured capillaries in her daughter's eyes. And when her period stopped and waves of slime were shooting out of her mouth every morning, she cried as she'd never cried before in her life. She opened the Bible to Psalms. Her son was the first to wish her a good morning as she sat at the kitchen table studying a passage. She looked up, smiling at him, and asked if he'd slept well. She called him back over to her so she could look him in the eyes. He approached, his towel still around his neck, his hair wet. He smelled like bath soap. She examined him longer than the others to make sure his eyes were still perfectly white, despite all the soccer heading. "Is something wrong, Mama?" She nodded her head yes. "I'll shape you into a good brother to your sisters, Audi, and a good father to your children." He laughed a little and glanced at the big book next to her. She went on, "And what's left will be pure gold for the woman you love." Her son only half-understood her muttered words. She slammed the Bible shut. What had happened couldn't be prayed away but couldn't be permitted to repeat itself. She got up and opened the curtains. Is every day really a new day? Louise wasn't sure. All she knew was that it was high time again to put breakfast on the table.

Since Audi was two years younger than most of his middle school classmates, he'd had to work hard, again, to be accepted by the big boys. And they gave him tough jobs to do, not with his hands but with his head. But when it came to girls, he was dead last in the ranking, which was all about who was oldest and tallest and had the biggest muscles. The problem was that the big boys' girlfriends liked to invite him over to their houses to show their parents they were still innocent. He didn't understand what the big boys meant when they said, *I'm going to pop her cherry one day.* However hard he tried, he couldn't see any difference between girls who'd had their cherries popped and girls who hadn't. When he went to Heli for guidance, she promised him a book with the answers to all his questions. He read *Dotted Lines for Boys* several times, voraciously, and got the gist of what the big boys meant. At his all-boys' middle school downtown, all the things he'd learned about his body at the age of ten had made him kind of a prude, instead of the innocent baby he'd been before. Two years later, with a group of his classmates, he looked at pictures in dirty magazines that caused blood to rush to his head and down below. It cost a dime to enjoy a peek at something they had to hide from the priests who taught them. Even though he still wore the robes of an altar boy at family Mass each Sunday at the church in Amora, his soul was no longer snow white but stained. Confessing would have cost him his ten-cent joys, so he kept quiet and rigidly followed all the other rules at school. That was how he reached the top of his class. He knew that ever since Heli had moved abroad, he and no one else was the standard bearer of his mother's household.

He quickly showered, threw on his clothes, and bolted down his breakfast so he wouldn't be in Babs's way; then she might let him catch a ride into town with her in her school taxi. Babs couldn't make Mama laugh the way he did, but she had a dad with dough, and the difference was plain to see—she was moody in the morning and not inclined to make things easy for her family. He packed up his things, went to kiss his mother goodbye, calling as loud as possible, "Babs, I'm leaving." He waited a minute for her response. Didn't get one. He would walk to school. Maybe someone he knew would happen to see him and offer a ride. He saved the bus money Mother gave him for his ten-cent joys. The hardened dirt road along which the houses stood in a row, the fenced yards, a guard dog barking at him, a girl staring at him—one fine day, he'd drive out of his own garage down his own driveway, leaving a villa in which his own wife was expecting his own child, and he'd look back and wave at her. On the wide, asphalt road, his thoughts turned to Mama's dog that was run over. He hadn't managed to find a puppy for her yet. Thinking of his sister Heli, he picked up his pace. "Au! Audi!" Babs's voice. He looked up. She was standing beside the school taxi beckoning him. He ran over to her. "Get in," she ordered, letting him go first. Then she slid in next to him, wrapping an arm around him without saying a word. The people he saw through the front windshield looked livelier, cleaner, friendlier than they did from a crowded minibus. He felt the wind and, taking a deep breath, looked through the side window toward the sky. His eyes welled with tears as he realized his future would have to be in this country, close to the people who loved him. He snuggled up to Babs a little. They dropped him off downtown. "Thanks, Babsie." She smiled and said, "Do your best, kiddo." Happy, he strolled on. The schoolyard was dead quiet. He was much too early, but the cleaning crew had left the study halls open. He snuck inside. It smelled like bleach, and with each breath he took in the peace and quiet. He shrugged off his back-pack full of books and stationed himself at a corner table far from the entrance so he could see what rolled into the schoolyard and who might join him in the study hall. Some time to consider the question on his mind. For one, his biology teacher was a gorgeous woman, and anyway, he couldn't ask a question like his in a classroom full of horny teenage boys. He decided that in his future studies he would focus on subjects that would bring him closer to the answer. He grabbed his planner and a pen, jotting down in big letters, *Why is it that the genitalia of species that reproduce sexually fit together so precisely yet still show so much variation?* He erased and erased until he got the question right. *It's thanks to God*, Blaasbalg would say, but the "hot chick" who taught genetics had already mentioned the word "evolution." Some boys had laughed scornfully. He'd felt like cheering. There was something about animal and human reproduction that mesmerized him. He didn't know exactly what. It started with the reproductive organs. The schoolyard filled up with people. Every boy walking there was the result of sexual activity. It made him chuckle. Planner in bag. Time to head outside. He knew exactly what he'd grow up to be: a rich man who did research in his free time, to figure out the things he wanted to know before he died. But how do you get rich in a poor community? Outside, he found his classmates by the bike racks. He ran over to them to catch a glimpse of something that would make his animal blood surge to his brain. He looked. No vulva to be seen. Dirty pictures of a different kind: older guys doing it with boys. It scared him, and he ran off to the peddlers by the gate to find something sweet. "Cornmeal pudding, please," he said to the woman's bright black face. She filled a paper cup for him, adding a dash of vanilla milk.

"Here you go," she said. Audi took the cup. Amused, he placed his dime in the palm of her hand.

"Can I talk to you for a minute?" Babs looked up. It was Derik, the program director, approaching hesitantly. She stayed put, looking him straight in the eye. "Talk to me? About what?" He scratched his chin gingerly, glancing around. "About Heli, your dear sister." She blew her top. "I'm not Heli, I'm not my mother, I'm not the woman you're married to, I don't want anything to do with your affairs, I don't want to be bothered, I'm just here to graduate from this program!" Derik strode off without another word. She remained planted there, with the feeling that what had just happened was all in her head. But she could still see Derik, heading for the administrative office. He really had come up to her. He had started the conversation. Above her head, she saw yellow blossoms flickering against the blue of the sky. It wasn't the butter yellow of the house where she'd been conceived, come into the world, and horsed around with her father. The blossoms were masala yellow with an orange interior to attract bees. Her mother led a privileged life in their creamy yellow house, because she had a man who met all her material needs. And even though Boyce had a wife with children who were getting older, he felt at home with her mother Louise. She walked to gym as slowly as possible but had no interest in running around. Her school friends were waiting for the gym teacher. "You're quiet today," one of them remarked. She nodded. "Are you coming up with an excuse to skip gym today, Babs?" said another. She nodded again. "Don't say you're having your period again, because

214

then he'll make you participate anyway, that womanizer."
They laugh. She doesn't. Her period? No! The run-in with
Derik had rattled her. She was so mad at him. It was his
fault that everything at home was so different now. Even
fried eggs tasted different, and her mother was no longer
the same woman. Her father had assured her there was
no fighting it. Her mother, Louise, remained friendly and
stunningly attractive even when she was withering away
on the inside. He'd been through it and finally agreed to
separate because letting her go would keep her healthy.
Her mother, sick with grief? Was he crazy? The week
before, Boyce had taken her to the bank to take care of
some business and then driven her to the big yellow house.
The yard was overgrown, and the house looked deserted.
No one lived there. It was still Boyce's property. She
didn't want to look inside. As Boyce gazed at the house,
he announced, "I know exactly who your little brother's
father is and also that it wasn't your mother's choice." At
that moment, she'd asked nothing, said nothing, kept her
mouth shut, but the news hit her hard. Over dinner on
Saturday at his usual restaurant, she'd brought up the subject again, asking him not to reveal what he knew to anyone but Audi himself. "When the time is right," Boyce
replied. She trusted him. He'd always kept his word. The
gym teacher asked whether she was planning to join their
baseball game. Maybe he'd noticed she seemed to have
no intention of following the others into the locker room.
He moved in closer and said, "I miss your sister. Tell her
I said hello the next time you write to her." And he left
her alone. She could hear the girls' excited voices. The
boys laughed loudly, maybe over nothing. Everyone loved
the gym teacher. She didn't. She loved her father and

no other man. Her classmates ran onto the sports field, whooping and shouting. Babs waved at them and took a seat on the bleachers. Watching. Waiting. And day-dreaming, of course.

Kolera sent word to Doctor Albert that Laura could go to Zorg en Hoop for one day but not until the week after her birthday. She and Grandmother took the news in stride. They would visit Laura together with lots of goodies and tell her she could come home for a day. A birthday present? "Maybe she'll refuse," Albert warned, having heard that Laura preferred not to show herself outside the facility walls. Grandma saw that very differently: her daughter didn't want to be driven out in an ambulance, but to leave the hospital well dressed and not reeking of the institutional kitchen. And as a mother, Bee had never been able to demand all that of Kolera, because of her categorical refusal to speak with experts about Laura's condition. And she, as the granddaughter and niece of the people involved, could completely understand the sources of their suffering now that she'd met Laura for herself. She wondered if her grandmother still remembered what it was like when Laura was first taken away. "Have a seat, dear child." And Grandma went to find her tobacco box. And an ashtray too. It seemed they wouldn't have this conversation at the kitchen table but in the living room, with her grandmother on the sofa for greater physical comfort. First a cigar, and after taking a couple of puffs and blowing a lot of smoke, she said, "Imker, all that's left are scraps of memory, you know." She felt uneasy and kept saying, "It doesn't have to be now, Grandma." Grandmother sighed and let out a controlled cough. This was how it began: "My daughter came to tell me, with her father there beside me, that my brother Léon had behaved inappropriately with her when she was still a child. I went crazy with rage." "What was so inappropriate, Grandma?" "He'd touched her where he shouldn't have and had done the same thing to Scott's twins." "And what did Grandfather do when he heard about all this?" "Your grandfather said, 'Good thing Ethel didn't have to go through this.' But Anton did so much more than that! From then on, the sight of Léon made him sick." For a moment, her grandmother seemed to have reached the limits of her openheartedness. "What happened next?" she boldly encouraged her. Grandmother managed to add that she'd made Laura out to be a liar, screaming and cursing. "Léon? Impossible. Laura's lying!" Grandma could still hear herself raging. "One Good Friday. We'd done the Stations of the Cross at the downtown church together, Laura and I. When we got home, my daughter fell apart." Grandma paused, sunk in thought. Laura had fled the house and was still gone when night fell, was that right? The next time Bee saw her daughter again was at the military hospital, and no one could say what was wrong with her. "Dear Imker, my beautiful daughter sat staring into space without saying a word for months, and when she started talking again, it was to someone no one could see... And years went by. She still barely speaks to people at Kolera. Sometimes, she starts a conversation with me, and these days she talks to you too, Imker." Grandma continued puffing away, no longer speaking. As if everything had been said. She wondered what the point of the story was. Grandmother's scraps of memory and the cigar smoke fogged her mind. She remembered her mother talking to her, Babs, and Heli one rainy afternoon at the kitchen table, and she hadn't realized back then that it was actually about Laura. No one had permission to touch them underneath their clothes, her mother said, and their own hands shouldn't touch other people underneath their clothes. This talk was later repeated for their little brother's benefit. "Only one person in this house is sexually mature, and that's me, your mother." Once a month, her mother reminded her what they had to defend and protect as long as they lived—their bodies. On New Year's Eve, Louise took each child aside and checked if there'd been any incidents in the past year. Then she threw away their old underwear and gave each of them a new stack. Grandma listened to her tale with bated breath. Eyes narrowed to slits, she said in a halting voice, "Yes, Louise would have liked to cobble together a life partner for each of you, as God the Creator did for the world when He gave Adam an Eve, but that worked out badly, Imker." She sucked her teeth in disapproval. Her energy unflagging, Grandma clarified, "Your mother would be happiest marrying you all off to young men of her choice, and who can blame her?" But she had a more urgent question. "Grandma Bee, do you believe your brother Léon abused your daughter Laura?" No answer. "Imker, I can't help Laura." Then Imker leaned her head against her grandmother's forehead. "Grandma, are you in pain?" Her grandmother rasped, "Yes. My Laura was such a cheerful little thing."

Grandmother had gotten so light that she could be carried to the van. But she objected, saying walking wasn't a problem yet. Rogier's school friend made light of it, whistling as he carried a bucket of ginger beer, a bucket of almond drink, and white cake boxes filled with warm chicken turnovers to the cargo van. He was borrowing the van from a friend, he explained. And after he'd loaded the birthday provisions and Grandmother, dressed for the party, had come to the front gate of her house, he lifted her up in his arms with a flourish and placed her next to him in front. She climbed into the back with ease, also wearing an eye-catching floral dress. She and Grandmother had been on the go for the past few days, getting everything ready in time, and in between cooking and baking, they'd sat quietly on the patio, exchanging smiles, sometimes with a tear. "I hope she wears her new dress and smells nice." Dr. Albert loudly laughed off her grandmother's distress. She kept an eye on the party supplies, so that nothing would fall over. Albert suggested, "How about if we sing happy birthday as we carry the snacks inside?" Grandma had something else in mind. "Dr. Albert shouldn't come inside with us. He should never be seen with us." Albert thought this was a "grand idea" and promised to arrange it all with the guard. They looked out through the windows, all a little nervous, at the city center barreling by. It would have been better if her mother Louise had been there with Babs and Audi. It would have felt more like a real party if the purpose of the trip had been to take Laura away from a place where she could never feel safe and cared for. When she saw the palm grove, her heart began to race. Grandmother was crying audibly, worried she'd find her daughter medicated into a stupor, even though Albert had promised he wouldn't allow it. Grandmother thought Albert had too much confidence in his own clout, but Albert held his ground, promising that the medical director wasn't as much of a fool as he seemed and was happy to do them a favor. Even so, he looked tense as he drove through the gate. Stopped the van. Got out and went up to the guard. They talked. Without another word, the man in the khaki uniform took a seat behind the wheel and brought the vehicle right up to the doors of the visitors' hall. Two nurses came to meet them. Laura was nowhere to be found. Imker helped Grandmother out of the van, walking inside with her up the four-step staircase. They spotted her at the same time. Laura sat in a decorated chair at her regular table in her new dress, with her hair carefully trimmed and new sandals on her feet. Not staring into space but gazing with a smile at her mother, who'd begun humming a song of praise. The guard unloaded the van, with help from the nurses. She saw garlands and balloons all around the dining hall and realized it had been kept empty to give Laura some time alone with her mother Bee. She hung back, letting Grandma go on to where Laura sat waiting. And suddenly, a voice, loud and clear, "Are you taking me with you, Ma?" That night, everything that had happened kept looping through her mind. She had the feeling that Laura had understood how frail her mother Bernadette had become. And even if Laura was out of her mind, she knew better than anyone the difference between her radiant mother and the woman who stood at the table beside her, humming and humming. Someone had put on music, very soft. The other patients were let in, and she helped the nurses serve drinks in paper cups and snacks on napkins. The women were mostly quiet. They polished off the food they were served and lingered in the hall, staring at Laura and her mother. It was as if they, like her, wanted to see the impossible happen—Laura taking her mother's arm and walking off through the gate and out of sight forever. As if they were thinking, *If one of us can escape, maybe any of us could be freed one day.* It was such a disconcerting experience. Kolera in a party mood? Imker wondered if Dr. Albert had slipped her grandmother a sedative, because Grandma was clearly in a state of profound calm.

Someone calls to me from the living room: Rogier, who's visiting Lya and Winston. Rogier's wife Wonny is there too, well into her pregnancy, their first. I take a seat on a barstool slightly away from the group and wait. Winston is sipping whisky. Rogier takes the initiative. "My mother is terribly sick, most likely dying from smoking cigars and chewing tobacco." I listen as he claims he doesn't exactly know what's wrong with my grandmother. He tells us the disease is in her throat and could spread to her vocal cords, her tongue, her whole mouth. "The pain may become intolerable." He's not speaking as her son but as a physician. Yet it's still evident how shaken he is. "Winston and I will need to go to Paramaribo before the end of the year, and after that...?" I let my eyes drift across the walls, seeing for the first time what's on display there, such as a wood carving of our country's coat of arms. I don't feel sorrow but bitterness as I ask, "Has either of you called Grandma?" The response comes from Lya: "Yes, you should write and tell her you'd like to call." No reaction from the brothers. Lya's face turns red. "So you'll go there to see her and she'll be on her deathbed and then what?" It's Wonny's voice saying this, and she continues, "You two say goodbye and leave her in the hands of dear Imker?" Rogier shoots out of his chair. "My mother has to go to a hospital, and I'll see that she does." His voice sounds composed, but his hands are balled into fists. I say, "Rogier, your mother doesn't want to go to the hospital." He looks at me in silence. "We're not going to force her," Winston says, clearly nervous and trying to smooth things over. Then he asks if we need a stiff drink as much as he does. "Not me," I reply, my voice a little too loud, and I hop off the stool, saying, "First, you two go abroad and pretty much abandon her to her fate, and then from over here, you're trying to control her life in Zorg en Hoop. Which one of you ever asked Grandma what she felt or what she wanted?" And off I go. I stop in the kitchen, looking at the bottle on the cabinet. The orgeat syrup glows in the lamp light, uncompromisingly off-white, so deliciously sweet, smooth, and aromatic. Rogier calls me back and comes to find me. He says with emotion, "The thing is, when we leave, if she's dying at home, or maybe in a hospital, will we be able to say goodbye to her while she's still responsive? And then leave her behind on her deathbed just because we can't bear to stick around? I don't know what to do, Heli, I really don't." I walk back with him to the living room. Rogier and I understand each other. He says, "I don't want my mother to suffer agonizing pain and become horribly disfigured and waste away under terrible conditions." And I say, "Even so, we owe it to her to do as she wishes, and once she can't endure it anymore, then death will deliver her from her agony, right?" I don't tell him that when I said goodbye to her at the airport, Grandma explained to me in detail how sick she was and that she was sure she'd never see me again, and I asked if I could pass on a message to her sons in Holland, and she shook her head no and just cried and cried. I say timidly, "I'm sorry, but I don't have anything else to say." In the foyer, I grab my coat and go out into the fading sunlight, into the streets, my hands in my pockets, where I feel my keys and a handkerchief. The air crisp and tender against my cheeks. The houses draped in the stillness of an autumn evening. Hans has asked me to come to his house for tea sometime, because his parents are so curious about me. Maybe his invitation is an opening into a community I'm not familiar with. Do it? A dinner date with Catie tomorrow at the diner. There's no one at the bus stop. A couple walk past arm in arm. That's the spirit! I walk back to the others, but I don't want to. I have to. It's vital that no one but Grandma Bee choose the hour of her death.

Laura would have been the first Vanta to travel so far from home. The first to bring a Dutch person into the family. At first, Laura was thrilled about the prospect of traveling to join her fiancé, but when the time came for her to go, she refused. Years later, she was found on a bench on the waterfront, staring out at the harbor. No one could persuade her to get up and go, not even at midnight. She wouldn't speak. Her behavior started to attract attention, and as the story goes, she was "gently forced" to leave. And locked away. Her father and mother were stunned and dismayed. My mother and her brother lived in worry.

And shame. The change in their little sister rolled into the city like something horrible. Something no one could find words for. My grandparents' house fell apart. Every one of their children was trapped in a nightmare. Winston was fighting to keep his head above water in a turbulent divorce. Louise was pregnant again. Rogier suffered a nasty break below the knee playing basketball. No one knew how much they all were suffering until Laura fell apart right at the dock where they'd first arrived in the city. I watched my mother vomit into the sink each morning. I would wake with a start to the sound of retching. In my dreams, I heard Laura's voice asking to be let inside. I found Uncle Winston's socks under Mother's bed and hid them. I dreamed Rogier had lost his legs. And in between dreams, I stood guard by day over Imker, Babs, and our beautiful baby brother. Mother didn't mind that I was there when my grandfather's sister came by to say that the family was planning a Winti séance, with all the bells and whistles, in an attempt to turn the tide for the Vantas. "Not for me," my mother Louise insisted, and she walked away from the conversation. Mama later grumbled, "What a load of bullshit." And said to me directly, "Don't even think about it, child." My last visit to Grandma Bee on my own, before I left Paramaribo, was unforgettable. A final farewell? She gave me letters to take with me, sent from Holland and addressed to Laura Vanta. Never opened. Grandmother hopes I'll visit Bram's family. I know his address by heart. Now I've figured out how to get there, too. I want to go. But I don't dare. A residential area somewhere on the outskirts of Apeldoorn. Invite Hans along? Talk to Cate? I sit on the bed, brooding. Fresh outdoor air works miracles. After my walk around the block, I feel revitalized. I hear Rogier and his wife walking to their car. They can't see me standing here behind the lace curtains. I turn out the light. Rogier looks at the window of my room. His wife keeps him on a short leash, according to Winston: "One day, my little brother will wrestle free." *She loves him a lot*, I think, *anyone can see that*. Their car drives slowly down the street. I turn the lights in my room back on.

Grandma Bee had never considered baptisms import-ant. Her children hadn't inherited any burden of sin, so they never made a fuss about the event. Making children members of a religious community was always risky, but they could make a different choice later. She and Anton agreed about that much. So when her husband's half-brother left his plantation to come tell her that the "bad blood" of her English forefathers was festering in their children because they'd forced Africans into slavery, and that the bad blood could be washed away in rituals where they'd ask the "spirits of nature" for absolution, she was against it. How could she and her children have anything to do with events on plantations nearly a century ago? And just as that fellow was stuttering in broken Dutch, count on Anton to show up in a shabby army uniform. "My sister Bee, did you not also wash your children clean of original sin with baptismal water because Adam and Eve did naughty things according to that priest of yours?" Her husband's half-brother was trying to remind her of things no one would say to her face, things that certainly had happened—slave whippings, disfigurements, rape, murder. Grandma lacked the skills to enter into debate with a plantation man about colonial times, so again, her husband Anton bore the brunt of her outrage. Mixing the languages of her parental home, she gave him an unforgettable verbal thrashing. "My children and I have nothing to do with slavery, and neither do you, Anton!" And Anton had looked at her with his enormous eyes, the whites shining like German porcelain in his black face, and said soothingly, "You and I don't have much more to offer our children than this backward coastal city, because we have no money and no land and no family reaching far enough into the past to cushion our children if we let them fall through the cracks. And Bee, my dear wife, that has everything to do with slavery." And he personally sent his half-brother back to the Winti clan with the message that no bathwater of any kind, no forest herbs of any kind, no food, no drum, no dance, no deity of any kind would be able to assuage the pain of slavery, because only time could do that, and "time" is another word for "the future." He said the same thing to his granddaughter Heli when she got her teaching license. She had been so surprised to learn that there was at least one grandchild Anton adored. No, no, no one would bring idolatry into the home of Anton Vanta. His children's condition? Rogier's leg needed time to heal completely. Winston had married a girl that he couldn't provide for adequately, because even after five healthy children, she'd left him all alone and dirt poor. Louise didn't know how a woman was supposed to live in a city whose men would always seem foreign, because her parents were outsiders. But what Louise lost, she turned into a win for her children. And Laura? Anton believed Laura had an unfathomable dislike of her own beauty. Unfathomable? Bee had already left Anton when

Heli came to tell her that a deep conversation with her grandfather had done more for her than any fortune could. And Rogier had been born in Paramaribo, without any memories of Nickerie, she thought. A city boy through and through. And what came of that? Right, he was in a distant country for training as a medical specialist, and she'd never see his children, let alone get to know them. And Winston's children? Lost to the wind. Plucked out of the earth of her being, like pups of a mother plant, ready to grow and thrive anywhere. She wiped away tears. She wanted to see all her grandchildren scampering around her. Had she done something wrong? It was as her confessor had told her. "You, Bernadette Vanta-Julienne, have walked the straight and narrow, and that is a remarkable feat the world over." Sweet consolation? She missed hoofing it each day to the main church in the busy heart of the city. She missed incense and brass polish. The pews by the figure of Saint Anthony. Perhaps she asked too much of her God. Perhaps she asked too often. She'd never asked Him to take away her pain, which circulated like hot cooking oil from her uvula to her tongue, setting her head on fire. No, she turned to her cigars for that, sending herself up in smoke. Imker was right. There hadn't been any need to bombard Almighty God with the same prayer three times each day for years. But what else did she have to offer than the measured words of saints? She hadn't been asleep on the sofa, as Imker probably thought. She got up. The closing theme rang out, announcing the end of the radio day. Imker was sitting close by. "Shall I turn it off, Grandma?" She nodded. "Anything else I can do for you, Grandma?" She nodded again, as if afraid the heat in her throat would melt her vocal cords. She went to the kitchen, grabbed a notepad and pencil, and wrote, *Imker, I'll teach you how to bake a fiadu. It's not easy, but it's my favorite kind of cake.* She slid it over to Imker. "Sounds good, Grandma. As soon as the stores open again, I'll go pick up everything you need." But she shook her head, writing, *I want to do it now, with whatever we have in the house, because maybe I won't be around when the stores open.* Imker's eyes grew moist, but she said evenly, "All right, then, Grandma, now." But in a blink of Imker's eyes, she was lying face down with her head against the kitchen tabletop. She wasn't sleeping. She'd let herself slip into something even more sublime than her favorite cake. According to her granddaughter, it had only lasted for a few minutes; to her, it felt like an eternity. Imker stood before her, afraid. The pain in her throat, tongue, and head had completely vanished. She spoke to Imker, "Imker, I'm slowly going to God, will you stay with me until I'm gone completely?" She had her voice back, but she sounded different. Her granddaughter came closer. Hugged her tight with both arms as if she were a small child. It calmed her, but she wriggled out of it. It was so good to have sampled how her death might taste. She felt sure there was still enough time to bake her fiadu. And Grandma Bee wanted to enjoy it with this granddaughter.

Her sister Babs had perfect timing. She heard the lock rattle at the gate to Grandmother's house. "Imker, are you here?" "Babs?" Imker flew to the front door to let her little sister in. She threw the gate open with delight on her face. "Smells like something good is baking."

Babs said, nodding to the taxi driver that he could go. "May I come in?" She nodded. She struggled to hold back tears and keep a smile plastered on her face as she held her arms open wide for a hug, so Babs would know how much she'd missed her. Inside, she took her sister to the kitchen, where the fiadu was on display on a crystal cake platter, cooling off for their grandmother. Gesturing at the bedroom, she whispered "Ssshhh" in Babs's ear, adding, "Grandma talked me through how to make it, and now she's sleeping after a restless night." Babs nodded, following her back into the living room to let their grandmother rest, and asked, "How long do I have to wait to taste how yours turned out?" But she was on the go again with crushed ice, glasses, coasters, and a shaker, and she poured orgeat for them, white as milk and savory as fresh almonds. While they drank it, they glanced at each other. "Good stuff." Babs finally took a good look around, saying, "The perfect setup for Grandma." Imker just nodded, setting the glass down, searching for words to talk about their grandmother, to be close to her sister without betraying her grandmother's secret. "Wait here," and she went to see how Grandma was doing. Bee was asleep on her back with her mouth hanging open as if she were hungry. "She doesn't eat much anymore," she whispered to Babs, and she stared at the pretty fiadu, made out of rolls of buttery dough and colorful candied fruit soaked in liqueur. "My fiadu should be as brown as my daughter Louise," Grandmother had cautioned as she slid the cake into the preheated oven to cook. And she and her little sister sat together again, with homemade shortbread cookies and a container of cheese sables for her to take with her. "You must make sure Mama comes to see Grandma, today, tomorrow, the day after, as soon as possible, because Grandma misses her so much." Babs jumped up, asking, "Shall I go back to Amora right away?" Her cheeks were flushed red. She shook her head, saying, "Mama never lets anyone rush her, so stay with us for a while, then you might have a chance to talk to Grandma." Babs paced around and then sat down again. "I missed you so bad all of a sudden that by the time the first break came around I just had to cut class. And I'd already sat out gym class, and Derik had ruined my whole day first thing in the morning." An awkward silence fell between them. Would they talk about Heli? Grandmother had received a big postcard and a signed letter from their sister and placed it under her pillow, explaining, "I want to enjoy it first without knowing what it says, and then I'll enjoy it again when I read it." "That's Grandma," they both mumbled at the same time. Babs, still not quite over her irritation about the incident at school, tripped over her words as she told the story. "Heli was sent away, but she's still haunting us, Imker." She wholeheartedly agreed. "What's new with you, then?" Babs said Boyce had promised her a car of her own, and oh, she just couldn't keep quiet about it: Boyce knew Audi's father. They looked each other straight in the eye without another word, until her little sister said something even bolder: "And now I want to know how a sweetheart like you could have a mother like ours." Again, their eyes locked in dead silence. Even without speaking, she remained an attentive hostess, setting out more tasty things to eat and drink, and as she gazed at the browned cake, she thought, *I'd rather not have a father at all*. She walked over to the cake and put a dome over it, as if defending their mother against her little sister's jabs. Still, she felt like spoiling Babs and suddenly knew how. Pulling her off the sofa, she led her to the kitchen table. She propped the kitchen door wide open and the trade wind breezed in, filling the house with sea air. "What are you going to do?" Babs asked when she tied on an apron. "I'll make nasi goreng for you, entirely Javanese style." Babs started laughing, and asked, "Do you need my help now that Umar isn't around?" She gave her little sister a hug, saying, "Have a seat, kid, and write a nice letter to Grandma." Babs went to do just that, grabbing some chewing gum from her purse, going out across the patio to the yard, leaning against the wall around the property, and staring pensively into the house. She put on the rice, thinking about her job at the fabric store and her Saturday outings afterward with Umar. She also wondered who she should ask to look after Grandmother on Saturday during her absence. Audi? She discussed it with her little sister, and both felt strongly it shouldn't be Louise. Their mother had the right to sleep in on Saturday mornings and take it easy until she went out that night with Lester. When the school taxi picked Babs up at her grandmother's gate at exactly two o'clock in the afternoon, Grandma was still in bed, and the cake remained untouched. Babs had enjoyed the treats that Imker had served her, had a long talk with her, and left a letter for her "Dear Grandmother Bernadette." Her little sister carefully locked the gate, walked to the taxi, quickly ducked inside, sat down, scooted over to the window, and waved at her. "That's the spirit," Heli would've said. In the kitchen, she found her grandmother looking at the licked-clean plates, seated in the chair where Babs had been. Oh, Grandma. "I didn't want your sister to see me looking like something the cat dragged in," her grandmother explained apologetically. "Babs has a sharp wit, you know." She slid her little sister's letter over to her grandmother. "From Babsie, Grandma." As her grandmother nodded and started reading, she walked to the place where Babs had leaned against the wall, thinking, *There are a thousand and one ways to love, but one thing springs eternal in everyone, including Grandma: the desire to live on in the thoughts of loved ones, even when they're beyond arm's reach, or have passed out of reach altogether.* Grandmother sat, letter in hand. Pensive. Smiling. Then she uncovered the cake and kept her eyes on Grandma until she said, "But Imker, you could've cut the cake for Babs." She stood in the bright sunlight in the doorway and shook her head, saying in her best English, "No, no, my granny first," and then going back to Dutch, "Want a taste? Yes? Now?" A big knife held firmly in her hand, she cut into the cake and placed a rectangular piece on a moss green cake dish, handing it over with a bow. "Here you are, I hope you enjoy it." Grandmother looked and looked and said, "Brown as your mother on the outside, and the inside off-white, like you and me." She poured a splash of sweet condensed milk, heated up the way Grandma liked it, over the cake, and then waited. She hadn't forgotten the pain in Grandmother's throat earlier that day. Grandmother cut a small piece with her fork and brought it to her lips. It took a moment. "Imker, our fiadu is soft like young life. It's bound to turn dry and crusty in time, but so rich, so delicious, as long as it lasts." Delighted, Imker took a piece of cake for herself, chewed, and had to close her eyes in sudden joy.

Could one stroke of bad luck after another make even a mother like Louise Vanta sink so low as to do something that would hurt her children? So profound was Bohr Libretti's empathy for the lives of women in the city that had offered his parents safe haven that he had become a gynecologist. After one too many at a party, he'd confess to the bodily urges that still tormented him every workday, whenever he slid his high stool in front of a "frighteningly beautiful Surinamese fox" lying helplessly on his examination table with her legs spread wide. He'd grown stronger over the years, and now that he'd had various children of his own with various desirable ladies, sex was no longer a necessity for him, more like a possibility. But once he'd set his sights on a woman, his craving would sometimes hound him until he smashed through her boundaries with the force of his male body and his authority as a physician. In Louise's case, he'd apologized outright, then and there. He'd even sworn he would always keep his distance from her and not stay so chummy with Boyce. He'd offered her a sum of money if she'd only forgive him for what had come over him; in her own house, he'd forced her to have sex with him on the bed she shared with Boyce, his only childhood friend and reliable business partner, the father of her youngest child Babs. She'd listened and refused his money, calling him a dirty bastard. Later she found out she was carrying his child. She refused to consider an abortion, so she had to leave the big yellow house behind unexpectedly and return to her childhood home, a dreadful comedown after she'd brought two little girls into the world under her parents' roof. And Babs, Boyce's daughter, born in the yellow house, made three, and now she was pregnant with a fourth and on her own.

And then, after Audi's birth and clashes with her family that took the wind out of her, she'd finally thought she'd found a place of her own, where her girls and baby boy would no longer be confronted with Laura's confusion—but she was sent back to square one. This time she'd have to terminate the pregnancy and fast. Somewhere downtown, a skilled gynecologist had a flourishing practice. And he owed her one.

And when his assistant brought her in, he turned bright red and stared at her, speechless. She waited until the assistant left and, getting straight to the point, let him know she'd come for a "quick, safe abortion." "You? Louise Vanta? An abortion?" His voice cracked. "Yes!" She'd lose her mind otherwise, like her little sister Laura, who'd just been admitted to an asylum. He resisted, insisting that as a doctor, he couldn't terminate a pregnancy except on medical grounds. She warned him he was obligated to help her, and without delay. She'd have to lie on the exam table, he told her, so that he could examine her uterus to find out how far along she was. She hissed, "Bohr Libretti, nine weeks ago, my brother raped me in my own bed, and three years ago, you did the same, so don't lay a finger on me except to rid me of this fetus, promise me now." He took her hands and said, "Louise, I promise." And she went behind a screen to remove her clothing, and then, without hesitation, lay down on the table and spread her legs. Yes, she was pregnant. He helped her get rid of the fetus a week later at his clinic, so she didn't have to spend a single night in the hospital. He performed a D&C, scraping her womb clean and making sure she hardly felt a thing. Two snow-white interns from New York stood next to him. After the surgery, he had her rest for a few hours under his supervision, and afterward, he personally drove her to Dwarsstraat in his own car. He promised she could always count on him. The most important thing he did was introduce her to a variety of contraceptives. Even then, she didn't mention she'd borne him a son.

Babs's news about her mother Bee was enough to make Louise's nerves light up with pain, and the pain was like entrance music for the horror. She wished she could have remained her mother's dream come true, as she'd been until age fifteen, instead of having to become an unwed mother, raising her children on her own. Her sheltered upbringing up to that point had left her too ignorant of the facts of a woman's life to find her way in the complicated community of her coastal city, which was still in the slow process of throwing off the legacy of colonialism. She'd listened to Babs and promised to go to Zorg en Hoop as soon as possible. Had to put up with Babs's whining: "Audi and I will be fine without you, so go tomorrow, right after work." She didn't respond. It was easy for Babs to talk—with a wealthy father and a boyfriend, she'd never lacked for anything. Sleep on it, first, then decide how and when. That was what she always did, and it had never yet brought disaster to her household. "Your mother is lying there almost dead," Babs barked at her. But in the same breath, her daughter apologized for this coarse behavior, "Sorry, Mama, I didn't even get to see Grandma, she was fast asleep after a rough night." She recognized an old reproach in her daughter's voice. She was so attuned to the melodies of her children's voices that as soon as they spoke she knew their moods. Babs knew that Boyce loved Grandma dearly and was thinking, above all, of what he would want. And what was wrong with that? That very evening, before her daughter went to bed, she reassured her about Grandma Bee. "Babs, I'll go to Zorg en Hoop tomorrow afternoon, God willing. Now sleep tight."

After the abortion, she'd promised herself she'd never fall into the hands of any man. She knew what pleasure she was sacrificing, even if it had been forced on her. Her children had just happened to her, and she didn't have time to get to know every one of them. They were like beloved pets she cared for as best she could. What was she supposed to do with those eyes that were constantly seeking something deep inside her, something unbreakable as diamond, something that could melt like gold, something she had but couldn't get to herself? At her job with the feisty preschoolers, she had a school schedule to cling to; at home with her own four little ones, she had to improvise. She was so relieved whenever they came together as a family in an intense game of rag dolls and dollhouses. Then Heli outgrew childish things and started demanding her attention. Her eldest wanted to be with her, help her in the kitchen, chat with her in the early evening. She felt a warmth that moved and troubled her. "Go do your homework, Heli." She was really asking her own self to leave her alone. And after she slapped her, so hard her hand was sore for days, her resistance to Heli broke down. She understood that her four children held her future inside them, that the time had come to get to know her firstborn and the others, to learn to appreciate them as chunks of time opening worlds of being, where no clock, no calendar, no time limit existed. She lost sleep over it. Resolved to do "fun things" with the children on weekends. It didn't happen. She was tired. Too tired even to go to her parents to ask how her little sister's intake had gone, and too tired to be able to sense what role she could play in all that. She was even too tired and too penniless to make sure her girls dressed up and went to children's Mass on Sundays. She enjoyed her work with the rich folks' kids at the private nursery school. She came home drained. At night her sleep was deep. Each morning, she faithfully opened up the Bible and sat in silence, asking the God of the Bible for help. She asked forgiveness for not letting her sister Laura into the house that night. For striking an innocent child. For enjoying a forced, forbidden lust. And each time she muttered, "Make each of my children better than I am, God the Father." And she understood it was her duty to help make that happen. She had applied for a job at a school outside Paramaribo, run by the municipal government, where she would earn a higher salary. She was summoned for an interview. She was hired. A post in Nieuw Nickerie. Mother Bee cried with happiness. Father held back his tears in his eyes like crystal. The children didn't know what awaited them but were excited by talk of the long boat trip, which they'd make with her as soon as the long vacation started again. Louise Vanta herself was shocked with relief.

I sit in a Surinamese diner in downtown Holland, listening to my Cate, who's gesticulating wildly, trying to give an impression of what a school day in Utrecht provokes in her. It's chilly in the diner. I shiver, listening carefully. "Mothers bring their children to class, personally remove their coats and scarves and hats and ear warmers and gloves, hug them, and sometimes leave with tears smudging their mascara. Can you believe it, Heli?" Yes, I know how different it was at the primary school in Beekhuizen. Back there, the Surinamese mothers left their houses on foot early in the morning and went by minibus to the colossal residences in the suburbs to support their households as maids for families of strangers. Their slightly older children kept the little ones quiet and sometimes dragged them to school, where they usually entered Cate's classroom crying and snotty nosed. That's why Cate made each school day into a party for the preschoolers in her class. I did the same for my teenaged students, who were often the older sisters of children in Cate's class. "And what could be nicer?" I ask innocently. Cate shrugs, "My paycheck, girl." She sounds indifferent. I know she always stresses that she doesn't want to get into a debate about the children entrusted to her care—no way, no how. "How do you like your colleagues?" She looks up from her plate of bami goreng. "They'll have to open up to me eventually, Heli. You know from experience how pushy I can be, right?" I don't nod. I have my hands around a bowl of saoto soup. What I know, as one of her co-workers, is that she can be overwhelmingly affectionate and wickedly resentful. I dig into my baked cassava and pecel salad. The peanut sauce burns my lips and is fresh and delicious. I want to enjoy my food and not have to talk. Not Cate. She rattles off a story about putting the boyfriend who followed her to the Netherlands on ice, which means none of his nonsense and absolutely no sex until he understands that she wants a family and not a romp in the sack. "Is he giving up on you?" She shakes her head, her hair cut short for the wintry gusts of wind. "He went scurrying off, but he'll keep calling every night until he falls for some Dutch whore who'll blow him until he forgets me!" I take a spoonful of my soup, which has gotten pretty cold, but I can feel her anger blazing. "So, seen anything that caught your eye, Heli?" I nearly choke. Look up and shake my head in denial. "Still waiting for that creep?" I nod. "Do you plan to stay with your family?" I shake my head. "No?" She falls silent. We finish our plates.

Arm in arm, we head toward the shopping center in Utrecht. Window shopping for clothes. And I let Cate lead me from one fashion boutique to another, enjoying myself as if I had bags of money to give away. Every now and then Cate disappears into a dressing room, hands full of hangers. Comes and asks, "Pretty?" I always answer right away, "Yes!" She has good taste, and she knows exactly what she wants. I don't try anything on. I look. I see something I think would look good on me, but I don't have a job. Hour after hour of window shopping, and I find out where they have the winter coat I want. Also how much it costs. It's Wednesday afternoon, and the shop is teeming with children, mothers, women, giggling teenagers. Cate wants to go on to a car lot outside of town. On the bus ride over, I confide in her about Laura's situation. Tell her I want to look up Bram's family in Apeldoorn for my grandmother. Catie wants to accompany me there. She also wants to help me find the perfect place to live. "Maybe we could rent something together?" she suggests. "You want to move out of your friends' house?" She nods, saying, "Lovely people, but sometimes he hits her." We fall quiet. We get off the bus and stroll over to the car lot. "Finding a good car seems so difficult," she says, laughing. "Heli, snagging a man seems easier." I say nothing. I listen as she says, "My mother claims that a woman must learn to adapt if she wants a good marriage, but who can have a good life with a man who keeps walking out, Heli?" I don't know. I have no understanding of men, no understanding of cars. A salesman hurries over to us. "Oh, welcome, lovely ladies, can I help you find a handsome car?" He's a real-life Adonis. We smirk at each other and follow him through the abundance of shining automobiles.

When Cate has boarded her bus to Overvecht and I'm finding my way to Central Station for the bus to Oog in Al, I hear someone calling my name. I look around and see him standing there. A young man from the Surinamese study group comes running over to me. "Do you want to grab a drink somewhere?" "No," I say firmly, smiling not at him but at his sculptured Afro. "I think you're cute," he says. I shoot right back, "You're not the only one." His smile remains on his lips as if frozen as he says, "People say you're Derik's other woman." I nod yes, then ask, "May I go now?" He nods and I walk on, because it's starting to get dark. I've already told Lya I won't be home for dinner, but I want to be back before it gets too late. Maybe I should be more involved with the Surinamese students in my study group, but it's tough.

If I go and sit with them, they maintain a stoic silence. Derik was their teacher and their training program director. I can't bend space and time—what's done is done. In any case, I'd rather see more of Holland than the faces of familiar compatriots. Another fear weighs on my mind as well. At the library, the morning paper was open to a headline in capital letters: SURINAMESE MAN UNDER THE INFLUENCE OF DRUGS ATTACKS GIRLFRIEND WITH MEAT CLEAVER. And still we must be our brother's keeper, a guy said to me, handing me a free pocket Bible. Everyone got one. He's a seminary student. I think he's too friendly. He smokes a pipe. He's told us he's into guys. A long wait at the bus stop. The cold torments me. I sorely miss my hometown. The crowded bus is the last thing I'm in the mood for. I squeeze my way over to a drop grip because there aren't any seats free. Derik leaps into my thoughts, warming me up. The bus ride is oppressive. Unknown people breathing into my face. Sweaty odors from complete strangers in my hair. The stop where I get off is dark and deserted. The taillights of the enormous bus. The quiet streets. The deaf-mute houses. I'm mad at Mama. Don't want this kind of life. In the hallway, next to Lya and Winston's jackets, I wipe away tears.

I'm sitting on the front stoop of our house after school one day, leaning against the closed front door, with Imker beside me. Our schoolbags in our laps. Our little brother's babysitter looking after Babs. Mother isn't here yet, but because she's always been here after school, I know I have to wait. We kill time watching all the vehicles pass by.

Then a car pulls up to the curb, right next to our stoop. Fear. The driver gets out and lets someone out of the back. It's my mother. She rises to her feet and smiles. She takes her purse from the driver, comes over to us, and hands me the house keys. "Turn the big key in the lock, Heli, to the left, two times." As I follow her instructions to the letter, I hear the voice of the babysitter. And the front door pops open. Mama goes inside first, then the babysitter with Babs and Audi in tow. I let Imker go in before me too, so that I can look at the car that brought my mother to us as it drives away. I close the door. Lock it. Turn the key twice. I face Mama. Suddenly, there's pounding and shouting at the door. Uncle Winston's voice. I don't move. Mother looks at me as she tries to stretch out on the sofa in the living room. In the kitchen, the babysitter is warming up lunch for us. I go stand near the door, screaming as loud as possible at my mother's brother, "Mama doesn't want you in here with us!" It grows quiet, and everyone stares at me. Mother nods in approval, closing her eyes and leaning back. Imker stands beside her and slides the shoes off her feet. Babs bends toward Mother's face and kisses her. I pick my little brother up and go to the window facing the street.

Winston's white car drove off and vanished from view. A Friday afternoon. The babysitter, who had a little house behind ours, made sure that our mother could remain on bed rest until Monday so she was strong enough to go to work. Everything remained the same. Nothing had happened. I had a recurring dream that Grandma wrang the necks of her pigeons to make a restorative soup for my mother. I gathered the windblown feathers to make a cushion for my little sisters, who'd get a dollhouse on December 6, Saint Nicholas Day. There's no year I remember in greater detail than the year on Dwarsstraat. The months calmly dragged on. When the long dry season vacation began, Mother left Paramaribo with us for her new job. We went to live in the birthplace of her mother, her grandmother, and her pure Scottish great-grandmother. I taught Babs and Imker English-language songs that Grandmother Bee had taught me for imprinting the English alphabet in your mind. We always broke into giggles at "B" for "bee."

Her mother Louise and grandmother Bernadette were seated at the table side by side as the water for fresh tea whistled in the kettle and Imker tried to cut a piece of fiadu, place it neatly on a moss green plate, and lay the cake fork next to it without collapsing from the tension. Mama and Grandma had no appetite for a hot meal, but they'd both said yes to a piece of fiadu. Mama hadn't been there long and, after greeting Grandma with a kiss on the forehead, had sat down opposite Bee, perhaps to get a good look. She discreetly slid the tea over to the ladies, asking if they'd rather be left alone. No response. No need to go, then? She slid a chair over to Grandma and sat down. She herself had neither cake nor tea. Nor any appetite for anything. She was the one who'd asked her mother to come to Zorg en Hoop right away. Grandma looked at Louise, who met her gaze. "Would you like warm milk with your cake?" "Yes," Grandma said. And she got up to fetch it for her grandmother. "Are you glad

Imker's here?" her mother asked softly. Her grandmother bellowed, "Imker? Imker, your Imker, is what keeps me going, Louise." The words seemed to come straight from the depths of Grandma's tumbledown lungs. "May I ask how you're doing, Ma?" The answer came right away: "Fine, as long as Imker's with me, because I refuse to go to the hospital." And with the fingers of one hand, Grandma started tearing bits off the fiadu, touching them to the lukewarm puddle of milk on her plate, and carefully lifting them to her mouth. At the same time, she gestured with her right hand for Imker to turn on the radio, so that she could hear the news and obituaries. "Not too loud," warned Louise, who wasn't fond of intrusive radio voices in her own quiet house in Amora. And when Mama had finished her cake and tea and the radio announcements were over, she told Imker to turn it off again. "No," Grandmother said firmly, adding, "Just turn it down low, Imker." The radio was Heli's and represented Grandpa Anton and the sunny days when they were a family together at the table. Her mother and her grandmother clearly had things to thrash out at the eleventh hour. She pondered the situation and decided to leave the women alone and go outside, into town if she had to, maybe to the river to get some air. She got dressed in a shirt, jeans, and sneakers. And she left.

First, she went to the training institute, where she was still enrolled as a student, to explain that she'd be absent for a few months to take care of her sick grandmother. No problems there. The secretary said, "Imker, you'll remain registered as a student, so you still have the right to your scholarship." It came to sixty guilders a month, but when a thick sandwich cost just thirty cents, sixty guilders in her pocket each month was nothing to sneeze at. She'd been just in the nick of time, because the secretary was locking up for the day. Two o'clock in the afternoon. Rush hour. Everyone going home. She flagged down a minibus, squeezing between seated students, and rode downtown. Got off and walked to the waterfront to see the river rising as high tide approached. She had no relatives she could barge in on and sit down and eat with. Even Great-Uncle Scott had returned to Nieuw Nickerie with his wife and sent his daughters to boarding school. Uncle Léon had a shop that was always filled with mothers hastily dropping off broken children's shoes to be repaired, and with other customers who took all the time in the world—retired folks, bums, even whores. No friendship she'd ever struck up over there had survived the voyage to Paramaribo. Umar had confided in her that in the Javanese-Surinamese kampong where his parents were born, friendship was stronger than blood ties. "My parents are nice people, Imker, but they've seen their young women and girls lured out of the city by Negroes, coolies, white farmboys, and other sons of bitches, and sometimes one of our girls never came back." Murdered? Run away? Once, she'd asked him to take her to one of the kampongs. She seldom encountered Hindustani or Muslim girls and never with their young men—except at the market or sometimes in a store, and of course on the street where they crossed paths without really seeing each other. She watched the river waves crash against the wall. Grandpa Anton had said Paramaribo was a godforsaken coastal city because the foreigners who'd founded it had

245

disappeared without a trace after the abolishment of slavery around 1863. Did she now live in a ghost town kept alive by people caged in on all sides? Rivers, mountain ranges, the ocean, and poverty always stood in the way. The bell of the shaved ice cart rang out nearby. She got up from the bench to buy a snow cone with cherry syrup. The young man had a full beard of jet-black coily hair, a brilliant smile, and bright eyes. He kept smiling as he handed over her order, tucked away the dime, and moved on. It cooled her down some, slurping and sucking on her snow cone. It melted away too fast. Did she still want a diner of her own someday? Maybe she was sitting in the same place Laura had once sat, day and night, because even her only sister had kept the door locked. Church bells nearby. She felt as turbulent as the river water. She needed to get back to her mother and grandmother. It was Tuesday, and at seven o'clock that night, Grandmother's favorite Mass would start at the church downtown. Agitated, she waved down a minibus.

A full thirty minutes before the service began, they took their seats in the Church of the Saint Anthony of Padua. Mama Louise, Grandma Bee, Granddaughter Imker. Father Overtoon had a good view of them in the pews, so close together, in the second row from the pulpit. It hadn't been difficult for her to get the ladies to church. Grandma had even said a long-cherished wish was coming true. When the church had filled up, the priest and altar boy appeared, bells ringing. Her grandmother rested her right side against her, as light as a butterfly, but clearly strong enough to murmur along with the prayers. She heard her mother singing along in a velvety alto voice. There were many hymns. The sermon was brief and direct: *Seek, and you shall find, and Holy Saint Anthony will help you in all your searching and in holding on to the good things, in Christ's name.* Had Grandma and her eldest daughter put their differences behind them? She dropped a substantial donation into the church offering bag. They were the last ones to leave the church. Waiting outside was their taxi, which would first take her mother to Amora and then drop her and her grandmother off at home. But Grandma Bee still needed a little more time; she took a long, slow, final look at the sanctuary into which she'd poured her heart and soul for so many years, and she let her tears flow freely. Imker gave her grandmother her own handkerchief.

Audi had been nervous for days. He couldn't turn his thoughts from the secret his sister had told him: *My father knows who your father is and has met him!* A storm of blood raged through him, and he was afraid his heart would jump out of his chest like a cork popping out of a bottle of champagne. But he'd had to promise to quit pestering Mama about things she didn't want to reveal to anyone. He and Babs had made the most of the hours at home by themselves without Louise and the others. They'd opened the living room windows wide, removed the mesh insect screens, and blasted the portable radio. They'd eaten roti with heavily seasoned curried lamb straight out of the carton using their fingers, and they'd drunk Coca-Cola straight from the can. They hadn't had their meals at the kitchen table but seated on the velvet sofas, and because their mother carefully guarded her off-white throw pillows, this was an act of rebellion. They scoured their hands and teeth with nail brushes and tongue scrapers, never knowing if their mother would barge in and shout, "Something smells funny about you two!" As they waited for Louise, Babs started talking about her. Facts spilled out like scraps of an exotic meal that had remained undigested in someone's stomach since even before his birth. "Boyce made friends with Laura, who had her gold jewelry crafted at his atelier, and when she and Bram went to buy engagement rings, they invited Boyce to the party at Jacobusrust out of the blue, and that was where Boyce spoke to our mother for the first time," Babs revealed. "My father was enchanted with the Vanta family. He couldn't get Louise out of his head. He didn't ask her out. He visited her every evening at her parents' house. He got to know her children Heli and Imker." He could still hear his sister talking and talking while his math teacher explained logarithms; he heard her talking even over the roar of downtown traffic; he listened to her voice as he lay motionless in bed at night. "Louise Vanta looked stunning in a military uniform and was serving as a telegraph operator. She had fun with the other women working there, and friendships blossomed. She didn't want a relationship with Boyce, because then she'd have to give up her job and possibly her freedom. Boyce wanted her so bad that he made her an offer no woman could refuse—a huge, luxuriously furnished house to live in and party in, a housekeeper, a chauffeur for errands, plus the chance to stay at home to care for her little girls. And he wanted her to bear his child. Her house became his base of operations. He welcomed his friends there for dinner and to slide the mah-jongg tiles with him. Grandmother was delighted. Crazy about him, too." And raising her voice, Babs added, "I was born in those good times," and softly, "then Mama got pregnant with you, and the good times were over." Even though they stared at each other in silence for a while, not knowing who needed consolation most, no one was accusing or attacking anyone. The looks they gave their mother when they sat at the table together were fraught with meaning. Had Mama loved his dad so much that she'd broken up with the man who'd given her a good life? And imagine if Boyce died all of a sudden before he finished his final exams, then he'd be left behind in ignorance. He had to come up with a way to force Babs's father to give up the name and address of the man who'd brought down misfortune on his mother. His old ten-cent joys now filled him with contempt, and even his relentless struggle with the details of sexual reproduction among humans and animals fell by the wayside. He'd always known there was some man walking around downtown who was the father he'd never met. His arrival in the human world had caused an irreparable rift, breaking open the cracks in the relationship between Grandma Bee and her daughter Louise. He told himself he would give his mother a cute puppy for Christmas to hold against her heart. And suddenly Babs came up with the solution: a friend from the rich folks' private middle school she'd attended was moving to the Netherlands with her parents, and the family couldn't take all their guard dogs along because the house waiting for them there was no split-level villa with an enormous yard. Any chance Babs wanted a big, strong guard dog? So he could let Mama know that she'd soon hear barking once again as she approached her front gate after work. Audi waited for just the right moment to deliver the news.

At her son Winston's house, Bee had done the house-keeping to have something to do and to make sure he wouldn't let things slide. Then he found Lya. And Lya didn't think much of her cleaning and complained about the smell of cigars, which she said could lead Winston to start smoking again. Lya didn't even want her to cook; she preferred to do it herself. Still, Lya was grateful to her mother-in-law for supporting Winston when everyone else had let him down. For two years she'd cared for him and encouraged him to make a fresh start, to follow the example of the wife who'd left him. She'd never under-stood Winston. Not even when he was a toddler. Stiff willy at bath time. Constantly seeking self-gratification. Always sucking his thumb with the other hand in his underwear. Her other little boy, Rogier, hadn't done any of that. Louise had sent her daughter Heli to his house in Holland but refused to talk about him. There were knots in the thread of her life, and some she just couldn't pick apart. All the experiences she had to leave behind unspo-ken—it was just a bit too much. Sitting opposite Louise and trying to get through to her with questions like "Do I know Imker's father?" and "Have you forgiven him?" was harder than accepting that smoking her scrumptious cigars and chewing tobacco had led to her cancer. And then Louise had started in with little remarks about Laura and Ethel, how losing her two younger sisters had shat-tered her own happiness in life, yes, shattered, because it would never be whole again. "Ma, it's painful to see how little remains of your three daughters, don't you think?" And when she tried to contradict this with a compliment—"But you're so strong"—Louise lashed out: "My life is hard, exhausting, and now that my daughter's in Holland, it's sad, too. I want my children to have a happy life, but everything is getting out of hand, Ma!" Then she got up to make a pot of fresh lemon tea and serve a big hunk of fiadu to the only daughter of hers who had become an unfettered city Creole. She admitted in passing to having given Heli the unopened letters from Bram to return to him, by mail if the girl preferred. Louise asked if she knew why Laura hadn't gone to Holland, no matter how much her fiancé Bram had pushed for it. She was no longer sure of the sequence of events. The long and short of it was that Bram's parents had written to her and Anton to keep Laura in Paramaribo, explaining that otherwise Laura would fall to pieces in the Netherlands, where their family had been torn apart and they were struggling to emerge from the horrors of the war. "Did you really think that letter remained a secret?" Louise asked. Laura had even shown Louise a wedding photo of Bram with a Jewish girl and then set it on fire in the backyard of the big yellow house, yes, burned it right in front of Louise, who had been visibly pregnant with Babs. And then Laura had told her sister something that really soured the relationship between them. "What was it, Louise, what was it?" The big yellow house and the kind of life they led there could make people envious—even close relatives, apparently. Laura had told Louise that, as it so happened, Boyce had been hiding from everyone that he had another woman somewhere on the outskirts of Paramaribo, raising his teenage children. And

251

her eldest daughter was pained to the depths of her soul. Laura had known from the start and kept mum. "Do you still hate Laura?" she asked Louise.

The Hindustanis married off their children. So did the other Asians, as well as the Lebanese and Portuguese, and even the Dutch farmers, Aram's people, chose suitable life partners for their children. Preferably overseas. But what kind of dowry could Louise scrape together for her daughters? No cows, no jewelry, no money, no property, no furniture. They shared a laugh about it, thinking of Imker, who was clearly in love with the young Muslim Umar. And she listed the things her granddaughter had to offer: good looks, a devoted nature, virginity. But qualities like those weren't nearly enough, in most arranged marriage systems, to bag the daughter a husband and get her out of the house. They laughed and nibbled away at their fiadu. And that's why Imker found her mother so relaxed when she showed up and proposed they attend the Saint Anthony service. After church, they were driven home through a city center lit by streetlamps and the occasional neon sign, through the slow traffic in the nearly empty streets, and because she seldom went downtown at night, she cried, moved by the atmosphere of the city she'd grown to love. She would never return to her village of birth again. She would never drop in on the old nuns at the convent again. Paramaribo had opened its arms to her. No one could see her tears well up like holy water, conferring a blessing on something that might be called happiness. If only they could ride on until they reached the heavenly realms and then leave her behind there in the darkness of her God. That same night, as they lay in the same room, she asked Imker if she ever felt happy. "Yes," her granddaughter replied immediately, "But Grandma, I don't know what it'll be like when you're gone." She thought, *Maybe your heart lies in nursing the sick instead of teaching children, and that's where you'll find your happiness.* She didn't say it out loud. How could she, who could hardly stay on her feet anymore, go on tending the flame of her granddaughter's life, even from beyond the grave? And Grandmother Bee considered the events of their lives and prayed for mercy. And pleaded for a happy life for all her grandchildren.

This time Louise Vanta went to Kolera not to anonymously drop off something tasty for Laura at the security booth as she sometimes did, but to see her little sister in person. She hadn't inquired in advance how Laura was doing that day either. This visit was different. Her boyfriend Lester dropped her off at the gate, and they agreed on a place in town he could wait for her. "Take your time, Louise," he whispered kindly as she got out of the car. There she was. Straight-backed. Hushed. She stared at her surroundings, the walls, the crushed shell pathway leading inside. An odor that said "old age" blew into her face. She continued along the footpath. She saw silhouettes of women. She peered into the distance, seeking out her sister, because she couldn't bring herself to go up the steps and inside. A woman asked who she'd come to see. She gave a name. "Laura, visitor for you." And then there she was in a floral dress, as if it were still her birthday, and she slowly walked to the footpath. "Come inside, Louise." It almost sounded like a question, asked in a light Nickerie accent. A wrinkle of ten years lay between Laura and her. *Hi, Laura!* She couldn't speak. Her eyes spoke for her. She wished it weren't just patients but visitors too who were allowed to engage in disorderly behavior, because then she could have rolled around on the ground screaming. She felt as if the world had been thrown off its axis, and she thought, *Don't fall over.* She walked up the front steps and right up to her little sister, and laid her hands around her neck under the hairline, one finger stroking the skin next to Laura's ear. They stood face to face. They didn't move. They saw tears in each other's eyes. They heard air finding its way out through their nostrils. And other women gathered around them. With both hands, she started stroking her sister's face—her lips, her eyebrows, her cheeks, her chin—but she was still too scared to hug Laura. "Who are you?" a woman asked. "I'm Louise," she said, and Laura added, "My sister, that's what you are." She hadn't brought anything for her to eat, to drink, to smoke. "Do you still live on Dwarsstraat?" She shook her head. A nurse chased away the onlookers. Asked if she knew visits weren't allowed on Friday afternoons. "The new medical director observes Shabbat." No, she couldn't have known. "Can you come back tomorrow, Louise?" She answered, her mouth close to Laura's ear, "Yes, Laura, I'll definitely come back to you tomorrow." And her sister wriggled free from their halo of their tender reunion, walked away without looking back, and left her standing with empty hands and fingers damp with fear.

She took her time walking to the parking lot where her boyfriend was waiting in his car. Her feet hurt wearing heels. She needed a bath and clean clothes. She needed orange butter lotion to anoint her body with. Her boyfriend Lester took the lead. She let him. Her mind seemed empty, as if a feeling too big for the space in her head was trying to force its way in. He stopped at the army base to pick up a hot meal and drinks at the restaurant. She sat in the car and waited for him and for everything still to come. Laura's face: bright eyes fighting back tears, wide parched lips, hollow cheeks above a pronounced jawline, forehead partially covered by curly hair. Supported by a long, slender neck. Her little sister had spent ten years in confinement since that terrible night she hadn't opened the door. Afterward, it had rained as if the city were grieving, and lightning had flashed as if the heavens were furious. With her? It was quiet downtown, and the pavement was radiating heat. Women had wrapped their heads in stylish scarves for protection from the burning sun and were hurrying home to their children. The oil painting of her in the nude still hung in Lester's air-conditioned living room. When he couldn't sleep at night, he would paint, his mouth longing for his clarinet or trombone, and in the worst case, he would rustle up a bottle of Carta Negra Rum, distilled by Mr. Emilio Bacardi. A man of refined tastes: she stopped in front of his oil painting and recognized the contours of her own body. During the long, slow years in Nickerie, she'd abstained from sex so she could focus on getting to know her children, each one individually. And then, by some happy coincidence, there was a military band on the boat back to Paramaribo and she struck up a conversation with a gentleman in fatigues who couldn't keep his eyes off her. A longing to be touched awoke in her, keeping her from sleeping and pulling her into dreams that made her body shudder with lust. They ate rice, pea soup, and strips of grilled chicken, and they drank rum and Coke. She looked at him: the curly stubble on his broad chin, his strong mouth, the thick eyebrows that framed his piercing eyes, the white T-shirt taut against his upper body, making him look more like a sculpture than a man at the table. Against the wall behind him was an enormous piano; nearby in the corner was a wind instrument she'd never seen before. "That's a saxophone," he said, immediately adding, "I have so much time for it because you don't want to live with me, Louise." She smiled, her teeth flashing, and saw through a side window the periwinkle shrubs in blossom, vivid purple and white flowers all along the low hedge. He kept asking even though by this time he could whistle her answer: "My children need a fixed point in their lives, a haven they can return to, no matter what or when, and that haven is me." And even when he swore to her he'd be a good stepfather, it was clear to her that a mother shouldn't be so foolish as to place three pretty girls on the verge of adulthood under the control of a powerful man who wasn't their father and, on top of that, had a drinking problem. She hadn't said as much to him because she wanted to keep him as her lover, and she was willing to give herself to him completely. Sometimes some young thing would get Lester in her sights and refuse to give up, and sometimes he let it go on too long, but as soon as she so much as mentioned it, he would freeze out the girl completely. By this point, their relationship had been going on for almost four years. Almost long enough for her to be able to talk to him about the pain still at work inside her, but not quite. She cleared the table. He put on some instrumental music, the kind that reminded her of Laura. She wanted to feel him. She waited until he was craving her. She went to the bathroom to shower until she was soft, supple, sleepy, receptive, but, most of all, cleansed of the past. Lester in the bathroom with her. Naked. Massaging her shoulders, her back. She leaned against him. Heated up at the touch of his sex along the crevice of her ass. She turned to face him. Their mouths drew together, he picked her up, and with her legs tight against his hips, he slid inside. He grew and grew in her vagina, and they didn't move until he carried her to his bed to release his load into her, thrusting and twitching. She went slack, like a block of sculpting clay that softens as it's shaped in an artist's hands. She shook her hair loose; she stretched as if thanking the heavens. She lay on her back. He on his side against her. He stroked her chin, stroked her breasts, her navel, the hairy trail along her cleft. He hummed along to the music playing in the living room, which she could just barely hear. And naked, Louise and Lester fell asleep side by side.

Number nine on Anton Wachterlaan is a spacious, freestanding house, much like the others that line the broad street. I should have just sent a postcard instead and waited for an invitation or a rejection. No one to be seen, although the curtain at a window stirs suddenly. Someone's watching me. And no wonder—I'm loitering in the street observing them. I don't see any way to ring the doorbell. Can't make heads or tails of houses like these, with gigantic front yards and low front hedgerows. Just walk on. A sprawling lawn? A driveway to a double garage? A gray tile footpath to the front door, concealed by an evergreen hedge. Why is a stranger coming to this address to discuss intimate events from long ago? Should I shout? And if no one comes, knock hard on the door? And what if even then nothing happens? I've walked so far past the house in my evil mood that I reach a dead end. Tennis courts. A big clubhouse, players in white. Boldly, I walk over. I'm attractive, well spoken, well dressed, with nothing to lose. Foolish to be so impatient, unwilling to wait until Cate could come along on this mission. A sign: MEMBERS ONLY. I hesitate but push the entrance door open. Quarter to eleven on the clock above the bar. Athletes with tennis bags and a man at the bar, by the register. Eyebrows raised, he looks at me. "Are you lost?" Everyone looks up. I stride over to him, saying, "No, do I seem confused?" He doesn't respond. "Can I order a cup of coffee and a stroopwafel?" He cocks his head at little table, keeping his eyes on me. I remove my coat, hang it over the empty chair, and sit down at the square table where he wants me. The athletes leave. He stands beside me. "Coffee and stroopwafel, miss. Would you like to pay now?" He's changed his tone for the better. And his attitude. I carefully count out the coins. He leaves. Comes back. "Your stroopwafel, almost forgot." A smile. I relax. I think, *Could this be the grandson of Bram's parents? Did Bram have brothers, sisters?* I see the waiter, dressed in a tracksuit, still looking mainly at me and not at the others who come inside, order a coffee, down it quickly, and head to the courts. There's no one else. Just him and me. "Excuse me, sir, do you know these people?" Standing next to a barstool, I show him the address on a letter. He looks at me, this time more probingly. "They still live there, yes, but they're not members. Bram was not like the others, but not a tennis player either." He talks fast. "Does Bram still live there?" He shakes his head, saying, "Bram's a renowned poet in Apeldoorn." I thank him and return to my cup of coffee, which is now cold and bitter. Gulp it down. The waiter comes over to the table, takes the cup and saucer, pauses before saying, "Their name is in the telephone book, maybe call?" I nod. "You're from Suriname?" "No, Utrecht." He smiles, dimpling his cheeks, and hurries off to serve the other customers. I'd rather not call if I don't have to. When I prepared, I was expecting to speak to them at their door. Except for my coat, everything on my body has just been bought, and I've had my hair done by Lya's hairdresser. Just as I decide I'll take the risk of calling, he comes back with a telephone book, pencil, and paper. He stands with his lower body right next to me. I see the sizeable bulge at his crotch. A shiver. Don't look up. Voice firm: "I'll look up the number, sir, but would you mind calling and saying that a woman from Paramaribo is here with you with a message for the family?" And to my surprise, he agrees. An hour later, I'm in the living room of a husband and wife, somewhat elderly. The people who wouldn't accept our Laura into their family as a daughter-in-law. I'm nervous. So are they. I hand her the letters, and she passes them straight on to her husband. "How is Laura?" she asks tentatively. My response is, "Why did you turn her away?" The husband sits with the unopened envelopes in hand. "Our son will be surprised," he mumbles a couple of times. But it's not my intention to while away the day there, and if they have no immediate answer to my question, then I'll be on my way—no coffee for me, thanks.

Then the wife begins to talk. And two hours later, I'm asked to stay for lunch. I'm too full, so I decline. Time to go. We've promised each other everything we can: letters, lunches, phone calls, a helping hand in emergencies. Bram's mother enfolds me in a warm hug. Bram's father doesn't drive me to the train station but gets on the highway to Utrecht. We pass the trip in silence. Suits me just fine. I feel hurt. He knows. They forced their son to marry a Jewish girl instead of Laura Vanta. I didn't dare ask how that had worked out. "Oog in Al," I say. "I'll take Bram the letters that you brought back, thank you for your trouble." I love car trips that seem to last forever, especially when the driver doesn't talk. I was made to be sent to the moon and even beyond the reach of sunlight. I daydream about extraterrestrial things. He stops at the house where I'm staying. "Sir, can you tell me about the Nazis?" A long pause. "Go to the library, but don't dig too deep." He gets out of the car, opens the door for me, and lets me out. Suddenly, he stares at me intently, saying, "What the Nazis did will never happen again. We don't sleep. Shall I give your regards to Bram?" His voice echoes inside me. I nod. A handshake. He drives off. I don't watch. I hurry to the front door. "Who's the man in the expensive car?" Winston asks. Lya's listening. "Our Laura's almost-father-in-law," I answer, then softer, "Laura could've been a ray of sunshine in that family. They're still in deep mourning after all those Nazi massacres." They stare at me. Even Winston doesn't know what to say. "Have a whiskey, Heli." I gesture at the bottle of orgeat syrup atop their kitchen cabinet, saying, "Grandma deserves a long letter from me, and I'll tell her you both said hello." I storm up the stairs to my room.

In Nickerie, one of my schoolmates had taken me to stand atop the seawall and see the ocean roll in. It was rainy, but no rain was falling. We biked from the capital city along sugarcane fields and down a long, compacted sand and gravel path to the coast. We biked in a line to leave room for large vehicles. Where we could, we stopped to hear the roar of the Atlantic. It was usually blustery by the seawall, and the dikes kept the pounding waves away from the loamy coast. He was in love with me. I thought he was handsome and adorably shy. There was no one else in sight on the concrete dike. Even the debris that the waves tossed onto the dike was consumed again at high tide: branches with leaves, uprooted bushes, driftwood, barrels, bottles. It was creepy. We walked hand in hand across the seawall for the last time, because Louise Vanta's family was preparing to pull up roots and leave Nieuw Nickerie. I was ready to go. He knew a place where we could sit undisturbed and gaze out at the waves of seafoam without getting splashed. I meekly followed. We started messing around. He firmly forced me to the ground. What had seemed a game at first became gravely serious.

He's turned on, his hand groping under my skirt, pulling down my panties. I keep my legs locked together, no matter how hard he tries to wedge a knee between them. I don't scream. I don't call for help. I physically resist. He unzips his pants, and out pops his penis. I struggle not to give in to my own surge of lust. "Touch me," he pleads, taking my hand. I feel him. He's panting. He strokes himself vigorously. Lies on top of me. Calms down. Rises up. It's the first time I've seen a grown man's member: big, thick, rearing. I want to touch it, grab it. Don't dare. I see sperm spurt onto the concrete. Then he presses against me. We French kiss, long and hard, both my hands finally enveloping his sex. Hand in hand, we walk back a few paces and stare into the distance—as far as we can see, the frothy crests of high waves, and clouds sinking into the ocean at the horizon. "I want to marry you," he said. "I'll send my father to talk to your mother." I didn't respond. He'd unleashed something in me I'd never felt before. In silence, we rode our bikes back to the gate of my house. There were spots of blood on my skirt. His underwear was soaked. It made my underbelly ache to let him go. Did I love him?

The memory flooded over me as the young man at the tennis clubhouse brought me my coffee and stroopwafel, telephone book, pencil, paper. He stood in front of me with his crotch at the level of my mouth. I could see his sex grow tight in his training shorts. I was so wet. I couldn't think of anything but a penis growing hard for me. I can't even write a letter to Grandma, Mama, Derik. I want something that has never risen up so forcefully in me before. In the early evening, my uncle and his wife leave to play bridge with friends. An hour later, I stand at the living room window peering out into the street. They say Laura sometimes screams with longing for a man. She can't be the only woman ever to feel that way, almost out of control. I grab the book Lya's reading and pick up where she left off. It's Hemingway, *The Old Man and the Sea*. I let the story carry me along until I start to doze off. Close the novel, bookmark my place. Climb the stairs.

Shower. The sheets are dry and warm. I think about the tennis club. Get wet between my legs. Exploring with the fingers of my right hand, I'm startled to feel my hips quivering. Horny? Am I?

Six

Grandmother tore the month of October off the calendar so she could see the empty squares of November whenever she opened her eyes in the morning. She wanted to stay in bed for a change and doze off as if slowly falling into a deep well. Tumbling into life itself, bounded yet bottomless? Rogier's wife had given birth to a son. Imker had pinned the birth announcement with a photo of her grandson onto the calendar. She didn't dare take a close look. Imker couldn't have thought of a better place to put it? She'd often gazed at how a month was divided into squares, each representing a day. Her squares would stay empty—unless she could muster the strength to go to church to do something other than pray. She no longer had it in her to trek across town. She'd be swept up by the trade winds like an empty plastic bag and set down who knows where—anywhere but where she wanted to be. Lying in her own bed was safe. Sitting up sometimes gave her back pain. She dozed off to houses where she'd worked hard for her family. She dreamed of conversations with peddlers who carried wicker baskets of clucking chickens, of stopping fishermen at her gate so she could examine the floundering catch they were selling. She saw the tomatoes, bananas, bunches of beet greens, strings of yardlong beans, papayas, soursops in the wide baskets of the women, who always kept their heads covered and sometimes wore veils. She could touch their bounty, in a sleep she feared was not drawing her into dreams but laying morsels of her own daily life on her tongue so she could savor them before they dissolved. Like the fragments of the Netherlands she'd seen in slides, small plastic squares that stirred so much emotion in her whenever bright light shone on them. She saw death as a woman sitting in a chair, waiting. For her? The woman had no head. A strange dream vision? Moving in with her son Winston had distanced her from her friends. In that suburb with barking guard dogs in every driveway, no one ever came to the door anymore with rumors, stories, products, gifts. And that had never changed. She still didn't have a single friend of her own generation to pick over her dreams with. A woman without a head waiting in a chair? Her bedroom had no chair, just a small bedside table from long ago with a home stoup filled with holy water for wetting your fingers before making the sign of the cross. Maybe her granddaughter would know what it meant. Imker had brought home coursework from her teachers so she wouldn't fall too far behind. She had given her granddaughter permission to invite Umar into the house after they were done in town on Saturday. Imagine Imker's surprise. Just as she'd grown attached to the figure of Saint Anthony, brass vessels, clouds of incense, and downtown sidewalks, she'd coiled herself around Imker's presence like a hungry ivy plant in search of sunlight.

On Saturday, Audi shyly came in to see her. His sister had let him inside as she left for her job at the fabric store. "Hi, Grandma Bee!" Imker had prepared sandwiches, fruit juice, and milk for her little brother. He was free to play out in the empty yard, but his homework came first. And so her grandson spent hours and hours at her house, by her side. Just in case. She got out of bed to go to the bathroom, and he hopped to his feet. "Can I help you, Grandma?" She took a long look at him, memorizing his face. Broke into a smile. "No, thank you, dear boy." She knew he was following Imker's instructions to the letter, and those boiled down to *Don't let Grandmother out of eyesight or earshot.* Even so, she asked him to turn the radio on at high volume to bring some music and outside voices into her bedroom. In the mirror above the bathroom sink, she stared at her own face for a long time, seeing the head that probably fit the seated woman in her dream. *Erbarme dich* streamed out of the radio, with a series of birthday wishes for a 100-year-old. She wouldn't make it to seventy. A funeral procession was in the making, to lovingly lay her to rest once her body gave out. She wouldn't hesitate to succumb to the magnetic power of whatever it was deep under the earth that was pulling her in. She didn't need a tombstone—just a bed of portulaca flowers. The dreams that ferried her to and from beloved people and places were helping her prepare for a separation she couldn't imagine, except that her pain would end, fall silent, vanish if it had never been. Just like after delivering Laura. Maybe the headless woman was her daughter Ethel, a woman she wouldn't even recognize if she came to the door. Maybe Ethel had been killed, beheaded in a war overseas because of her skin color? Half-asleep and excited, Anton had once told her his dream: *Our daughter Ethel is living in an African country with her husband and children.* No one could take that dream from him. Even on his deathbed in the hospital, he'd muttered that he could see Ethel with people who looked like her, and like his parents, his ancestors, and that those people were calling to him, using a name he'd never heard before and couldn't even pronounce. Anton died peacefully with a renewed faith in the future of his progeny and in the past of his plantation. What she would experience during this transition was a mystery. For who could say—the headless woman could be her own mother after all, a woman who died so young of a sickness that began in her chest and moved upward. She'd hoped for dreams of sitting in her mother's lap and being able to stroke her mother's face. Her hands still remembered how it had felt. Soft. Cool. Hers alone. But over the years, the features of her mother's face had slipped Grandmother Vanta-Julienne's mind completely.

"At a convenience store, an older man asks me if I'll pull up my skirt. I ask, 'Why?' He says, 'To see if you have room in your tummy for treats.' I lift my skirt. He bends down, takes a peek, and gives me some candy. I run back home to Mama, show her the sweets, tell her what happened. Mama races to the store, reads the riot act, returns home furious. 'You're not allowed to go in there anymore!'" This must have been when Imker was about eight years old. She had been recounting the incident to Umar. Narrowing his eyes, he said, "Some men are like that, and that guy Derik your sister dates is one of them." She got mad, hissing, "Heli wasn't a minor, no matter how much older he is!" Practically a squabble. He said nothing. Scowling but still at his side, she passed the fish stalls, which reeked of gutted giants and their blood. Yet she was the one who'd wanted to buy kwi-kwi fish for pepre watra soup. Umar stopped in front of a bucket. "You want live ones?" She bought ten without even checking their condition. And quick, quick, back to Grandmother's house to take over from Audi and get started on the spicy fish soup. But Umar didn't drive to Zorg en Hoop right away. He took her to the waterfront. And sitting on his moped, with her standing next to him, he talked about how the headlights on his brother's Volkswagen and a blinding police flashlight had stopped Derik from screwing Heli. He'd followed the car they were in until it pulled over. He'd aimed a beam of bright light straight into the car. And Derik had kept moving on, driving away with Heli, and the two cars toured the city as Umar pursued them... She listened, embarrassed for him and for herself. It was her fault Umar was telling her about Heli's intimate affairs. She wanted to go home to Grandmother immediately. She had dredged up the wrong memory from her Nickerian childhood. She could've mentioned the Phagwa festivities and floats, the street parties at Eid al-Fitr, the kiddie parties at home, so many joys that had ended for all time when they moved to Paramaribo. She was reunited with her country's many colorful communities at the market, where all the products of their soil and water were hawked by a diverse range of compatriots. What she'd really wanted to ask Umar was how his childhood had been as the son of warung owners in Moengo, where white Yankees had hundreds of helmeted shift

269

workers blasting bauxite out of the ground beneath their feet day in and day out, as they barked orders in American English. Had his father been a manager? Had he carved little hearts out of bauxite for a girl? She'd wanted to get through to him, make it clear she was no longer a little girl under her mother's thumb. And he'd brought the conversation straight back to Heli. Couldn't he understand that the two of them had to get on with life without the young woman they'd looked up to for years?

In Grandma's kitchen, Umar removed the fish from their plastic packaging, asked for a good kitchen knife, and went out into the backyard, coming back fifteen minutes later with ten cleaned kwi-kwi fish—hard fins gone, gills gone, bellies emptied out, rinsed under the outdoor spigot. The waste neatly wrapped in an old newspaper, which he disposed of in the trash barrel outside. Audi sat on the sofa in the living room with Grandmother, listening to a radio serial, *Linda's First Love*. She and Umar had the kitchen to themselves. He helped clear out the ice box, clean it with soapy water, and refill it while she started the soup. He asked, "How can I help?" He diced garlic, onions, vegetables, peppers, and salted meat on a cutting board. Filled a large pot with tap water. Turned the burner up high. And when the kitchen was filled with the aromas rising from the stove, he said cheerfully, "Would you be willing to marry me one fine day, Imker?" She smiled at him but couldn't speak a word. He waited, eyes wide. She nodded her head yes. He didn't get up to kiss her but stayed hunkered down in the light of the late-afternoon sun on the patio where she stood in her apron, kitchen towel in hand. Nor did he slide his hand into his shirt pocket to pull out a shiny ring for her. Visibly relieved, he said, "I'll drive your little brother back to your mother's house right now and tell your mother you said you'll marry me." He jumped to his feet, went to the soup pot, scooped the fish onto a platter, scraped off the scales, removed the bones, and returned the fish to the pot with the heat turned low. She'd never seen him so domestic before. And when she'd imagined a marriage proposal, it had gone very differently. He noticed her silence and retreated to the far corner of the kitchen, as far away from her as possible. "Look, Imker, you're still underage for the next few months." She stared at him open-mouthed. He stared back. "You two smell like fish!" It was Audi, cheerfully entering the kitchen and looking from him to her in surprise. "That's all right," Umar said, adding, "Pack your things, we're going to your mother's house, and on the way, we'll grab a manly meal, blood sausage or something." And teasingly, with his mouth next to her ear, "Pepre watra soup without a spicy Madame Jeanette pepper isn't guy food." Suddenly she couldn't cope with boys of twenty-three and thirteen and went to sit next to Grandma. She couldn't handle a Madame Jeanette herself, so she wasn't about to use one in soup for a woman with terrible pain in her throat. There was a sort of calm in her that had made her speechless. After Audi and Umar had driven off on the noisy moped, Grandmother, who'd said almost nothing for days, asked, "Did something happen?" She scooted closer, saying, "Grandma, he asked me to marry him!" "Marriage?" Grandmother tried to smile. "And you turned him down?" She shook her head. "But it won't happen for years, Grandma." Grandmother tried to stand up but plopped back down on the sofa. "Muslims marry young, child." Taken aback, she couldn't think what to say except, "Shall I get us some soup?" Grandmother nodded, coughed, said, "No sex before the wedding, Imker?" She grabbed Grandma's hand, got on her knees, and said, "Grandma, I promise." She stood up again and felt as if she had to catch her breath. And as she marched over to the pot of soup, she heard Grandmother saying, "Imker, be sure to strain my serving first." She laughed in surprise. She'd expected to hear "Congratulations." But no. Was it somehow connected to Laura's engagement party? She returned to the kitchen. "Yes, dear Grandma."

She recalled how Louise and Umar had kept a close eye on Heli for months. Whenever her mother knew Heli was planning to go into town in the late afternoon, she'd had to bike over to Umar's house with the news. She'd hated to be dragged into it, but it was nice to see him. He never said much to her. Always the same thing: "I'll take care of it. Tell your mother I said hello!" She'd head home. But he would watch her leave. She noticed when she looked back. She'd asked Heli what kind of boy he was, but her sister's responses had been evasive. It was clear he didn't mean much to Heli. Mother raved about him. "Umar? Well-mannered, trustworthy, generous, funny, good-looking." She rarely brought up his Javanese background. Still, Heli had said, "I'm not into Asians, Mama." And Louise: "Well, you'd best try, Heli." She was there the time Babs snapped, "We'll choose our own husbands, Mama," rejecting her mother's unwanted advice. Louise didn't bat an eyelid. Babs was just fifteen and had told her mother she was in love with a rich white boy years older—a buru, the descendant of poor Dutch farmers. And Louise: "Just as long as he knows you're underage." Mama had drawn lines that her children were forbidden to cross. How would she react to Umar's proposal? A comment from Grandma reminded her of how Louise had made her three daughters brush their teeth and take a shower together every day in the enormous bathroom at their house in Nickerie. And how Mama had stood outside the shower with a pile of dry clothes, never failing to say, "Don't forget to wash your vajayjay, yep, a little soap on your washcloth, rub gently, yep, under the shower, don't be scared, your jayjay is yours, yours alone, no one else's." Her voice grew soft as she spoke, and Grandma came closer so she wouldn't miss a word. "After the shower, Mama would come into the bathroom to scrub our behinds. We just couldn't stop giggling. Then she'd wipe us dry with fresh-smelling towels, and if she was in a good mood, she'd dust us with powder like babies. In the room we all shared, with mosquito nets above each bed, we slept in our pajamas like angels. But in the morning, I would feel right away to make sure my jayjay was still there, because who the hell was this 'no one else'?" As she recounted this story, Grandma Bee listened almost breathlessly, wearing a smile that only broadened. How had her mother reacted to Umar's proposal? She and Grandmother were both wondering. But they spent the Saturday afternoon in silence. And later, tossing in her sleeping bag, she thought, *Was everything Umar said just a joke? Couldn't he at least have given me a kiss?* With these questions looping through her mind, Imker fell asleep.

Louise was being tugged out of her routine. Her influence over her children's actions was obviously weakening. Heli's letters were proof of her daughter's independence, delivering a veiled reproach at being sent to a country her mother had never even visited: "Above all, Mama, don't force me to see my father regularly, because I'm not interested." It hit her hard, but how could she make her daughter do what she hadn't even deigned to do herself? In the land of their birth, having a father around wasn't nearly as vital as knowing your mother was there for you. In Holland, she'd been told time and again, everything turned on the questions, *Who is your father, and what does he do for a living?* Heli could answer those questions, and maybe that was enough. Her mind was on other matters. She'd been reunited with her sister Laura, in a place where no woman wanted to go: inside the barbed-wire fence at the world's end. Now it was her duty to lighten her sister's undeserved suffering by spending time with her, as much as possible, or even if it became impossible. Her walks to and from work felt weightier, and nothing she did with her preschoolers was free of pain. Laura had been a model educator. And when she sat reading her Bible in the early morning, she could no longer connect with the meaning of the ritual, having seen how hopelessly distraught her little sister was. These weren't feelings she could discuss with anyone. Just like her father Anton, she held her back straight, deflecting every intrusion with a blinding smile. When she lay in bed for a siesta, her thoughts would drift to the fenced-off grounds where Laura wandered, staring at the gate, sometimes with a cigarette between her nicotine-stained fingers. Panic overcame her as she thought about her daughters and their future. Her son would find his way effortlessly in a world that put men first in every respect. She had made the situation crystal-clear to the boys who'd fallen in love with her daughters: Heli, Imker, and Babs were free to choose their own life partners but weren't yet available. They were still under their mother's supervision until they came of age, and hadn't yet chosen careers or earned the relevant degrees. When they strayed from the path, they needed a course correction, as in the case of her eldest daughter. Yet it was Heli, more than anyone else, who'd always respected her parental authority.

Dr. Albert visited her at work one Thursday and offered her a ride home, which she accepted. Their conversation was about her mother Bernadette; she was tough, he said, but in his professional opinion, the end was clearly in sight, and Bernadette's sons wanted to fly to Suriname to say goodbye. She didn't have the impression her mother was doing so badly, and she told him so. They sat talking in his car by the gate of her house. He insisted on a checkup at the hospital where he worked, a thorough examination by a specialist to clarify the situation. Her mother had told her that was the last thing she wanted. Her eyes filled with tears as she gazed out through the windshield into the street at happy schoolchildren finding their way home. Albert also brought up her recent visits to Laura, but she didn't respond to that at all. As a classmate of her brother Rogier, he was an old acquaintance of the Vanta family, but that didn't make him one of her close friends. With her hand on the handle of his car door, she said, "Albert, as long as my mother is capable of making her own decisions about her body and her life, I won't get in the way." And then he said something truly strange. Adamantly: "Perhaps your mother is waiting for someone to force her to see a specialist at the hospital." She pushed the door open, got out, and replied, "I need to go make dinner for Audi and Babs. Go talk to my mother yourself, but don't force anything, Albert." She closed the door a bit too hard, to make it clear that Winston and Rogier had no influence over her. Nevertheless, Louise Vanta decided she'd discuss the situation with the school doctor. Her mother's last bit of freedom was at stake.

Babs asked her father about his parents. She asked about his childhood. She wanted to know if he had brothers or sisters. She'd gotten the idea after spending time with Grandma Bee. She and Grandma had been like strangers to each other for years. Domestic circumstances? Boyce introduced her to his other children, calling them his "first batch," but wouldn't talk about his parents. She asked her mother if she'd ever met Boyce's parents, but Louise had felt it was normal for a grown man not to bring his mother and father along into a new relationship. "If children want to learn more about their roots, then they'll find a way," Mama said, "leapfrogging straight over their birth parents if they have to." Louise had obviously given careful thought to how she formed her own family and had no need for still more relatives. As for her, she felt claustrophobic in their household of five, now reduced to three. Over a bowl of steaming fish ball soup, her father stared at her for a long time before he started talking, practically whispering. She listened discreetly. He paused. She understood why he'd rather not discuss his parents. Complicated race relations, which did more to separate people than to unite them. The words that exposed all that to the light of day were offensive to everyone involved. In a city as small as Paramaribo, the dividing lines between ethnic groups were sharp and often unyielding. She hadn't realized how unyielding. How sharp they were—that she saw each day at the private schools she'd been to. She promised Boyce she wouldn't do anything to try to find out more. Her father's personal history was a constant burden on him, present each time they met like a lap dog that never barks. She had her own escape route. One time she and Aram went to a matinee showing of a Western; another time he drove her far out of town, along the estates of Dutch cattle breeders and Asian horticulturalists, along woodlands, and along bauxite embankments worn smooth. These were the outer limits of her existence. It made her feel rebellious. She was still a child of her country and always would be, she told Aram, but she would bring her own children into the world somewhere else. He replied, "In other parts of the world, there's always war and bloodshed, famine brought on by natural disasters, unspeakable suffering that never ends." His arguments were convincing, at least to himself: "The Surinamese are descended from people who observed that the rest of the planet is even worse." He didn't intend to settle down anywhere else, he told her, not for anything or anyone. Yet he kept planning for a future in which Babs, and she alone, was his wife. It made her happy and sad all at once. He loved her the same way he loved his country, with a heart afraid to choose the unknown. She knew without a doubt that both would disappoint him in the long run—Suriname and Babs Vanta. She wanted to see more of her ancestors' cultural heritage—not so much in the Netherlands, but in other European countries and still other continents. She could study foreign languages, become an interpreter, and feel at home everywhere. And somewhere on the way toward that possibility, she was sure to find a suitable life partner. Imker had pointed out to her that even though their grandmother's relatives had faded from their lives over time, they could be tracked down. Imker also knew exactly which river ran along the plantation where the name Vanta had first come into use in the days of slavery. Sometimes when Grandma couldn't sleep at night, she woke Imker up and told her to watch over her, so her sister had had the chance to hear anecdotes that no one knew, not even their mother Louise. Sometimes Imker passed on some of these stories to her, ever since she'd started dropping by regularly with treats for Grandmother, like the bottle of Dimple whiskey that Boyce had given to her for her grandmother last time he saw her. "Whiskey," Imker had said in surprise, but soon afterward she had to admit that a few sips helped their grandmother put off reaching for her next half-cigar. Besides, alcohol was said to be cleansing and relaxing. She brought over *Ebony* magazines for Imker with beautiful Afro-Americans and their success stories. The void created by Heli's departure slowly began to close, like a hole in the ground filling with sand and seawater. Babs slept better at night and woke in a good mood each morning.

One Saturday morning, Audi opened the front door because someone outside was calling out, "Mrs. Vanta, Mama Bee!" It was a man in a striped shirt with long

278

sleeves. He knew right away it was Babs's father Boyce, because his sister's room was full of pictures of the man. "Are you Audi?" A nod. "I'm Babsie's dad." And he let him inside. Boyce didn't sit down. He'd come to see Grandma. Years ago, she'd warmly welcomed him into her house, into her family. But it was almost ten o'clock, and Grandmother was still in bed. "Is she sleeping?" Boyce asked. "Wait," Audi said. He walked into the bedroom. Through the half-open door, he could see Grandma lying there. He whispered that a visitor had come to see her. No, not someone from church but Babs's father. "Tell Boyce to come to the doorway." He brought him. "Mama Bee," Boyce cried a few times, adding, "Is there anything I can do for you?" Audi was standing too far away to hear Grandma's response. He was standing by the open door to the patio in the backyard looking at this stranger. Light pants with sharp creases, white leather shoes without socks. He was looking at the back of the head of his mother's ex-partner, the man who knew exactly who his father was, not to mention where. Boyce had kicked off his shoes and gone into the room, crouching close by Grandma. "Would you like a chair?" Boyce: "Sure, thanks." A faint smell of whiskey and cigars lingered in the bedroom. He returned to the living room. Radio on. He had no idea how to handle the situation; on Saturdays his mother went to Kolera to take care of Laura, Imker helped out in the Lebanese shop, Babs was probably already on the way to where she and Boyce met up every week. And where was Audi? Not on the soccer field, not with the Sea Scouts, but close to the man he needed to talk to about his dad! His fascination with sexual reproduction in animals and humans might be understandable, yet how was it possible that he was suddenly eye to eye with the man he'd been longing to meet ever since Babs's confession? He'd racked his brains day and night, wondering when the right moment would arrive, and now look: Boyce was coming out of the room, walking toward him, confiding in him, "I'm sending someone to install a phone at your grandmother's." Then, with a smile, "Now I'd better go, or I'll be too late meeting your sister." He nodded, looking on breathlessly as Boyce slipped into his moccasins, passed through the front door and out of the gate to his car, got in, and drove off. He had a scream caught in his chest. *Stay, Boyce! Talk to me, Boyce!* His mother's gloomy silence had become too much for him. He would rake the yard, all of it, even if not one leaf had fallen. Grandma needed the raking noise to feel at ease, and as he passed her bedroom window, he heard tapping on the glass. He looked up. Grandmother beckoned him inside with her index finger. Put the rake down. Go to Grandma's bedroom, where the visitor's chair had been left behind. "Sit?" She nodded. "Audi, I've always thought that Mr. Boyce was not only Babs's father, but yours too. I believed he'd abandoned my pregnant daughter and Babs, but it turns out he didn't." Ears pricked. Blood rose to his head. Would Grandmother relieve him from his suspense by telling him the name of his own father? She said, "He wants to tell you where your father is, and I've asked him to do it soon." He didn't know what to say. He looked at her and nodded, even smiled, and got up to go back to raking the crushed shells. He thought of the Saturdays he'd gone through the bungalow with mop and bucket, wiping the floors and windows until they shone. The Saturday he'd learned to make coffee with a filter and waited until he could serve two cups with steamed milk without spilling. The Saturdays he'd made eggs over easy, spread Wijsman butter on slices of bread, and wolfed down his breakfast as if his life depended on it. He'd polished the wooden furniture and kitchen cabinets, scrubbed the grease off the gas stove and the kitchen cupboards, shaken out the placemats and orange tablecloth. Helped his grandmother to the bathroom, waited at the door. Cleaned the bathroom. Put dish towels, napkins, hand towels, bathroom towels, and his own brown shirt in the washing machine. Hung the clothes out to dry on the clothesline. Raked the yard, every inch. After Boyce's visit, it became another Saturday like those. And in the late afternoon, Imker found him in the living room with Grandma, listening quietly to a radio play in Sranantongo. Audi Vanta was fit to burst.

I completely forgot that I told the man from the tennis club which training program I'm enrolled in, after he gave me a detailed description of his sports medicine program at the university in the city where I'm staying. And suddenly there he is waiting for me. Our eyes meet with a shock. He launches his longing at me. I feel it in my underbelly. I freeze. He approaches me, asks if he can invite me for a drink somewhere nearby. I nod. I follow him to his car. Get in his car. There in the parking lot, he leans toward me and draws his mouth to my lips, and my hand gropes for the spot between his legs, which I've been fantasizing about ever since I met him. He moans. I want to cry with joy because his penis is so hard, and without hesitating, I pull open his fly and shatter to pieces with happiness and his sperm finds a path through my fingers to his underwear. I let go of him. He shifts in his seat. "Shall we go to a hotel nearby?" And again, I nod. He pulls out of the parking lot and drives out of town. Stops somewhere. Opens the door for me. Leads me inside arm in arm. He asks for a room for two nights, pays, and pulls me into the elevator, and then to the room, opens the door, shuts it behind us, sweeps away the covers. He slides my jacket off me and lays me on the bed. Takes off his clothes until he's completely naked. Pulls off my skirt, my underwear, my shoes and tosses them all on the other bed. Leans over me. I see his sex eagerly rising toward his belly, and I grab it. He shudders. He searches with his lips until he finds my vulva, opening it slowly with his tongue. Quivering, I take him into my mouth. I know what will happen, but I don't have words for it and don't recognize myself. I wish it wasn't me but someone else lying there with him. And when he gets up and pushes his tongue into my mouth, I die. For an instant. I keep my eyes shut. He licks my lips, my ears, my face. He lifts me up. Lays me down on my stomach. Slides a pillow under my hips. He sinks into me, grunting and piercing. I don't scream. I let him thrust his way inside. Our breathing is all I can hear. He pulls out. Asks me something. Turns me over. Lets his sperm run over my breasts. Comes with his mouth against mine. His eyes staring into mine. Kissing me. As if he understands speech has no place here. We shower. We use towels, toothpaste, and hotel toothbrushes in sealed packages. We pull on and step into our clothing. I comb my hair. He watches. Grab my purse. We leave the room, the hotel, hand in hand. I have him drop me off downtown. Am speechless for days. I'm a fire slowly burning out. I'm still tingling with pleasure from the waist down as if my nerves are on alert, waiting for more. I can't do anything but feel. Lya asks why I don't have much appetite. "Coming down with a cold," I say. Take aspirin. I send Cate a postcard asking if we can skip our Wednesday meeting for once. Scared of her questions.

A week later he's standing there again. Same time. Same place. I see him from behind because I've deliberately taken a side exit from the cafeteria. I stare at his figure. Unimposing. He's inconspicuously dressed. Last week, he paid for two nights in an expensive hotel despite knowing our stay would last only a couple of hours. At the reception desk, he gave the impression that I was his wife. I walk step by step toward him and call out his name. He startles visibly, turns around, brushes both hands over his close-cropped hair, and walks over to me. "Will you join me again?" I let him wrap an arm around me, and we head to his car. "I can't go on like this," I say softly. A deep breath, and then: "I need to finish my school year on a high note so I'll have my pick of scholarships, but now all I can think about is sex with you." He stands close to me, lifting my chin with a tender stroke of his fist: "I'm crazy about you." My hips ache for him. My labia throb. "I have a boyfriend who's flying from Paramaribo soon to see me." He keeps staring at me: "I broke off a bad engagement over a year ago. So now what?" I bring my body closer to his, pressing my face against his and holding it there for a moment. Then whisper, "I'm taking the bus to the library, babe." I pull away, walking out of the parking lot to the bus stop without a backward glance. He spent a few years working as a tennis instructor and is now studying sports medicine. Almost thirty? He looks awfully young. On the bus, I feel miserable. Fooling around with him feels over-poweringly fantastic and makes me hunger for more, but it won't ever be like that first time again. I tell him so at the library, where he's waiting for me. I even add, "You're the first I've allowed to penetrate me." He doesn't believe it, I'm sure, because there wasn't a spot of blood to be seen. I think back to the scuffle at the seawall in Nickerie and realize for the first time when I lost my maidenhead. He hands me his business card. I finally know his full name. "Heli Vanta," I mumble. He knows where I study. He knows where I live. "Can you play tennis?" I shake my head. "I'll teach you, as soon as it's spring." He kisses me lightly on the lips and disappears into the rush hour crowd. Spring? I work my way through the revolving door to the reading room. Derik has the right to a proper letter from me.

I'm allowed to check four books out of the library. They're novels and biographies about the last world war. I don't want to walk around in this country among people who experienced the violence of war, racist violence, not very long ago—without delving into the subject a little more deeply. Each day thirty pages per book. I can tolerate my classmates better now, their reluctance to open their hearts to my compatriots and me. Why are you sitting with the buckra students drinking tea instead of with us? I understand the question. Don't answer it. Am the living answer. When I'm with other people from Suriname, they bully me. When I'm with folks from Holland, they ignore

284

me. On a tourist postcard with a rural Dutch scene, I write to Imker and Grandma: OFF-WHITE = MY WINTER COAT *with all my love*. I feel Holland piercing between my legs and up into my heart and my head, and I like the feeling. I'll bring my mother, my little brother, and my two little sisters to this country, so they can sample the Dutch culture they find hovering just out of reach all over Paramaribo. *The Netherlands demands to be let in with all your senses, Mama.* I don't know how my mother feels about lines like these in my postcards. What I gleaned with difficulty from my schoolbooks is all around me for the taking in Utrecht. When I asked, my disgruntled primary school teacher told us that Holland was a teeny tiny patch of land, five times smaller than our country, and on top of that it was under sea level and would one day be gobbled up by the North Sea. Not a word from the diary of a young Jewish girl who'd hidden so she wouldn't be killed in a war that mainly targeted civilians. Nothing about the Dutch people who'd scrabbled upward, repairing the chaos. No references to such events anywhere in my education in Suriname. And when a teacher so much as attempted to discuss Multatuli's *Max Havelaar* at the teachers' college, he was bullied and fired and sent back to the Low Countries whence he came. I included the whole story in my class presentation in the Netherlands. My mother Louise and father Gordon had worn military uniforms and ridden in military vehicles through a city that had never known anything more serious than minor raids by men who'd escaped from slavery, raids it had brutally struck down. No one had wanted to flee to Suriname because, even though it was a safe haven, the country on the coast of the Amazon forest could not offer a more stable form of life than Europe's deranged, battle-weary civilization. *Mama, I've talked to people whose entire families were deliberately murdered in a war, and I'm not talking about something that happened a hundred years ago.* My mother writes back that I owe my very existence to the Second World War. She'd gotten to know my father at his barracks, which were overcrowded with Dutch and American soldiers. The soldiers handed out chocolate bars and filtered cigarettes left and right, and some young women who worked there went to astonishing lengths to attract their interest, even if for only for a night. Did that include Louise? She took cans of chocolate milk to Jacobusrust for her little brother Rogier, she tells me. My provocative reply is that Gordon was more sensible than she was: he ultimately chose to live in Holland. And she responds sincerely: *The Dutch and sex? Sickos! Be selective, Heli.* I don't know what she means. *Selective* was the slogan of the Dutch butcher shop where I always had to pick up ground beef on Wednesday for Mama's delectable meatballs. Stifling a laugh, I glance at the business card with "tennis instructor" written in orange letters, and I can't wait for spring to arrive.

Grandma has a telephone now, and the same benefactor has had one installed at my mother Louise's. It must have cost a lot of money to extend the Amora telephone cables all the way to Mama's pole. The police station, the doctor's clinic, the schools, the Catholic church and rectory, and the obstetrician have telephones, but those are clustered together along the main road through the new housing development. Boyce wanted to keep Grandma connected to her children, even overseas. He said, "I'll cover the installation fees and the monthly bills." The family was speechless with gratitude, and when he called to check if everything was working, they couldn't find words to thank him. Later in the week, other gifts were installed at Grandmother's: a sun awning over the patio out back against the outside wall of the kitchen, and even a set of two colorful lounge chairs for the yard. Imker and Babs giggled over this onslaught of assistance; Mama and Grandma kept as silent as the grave, and Audi had to keep telling the whole story of Boyce's visit to Grandma Bee. At Mother's and at Grandmother's, the telephones were installed in the kitchen, and the bells could be muted. Imker called Dr. Albert to give him the numbers, and he passed them on to Winston and Rogier. My mother couldn't wait to hear my voice again. She tells me the story of the new phones in great detail. I have no news to report other than, "I miss you all." Mother blurts, "You can always reach me, at work and at home. Are you praying, Heli?" I write down the numbers and hang up. Maybe I'll have to find a room for myself to maintain a little more distance from my mother. Derik is still determined to spend New Year's Eve with me, somewhere high above sea level in the snow. He studied in Holland but never found a suitable job there. The only reason for him to want to be in the Netherlands again is me.

Had Saint Anthony of Padua returned to her what she'd lost? Grandmother Bee asked her granddaughter to buy an enormous bouquet of fresh flowers and place them next to the figure of the saint. How else to express her gratitude but with flowers? As soon as Imker came close enough, she whispered, "There's been a miracle, child." She understood that a girl a few months short of eighteen didn't have the life experience to see what the miracle was. Her priest, who'd come over to see if he could be of service to her, might have realized that she was saying, "Father Teloor, I'm completely ready to go." He heard her confession in her bedroom. She confided in him that she'd sometimes cursed Boyce and now understood how wrong she had been. Even though she had apologized to Boyce, her mind was set on performing an act of repentance, such as praying a couple of chaplets in profound solitude. No point in any more than that—Saint Anthony had brought Boyce back to her, and God had restored their relationship. Their prayer was brief. Bernadette Vanta née Julienne was ready to go. The priest spoke words of encouragement, reminding her pointedly to keep enjoying the comforts that came her way. He complimented her on the lounge chairs, the sun awning, and the telephone, and told her the parishioners said a daily prayer for Imker, because they so admired her dedication. "Yes, Imker is such a sweetheart." And Father Teloor said, almost patronizingly, "Don't cry, you deserve it." He said a prayer of gratitude with her and left again. She sat up in bed, waiting for Imker, who'd gone out to rake the yard so as not to bother her and the elderly priest. She'd been brooding for days over something—she'd never been naked in front of her children before, and except during her pregnancies, she'd never shown anyone but her husband Anton the most intimate parts of her body, and now she'd gradually become so weak that she could no longer shower properly without help, and Imker was the obvious person to ask, but she felt so ashamed of her decrepit body. Crying. Sobbing, even. Longing for death with hopeless intensity. But it wouldn't come. It was Imker herself who offered to be more involved in dressing and bathing her. "And in the toilet, too, if you need help with that." She said, "I feel so ashamed." And her granddaughter said, "Me, too, Grandma." And then they couldn't help but laugh. But she felt so relieved after the first shower, because Imker was as naked as she was, splashing water in every direction. She sat on a plastic stool while her granddaughter soaped her up and had both hands free to use the handheld showerhead. Afterward, there was no shame and no hopeless longing for death. After a shower with Imker, she would stretch out on the lounge chair under the sun awning in clean clothes, enjoying the breeze, the kiskadee birds hopping in the sand, and the thought that God was palpable in everything others did for her.

She was taken by surprise when Heli called from Holland to hear her voice and ask if she could find Ethel's birth certificate. The father of Laura's long-ago fiancé wanted to do right by the Vanta family and locate Ethel. He knew how, because he spent much of his time tracking down missing victims of the war. A few sips of Dimple whiskey helped to relax the spasm in her head. Dreams helped her see Ethel as she was before Anton essentially sold his favorite child to German missionaries. They told him Ethel would have a wonderful life, a guarantee that was priceless to him. Tearing a hole in their family meant nothing to him. Locate Ethel? Imker went over the possibilities, and Louise came up with the suggestion of involving Dr. Albert, saying that if that didn't work, she'd ask Lester to pick up the birth certificate in Nieuw Nickerie. Both men flew to the Nickerie district once a week for work. Albert trained midwives to care for new mothers, and Lester taught a folk music class for brass players. Perhaps no one in her house had faith that Ethel would ever turn up, not even with a man on the case who always found who he was looking for, or at least their trail. But he was bound and determined to find Ethel Vanta. "Goodness gracious, Grandma, what will we do if Ethel's found?" She knew the answer right away, without speaking it aloud: her daughter would refuse to be taken away from everything she knew a second time. It would be enough to know that Ethel was still alive and hopefully in good health. She'd let the others take care of the details. And that was roughly what she told her granddaughter. She closed her eyes more and more often during the day, tumbling into a slumber of forgotten experiences. She let Imker take care of her. Babs read to her from the newspaper. On Saturday afternoon, she listened to the radio serials with Audi. On Thursday, Imker baked a quiche for Laura, following her grandmother's spoken instructions. "A post-Shabbat pie for Kolera?" Sometimes, she made weird remarks to get a laugh out of Imker. At the home stoup filled with holy water, she looked at the pinned-up photo of her youngest grandchild and said a special Our Father for his parents Rogier and Wonny. Dipping her right hand in the water, she roguishly whispered, "Father, Son, Mother, amen!" She didn't need anything anymore. Very occasionally, Grandmother would ask for half a cigar, and she knew that even as she smoked it, Imker would stay close to her side.

Once again, Rogier's old classmate was waiting for Louise at the school gate, this time with birth certificates carefully folded up in brown envelopes. "I didn't have any trouble getting them," he said, even though the ladies at the office had spent a long time searching. "And look, I've brought along birth certificates for all the Vanta children born in Nickerie because—" And he handed over the second envelope: "You never know if you'll need them one day." "This is just perfect," she said, thanking him for his trouble. Rogier had never met Ethel. Laura had completely forgotten about her vanished sister. She and her brother Winston had known Ethel, seen her each day for years as children, but even Laura's appearance had changed almost beyond recognition in the space of ten years. Still, they sent the original documents to Heli in Utrecht by registered mail. At work, only her nursery school students noticed she wasn't always focused on them. One of them would say, "Teacher is tired, sshhh." She wasn't tired. Sleeping dogs had been awakened, and she could hear them barking and growling. To make matters worse, her own children's feelings had become a mystery to her; they kept walking on eggshells around her and discussing their lives with each other instead—not even under her roof, but at their grandmother's. She could take the words of her nursery school students with a grain of salt, or distract them by teaching them a new song. But she no longer even dared to hug her own children; they had drifted so far away, even if they did keep their eyes on her when she was with them. Her schoolchildren shrieked with laughter when she brought them outside to play hopscotch, afterward grabbing their schoolbags with sweaty faces to skip over to their own mothers. Watching them leave, she sometimes longed to be a child again so she could start all over. She expressed this thought to the school doctor, who sighed and responded that the experiences retained for years in a woman's body are part of what makes motherhood more than a purely physical thing. "Just look at me—I became a true healer only after years on the job, even though my licenses were on display in elegant frames in my consultation room from my very first day." The doctor had decided that instead of having nine children like her own mother, she would bring just one child into the world. As the youngest of the nine, she'd experienced how drained her mother was in the end. "Yes, Louise Vanta, even children learn from what goes wrong in their family." She'd received support from the same quarter for the position that Grandmother Bee shouldn't be forced to see a doctor if she didn't want to. The school doctor had ruthlessly zeroed in on the crucial point: "Is your mother a burden to your family, Louise?"

Mrs. Vanta-Julienne had grieved—and not quietly, either—when she found out Louise, the dream daughter, was pregnant. Wailing, Bee had walked the back alleys of Jacobusrust as if she expected to run into the bastard who'd done the dirty deed. But Anton brought her mother back to her senses by telling her the name, first and last, of the biological father. A military man? A sailor? Louise really couldn't do any better? Winston brought their mother boxes of Havana cigars and pretty match-books, because smoking calmed Bee down and maybe even comforted her. And he let Louise spend the final months of her pregnancy with him and his wife Susanne in their colossal three-story house on the condition that she wouldn't see the father of her child until after the delivery. A Sunday afternoon. At the military hospital, because Anton had gone to his superiors and demanded her admission there. She and the midwife and a nursing assistant. A doctor, too, who kept a close eye on everything. It hurt. Bleeding. No complications. Nothing tore. It was a girl. Her name was Heli. Heli? Helium is vital to the emergence of life. The midwife placed the newborn in her arms, saying, "Hold your daughter close to your heart, Louise Vanta." Winston and his wife stopped by with Dutch grapes, gleaming red apples, pears like perfect wombs. Susanne made an attractive arrangement on the side table by the bed. They congratulated her with kisses and stayed beside the cradle for a long while, admiring her little one. Then they headed homeward, leaving her behind. During the morning visiting hours, her father Anton came by in military dress. She saw tears in his enormous eyes. He had brought a big pack of diapers and stammered, "They were in the warehouse for a long time, and the white has changed to off-white, but after a couple of washes, they'll be good as new, Louise." He too spent a long time beside the baby's crib. "Her name's Heli, Pa." She couldn't see if the unusual name made him smile until he was leaving and said, too loud, "Your Heli brings back memories of our Ethel." And then he was gone. Had her father meant that just like their vanished housemate Ethel, Heli was sweet but unwanted? A lady she'd made friends with at the army base stopped by one afternoon to drop off an envelope of money from Heli's father. No one could have stopped him from seeing her and his child. When she left the hospital one rainy morning, he was standing by the exit in civilian clothes with a bouquet of roses. Her brother boomed, "Gordon's been kicked out of the military because he got *another* girl pregnant, so don't give him a second glance, Louise!" She sat down in the back of the car, took their child from the nursing assistant, waited until her suitcase was in the trunk, and then searched for Heli's father with her eyes. Gordon stood there with the flowers, waving. He couldn't have imagined how profoundly he'd changed her body and her life. In a rush of deep sorrow, she told her brother, "Take me to Jacobusrust, where my mother is waiting for us." "Jacobusrust?" Winston repeated, taken aback. "We've already arranged a room for the both of you at my house." But her mother Bee had not failed to do the same in their childhood home. And on the day she would see Laura again after ten years, she asked to be taken to Jacobusrust first. It was hot. She was assaulted by images from long ago. The houses were gone, the rubble cleared away. Yet somehow the neighborhood she knew was still there. If the government ever set up a gigantic house for the elderly in Jacobusrust, she would sign up for the waiting list at once, so she could qualify for a room with big, glass windows looking out on the broad street, which was certain to recognize her as soon as she arrived, and as long as she lived there, she'd never lose her way. No place in the world was more real. She saw Laura sitting on the level front patio with straightened hair over her ears, eyebrows reshaped, lips painted a deep red, nails brightly polished, mouth open as she sang along, *I'm glad that you're happy with somebody else, but I'm sorry it couldn't be me.* But as she wandered through the memories of her own little past, she found herself sucked into a black hole: Gordon was on the verge of leaving for Venezuela to go work for an oil company, and he'd promised to come over to say goodbye to Heli even though he'd been pressured into marrying the young woman with whom he'd conceived another child; she stared for hours at the gate, waiting out front on the level patio at Jacobusrust, but he never came… She, Louise Vanta, had waited in vain. The lines that stuck with her from that worn-out 45-rpm Doris Day record were different from Laura's. She walked to the window and pulled the curtains open: *I cried when we parted but I don't blame you, you just did what your heart told you to.* Her voice cracked. Louise's eyes fixed on her own gate, where she'd broken to pieces when Heli crouched to pet their guard dog Leika goodbye, and had stayed crouched there as the minutes passed.

Audi slid back into his ten-cent joys with his classmates at school. His mind didn't join in, but the dirty pictures triggered something somewhere in his brain that sometimes yanked him awake at night with a force that felt familiar but was completely new to him. He did what he'd seen others do. He was burning with lust. He hid his stained pajamas in a paper bag, shoved them down among his schoolbooks, and carried them around in his backpack until Saturday at Grandmother's house, where he had the chance to wash the sheets, hang them out to dry, bring them back inside, and fold them. No one noticed his underwear or his blue pajamas and striped pillowcases waving in the wind among Grandma and Imker's white sheets. In less than two hours, they were dry and neatly stored away, long before his sister and Umar arrived with groceries and took over the kitchen and backyard. Mother, who picked out and bought his clothing, knew he was growing fast, but she obviously knew more about his clothing sizes than she did about his budding manliness. And as a budding man, he was taking his fate into his own hands. He had stomach cramps and had to poop all the time, he told the principal—an excuse to play hooky for a day after two hours of biology lessons about fruit flies. He had new clothes on—slim-fit jeans, a black shirt, and polished black shoes on his bare feet. He chewed mint gum as he walked to freshen his breath. He sought out the shady side of the street so he wouldn't get sweaty. When he arrived at the jewelry store, he began to have doubts. Took a deep breath. Moved by a feeling stronger than his will, he pushed the glass door open, flinched at the cold draft from the air-conditioned interior, pulled himself together, and peered straight into the eyes of the man he'd come to see, who slid his safety goggles down to his neck and pulled off his work apron. He sensed the others waiting in suspense as they looked up from their work. "Babs's baby brother," Boyce said, leading him to an office in the back. "Take me to my father, I can't wait any longer!" The man who'd once lived with his mother was silent for a few minutes, then said, "Well, Audi, I don't know if you'll get to speak to him today, but this way the two of you will know about each other once and for all, right?" Boyce told the others something urgent had come up and led Audi outside and down the street to a car he recognized by its unusual hubcaps. Get in, he told himself. Don't say anything. Don't give in to the sudden wave of shame. His eyes looking down at the pavement. How could he have known that Boyce also had a score to settle with the man they were going to visit?

A few days later when it was Saturday again and he'd brought the laundry inside and even folded it, he asked Grandmother Bee to listen to him carefully. The wind was savage, an earth-cleansing gale, and the air promised rain. "Is it something good?" "Maybe," he answered, adding, "May I sit on the floor next to you?" And then, for the first time, he spilled the whole story. Boyce had taken him to a gynecologist's clinic at the military hospital, produced a notebook, scrawled something on a blank page, folded it, and asked a staff member to hand it to the doctor immediately. Not long afterward, a man in a white doctor's coat came walking down the hall. Boyce rose from his chair to meet the doctor. Everyone could hear his words: "Bohr Libretti, take a good look at your and Louise Vanta's son!" And the three of them stood there in the hallway, out of sight of the full waiting rooms. He felt the urge to run away, but then his whole ordeal would have been for nothing. He stood his ground, waiting for the sound of his father's voice. Finally: "Let's meet up at one-thirty at that restaurant on Herenstraat. I'll make the reservation myself." And at last, a good look at him, a hand on his shoulder, a personable "What's your name? Audi?" And Bohr went back to his scheduled appointments. Boyce, looking pale, headed back to his store downtown. Alone and on hold. He endured the slowest hours of his life before Boyce picked him up again and drove to Herenstraat. "And did it change anything for you, sweetheart?" With his grandmother so close by, nothing had changed. He was silent. Grandma: "Time will tell, Audi." He got up and did some stretches. "Do you mind me telling you, Grandma?" She said, "I'm in seventh heaven." He wiped away his tears, because he didn't know how to tell his mother what he'd found so easy to confide to his grandmother.

One Sunday when Mother came home from early Mass and started preparing to cook, he asked if she could possibly change his hairstyle from an Afro to something more Rasta. She needed to make a marinade for the chicken first, so she tied her kitchen apron over her Sunday dress. He lingered beside her, watching her hands nimbly grind and blend garlic, chives, ginger, masala, sugar, salt, vinegar, coriander, paprika, pepper, and olive oil into a pungent mixture. He sneezed. A platter with pieces of chicken, and his mother said, "Give your hands a good washing, Audi, and work this marinade into the meat." It didn't sound like a request. He sprang into action. She went off to change clothes. Braiding his hair would take a long time, and he'd have to sit on the floor in the living room on a soft rug between her legs, her on the sofa with a big comb and a jar of water. He kneaded the meat as if it were bread dough until his mother reappeared in pants and a T-shirt. She whisked away the platter into the meat safe to let it rest. He huffed and puffed as he rubbed dish soap into his hands, trying to get them really

298

clean, but he couldn't get the yellowish tinge out of his nails. Feeling belligerent, he shouted, "I had such a great lunch with Babs's father and his childhood friend Bohr the other day!" His mother stopped short and said in a pinched tone, "I don't understand you, Audi." And with a vessel of tap water in her hand, she went to the sofa. He didn't sprawl on the floor. He sat down next to her. "Talk to me," she demanded. He wanted to grab her hand, didn't dare, brought his own two hands together as if in prayer, saying, "Mama, my father wanted me to tell you hello. For years, he's regretted what he did to you and Boyce. Now he's seen me, touched me, spoken to me, and he's a happy man once again; he said so at lunch. Boyce was there too." His mother said nothing. He reached into his pocket, slipped a ring onto his finger, a thick one made of pure gold, and showed her his hand. "Nice, huh?" She said nothing. "My father wants me to have his last name." Still nothing. "My father promised me a monthly allowance." Sighing deeply, she said, "Do you still want your hair done or not? You do? Then take a seat on the rug." He obediently slid to the floor between her legs. "What did you have to eat?" He scoffed, "What do you think? Pasta and more pasta, to celebrate his roots, I guess." Laughter. "Mama, my father wants me to meet his parents." He swung around so he could see her face. "He's a good-looking man." She pretended to shudder. "He was a son of a bitch." He didn't have any response to that. He stretched out his legs, resting his hands on his mother's slippers and feeling her toes. She got to work with the comb; it would hurt quite a bit and take a long time. "People who want to look good have to suffer for it, but people who hide their beauty come closer to happiness." "You're wise, my son," Mother said, continuing to untangle his coily hair. "Bohr will be surprised by my Rasta look, Mama, but you'll still love me no matter what, right?" Without hesitation: "Yes, my boy. Satisfied?" Audi smiled, content.

November started off cold with lots of wind and rain. I bought fur-lined boots that nearly reached my knees. Went with Lya to a specialty shop for winter underwear, gloves, and lambswool sweaters, a scarf, a hat with earflaps. And finally, my own winter coat. I can't afford to catch a cold, come down with a bladder infection, or develop aches and pains. I gulp down cod-liver oil and vitamin pills every day. I force myself to finish an apple each morning and learn to like yogurt. Lya works in a hospital as an anesthesiologist and monitors the vitality of her housemates. She doesn't ask if I want to see a doctor. She doesn't ask if I want to get on the pill. Cate asks questions like those one Wednesday afternoon as we wander through the rain under an umbrella. Cate wants to take me to her doctor for contraceptives. I offer no resistance. And not a word about my tennis instructor. She'll schedule the appointment for me, she offers. Then she says cheerfully, "Hot Venus is getting it on with Thick Penis again!" My reaction is immediate: "Hhhmmm, do I hear wedding bells?" Drivers honking their horns excitedly. We cross a busy shopping street at the wrong spot, dash into a department store, look for the café inside. Sit down. Order hot cocoa. "No whipped cream for me, please." I stretch my arms toward the sky. Cate explains earnestly that masturbating puts her in a bad mood, that his dick is better than her finger. I nod consolingly but try to steer the conversation away from the realm of the underbelly. I tell her that my two uncles are packed and ready to leave for Paramaribo whenever the time comes. Confide in her that I'm looking for my mother's sister, who's lived somewhere in Germany since childhood. And also blab that Derik's taking me on a ski vacation during winter break. She looks, listens, drains her mug of cocoa. As well as mine, which does have whipped cream on top. And then she starts in. "Heli, I can get a furnished apartment in Overvecht. There's a nice Surinamese community there, shall the two of us pool our money? Freedom and our own four walls, what do you say?" The elementary schools close early on Wednesday afternoons, and the restaurant is filling with mothers and children. I love the hum of their presence. Look around to store a few of their faces in my mind. "Cate, I don't want to live with other people from our country on some kind of Surinamibo reservation; I want to sample the Dutch way of life, understand it and absorb it." My voice falters, "Besides, you'll soon have a live-in husband and I'd be a third wheel. That's two times no." Catie shrugs, a gesture of incomprehension, but doesn't seem to know what else to say to convince me. All the same, she winds an arm tight around mine, and we walk, intertwined, through the blustery city center. I don't dare ask why she doesn't just go live with her boyfriend. Suddenly: "He beats her, Heli, that makes me sick!" Cate urgently needs to move, that much is clear, but... "Why doesn't she move out with you then?" No explanation. Saying nothing, we walk on and on. It feels strange, dreading something that happened in the past.

One evening—the first time I got home to Amora late, around midnight, after meeting up with Derik—my mother pounced the moment I pushed the door open and was on the verge of beating me. She raised her hand, possibly on impulse, but didn't strike. Then she apologized. "No one is allowed to hurt you, Heli, no one!" And I fled to my room. Her whole body told me I was breaking her heart. What's more, the neighborhood was still abuzz with the news of the murder the week before of the stunningly beautiful woman across the street, killed by her own husband, who had been constantly suspicious and uncontrollably possessive. I can't recall any other violence so close by. Laura jumps like hiccups in my body: on the night when she had no place to go, her sister wouldn't let her in. I stack up the books to return to the library. Cate said that she absolutely doesn't want to live alone, that she's scared something terrible will happen if she does. Her mother is Jewish, but she doesn't want to talk about that. "I come from a big family," she explains whenever anyone asks why she always surrounds herself with other people. She's not lying. Her parents' house is always full of music, good food, and the heartwarming chatter of brothers and sisters. I pick up the books and stuff them into a nylon bag. Should I rent a place with Cate after all? She asked me if I masturbate. "No, a lot of fuss about nothing," I answered. I've never yet tried anything like that. At the end of our last meeting, we parted ways cackling with laughter. I never knew my old co-worker Cate was so charming. There's friendship there. I stare out the window. Missing Paramaribo. I've put everything in place for yet another day at Orange-Nassau. Lights out. Super comforting to be in bed in the guest room as Mama's brother and his wife watch a movie in the living room. Yet I'm scared every time the telephone rings. Maybe it's my mother. "Are you still praying?"

"An aide? Is your father an aide?" Imker's voice cracked. This title was given to the chief assistant of the district physician, who lived next door to the health unit. Umar went on talking softly. He'd brought his parents to Paramaribo so they could get acquainted with his steady girlfriend. But he hadn't discussed the plan with her beforehand. And she was unwilling to upend her weekend routine. Her top priority wasn't Umar, but her grandmother. She and Umar had just finished clearing the table after a hot afternoon meal with Grandma and Audi when they heard knocking. She broke into a sweat, because she knew without a doubt it was her boyfriend's parents at the door. Audi shouted, "For you, Umar!" And he called back, "Let them in, Audi!" Her: "Your mother and father?" He nodded so hard that his straight hair danced around his head. He hurried off. She ran to the bathroom, quickly brushed her teeth and washed her face. As she combed her hair, her eyes looked wild in the mirror, she noticed before racing to the living room. There she was startled to find them still on their feet, gazing down with compassion at Grandma Bee, who had fallen into a deep slumber on the sofa. The kitchen, maybe? Or farther away: the terrace with the awning and lounge chairs? They sat down at the kitchen table. Audi stayed with Grandma. Umar started talking, his eyes on his father. "She's the girl I want to marry." "Her?" Finally, she looked openly at the guests.

303

"Can I get you anything to drink?" The heavy voice of the bearded man, "My wife is hard of hearing." "Are you Umar's father?" His wife nodded. "We wanted to meet you, then we'll be on our way again." Umar said nothing but fixed his gaze on his mother, whose thick knot of hair was held in place with a gold hairpin. A beautiful woman, who sat back in amusement and said, "Umar talks about you, and now that we're spending the weekend in town we wanted to meet you." She nodded at the woman. Didn't know what to say. How loud could she talk without being rude? They stood up again, shook her hand, and went out through the kitchen into the yard and back to the street. Their son followed. She walked through the house to the front window looking out on the street and watched them get into their fancy car and drive off. He came back. She asked, "What just happened, Umar?" Him, reluctant: "Javanese people from the sticks don't find it easy to visit sophisticated Creoles in the capital, you know." She'd never thought about that before. "So, what now, Umar?" Her voice had an edge. He smiled, saying, "Imker, now my parents know they no longer have to find a girl of marriageable age for me." She was flabbergasted. Ashamed, too, that she hadn't learned more about his background. She'd behaved as if she didn't know he came from an Islamic community. "Are you a Muslim?" she asked. He shook his head. "But your parents are?" He nodded, saying firmly, "I want my sons circumcised. Is that a problem?" She sighed in relief. It seemed nothing had really changed. He gave her little brother a ride back to Amora Village on his moped, leaving her with a bit of advice from his parents. "Imker, my father's been an aide for twenty years and has plenty of experience with sick people. From the way your grandma was sleeping, he could tell she doesn't have much longer. You have to get help from a doctor." Audi heard this too. And, like her, was unmoved. She watched the boys ride off until she no longer heard the moped. Inside the house, her grandmother still lay on the sofa sleeping. She looked at her, listened to her steady breathing. Did Grandma hurt even in her sleep? Head of the health unit in Mungo and renowned restaurateur. Good advice is precious. But her grandmother had confided in her that she wanted to die in her own home. She stared and stared, rooted to the spot. "Why are you looking at me like that, Imker?" Grandma Bee asked without opening her eyes. She couldn't say the truth and stammered, "I want to mop the floor without disturbing you, Grandma." Her grandmother looked up at her. "Go ahead, you can tell me later who you just let inside."

Grandma's house and everything in it was hers. By notarized deed. In return, she had to take good care of Laura. She and Grandma were the only ones who knew, besides the notary. She didn't want to think about it, but as soon as she had rinsed away the mundane matters of the day under the shower and toweled herself dry, rubbed on some mildly scented eucalyptus oil, pulled on her pajamas, and turned on the outdoor light, she couldn't help thinking about the fact that she now had housing for the rest of her life. When at last she lay in her bed next to Grandma's, she was overwhelmed by questions she couldn't ask. Grandma was less and less able to move her jaw to chew and speak without pain; slipping her tongue into a small glass of whiskey dulled her pain the same way a big cigar had for years. She'd told her grandmother that Umar's mother was hard of hearing and that had made him learn to keep quiet and that she didn't mind spending long stretches of time with him because he rarely spoke. She meant: *Grandmother, don't talk if it hurts.* Grandmother dismissed her concern, saying, "Imker, my vocal cords and my tongue work even if talking hurts, and I need to hear my own voice. I used to sing so much when I was alone in this house." A woman with a used-up body who's this close to dying in her sleep might as well use up her voice too, Grandma believed. She wished the aide had seen her grandmother Bernadette Vanta awake, not asleep. Grandmother dived into talking about how she wanted to be buried. "Imagine, child, that I suddenly lose my voice entirely, like some people turning slowly deaf, which is what happened to my father Julienne." She let a silence fall before thoughtfully saying, "Grandma, we still have to plan Laura's visit, right?" She couldn't guess how this remark affected Laura's mother, because she couldn't see her grandmother's face from her cot. And it remained dead quiet until Imker fell asleep.

Talking with jaw pain about painful subjects. It was just too much. That was what Bee told Doctor Albert, who'd stopped by to visit her. He said he'd arrange for painkillers, but they might slow down her bowel movements, making it harder to go. He whispered, "What you have is difficult to manage, you know that." She nodded. He thought she was brave, and thanks to Imker's help, she was doing as well as could be expected. "No more smoking. Alcohol is not as bad. There are pills for the pain—and morphine, if necessary." She could hear him placing a call to Holland. "Here's Rogier on the line, Mrs. Vanta." She didn't want to talk to her son on the phone. "Perhaps it's time you came here," she heard Albert saying. She sat outside under the sun awning—washed, dressed, hair combed, rubbed with lavender lotion. Imker had even put warm socks on her feet, because she'd been complaining that they were cold. The radio brought the Sunday morning family Mass into her house. The trade wind brought an ocean of memories. The surrounding silence pulled her into slumber, and she wandered through the houses where she'd once lived. Sometimes, she startled awake because she thought she was walking through the city center. Sometimes, her dream of the headless woman lingered in her mind. When she'd gotten pregnant in Paramaribo for the first time in years, her brothers had given her two rocking chairs. She would sit with Rogier in her arms and Laura in Anton's lap. They'd rock their youngest children to sleep without the slightest sound. They'd rock slowly in their wooden chairs with wicker seats, back and forth in their living room that gleamed with brass, with a three-legged table between them, topped with a spotless white cloth edged with handsewn embroidery. The children would fall asleep against their chests, and the two of them would gaze at the rose bushes by the locked gate of their front yard. The ideal Sunday morning with little Laura and Rogier in their last house together in Jacobusrust. When the houses there were torn down, she'd gone to look around. Those defenseless repositories of memory, razed to the ground. *Bricks and tropical hardwood can feel, too*, she thought, upset. She filled a little jam pot with shells from her garden and stuck a Band-Aid on the white screw-on lid with a word in black letters: OFF-WHITE. She stashed the jar among her clothes in a trunk, next to Laura's jewelry, which Kolera had released to her for safekeeping. She wouldn't force her daughter to leave the institution for a day to stay with her. She couldn't do such a thing to her. She'd once had to watch as two nursing assistants practically dragged Laura out of the house one afternoon at Jacobusrust. Years later, it still tormented her soul. God knew it did. God had brought Louise back to Laura. And since then, she'd been able to mentally let go of her child, that girl who'd bloomed like a rose into womanhood. Her brothers had told her Laura resembled their mother, and the likeness had grown over the years. Mother? She hadn't yet started to fall apart, but before everything was over and done, the last image she'd see would be Laura, the apple of her eye. The woman who had lost her head? The head that had started spinning? The lady who'd let her head run away with her? At the table with Imker, she wanted to discuss her funeral, but she couldn't get a word out. It was the powerful resistance of damaged tissue. And actually, maybe she was frightened to speak of her own death. During every delivery, she'd been deathly afraid she would die. She knew fear was worse than pain. She couldn't even manage to eat her soft-boiled egg. No appetite. Her body was no longer fighting to live. She could feel it.

She welcomed the message that her sons were doing their best to reach her bedside before the busy December holidays began. The news had reached Imker over the telephone. It gave her the courage to choke down the food her granddaughter had lovingly prepared for her, even though eating hurt and the drinking straw was so awkward. She didn't want to look a fright when the boys arrived. She wanted to shine once more in her role as their mother, even if she was no longer the sparkling frame around their lives. Childbirth was the only time when her husband Anton said to her, "Bee, I love you so much." But in the presence of their children, he'd seized every opportunity to express his appreciation for the "lady of the Vanta household," comparing her to everything precious: diamonds, gold, crystal, sunlight. As far as he was concerned, his slender bride was "the best of the best" as a wife and a mother. She'd never said aloud that she loved him. Even when her father was traveling back to Paris and asked her if he'd brought her a good husband, she couldn't bring herself to say that she'd grown awfully attached to Anton, because she didn't know if it was true. Instead, she had followed her father around wailing, "Papa, you're taking my heart with you, how can I go on?" Her mother, spirited away to die in a hospital bed. Her father, far away but certain to return; after all, he'd promised her with her hands on his heart. But ship after ship arrived without him, and each new week brought an increasingly bitter aftertaste. For five times nine months, the little hearts of the children who'd grown deep inside her had made her as soft and sweet as custard, time and again, time and again, until the moment her water broke and she screamed for her own mother and father. Then Anton was there with his face as dark as the solace of night, leaning over her with eyes bright as daylight, "I love you so much, Bee." Soft as salve. Knowing another person truly loved her didn't take the pain away but did give her confidence that the feeling would pass. And that was why she asked one Thursday morning over a breakfast of thin oatmeal, "Imker, do you know what love is?" Imker, who usually remained unruffled, seemed shocked, looking around almost dazed, but then the girl gazed straight into her inquisitive eyes and firmly answered, "Grandma, my love is like a house where the two of us live." She nodded. Understood. She was also relieved because Imker had given her the words to tell others how things were: her heart, too, had come into its own in the houses she shared with her husband and children. The houses were like the interior of her departed mother. She said, "Imker, I've died of utter misery so many times in my life, but you make me realize I've been reborn every time." Granddaughter nodded, "Understood, Grandma." Did she have any voice left? Perhaps not much. Was she in pain? Yes. The day passed by in silence again, without her having been able to savor it.

Her boyfriend Lester had brought her a new wristwatch. He "urgently" wanted to give her something, he'd said. Louise Vanta was surprised. She never would have chosen such a thing on her own—a large black dial with gold numbers and hands, attached to a black leather wristband. From now on, she would have both the time and date on her right wrist. She often checked how far the day had advanced, and on Mondays she would go through the days of the week with her schoolchildren: Monday, November 16th. Is it anyone's birthday today? She also told them what time it was when the bell rang for snack time and at the end of their school day. And she'd taught the children to read clocks and calendars. They clung to her every word: "We live on a ball that spins around the sun like a top and makes a circle of months." Then she had one of them recite the months of the year. And she put the calendar away again. They didn't ask questions. They were thoughtful afterward, and kind to each other. As if they sensed that everything flies by if you let your mind wander. One Friday, they'd gone home with hand-made wall clocks made of colorful cardboard. A week's work. Whenever one of them came to her desk to ask her something, she would see the child's eyes drawn to the striking object on her wrist. Children notice everything they can recognize, and sometimes a little boy would boast, "Teacher, my mother has a nice wristwatch, too." She'd strapped her gold watch, with its dial as small and square as a five-cent coin, onto her daughter Heli's wrist at the airport in Zanderij. And as soon as she returned to school and the children saw her again, a few little pests asked her, "Teacher, where's your watch?" Before she could even respond, a little girl said, "Teacher Louise's watch is off to the Netherlands." Children easily under-stood the things that adults did on impulse. When she was offered the chance to go on studying after earning her preschool certificate, she refused. Her heart was tied to the toddlers, who were leaving home for the first time to enter the workaday world, a transition that often brought children a lot of sadness. But by the end of the school year, she'd become a second mother to her little ones and left them hankering for their return to school after the long vacation. Her job had given her motherhood depth and offered her a framework for childrearing developed not by herself but by world-renowned experts. Above all, her profession offered her the chance to experience more of her home country through close contact with other language groups and families with less familiar lifestyles. Each day, she went to work excited. The national government paid much less than private schools but offered reliable benefits: free transportation to and from work, free medical care, a retirement plan, and even free, high-quality housing outside the capital. She insisted that her own daughters secure teaching certificates, so she could feel she'd done her duty by them—how they found and chose their life partners was out of their mother's hands. For all those years, she'd never once failed to read the Bible in the morning; the passages consoled her, encouraged her, and most of all, made it clear that human existence, for men and women, in every time and place, is like a struggle against essential elements: water, wind, fire, and human passions. She prayed with her children right before going to bed: *God, grant each of us only a small, quiet life. Amen.* And what if, in spite of all that, something went wrong?

She'd taken her grown little sister Laura under her wing as soon as they first made eye contact again at Kolera. She'd done the same during their childhood years, as their mother Bee grew more and more agitated after the difficult birth of Laura, because Bee's father Julienne still hadn't come home from France. His children no longer even heard from him. Raging with grief, Bee kept hoping for signs of his return. How could God torment her like this? Their mother screamed to God for help and shouted at their father Anton, words that must have cut him deeply, because she saw tears running down his cheeks. She took Laura away from the fighting, took the toddler into their bedroom, closing the door so they wouldn't have to hear anything. There they made animals and dolls with scraps of fabric, singing songs as they worked, and she made up stories that captivated her little sister and made her laugh. No one could see how much she missed Ethel. No one was willing to answer her questions about the disappearance of blonde Ethel Vanta. Not even the teacher at school. And the first few nights in their bedroom without the seven-year-old were so awful that the thought of them still made her sick. What had the first few weeks, months, years been like? She stood at the window, her eyes combing the distant horizon, the starry night, staring at trees, at the moon, crying, calling, screaming, "Ethel, come back!" She sat for hours at the sewing machine that had once belonged to Mama's mother, stitching together clothing for her little sister Laura's rag dolls. Everyone noticed that the cuddly toys were dark brown like Ethel, with light braids fashioned from scraps of blond rope, bright white buttons for eyes, and a mouth of rust-brown rhinestones. She never allowed the rag doll to leave her room and even named it after Ethel. Was the adult Ethel beautiful to behold? Would Bram's father find her somewhere in Europe? She would give anything to have Ethel back at home. She couldn't wait to tell her sister about everything that had happened in the years of their separation. Caught up in her memories, she fell asleep. She dreamed of their first house in Paramaribo, how she searched among the strange furniture for her own rag dolls but couldn't find them. They were still packed away in moving boxes under a tarpaulin. Then she woke up in tears in the middle of the night. And she sat up and looked at the other bed where she saw her little sister Laura soundly sleeping. She needed a sip of water. She heard a cat yowling for a tom. She sat up and took a sip of water. Paramaribo had nothing to offer Ethel, except for a wide river mouth and at least one blood relative who had gone on calling, *Ethel, we love you!* And Louise fell back to sleep.

It wasn't exactly a puppy that Babs showed up with. He was glossy black with reddish-brown ears and paws and some brown spots on his face. His eyes sparkled, and he wagged his tail almost endlessly. He didn't bark but panted a little and yapped now and then. Maybe the kennel was too warm for him. Her mother had decided that the dog should stay in Zorg en Hoop until the Christmas break, because there would always be someone at home there, which wasn't the case at her house in Amora. She simply couldn't resist the dog any longer, and after emotional farewell kisses for the family going to Holland, she was driven to Grandma's with Biko in his kennel. She had also been given a water bowl and food dish, dry dog food in bags, soft canned food, a collar, a chain, and his own blanket. After they arrived, he started to whine and seemed inconsolable; he wouldn't be able to smell his mother and his two littermates ever again. Louise's neighbors had four dogs that roamed freely in their fenced-in yard, so he would have buddies in Amora, but Grandmother's yard had brick walls some six feet high. And there wasn't anything to see there besides crushed shells, some marigold bushes, and some planters with rampant parsley growing tall along bamboo sticks. Winter break was weeks away, and they weren't about to let Biko die of sadness. Her grandmother and Imker let him snoop around every corner of the yard, snuffling, whining, growling, until he came across his own blanket on the patio's tiled floor and lay down, eyes on the door to the kitchen, ears pricked up. He even left his food dish and fresh water untouched. Grandma couldn't restrain her tears when she heard his life story. "Are they going to the airport this afternoon? Yes? We'll be good to him, right, Imker? The steel gate to the street will stay locked from now on, right, Imker?" And she was treated to tea and fresh sequilhos. Her mother Louise was required to live close to the school where she worked, but that didn't mean that she could get a house within sight of the schoolyard. Biko needed twenty-four-hour care and attention right away. She discussed the situation with Grandma and Imker, their eyes on the dog, who looked as if he knew what he'd lost. Imker chained the dog to a steel ring cemented into the garden wall along the side of the house. Biko let her do it. Aram picked her up to buy Christmas lights for his house. "Would you mind if I pick up a few things for your house too, Grandma?" "A star," Grandmother said. "No flashing lights," Imker said, "and nothing that would confuse Biko." Petting the dog, grabbing an extra cookie for Aram, and still chewing on her last mouthful of crumbs, she saw herself out the door. She slid into the car next to Aram. "Look," he said softly. She saw a woman standing by Grandmother's neighbors' front gate. "She kept wandering over to your grandmother's gate. Do you know her?" She thought she recognized the woman right away, but she said nothing. She slipped out of the car and went over

315

to her, saying softly, "Laura, are you looking for your mother?" The woman nodded energetically. "Come on, I'll take you inside your mother's house; come with me." She hadn't seen her mother's sister for such a long time, but the dress and sandals had once been Heli's, and she'd recognized them at once. She pushed the gate open and, without delay, escorted the woman around the bungalow to the patio. Wild barking. "It's me," she called out, and she gripped the woman's hand tight, pulled her inside, and led her to the kitchen table. Biko wouldn't stop barking. Imker and Grandmother looked stunned. She stuttered, "Laura was just standing and standing at the gate." Imker shouted, "That's not Laura!" And Grandmother rasped, "I recognize that woman. She's always running away from the hospital." And Imker asked, "What's your name?" But the woman didn't respond. "She has Heli's clothes on, you see that?" "Yes, Mama took them to Kolera." Babs stopped talking, terrified, then asked, "What are we supposed to do with her?" Grandmother kept her eyes glued on the visitor. "Alma, how's Laura doing?" she asked. "Fine," the woman said, taking a seat. Babs needed to leave. "Do you want me to take her back out to the street or something?" Grandmother shook her head. "Go do your Christmas shopping, Babs." And she left again. Aram drove straight across town until they reached the Garden of Palms, and then slowly passed the food trucks until they arrived at the security booth. He'd promised to report that a patient had run off and where she could be found. She looked on. She didn't tell Aram that she no longer knew what her mother's sister looked like after years locked away behind the high walls. She'd been only a preschooler when she'd seen Laura for the last time. She felt like buying Saint

316

Nicholas Day presents for her family. Their mother Louise never did much for the holiday, except at school with her toddlers. At home, she gave each child their first initial in milk chocolate. She thought, "I want to bring Laura a big present, but what?" On the way to the shopping district, Aram told her what the security guard had said: "Alma is a revolving door of a lady, she comes, and she goes. We'll go pick her up right away." The guard wasn't a doctor. Still, she thought, "And why couldn't our Laura even visit her mother for half a day?" She kept quiet. She'd hoped that Saint Nicholas Day songs and Christmas sales would improve her mood, but what she felt was disgust. Aram didn't insist on running his errands first. She bought white bathrobes with matching towels and washcloths for Imker and Grandmother. Grandma's had a big handcrafted star, gold, not white. House slippers, too. Perfume and two housecoats for her mother. For Audi, Aram picked out underwear. "And what about you?" he asked, more teasing than worried. "I'm on my period and just want to sleep," she said, nestling against him, adding, "I'm getting ten packs of sanitary pads for Mother and me." Aram helped carry everything to the cash register. "Are you in the mood for a present?" He brought his face close to hers. "Yes," she said, "but I want something that doesn't cost any money." He wrapped an arm around her as if he knew that it wasn't her monthly bleeding but the revolving door lady who'd plunged her into pain. Wrapped gifts in the trunk. "Drive me to the river, Aram." He drove her out of the city, until the highway of shimmering black asphalt gave way to off-white shells and sand and onward, until they couldn't drive any farther. The ferryboat had just left. They got out of the car and walked onto the bridge and went on until they stood in the middle of the bridge overlooking the river. It was low tide. In the distance, the ocean glittered. Across the river, only the forest's edge. She looked at the anchored canoes bobbing up and down. She stared unabashedly at people living the consequences of her homeland's scarcities. She knew that Aram enjoyed what was intangible and moved through time in a million forms. The avocado fruit needed more time to ripen than sapodilla; rose bushes grew more slowly than periwinkles, and Aram ate much more slowly than she did. For three generations or more, his family had possessed the exclusive right to fly helicopters in the airspace above her country. He was the only son who'd refused to become a professional aviator. In Texas, he'd trained as a helicopter mechanic and earned a pilot's license on the side. He liked to listen in on air traffic control communications, and aircraft were dearer to him than his own life. "You should come flying with me at least once, Babs," he'd suggested. Then she'd see from overhead that she didn't live in a city but in a coastal country with a vast Amazon forest. What gave him pleasure frightened her. It was her enduring belief that she'd been born into the wrong family, the wrong country, the wrong epoch. And yet she and Aram could stand next to each other here at Leonsberg and catch their breath. *But for how much longer*, Babs wondered, reaching for his hand.

Seven

Winston and Lya are waiting for me. That's really quite unusual. A young white man with very close-cropped hair left a present for me with the neighbors early this morning. A big package. They never celebrate Saint Nicholas Day, maybe because they don't have children at home. They've told me there's no escaping it at work. The package is in the kitchen. Winston knows for sure it wasn't dropped off by Hans, the boy who often walks me home from the bus stop and invited me to spend Saint Nicholas Eve with his family. It was a young man in a gray Opel sports car. I glance at the bottle of orgeat syrup on top of the kitchen cabinet, tear open the wrapping paper covered with tiny Black Peters and Santa Clauses right in front of Winston and Lya, and goodness gracious, it's a white tennis bag and, inside it, a whole lot of used and brand-new tennis balls, and look at this, a gift card of "unlimited value" for tennis equipment at "participating stores." "What's his name?" Winston asks. "How do you know him?" Lya asks. Their eyes bore into me. My breath quickens. I get a grip on myself and tell part of the story. They're reassured and tell me to take the equipment to the guest room. I'm so excited, and December has scarcely even begun. I have two unread letters from Derik with me and a brown envelope with no return address. I've also finally cleared the junk mail about holiday sales out of my post office box and brought it along. In the brown envelope that I rip open is an urgent request to get in touch with the man searching for Ethel. A telephone number is enclosed. I feel relieved. My hands grope through the tennis balls. Cate told me yesterday that a medical examiner had forced her to lie down on his examination table, stark naked, and probed her with his fingers for an awfully long time. She could see that he was getting off on it. Her eyes were full of tears. His wrinkled face turned bright red, and his mouth fell open. Cate was embarrassed by the brazen attack on her body, but: "Heli, all of a sudden, what that creep was doing to me felt so incredible, so pleasurable because when he realized that I wasn't resisting, he bent down to my crotch and started to lick and lick me between my legs, Heli, and I just about died of ecstasy!" *My God*, I thought. "He gave me cleaning wipes to take to the changing room." I wanted to bray in disapproval. But instead, I quietly listened to Cate as my sluices opened down below, the soles of my feet itched, my knees buckled, and my labia wanted to suck my Dutchman inside. I was desperate with lust. And now here are his hard balls in front of me. And suddenly I can't stop myself anymore. I storm out the house, claiming that I've left a textbook behind somewhere, wanting to race out of Oog in Al, and as soon as the bus drops me off downtown, I flag down a taxi, jump inside. "Where to?" "Apeldoorn, sir." Onto the highway. It takes so long. Cars and massive vans everywhere. I monitor the taxi meter. How much cash do I have on me? The ride goes on and on. I feel ashamed. I should have stayed right where I was. My shame grows. I don't see him at the courts. No one around anywhere I look. It's drizzling. The gravel surface is darker than I remember it being the first time. His car is next to the door. FOR MEMBERS ONLY. "It's been drizzling all day long," the taxi driver says, and asks if he should wait. I pay for the ride. He drives away. I slip inside the clubhouse. He's standing at the bar. Empty tables and stools. He notices me. I reach out to him. Embracing, we rub each other warm, hot. He locks the front door and takes me to a workspace. French kissing, undressing, and he lays me down carefully on top of a huge desk, leans over me, runs his wet tongue over my face, strokes my hips, and then his hard cock in my face. I grip, bite, lick, feeling his ravenous mouth between my legs, his rough tongue flicking past, and I scream, cry out, more, deeper, as I draw him inside. He moans for minutes, stands up, raises and spreads my legs, and cautiously drives himself into me. I shudder. My anus is on fire. His penis pulses, fuller, harder, deeper, warmer. His fingers thrust, stroking my dripping wet insides until we meet each other's eyes. I enfold his waist with the strength of my thighs. He grabs my hands. We're locked together. Everything stands still. I want it to go on and on. I feel the precious metal of my mother's wristwatch. Cry. He goes to make coffee, and I finally see where I've wound up. The work room is spacious with modern furniture. There are four exercise machines, rolled up meditation mats, knuckle guards, and things I don't recognize. I go to the toilet. There's a shower. I stand under the hot jet of water. He brings me coffee, clean towels, even a new toothbrush, toothpaste. He takes a shower, too. A little while later, I'm dressed and sitting at his bar, and the mailman comes to the door. He lets the man inside, serves him fresh coffee with whipped cream, receives the deliveries addressed to the tennis club. The heat is on high. I don't know what to say. I don't know what to do. It's starting to get dark. He wants to take me out to eat. I'm not hungry. I call home to say I've been held up and won't be back for dinner. The lust in my womb has not been sated. I want to feel more everywhere he can touch me, melt with desire until I'm as soft as the strings of sperm that shoot out of him. I want to fuck him in the dark, to the point of bleeding if that's what it takes. He lets the mailman out, locks the door, draws close to me, takes my left hand, presses it to his crotch. I grip it, fondle it, and he pushes his tongue into my mouth. With both hands, I hold him by the balls, saying, "I need you to fuck me!" He lifts me off my feet.

Lya and Winston are watching the news when I let them know I'm home. "Were you with him?" Winston calls out. "Yes," I call back, adding, "It took a long time, my Dutch dinner, delicious, though!" As I say this, I look up at Grandmother Bee's orgeat syrup. "I love that man," I whisper. He drove me to the emergency pharmacy after- ward to pick up the morning-after pill for me. He and the cheerful pharmacist had gone to the same school; they were both born in the city where they live and work. He drove me to Utrecht. Dropped me off at home. Kiss. Sped off in his gray car. I still have unopened letters from Derik to read. In the brown envelope, a short, handwrit- ten note from Bram's father. The family has been located. The trail leads to Scotland. More to come. One more day and then I'll join my school friend Hans at his house for

Saint Nicholas Eve. I still need to make up rhymes to go with the presents I'm taking with me. The scorching heat of a desire that rages for more is licking at the edges of my thoughts. I'm so wet. How will I make it through this school year calm and dry with my ferocious sportsman? Get on the pill, Cate would say. And I record in my diary for December 5th: take the pill every day. My mother takes it too. So does Babs, to regulate her cycle. I lay my diary on my navel under the comforter. Lights out. He's lying on top of me, and I feel him getting hard. It's not him but sleep that takes me.

Even before they could get into a real conversation with the woman from Kolera, a van arrived at Zorg en Hoop with a man inside. No resistance, no dismay, no anger, not a word. Alma went along with the orderly without even saying goodbye to Grandma and Imker. Imker said, "Grandma, Alma's fighting spirit must have been broken a long time ago." Her granddaughter was right. "Give Biko some wet food—meat, I mean." Imker got up, asked for the keys to the gate, and went out to lock it. Biko was chained up, tuckered out from barking. "Can I untie him?" She nodded, and when he was released, he ran around everywhere looking for his family, a tree to pee on, a place to poop. She and her granddaughter watched everything Biko did, penned up within their walls. He howled because he couldn't find what he was searching for, but took comfort in the fresh meat that Imker brought him. "He's almost like my girl," Grandmother said. "Laura takes comfort in whatever we bring her." This comparison didn't seem to sit well with Imker. She let out an angry "Laura should run away!" As if that wasn't exactly what her daughter had done. "If you ask me, no other woman in the place has escaped as often as Laura." Her voice rasped, "To keep her inside, they confiscated her clothing, and my daughter won't so much as go out to the gate in one of those hospital gowns." Talking hurt. She reached for the whiskey bottle, and when Imker slid it closer, slowly unscrewed the top and poured herself half a teacup. She didn't sip it. She tossed it back in one go. Her eyes watered, her tongue grew thick. It didn't go down the wrong way and make her cough. The comforting drink trickled down her throat and brought back the fire inside her. Biko came into the kitchen. Lay down by the legs of the chair where she sat. She stiffly bent over. Petted the dog. Imker asked if she was hungry. She shook her head. What was about to happen was this: Bram had called her house from Holland to get permission to visit Laura. But what did Bram know, these days, about the woman he'd proposed to so long ago that Imker embodied all their years apart? Grandmother shivered. "Imker, how old are you? Out of sight for almost eighteen years and now he's popping up again." Her granddaughter, almost eighteen and unafraid of the future, bustled about the kitchen. "Let Bram fly over, Grandma, so your daughter can see what remains of her fiancé." Laughter. "Grandma, when she sees Bram, your daughter can take the Laura who wasn't allowed to go to Holland and dump her in the river once and for all." Another burst of laughter. And without even wanting to hear her protests, Imker grabbed the telephone. "Grandma, I'm going to call him back to give him the okay, all right?" It was a joke. Imker didn't take the receiver off the hook but went to recline on a

324

sun lounger under the awning. She got up, too, following her granddaughter. Biko shuffled after her, staying close. She stretched out on another lounger Boyce had given her, in the northeast wind. Dog on the blanket. Yes, it was all right if Bram flew over to Paramaribo. She still couldn't quite wrap her head around it, but fine. Louise's girls were excited. Her almost-son-in-law had asked Heli what Laura needed the most. "Do you know what Heli answered, Grandma Bee? Sex!" The two of them burst into laughter.

As if Laura'd had no other worshippers after Bram. Every year, some guy who was smitten with her daughter showed up at the gate. Laura had kept up with her singing, too—often with a trio, sometimes in a choir, and usually as a soloist in a jazz band. No one had any reason to presume that a lady with so much joie de vivre, who moved so effortlessly through life, would ever end up in Kolera. Once it had happened and her daughter was stuck there, her friendships slowly fell by the wayside. It hurt too much to discuss that heartache with her aching jaw. She searched her mind for a landmark to organize her memories around. Elections. A Green People's Party. The whole city littered with pamphlets. "Laura joined a young politician who was campaigning for a presidential candidate known to his adoring followers as Jopie. She formed a club with other young women that provided entertainment throughout the campaign, performing songs about the country, its party politics, and, of course, love. The politician lost the support of his party. He turned to alcohol. Threw tantrums. Put pressure on her to binge drink with him after his failure. Then something must have happened that made her snap. A rape? Did he beat her? She returned home from her job as a teacher in Saramacca a broken woman. Never wanted to see him again. Insisted on pressing charges against him. Gave us a hard time because her brother and sister were so enthusiastic about the new party. The city filled with cheering people dressed in their party colors, and even Louise was happy with the election results. At long last, a black man was the people's political leader. The party hadn't gained a majority but had gotten so much bigger. Then came Good Friday, after the election results and the hullabaloo—all you heard on Anton's radio all the livelong day was a lot of hot air about who'd won and why. Laura had been extremely rude to your family when you came to visit and it was eating away at her, Imker. I invited her to the Stations of the Cross, and there in that church downtown, something within her must have caught fire. When she got back home, she threw out everything, I mean everything, and as if in a drunken rage, she talked about the politician and what he'd done to her, and even hurled my brother's name into the fire like kindling, claiming he'd abused her when she was a child. Léon? Impossible. Was Laura crazy? Then so was I! We screamed at each other so violently that the neighbors came to look. Your grandfather didn't have the first notion what to do with us. He asked Laura to hush or else leave Jacobusrust. She left. And that must have been the night Laura knocked on your door at Dwarsstraat. She wanted to apologize, I think." Her voice broke. She was exhausted. Imker looked up. As if these last words were sinking in for her granddaughter like the stings from a swarm of wild bees. Imker looked stunned. In a trance, almost. Her eyes bulged like those of her grandfather Anton whenever he realized something. "Grandmother, who is my father?" The coughing wouldn't stop. Imker leaped up to help. A lump in her throat. The taste of blood. Gasping for breath. "Spit, Grandma!" She was slipping away. Felt her weight on the lounge chair growing lighter. Biko whined softly. She felt the dog licking her hand, the wind stroking her face, her neck, her head. She caught her breath. Imker in tears.

The Saint Nicholas Day gifts from her granddaughter Babs escaped her notice until Umar hung up the Christmas star one evening. It cheered her heart. Maybe the morphine injection that Doctor Albert had given her days earlier was finally wearing off completely. She could see the gold glittering, count the points of the star, understand that this was a work of art made from paper by loving hands. For days, everything had seemed out of focus, hazy, distant. Sounds and tastes and, yes, even her feelings had seemed drowned in her head. Now the world was in arm's reach again. Imker brought her polenta with honey, and she even smelled a dash of nutmeg. She was going to die, just as a new chapter was beginning for the Vantas, maybe even a happy one, but either way, she was close to the granddaughter with whom her bond remained strongest. She took small bites. Finished the entire bowl. She fluffed the pillows and lay down on her back. Biko wasn't lying on the patio but preferred her bedroom, facing the back door. With him nearby, she could fearlessly tumble back to the Winti séance, which had not disappeared from her thoughts since the morphine. Far from Paramaribo without electricity. A hut made of twigs and leaves among trees and shrubbery. She and Anton next to each other on a wooden bench, her son Winston and daughter Laura on another bench. Adults in colorful shawls, men with bare torsos next to wooden drums, women with headscarves carrying sloshing buckets of water with fragrant herbs. The master of ceremonies, wearing a European-style suit. He assured them that Anton's ancestors had something to say and that "Dame Bee" might also receive a message from her father, mother, and earlier generations in the afterlife. They sat stiff and cold like pillars, standing out, because everyone else was in a flurry of movement. They remained silent as the others spoke, laughed, sang. For them, it was a way of mourning. For the others, a party. Everything got louder—the singing, the handclapping, the foot-stomping, the drumming. She and her children stopped up their ears with their fingers. The man in the European suit had painted his face chalk-white, and a fringed shawl was draped over his shoulders, so beautiful. She remembered the woman with strong buttocks who'd unexpectedly come dancing toward them, slow and restrained, and suddenly dropped to the hard, dry clay floor. A man pulled the dancer back on her feet, and a woman brought a gourd filled with a reddish drink, which the dancer sucked in then spit out. And returned to dancing, but more and more wildly, until she screamed, the dancer did, and everything held still. She stared out ahead of her and spoke. She must have spoken to Anton in a plantation language, because Bee didn't understand a word of it. She listened intently just like the others surrounding the dancer. Impatient, Anton said, "What is this woman saying?" And she whispered, "I want to go home." Laura and Winston, like all the guests, were offered pieces of cake, which they refused. The women went around with trays of pastries. Others began to stomp, shaking their rear ends, waving, and humming along with the musicians. Guests had come from everywhere to dance in this circle. Strangers were also looking on, the light in their eyes like jewels in their faces. Anton pulled a flask out of his pants pocket and took a few sips of gin. He stood and turned to the dancer, who was still speaking to him. "You're talking to someone who doesn't understand you, so shut your mouth, woman!" The words sounded rude and domineering. The woman, breathing heavily, began wandering aimlessly and was removed by the master of ceremonies. Laura and Winston also got up. Even before it got dark, Anton Vanta's family was escorted back to the path where a car waited to take them back to Paramaribo. Anton kept pouting along the way. Grumbling and drinking gin. She and the children wisely said nothing. The Winti séance seemed to have been forgotten until, years and years later, the dancer's gibberish began to look like a premonition. Laura, a grown woman, living at Kolera? Winston without a job and divorced? Louise with troubles of her own? To many people, it was simply cause and effect. She was bombarded with accusations from the plantation. Conceited? Lacking in faith? Had her daughter Louise, by refusing to attend the séance, offended the gods of the Africans forced into slave labor? Head held high, Anton went to his job at the army base. She stayed behind at home in doubt and sought out a priest. Found Father Teloor in the downtown church. Went to confession. Left the Moravian community and became Catholic again. One by one, her children followed suit.

She saw Imker looking at her from the doorway. She had to blink her eyes a few times to land back in Zorg en Hoop. "When is Bram coming?" she asked drowsily. "Any week now, Grandma." "Will I still be around then?" "Yes, Grandma." And Imker came up to her, crouched down, grabbed her feet, and started gently massaging them. It warmed her. "Look at me, Imker? Stay with me when they prepare my body. Stay close when I'm laid in the coffin. Stay and watch when they carry me to the church and to the cemetery. Stay until I'm completely covered with sand. Don't cry, Imker, you don't have to promise anything, I just want you to hold me close in your thoughts for a long time to come, please…" Grandma Bee couldn't stop her tears.

Audi didn't know exactly why Babs and her boyfriend wanted to take him along to the international airport. The airstrips at Zorg en Hoop were more familiar to him and didn't make him feel upset and queasy. Zanderij was the place where his sister and friend had disappeared from their daily lives in a puff of smoke. She'd sent him postcards. He'd given no sign of life—not a card, not a note, not a letter. During the ride in Aram's minibus, alone all the way in the back, so much emotion broke loose. Tears in his eyes. Fear he'd never see her again. Pain because there was no one else he could go to when he needed to ask tough questions or pour his heart out. He'd discovered Bohr Libretti, the Adonis who'd fiendishly fertilized his mother and must have known damn well for years that he had a son and not only his four daughters from various relationships, including one stunning girl who brought the television news to their living room every evening. Now he understood his mother's impulses better than before. His time with Grandma had made him so much wiser. Heli should see him now! The crowd near the departure terminals sucked him in. Fear gave way to excitement. Anger gave way to joy. Babs had slipped him photos of the man they needed to look out for. Bram looked different now than during his engagement party with Laura. "The man is a poet but looks more like a wizard with that full beard and fur hat," Aram chuckled. "Butterflies in my stomach," Babs said now, having barely uttered a word during the hourlong drive, same as him. They got out. Aram parked the car. She threw an arm over his shoulders and they made their way to the arrival hall with Aram, who had a special airport pass because of his job and would pick out Bram from among the approaching wave of passengers loaded with hand luggage. "A pale face will stand out," Aram joked. Then: "Look, I see him; he's shaved his beard, khaki suit, military green hat." "Go grab him and bring him straight back to the car. We'll wait there." Babs had spoken. She walked back, with him in tow, to the car, which displayed the name of Aram's family's business. "Oh, I can't stand airports, Audi." He nodded. She leaned against the van. There was nothing to say, so she stared straight ahead, looking sad. The arrangement was that Aram, who was in the tourist trade, would get Bram oriented and then leave him to pursue his Laura mission without interference. Babs still couldn't muster the courage to visit her aunt, she admitted. He'd walked along the walls of the complex a few times when he had study hall, to escape hearing the other boys boast about the city girls they'd nailed at night on the benches in the Garden of Palms. He avoided the

Garden of Palms. He'd strolled past the market stalls toward Kolera, bought cans of soda, and brought them to the security guard. "Give these to the nurses inside for my Aunt Laura, okay?" Sometimes, he slid a half pack of cigarettes over to the guard. The man in the denim blue suit with a transistor radio at the gate of the madhouse, a former barracks for cholera victims, asked, "Why don't you ever bring this stuff inside yourself, little buddy?" He shook his head, "Man, no one even knows me in there because I wasn't even born when she was admitted." The man looked at him from his stool in the security booth and promised not to bug him with tough questions. A handshake. Had he done the right thing? He pitied Laura. He felt so sorry for the girls and women of Paramaribo. "Don't be silly, Audi," Heli would've said, looking him straight in the eyes. "Nowhere else in our country are women and girls as independent as in this coastal city." He was curious what she would say about his obsession with the sex organs of animals and humans. During the ride back—Bram seated next to Aram, and he in the back seat next to Babs—he heard their guest remark, "The women in your country, man, they're so beautiful, so strong." No one responded. His father came to mind. Bohr Libretti had invited him to go fishing on Saturday evening. He hated hooking fish and had slowly been gathering the strength to refuse. Besides, he spent each Saturday entirely in the service of Grandmother Bee. And Imker. And guard dog Biko. Bohr slipped him money every time they saw each other—"catching up on maintenance." Money wasn't everything, but the gesture touched him every time. He took it. He shared it with his mother. In the Scouts group, he told everyone his father was a gynecologist who worked hard and earned good money, and

332

his status there significantly improved. Mama was right: money may be dirty, but it sure cleans up your life. When he turned eighteen, he would change his last name from Vanta to Libretti. It didn't have a familiar ring to it yet. Since Heli's departure, he'd learned so much about ties of blood and needed more time to absorb it all. Bohr Libretti had invited him to attend an anatomy lesson he taught at the hospital. Guests and students from the medical school. His pa, a professor? He was wild with happiness when Bohr also told him in advance it would be about reproductive organs. A penis with testicles? A vulva with a uterus and ovaries? He and his father shared a light meal in the hospital cafeteria. Over the roast kubi fish, he was brave enough to ask, "Were you aware of my existence?" "Yes, of course, half the town told me about you, kid." Him: "Then where were you?" Libretti: "You don't have a child until the woman says it's your child." Him: "My mother still hasn't said that." Bohr Libretti put down his fork, wiped his lips with a paper napkin, and rubbed his hands in a wringing gesture to warm them, all the while looking him in the eyes, his words painfully slow. "Yes, but I had the good fortune that you yourself reported for duty as a Libretti. I know for certain I'm your father, Audi Vanta." Sometimes, a real-life experience seemed more like a scrap of a dream. The whole time he listened to his father's confession, Audi was holding the kubi stone he'd found in the head of the roast fish. *I know for certain. I know for certain.* And on the way back from the airport with Bram and the others, he could still feel the pressure of the chalk-white stone in his pants pocket.

Imker had a hard time getting through the Saturday. In the morning, she fell over a stack of discarded cardboard boxes in the fabric store, hurting her right hand. The day went by excruciatingly slowly. And to top it off, she was having her period. She did manage to help four women choose the right fabric for party dresses, and each customer received an extra yard of fabric as a December gift from the company. Making other people happy kept her on her feet. But when Umar came strolling in half an hour late, she snapped, "I hate it when people keep me waiting, Umar!" He took the shopping list from her hand and found folded inside it the money Grandmother had given her. He had borrowed his brother's pickup truck, and cars went slower than mopeds on the single-lane highway. He got no sympathy from her. He suggested driving to her grandmother's to pick up Audi before they ran errands. She refused. She loved the street vendors with their sales pitches in a language she seldom used; she examined their fresh products with delight, and the swarming and cackling of poultry and customers amused her. And how splendid it was to be outside after Grandma's episode. It had kept her from sleeping. Six days awake at Grandma's bedside. The pickup truck bounced through the crammed shopping streets to the parking lot. The market was by the river, and even though she didn't see the running water, it filled her with new energy. She got out. Looked at the truck. "Do you plan to buy a truck just like your brother's?" She sounded scornful. Umar grabbed her left hand and guided her through the throng of people. Not until they reached the familiar market stalls did he reply, "Yes, I think a little truck like this one will be just right for you and me in the future." She said with a laugh, "Our future is now, man." He chuckled. "Then I'll buy a truck next week in whatever color you like." She hesitated. "Whatever you prefer, but a van would be better for us, don't you think?" He said nothing, and their attention returned to their errands. They didn't notice Babs and Aram until her brother and sister were right beside them with a Dutchman. "Bram," she said, surprised. "Imker?" She smiled at him. No hugs. Handshakes. "Are you ready for tomorrow?" He looked at her, ran his hand over the stubble on his chin, then said, "Four times. I've already visited her four times. It was wonderful." Everyone seemed to be holding their breath. Umar announced he was going to buy fish. Aram said, "I'll join you." Bram, Babs, and Imker were next to a food stand piled high with tomatoes, parsley, peppers, yardlong beans, bitter melon, eggplant, bananas. "Did she recognize you?" Babs leaned in to hear every detail of his response over all the noise around them. "Out of nowhere, she called out my first and last name, said I'd gotten fat and old." She threw a stunned glance at Babs, who shook her head, amazed, saying, "It's time for me to pay a visit to Kolera, too." Bram: "Tomorrow, I'll stop by the house in Zorg en Hoop, Imker, but I don't know if your grandmother is ready for me." She gave an understanding nod. "Bram, I don't know, either." He said goodbye and walked on as if the market wasn't foreign to him. They watched him go. Speechless. Then rushed off to find their boyfriends.

And her grandmother's shame ran so deep. Bee's golden girl had tumbled into nonexistence. After a while, no one asked where Laura was or how it was going there. Bitter years, which Grandma had endured by getting more involved in the downtown church, until she'd become too weak to leave home. She understood her grandmother's feelings. She called Bram to notify him that Bee needed another day or two to prepare before seeing him. How'd he been spending his time, she asked. Taking short walks with Laura. Sitting with her on the benches in the palm garden. Listening to the rustling of the palms. Breathing in the sea air. He would stroke her hands, her face, and she'd lean against him until they walked back to the institution, arm in arm. He spent the rest of his time alone in his hotel room. He had a lot to think about. As he told her all this, he sounded cheerful. She and Bram promised to keep in touch. Was he still in love with Laura? She hung up the telephone. Umar was out for a walk with Biko. Audi was pacing around. Grandmother lay in bed napping. Pain in her injured hand. She wished she could turn in early. Couldn't. Umar, back in the kitchen. Biko on his leash, barking. First, fresh water and meat for the dog. Make the boys wash their hands with green soap before sitting down to dinner together. Umar had bought roti with curry at the market. They peeled the plastic away with their fingers and slowly polished off their lamb, potatoes, and yardlong beans in pepper sauce. Eating with attention, because it was unusual food for them, prepared by strangers. Three gleaming glasses by a carafe of water in which ice cubes danced. She loved these men next to her. She loved this house with its spacious living room, the enormous kitchen, the double-sized bedroom. She loved the light green walls, the stained wood floors covered with Marmoleum, the green tiles in the kitchen and bathroom. She loved the patio too, and the rotary clothesline that stood on the crushed shells. Big windows everywhere that couldn't be opened but were fitted with ventilation louvers. The patio connecting the kitchen to the yard around it, letting in sea air through a double sliding door with tinted double glass. Winston had left his mother behind in a miniature fort with high walls and an iron gate. She wanted to get two cats for the house as soon as her mother came to pick up Biko. Grandma had no objection. "Eat up," Umar admonished her. She nodded. So much for her daydream. The boys brought their food scraps and packaging to the big trash can outside and were ready to leave. Audi needed to be home in Amora by eight o'clock sharp. On Saturday evenings, all of Louise's children pitched in so their mother could go out with her boyfriend Lester. She waved goodbye to them and locked the gate. The wide street on which the bungalow stood appeared abandoned. There were parked cars belonging to neighbors she hadn't met yet. Maybe someday there'd be a brightly colored pickup truck parked at her gate. Every night. She heard the little bell that Grandma had on her night table for emergencies. Hurried inside. "Do you need the toilet, Grandma?" Lights on everywhere. Grandmother sitting on the bed, her feet on the fuzzy rug, her hands in her hair. "Imker, I don't know for certain who your father is, but your mother sure does. But it's better if you don't ask her, please." She nodded. Grandmother, louder: "Did you hear me?" Imker crouched down, closer to her. "Yes, Grandma, I won't ask your daughter Louise who my father is, all right?" Grandma grabbed her rosary, adding, "And don't ask anyone else either, understand?" She left the room. Came back, tense. "I'm going to train to become a nurse, Grandma, but my mother can't find out."

337

Not a word in return. She got ready for bed. She saw Grandmother mumbling. Praying was not her thing. God was not her concern. Churches held no attraction for her. As she lay zipped up in her sleeping bag, she couldn't fall asleep. Then she tried to imagine how it would be twenty years later in her country, her city, her grandmother's house, which would be her home. Her grandmother Bee dead and buried? Her mother Louise the grandmother of her children? Heli still abroad? And sleep brought Imker the peace she craved.

Louise Vanta picked up Bram at the chic hotel where he'd taken up residence. For one night only, a jazz band from Trinidad was performing at the army base. Bram came out to meet her in a loose-fitting shirt in bright tropical colors, snug pants, white shoes. He'd put on weight, but everything about him was still recognizable, especially his face, his voice, "Oh my goodness, Louise!" He gave her a big hug, right in front of Lester. "We're writing history, man," he said, grabbing her lover's hand. "The first time I saw Laura, she was performing the songs of jazz divas on the patio of this very hotel, on a sultry Saturday night just like this one." She looked around nervously for eavesdroppers. He paused for a moment, finally letting go of Lester's hand. More softly: "But time moved on long ago, and Laura and I were driven apart like continents that had once formed a single territory." He ran his hand over his stubble, shaking his head. "Maybe you can take her out one day to enjoy live music again?" Bram nodded, "Good idea, man, but where are you two taking me tonight?" And together they walked out of the lobby to

338

where Lester had parked, right up next to the front of the hotel. But Bram wouldn't just hop into the car. "Louise, where are we going?" He stopped on the bauxite footpath. "To the lodge for the Netherlands Armed Forces in Suriname." This was Lester, somewhat impatient. Bram moved into the light cast by a streetlamp. He looked at them as if they'd asked to hear one of his poems, and said in a raised voice, "I claimed to be homosexual to get out of military service in the armed forces; my chance to become a husband and father in this country was taken away from me by my grieving parents; almost all my blood relatives disappeared in a mass murder executed by armed forces." A passer-by stopped to gawk as Bram shouted, "How can I enjoy myself among soldiers?" It was she who said, in a soothing tone, "Then I can't provide you with any Saturday night entertainment, Bram, because Lester is a professional military musician, and he has to perform soon." Bram nodded, understanding, and said goodbye, shaking her hand and waving at Lester. Her: "How is Laura?" Bram: "She keeps asking where you are." And he walked off. Heading downtown. They could see his tropical shirt and white jeans shining in the dark. She would rather have had him with them so they could talk about Laura in more detail. Ever since he'd been visiting her sister each day, the medical staff at Kolera had advised her not to see Laura—"too many emotions in a confusing context," they'd said. "What do you mean?" she'd asked. They'd told her Laura might start thinking that Bram and Louise were dating each other outside the institution's walls, just when Laura had been doing so well recently. Her little sister, suspicious of her? She and Laura trusted each other blindly, even if they'd sometimes lashed out at each other. But she'd said "fine" and hung up the telephone. Her little sister was more or less the property of that place for as long as the national government paid for her care. She understood the lava flow of rage in constant motion under the lives of people like Bram, because she had a similar feeling about parts of her own life. One fine day, her sister would leave Kolera—in her coffin, if not before. She looked on in amusement as Lester prepared his instrument for the kaseko performance. An acquaintance joined them, whispering, "Louise, do you know Derik is so shameless he's planning to go to Holland to see your daughter, leaving behind his wife and children, that bastard." She wore her self-restraint like jewelry. Without even a glance at the woman, she smiled at Lester as she responded mildly, "My daughter Heli is a grown woman and no longer lives at home." That was all she needed to say; the woman backed off. But she felt defeated, and small. For years and years, her mother Bee had sought her refuge in the patron saint Anthony of Padua, transformed over time into a stone symbol, until Imker found her sick and abandoned. As for her, she was guided by passages from Old Testament stories, and, like her mother, by an unconditional faith in God's mercy. Even though Anton Vanta had maintained to his dying day that only time was merciful to man and beast. She gulped something back. Grabbed a handful of peanuts. Crushed them between her teeth. *Feeling pain doesn't always mean you're sick; feeling pain often means you're healing.* Her little brother Rogier had written those words in the big leatherbound family Bible that he'd brought her before departing for Holland to thank her for everything she'd meant to him. Through the whirling bodies of all the people losing themselves on the dance floor to the buoyant kaseko rhythms, she saw tanks, soldiers in uniform, military equipment, tense faces. The boxes of food and beverages, tobacco and alcohol, that she and others had stacked in the storerooms at the base. Mass murder. Gas chambers. Jews. Words she couldn't match to any images. Biking to Jacobusrust in the afternoon with panniers full of chocolate bars, cans of chocolate milk, corned beef, white bread, powdered milk, cigarettes. Rogier standing at the gate waiting for her, pushing open the latch, letting her and her bike inside. Helping to empty the panniers. Piling the packs of cigarettes next to her father Anton's radio. Reading the labels on the American products aloud with their mother in the kitchen. Drinking chocolate milk straight from the can and looking at her. Her brother's childlike happiness was contagious. Rogier had been conceived and born in the luxurious residence of a family who'd fled for fear of the Gestapo, knowing Suriname was Dutch territory and could be drawn into the conflict. In the large mirror in the Jacobusrust living room, she saw herself in the uniform of an army at war. And straight through the voice of the kaseko singer, she heard the quartermaster saying, "In Holland even the farmers hardly have enough to eat, so take as much as you like home to your family, Louise Vanta, because war is all or nothing." On the stage, her lover's saxophone filled the room with sharp sounds, and sweat broke out on his coffee-colored face: *Ma Fu San Ede Mi Musu Dede*, Why in God's name must I die? The singer's voice—wailing, taunting, flattering, but always charged with defiance. The band took five. The dance floor cleared out. Lester came walking over, lean and tall, with two glasses of whiskey on the rocks, gave her one of them, and sat down next to her. She could hear him catch his breath. They looked at each other, lifting their glasses: To our life!

I've summoned my friend Cate. "Awfully bad news, Catie." I can't wait until she's sitting across from me. The waiter brings us the daily special and disappears again, without ever taking our order. But what choice does a person have anyway, amid harsh gusts of wind and freezing cold? Cate looks pale from the rough weather and grimly takes off her gloves. "So, tell me." It comes out in a seamless screech: "Derik has left his family to continue his relationship with me, and I have to pick him up at Schiphol soon so we can fly off together!" Cate sighs, clearly relieved, gets up to order two bowls of peanut soup, comes back, sits, and takes the hat off her head. "What can I do to help, sweetie?" I look into her gold-varnished pupils, frowning to show I'm serious, and say, "You and I are going skiing together. That has to be the story that reaches your mother and my mother in Paramaribo, okay?" She slides her chair back. "I don't lie to my parents, Heli." A silence falls between us until the waiter comes to serve us the Creole delicacy. The bowls are set down before us, steaming, smelling of fresh parsley and ground peanuts. Cate takes a white napkin from the napkin holder, grabs a marker from her purse, and writes in red letters: *Fine, I'll help you escape into happiness*. And look: a complimentary plate of chicken satays is brought to our table, smothered in spicy peanut sauce. "Compliments of Sranan Sani Diner," says the Javanese woman, adding, "Enjoy your meal, ladies." Outside, the

downtown area reverberates with Saint Nicholas songs—
"If you're sweet, you get candy to eat. If you raise Cain,
you get caned…" It's so fundamentally human, we can't
help but get into the spirit. We don't just eat, we feast,
filling ourselves with so much good protein that we boldly
forge our winter plans. Warm with joy and deep satisfaction, we suit up our bodies and our heads again for winter.
In hats, gloves, and high spirits, we exit the diner, but not
without leaving a gigantic tip by the empty bowls. I'm
nervous. Cate's as stiff as frozen water. I ask about her
job. She mentions the date her winter break begins. I ask
about her boyfriend. She says she'd like to get an IUD
but has heard they can lead to infertility. I ask how things
are going with the married couple she's staying with. She
says, "They can't keep their hands off each other." At the
post office, we choose the same postcard. We write the
same message in the same red ink. As a postscript, Cate
sends my mother warm wishes in her own handwriting. I
do the same on her postcard under the note about our ski
trip in Austria. Blue airmail stickers and plenty of postage. To the mailbox. I slide in both postcards. I hug Cate,
turn around, and find myself staring straight into the
face of the man who turns me on. He's waiting. Should I
ignore him?

"Who the heck is that potato eater you were having such
an intimate conversation with?" Cate and I are sitting
together in front of the mirrors at the hair salon. "I'll
tell you soon, on the way to Schiphol." She sucks her
teeth loudly in disapproval. "Have you already bought
ski clothes?" she asks. The ladies doing our hair smile.

"We'll shop for them together, you and I," I answer, adding, "My exams come first, before everything else." Cate chuckles, "Expensive clothes from head to toe, that man." I say nothing, and our eyes meet in the mirror. I lift a finger to my lips. She does the same. I surrender to the hairdresser's hands and glances with a "Just trim the dead ends, because I need all my hair this winter, ma'am." But Cate and I don't stay quiet. Our hair cut and washed, each of us with her head under the dryer, we plan our ski trip down to the very last detail in Sranantongo. I can picture it unfolding before me: Catie calls Winston and Lya to pick me up; I go to her car with a suitcase; no, Winston insists on dragging my suitcase to the trunk to make sure there's another suitcase there, namely Cate's; he and Lya smile and wave as we drive off. It's like a dream, but I can never remember how it goes on from there. What will it be like at Schiphol when Derik and I are reunited?

At the Orange-Nassau training program, I bury my head in my books. I have an internship lined up at an elementary school in Amersfoort in January. I'm required to finish the semester with an oral presentation on a theme from Kohnstamm's theory of education. But I can't pick a topic. My teachers are grizzled old men. Not one woman instructor for us this year. In Paramaribo, I had two. One for biology and one for singing and music. Surinamese and Dutch. Our biology teacher was so dazzlingly beautiful that we were too shy to look at her. The boys wondered and argued about how she had made it all the way to a university degree without any hiccups while remaining happily married to a Surinamese man and giving birth to two children. That biology teacher, radiant with knowledge and beauty and marital bliss, gave me the idea that I might want to start a family someday. But that thought had never developed into a wish, let alone a longing. Marriage was for other people. Derik couldn't marry me; all he could do was try to be faithful to me, and keep me safe from the horny suitors who would swarm around me. My uncle and Lya are spending a long weekend in Paris. To visit an international art fair, I presume. I take ownership not of their house but of their bathroom, stewing in their extra-large bathtub. Soon every room in the house smells like English Roses bath lotion. I'm soaking my body until it's reborn, virginal, from the grotto of lewd pleasure into which it's descended. Then I hear him saying in whispered tones as Cate watched us, "I'm not getting married before forty, how about you?" I responded, "Go ahead and transform into oceans of time, and don't teach me tennis, teach me to swim." We smiled at each other. He'd just been to a wedding, which hadn't thrilled him. Wanted to kiss him. I drown in him each time we meet. This has to end. I prefer to keep my feet on the ground, as I do in my relationship with Derik, which has limits I can touch like a prisoner in a glass globe. Back in Suriname, it made my head spin now and then, and some people whispered that I would lose my mind if my mother didn't hurry and drag me out of that fiend's magnetic field. But wherever you go, there are experienced men with eyes that engulf young women. And a few also say things like this: "I enjoy putting my hands on other people's bodies and feeling the bones and muscles and helping them get stronger or recover." Sounds different from grace at a married couple's dinner table. It was really too much for my study buddy Hans to expect of me: to sit on their sofa on Saint Nicholas Eve, stuff myself with marzipan, and even get into the spirit enough to enjoy the televised antics of two clownish men. Yet I went along with the whole thing. Since then, Hans's parents have even invited me over for Christmas lunch to meet more of the family. I shudder. Apparently all their mature parental authority, their nurturing warmth like a crackling fire in the hearth, is just too much for me. It makes me panic. Hans doesn't upset my underbelly, but my young woman's heart, which is moved by good blood and personal ambition. A wedding is like a sacrament, meant for saints. Hans's dear parents are unable to see how unseemly I am. I let myself desire and am desired. And, for instance, I brave the cold of the cooled bathwater. Rinse in the ice-cold shower. Dry off in front of the full-length mirror. Seeing no one but myself for days is heartwarming.

The money Derik sent me by registered mail from Paramaribo, folded up in carbon paper in an official envelope, is enough for more than one winter outfit. I let the lady in the shop advise me on what to buy. Downhill skiing? No, I'm sure it must be hiking, cross-country skiing, something like that. And I select a wine-red outfit, black snowshoes, a black parka, along with red hats, socks, and gloves. The adorable blonde woman persuades me to buy special underclothes. I can barely resist the temptation to pick out warm pajamas for Derik. But I've locked him out of my heart, and my lips, and instead I buy a warm scarf as a present for Cate. Royal yellow is her favorite color. Then it suddenly occurs to me that I also owe a Christmas present to my housemates, though not from the specialty sporting goods store whose address was on the gift certificate from my Apeldoorn athlete. I find them a wicker basket filled with all sorts of winter treats, plus a good bottle of Dimple whiskey for the man of the house. I pay the delivery charges and supply the address and phone number at Oog in Al. With a light heart, I send off a letter to Derik to let him know I've taken care of everything. *I'll be at Schiphol when you arrive from SU, waiting by the currency exchange counter, possibly with Cate.* I would have preferred to wait someplace else, but Derik can have it his way. And I'll have a sharp-tongued friend with me just in case there are any shady guys hanging around. I'm well prepared and well equipped. Lya approves of my purchases, saying they're tasteful and remind her of vacations in her student years. She doesn't begrudge me this outburst of freedom. My uncle says nothing. He and Lya are staying at home this year, because a beloved family member in Suriname is gravely ill. "You mean Grandma?" "Yes, who else? Will you leave the phone number of the place where you're staying, Heli?" But his wife responds firmly, "No need for that. A vacation is a vacation." Has she guessed that the trip with Cate is just my cover story? As a man, does he have an instinct about what I'm up to? He narrows his eyes to near slits as he looks at me. But Winston's thinking about his mother at Zorg en Hoop. I escape his attention.

Washing Grandma was painful for Imker. In the shower, she explained she'd tripped at the fabric store. Once Bee was seated at the breakfast table, powdered and lotioned, dressed and combed, she laboriously brought out the words, "Imker, let me see that sore hand." She held it out to her grandmother at once. Grandma took the hand and examined it, softly probing, massaging. She sat down, amazed by the strength in Grandma's fingers. It went on for more than a quarter of an hour. Grandmother let go and slid a gold ring off her own right hand. "For you, Imker, so you don't trip and fall again." She protested, "The boys at the fabric shop are sometimes so sloppy with the cardboard trash, plastic packaging, and everything." Grandma said nothing, holding the ring out in her open hand. Imker, nervous: "Besides, that ring was a gift from your son. His name is engraved on it." Grandmother set the ring down on the table. "Yes, and from now on, this ring is yours and yours alone, Imker." She couldn't think how to respond except by stammering, "You're giving me too many presents, Grandma." And leaving the gift on the table, she went to the kitchen sink and cut a slice of white bread into bite-sized squares. Grandmother wanted milk bread spread with mashed sardines. The hand that was hurting felt more relaxed. The radio was announcing recent deaths. Grandmother hummed along to the background music. The ringing telephone startled them both. "Shall I answer it, Grandma? Yes?" It was Bram. "Yesterday, Laura brought up her mother." "What did she say?" She let him tell the whole story, and promised to talk to her grandmother about it. "That was Bram?" She took the plate with Bee's breakfast to the dining table, carefully setting everything down. "Was that Bram?" She nodded. "Eat something first, Grandma." But her grandmother was already leaning over her plate of mashed sardines, bringing little bites to her mouth with her fingers, saying, "Hhhmmm, good," and then, "Don't act like a hospital nurse, Imker, tell me why Bram called." She had no choice. Anyway, now that Grandma was eating, she could pass on what Bram had said in digestible mouthfuls. "He wants to come and visit you with Laura. Laura wants you to see her together with him. They asked for permission and got it." Her grandmother went on lifting tiny bits of food to her lips, smacking her lips to make it clear she'd recovered her appetite. As for her, she had two slices of bread with the sardine pâté, but added a dollop of sambal made by Umar's mother. She didn't talk for nearly an hour. She listened to the news, pop songs, the preacher's morning benediction. "Take your ring," her grandmother said suddenly. "Put it on your finger." She did as she was told. "Let me take a look at your hand." She slid her right hand toward her grandmother. It was quiet for a while. "Imker, when Bram flits off to Holland again, my daughter will really go crazy. And I'm going to die. You'll be left behind in double sorrow." They both fell quiet. She poured a cup of tea for Grandma and a glass of water for herself. Her grandmother reached for the whiskey, pouring a trickle into the hot tea. "You mean Laura and Bram can't visit?" Grandma shook her head, bestowing her approval. "No, they can come and have dinner with us, with me. After all, I'm longing to see Laura." The conversation proceeded in fits and starts. "Can they come this Sunday, Grandma?" Bee nodded as if she had no intention of stopping. Relieved, she tried to reassure her grandmother. "Oh, but Grandma, Laura doesn't just have Bram to rely on, she also has Mama and me, Babs, Audi, even Heli, and don't forget Umar and Aram." Grandmother raised her head, opened her eyes wide, and took a deep breath. "I've never told anyone what I really felt in my heart. Imker, I love you." She kept her eyes lowered. Grandma Bee: "That ring was a gift from your father, Imker." She felt tears. Didn't make a sound. So early in the day, the most she could bear was the sound of Biko rattling his chain. "Want another slice, Grandma? No?" And they looked at the dog. Biko would move to Amora at the end of the week along with all his things, beginning his new life at her mother's house. Umar had already claimed a couple of kittens from friends. She had everything but could find no words. She stared at the parsley plants poking out of the soil in the pot. Christmas vacation was coming for Umar, and this year he didn't want to spend it with his parents in Moengo but at the bungalow with her. He had plans for the featureless sea of crushed shells in Grandmother's yard: buttercups, limes, bananas, a vegetable patch, and the bright red flower called fayalobi. They'd go to the showroom together to get the new pickup truck. After that, they would throw themselves into bigi-krin, the big end-of-year cleanup day in Paramaribo, even though you could already eat off of Grandmother's floor—so spotless. With Grandma Bee's help, they'd try making chicken pot pie for when Laura came to eat with Bram. Just like the bungalow encircled by crushed shells and the gold ring engraved with her father's name, no one could ever take away the cooking and baking skills that Grandmother Bee had constantly been teaching her. Biko stirred, restless. She'd miss him something fierce. Grandmother had said it would be all right to bring the two cats to the house before the end of the year. She planned to send Christmas cards to her family in Amora, with best wishes from Umar, and a card to Heli in Utrecht with the jingle *Let It Snow, Let It Snow*. She went to make sure that the gate was locked tight, took the licked-clean pastry containers from Biko, brought fresh tap water, and removed his chain. He shook free, whimpered, jumped up against her, ran to Grandmother to be petted, and scampered through the rooms before racing out to the crushed shells to dig a hole somewhere for his poop. He'd have the dogs next door to play with at her mother's place. He was sure to adjust to his new housemates and yard in no time. Her eyes filled with tears. Was she happy and sad? Her mind a blank, Imker washed the dishes in a tub of warm, soapy water. Suddenly, the future looked a lot like the day unfolding around her.

Boyce beckoned to the waiter, calling out, "Get my daughter a Peking Duck Extra Special to take home, boys!" He turned back to her. "The house is still in good condition, Babs. It needs a new coat of paint. There's still furniture inside. The kitchen is ready for use. There are beds, yes, and even the crib you used to sleep in." He peered at her, an anxious look on his face. "Is it clean, Dad?" "Clean, you ask? Every year during bigi-krin, the house always gets a thorough cleaning from the same two people—a mother and her son. There are still lamps on the tables and paintings on the walls. It's just a matter of hooking up the water and lights, Babs." Boyce thrust a hand into his pants pocket and placed a bunch of keys on the table-cloth. She looked at his fingers glittering with gold dust. He abruptly stood up. He had urgent business. "Is it too much to ask of you?" He shook his head and leaned in close. "Make a man your life partner only if you love his family, too. I lost your mother but not my feelings for her family." And Boyce hurried to the door. She was left alone there, waiting for the Chinese specialty that her mother liked so much. She looked at the keys. A tag hung from the ring with the address of the house where she'd been born. Would her mother be willing to go back there with her, or even on her own, to wander around, to look without talking? Two days later, she went with the boys: her little brother Audi, her boyfriend Aram, her sister Imker's Umar, and Bram, the Dutchman. The house had been cleaned and tidied especially for their visit. Aram and Bram shouted from the kitchen that everything looked fine. She went to check. In every room, the smell of Lysol, bleach, even insecticide. Mosquitoes? She looked around, uneasy. Aram gently led her into the living room, the bedrooms, the bathroom. She found the crib in a bedroom next to a pink dresser and other baby things. It was almost unimaginable that the rooms hadn't been used in ten years. The double bed. Had her mother given birth there? Audi stayed with her as the others examined the wiring, the yard, and the exterior of the home where she had been born. "Bram can move in at a discount," Audi suggested. She stiffened, saying, "I'm no landlady. Bram won't have to pay for anything but his own water and electricity." Audi, surprised: "Is this house yours?" She nodded, grabbing his hand. "Real estate is my great grandfather Han Hong's specialty…" And she added defensively, "So Boyce is partly Chinese-Surinamese, so what? There's also some Jewish and white blood mixed in, and a little African ancestry. Anyway, I understand *your* dad's highest ambition is to be a rootless city boy." Audi went to the locked window, turned toward her, and listened with his hands hanging limp at his sides. "Paramaribo has always had a shortage of eligible bachelors with money, compared to all the fertile women around here, you see?" He shook his head doubtfully, saying, "Bohr Libretti's parents fled their hometown somewhere in southern Europe when they weren't even sixteen, Babs, and cooked and cleaned on cargo ships so they could stay together and alive. His mother brought my father into the world with the help of a black midwife, a difficult birth in the safe haven of our city, where their ship the *Bohr* happened to be docked for repairs. The midwife looked after my father and his mother for weeks in her own home. Their ship sailed away. Forever. The Librettis stayed to give their son opportunities they hadn't had in their hometown somewhere near Naples." Babs, aggressive: "Did they realize Paramaribo was a pit that no one can ever really climb out of, Audi?" But her brother hurried on, "Bohr's father became a dock worker, working his way up to chief customs officer, while his mother started a catering business for dock workers and soldiers." Someone was calling her, asking if she wanted to see the yard. It was Umar's voice. She whispered, "Umar is just a Muslim schoolteacher. If he really wanted to provide for our Imker, he could get another degree and make more money, but instead he wants to paint." She spoke quickly, coaxingly, "Come on, Audi, come with me, you and I haven't made out too badly at all with our fathers." And they went outside to find out if Bram wanted to move in, for as long as he liked. Bram wrapped her in an enthusiastic hug and even offered to pay for a fresh coat of paint on the outer walls. She had seen enough. In about thirty months, she'd be a legal adult and a house owner. She asked for the keys and handed them to Bram. "Let's go get coconut ice cream, boys, I'm melting in this heat." Umar wanted to show her more of the grounds and the surrounding yard, but she'd lost interest. "Make mine a beer," Bram said. "I second that," Aram said. "Me, three!" Audi yelled. Umar said nothing. Elated, they left the house Louise Vanta had once abandoned. When they were back at their cars, a woman with a surprisingly large mop of gray, curly hair approached them from a nearby house, asking, "Are you Louise's Babs?" Silence. "Yes, that's her," Aram answered affably. The woman came closer. "I was your mother's midwife. We were neighbors. It was a good home birth." No one said a word. The woman again: "For you, an envelope with photos of you and your two sisters in your backyard full of fayalobi." She forced back tears as she accepted the envelope. Trying to keep her voice even, she said, "Thank you, ma'am, so very much." The woman gazed at her, smiling, and said, "May I give you a hug?"

The Peking Duck Extra Special from her father. The black-and-white snapshots from the midwife. The crib in the nursery. Life seemed to be racing headlong into the future and into the past, both at once. Louise remained guarded, refusing to have any of the Peking Duck Extra Special and warning her, "Don't let Bram get on your nerves, Babs." Advice from a concerned mother, offered in a friendly tone. She still hadn't been able to bring herself to visit Mama's sister. She had no idea what a woman with a mixed-up brain looked like. Bram had assured her that Laura wasn't confused but had "turned inward." She couldn't imagine what that was like either. What look did she have in her eyes? How did her voice sound? Bram tried to reassure her. "I'm trying to help Laura become outgoing and cheerful again, and enjoy the little things." "But how?" "By spending time with her and finding a new place for her in everyday life." And beyond that? Didn't he have obligations in the Netherlands? She was the only one who asked him these kinds of questions and then actually waited for a clear response. He claimed to be a freelance copywriter and a poet, and after a failed marriage without children, he was free to go wherever he pleased. But he'd confided in Aram that, against his wishes, he'd inherited large sums of money from blood relatives he'd never gotten to know because of the war's devastating violence. Aram had liked Bram right away. She thought he was weird. Under her mother's wings and in her own social circles, she seldom came across people who didn't fit her expectations. Even though Bram's plan worried the Vanta family, she was happy to let him stay in the house where she'd crawled around and learned to walk. It pleased her to be able to do something for Laura, whose existence made her anxious. Her grades for the first semester were outstanding. Her mother would beam with pride. The students at the teachers' college were whispering that Derik had left for Holland for personal reasons. Chasing her sister Heli? She had to make sure Mama wouldn't find out. She herself hadn't mentioned it to anyone. She'd mailed a New Year's card to her sister in Utrecht with a very heartfelt message. The business oper-ated by Aram's family always threw a New Year's party in late January, and for the first time her mother had given her permission to attend. She could finally see all those wasp waists buzzing around Aram like honeybees. She was more nervous about it than she'd expected. She'd be sixteen in January. "Barely more than a child, really," Bram had said. She resented the remark but had to admit he was right. Yes, she was still growing up, and an older man could see that. She would need to remove the crib, which had come a long way from a foreign country for her birth, from the house where Bram was staying. She could donate it to an orphanage, along with her first bed and other baby things. The neighbor, as an experienced mid-wife, was sure to know of someplace. And so she woke up each morning without any dreams she could remember but with a head full of plans. On the salon table, next to the other postcards, lay a New Year's card from Heli with the message that she'd be going on a ski trip with Cate, her old co-worker from Fatima School. Walking in the snow? With that redheaded wild child? But Mama seemed indifferent to the news. Louise preferred to keep quiet about her deepest feelings, same as Babs.

Oog in Al. The front doorbell. It's Cate. A dark blue Mercedes on the street. "What's going on?" Cate apolo-gizes, "I don't trust my own little car on the highway to Schiphol, and we can't miss the flight." "A taxi?" "Yes." "Pricey?" "Doesn't matter." Winston grabs my suitcase, carries it over to the chauffeur who is waiting by the trunk, and looks on. Coat on, hat on, bye-bye. "Have a good trip!" Waving. Getting in. Car doors slam with a dull thud, and off we go, with the man in the dark suit in the driver's seat. Cate takes my hand. "What is this all about, Catie?" She chuckles. "I meant what I said." She

356

tells me more, and as we merge onto the highway, I see what she was afraid of. The traffic is unbelievable. Cars are speeding past. The tangle of roads makes my head spin. I unzip my travel bag and drop my present for Cate into her lap. "Beautiful wrapping paper, thanks, sweetie," she says. We barely talk. My eyes are glued to the road. "How much is this ride costing me?" Cate sighs. "The meter's right there, Heli. But actually, I've arranged a flat fee, and I'll chip in." I don't respond. The truth is, her decision not to drive us herself was a stroke of genius. "How will you get back home?" She doesn't answer, just rips off the pretty wrapping paper, touches the scarf, brings it to her face. "Lovely, Heli. Kiss, kiss." She scoots a little closer to me. I inhale the fragrance of her bath soap. "Don't get knocked up, all right?" I shake my head no. Only then do I take a good look at the sky. "A dazzling blue," I say. "But it's nearly freezing, ladies." The driver's voice. Schiphol in sight. I slip my hands out of my gloves and reach for my wallet. I'm all wound up. A kind of fear has me by the throat. "I'm scared," I whisper. "I'm here with you until he arrives." Her voice sounds fainter than usual. "The arrival terminal, ladies?" She doesn't respond. Butterflies in my underbelly. Getting out. Paying. Grabbing suitcases. It's incredibly busy. "Is everyone going on an ice-skating trip?" "No, miss. Dutch people go to the mountains." Mountains? I pay the friendly chauffeur.

Four hours later, Cate and I are sitting on bar stools sipping cappuccinos. We've checked in. Our suitcases have been handed over. Derik has given his ticket to my former co-worker. I can see it as if it's still happening, the way he walked up to us, smiling as he took me in his arms, and said, "She insisted on joining me with the children but left them with me at the hotel and disappeared without a trace, I still have no idea where she is, oh, I'm sorry, so sorry." I let go of him and walked back to where Cate was sitting. It wasn't busy at the currency exchange counter. Derik followed me. "So you can't come?" Catie's voice. "Then I'll go with Heli in your place." It was as if she had known this might happen. "Just give us the tickets and go, Derik." He rummaged in his inner pocket, pulled out the papers. I looked at him—my man, so handsome, always full of confidence. I felt pity for him. Admiration, too. A father who would never walk away from his offspring. I give him a kiss. "Go back to your children, Derik." His eyes filled with tears. The three of us can go to the travel agency and make the arrangements—but could you let me have a moment alone with Heli first?" We walked away from the meeting place by the foreign exchange counter. He and I. Cate trailing behind with two suitcases on wheels. I listened to everything Derik had to say. He'd be here waiting when we got back. Same place. The currency exchange counter. And also, "Enjoy the snow!"

The barstool in the café is uncomfortable. It's my first cappuccino ever. Cate and I keep shooting looks at each other. I gradually relax, smile, burst into laughter. I order another cappuccino and a stroopwafel to go with it. "What's in your suitcase, Cate?" She laughs, "Not much." "Do you need to call your housemates, Cate?" She leaves and comes back with two cups of coffee and a tray that

358

she slides onto the round table. "Heli, never before in my life has any man besides my father paid my way." I sip my coffee, enjoying it. Derik has given us spending money so we can make the best of his lost vacation. We grab our purses and head toward the gate for our flight. We agree to be inseparable for the next ten days. I feel great. It's like I'm dancing. "Kaseko," Cate whispers, excited.

I don't check a map. I don't want to know exactly which red dot we're located at. Keeping track of the travel itinerary is Cate's job; I meekly follow her to an arrivals hall with our suitcases. There's a man holding an orange sign with my name and Derik's in shiny black letters. He's suspicious at first, but our travel documents convince him to drive us and our luggage to a town blanketed in snow. I can't believe my eyes. We need our dark sunglasses during the drive to endure the blinding whiteness of our surroundings. I'm overwhelmed by the feeling that my experiences in the tropics were mere dreams and now, finally, reality is shining before me. It's clear why Derik wanted to bring me to this virgin landscape high above sea level. When I enter our room and discover the view of the mountain range, I know my mother's God has intervened. Cate comes up beside me and stares, too. "We're up high," I say. She doesn't see my tears. Everything is frozen in place. We can go up even higher on the lifts tomorrow. The nearby lake is breathtaking. Suddenly, she says, "Heli, who was the guy you were standing so close to and chatting with the other day at the post office?"

A skiing outfit for Cate. We have lunch at the hotel restaurant. We've slept off our euphoria. We have to find warm clothes nearby for my dear travel companion, whose suitcase contains nothing but two towels. Oh, and padded boots, too, just in case she had to take the train back to Utrecht. We want to stay close to the lodge the first day and figure out how and where to go hiking without risk of being caught by surprise by snow or other inclement weather. My mouth nearly drops open when I see all the skiers passing by. Even Cate watches in silence. To experience more fully how affluent Europeans spend their winters, we book a table at a well-known restaurant. We plan a trip to the sauna, massages, and a jazz concert at a night club. No group excursions. No separate dates that might lead to vacation flings. We won't be parting ways at this resort. I don't feel like talking about my romps with the tennis player. Cate shows no sign of wanting to discuss her Surinamese boyfriend. At Schiphol, we bought a pack of playing cards and two fat novels, same title, same author. No getting drunk or gorging ourselves on chocolate in the hotel room. An occasional blue movie from the hotel's collection to tickle our underbellies. But most of all, plenty of long, deep sleep. Bringing breakfast up to the room. We sleep so long and so soundly that we wonder if it was the built-up fatigue of bodies on tropical time. Still, we also take plenty of long walks. Cate and I make up all kinds of rules to live by, house rules really, as if we're secretly practicing for sharing an apartment someday. The maid has brought us four video tapes. Not pornography this time but instructional videos for downhill and cross-country skiing. We push one video after another into the VCR. We get a bowl of peanuts.

We watch. "Do you want to go skiing?" "No, you?" "I'd be terrified with nothing but snow and ice and wind all around me, how about you?" "Someplace warm next year? No other plans yet?" "The road to great vacations is paved with money I don't have, Cate." "Money and a dependable man to go with it," she replies. "A tough combination, right?" We laugh. More peanuts. We laugh ourselves to sleep, joking about impossible fantasies of happy love affairs. Each day glides effortlessly into evening, night, and a morning of new marvels and blissful serenity. We read each other titillating snippets from Jan Cremer's notorious book. We walk as far as the lake and back to the restaurant, where we sit by a huge fireplace eating roasted meat with potatoes baked in cream and fruit salad with a jug of mulled wine. We go to the sauna but don't get massages and then, back in our room, rub soothing avocado lotion into each other's backs. We paint each other's nails. Tell stories about our home country. And sometimes Cate starts in again about me flirting with the handsome Dutch guy at the post office. I keep my lips firmly sealed, even though I realize that over time she's become more to me than a co-worker I got along with in Paramaribo. On the last day of our trip, my period starts, and I'm a wreck. I don't want to go back to Holland. Cate teases me, saying, "But Heli, my little school kids need me." I suck my teeth. We are picked up right on time for our trip back. I'm torn from my dream landscape of carefree bliss. But in this life of ours, nothing remains unaltered: even a corpse goes on decomposing, and even winter will turn into spring. Cate comforts me with wisdom gleaned from a book she read recently. I turn in the keys to our room, and we sign out. "Enjoyed your stay, ladies?" asks the friendly platinum-blonde receptionist. We nod. We smile. We thank her for the service. A teenage boy in livery escorts us outside. The shuttle bus has picked up other people. Still plenty of space for Cate and me. We drive off. Slowly touching down in a new year after soaring free of the control of clocks and calendars. I don't want to fly back to the coast.

My first date with Derik was on one of Laura's Sunday afternoons. The third Sunday of each month, I would spend at least two hours with Mama's little sister, visiting her with a tiffin carrier full of delicious dishes, freshly made by my mother and paid for entirely from my salary. I was more nervous than usual because I'd be getting home much later than usual, and what was worse, I'd have to deceive my mother. Umar drove up on his expensive moped and offered me a ride downtown. I refused, saying, "I wear my hair loose, and I don't want it all messed up when I get to Kolera." He smiled, walked with me a while, and asked if he could pick me up from the institution at a certain time. It was hard to brush him off with a lie, a boy I'd sat next to at least six hours a day, five days a week, for three academic years. "I'm going to visit my grandfather in Jacobusrust afterward," I stammered. He smiled and gave a sympathetic nod. Then I flagged down a minibus and headed off. But where was the food container? Umar had been carrying it for me, and I'd left it with him. Tears. Goddamn it. Mama had put a lot of work into the bread pudding, meatloaf, and peanut cookies for Laura, and here I was showing up empty-handed. It was Sunday, there weren't many passengers, the bus made it downtown in no time, and the driver agreed to drop me off at the entrance to the mental hospital for a few extra coins. But I suspected that Umar was on his way with the food container. I got off at the regular bus stop. Waited. Sure enough, Umar vroomed to a halt next to me with the food container, smiling at me with his handsome front teeth. I felt uncomfortable. I still had some distance to go and refused to get on his bike, instead walking away without saying goodbye. He understood I wanted to be alone, and I didn't hear him take off but felt his eyes burning into my back. On my way there, I bought cigarettes and cold fruit juice for Laura. I was so nervous. When Kolera came into view, I paused for a moment. I had the perfume with me that Laura had always worn in her better years. I'd also brought a lovely group photo of her with her students in case she asked for it. She knew I was also a teacher. At the gate, the security guard waved me through, and as I walked on, I heard her friends shouting that I was on my way. Arms spread like a happy bird, she came up to me and gave me a hug. She took the food container, insisting, "Come with me!" I followed her to the visitors' lounge, saying hello to a nearby nurse. I had brought a spray can and a cloth with me and managed to clean a table. Laura waited until I was done. She took the spoon that a friendly nurse brought her. I helped her open the hamper, explained the contents, and stammered, "Enjoy your food, dear Laura." She was never greedy when I visited. She took careful bites and chewed slowly, enjoying her meal. She seemed more reserved than usual, and I didn't turn away from her penetrating looks. She nibbled away at the meatloaf until she'd had enough. Then she took a piece of bread pudding and dug in. I opened the bottle of orange juice and slid it over to her.

"Do you have cigarettes, too?" she asked. I nodded. And then she said, as if someone had whispered it to her, "You have a date with your pal Derik, right?" Her eyes sparkled restlessly. I gasped. I didn't ask how she knew. I nodded. My heart's great secret had leaked into the city and trickled down even to Kolera. My aunt tried a peanut cookie, taking small sips of juice. She asked for cigarettes, but before she took them, she got up to share the remaining food with two women who'd been watching her as she ate. I gave her a light. She inhaled deeply, closing her eyes. "Is there anything else you need?" I asked. Her eyes still shut, she said in a sultry voice, "A man, Heli." I looked around and saw women all around us. I pushed the whole pack of cigarettes over to her and slid a folded banknote into the empty slot. She saw and nodded. "You smell nice," she said, and I showed her the perfume, and she reached her hand toward me. I sprayed some on her wrist. "Just go to him," she whispered softly. "Just go, Heli." I gathered the napkins and the metal tiers that formed the tiffin carrier. Laura turned away as I got up, unwilling to say goodbye. I walked away. I never looked back. I always cry.

Derik's waiting at Schiphol. He comes up to us. Hugs me. Thanks Cate effusively. We chat a bit. Cate says goodbye to me. She has a train to catch, and wants to give me one last day with Derik. We embrace, almost sad. He wants to spend the night with me in a luxury hotel in Amsterdam. I protest. He's sympathetic and rolls my suitcase to his rental car. I follow in silence. We drive off. I say nothing about my trip, haven't bought him a present, and I demand that he drive straight to the city where I'm registered as staying. He suggests we stop somewhere near the house and catch up a little. I can't say no. He's been missing me for months, he says. "How about a restaurant along a country road?" Reluctantly, I get out of the car. We sit at a squeaky-clean table. It must not be mealtime. We're the only ones in the place. He says pea soup with all the trimmings will hit the spot in this cold weather. Fine. I wait until we're served. "What now?" My voice is unwelcoming. He hesitates, calmly stirring the soup with his eyes cast down. "You wanted to talk," I sternly remind him. He looks up and says, "I don't deserve you, Heli." I hold back my tears. "What am I doing in Holland?" My voice. His sniffling. The soup is getting cold. I go and ask the waiter to call me a taxi. "Right away, madam?" "Yes, have it pick me up out front right away, please." I head for the ladies' room, have second thoughts, and return to Derik. In the meantime, he's taken care of the bill. "I love you," I say. He sits. I stand beside him. He nods. Gets up. "You're even more beautiful now than you were in Paramaribo." I nod. I take his hand, stroking his fingers, and we leave. Derik takes my luggage out of his trunk and carries my suitcase and travel bag to the trunk of the dark taxi. "Do you need money?" he asks. "No," I say. Kiss him on the mouth. Get in. Derik doesn't move. The chauffeur drives off. *Don't look back*, I think.

No one at home. In the living room I see my Christmas gift to my mother's brother and his wife Lya. They've opened the whiskey; it gives off a golden glow in the elegant triangular bottle. On the kitchen counter, a big sheet of paper with my name on it. HAD TO RUSH OFF

TO PARAMARIBO BECAUSE OF GRANDMA. I look at the bottle of orgeat syrup. It's as if the contents have separated into light and dark portions. With a five-hour time difference, it's eleven in the morning in my homeland. Call them. Imker's on the line right away. "Grandma Bee has fallen into a coma, but everyone is with her, including Laura and Bram, and even Rogier and his wife with their baby boy Johan-Anton, and Grandma will stay right here in her own home with us." It takes me a moment before I can say it: "Tell Grandma I love her and I hope to see her again one day, no matter what, no matter where." "I promise I will," Imker says, and, "Bye, Heli." I stand there. Hang up the receiver. Carry the suitcase to the guest room. Stop in the toilet on the way to change my sanitary pad. I stare at the traces of the bloody sludge my womb expels each month. Grandma Bee will never see any of my children. Wash my hands and face with soap and cold water. Open a window to let winter in. Mail for me on my desk. Rip a certain letter open. "For the past year, Ethel Vanta has been living with her husband and two children in Ghana. He's an internist. She's a pharmacist." *Don't collapse*, I think to myself. Coffee. Carefully, carefully, down the steps to the kitchen. And I'm stunned. Goosebumps from head to toe. The bottle of orgeat has cracked. Grandma's syrup is oozing along the cupboards and counter toward the tiled floor, slow as heavy honey. A pool of off-white beginning to harden. I crouch down. Dip my index finger. Lick and dip, lick and dip. Just as sweet as my grandmother's always been to me. "Grandma Bee," I whisper. The bottle is empty now. All around me, the fragrance of almonds.